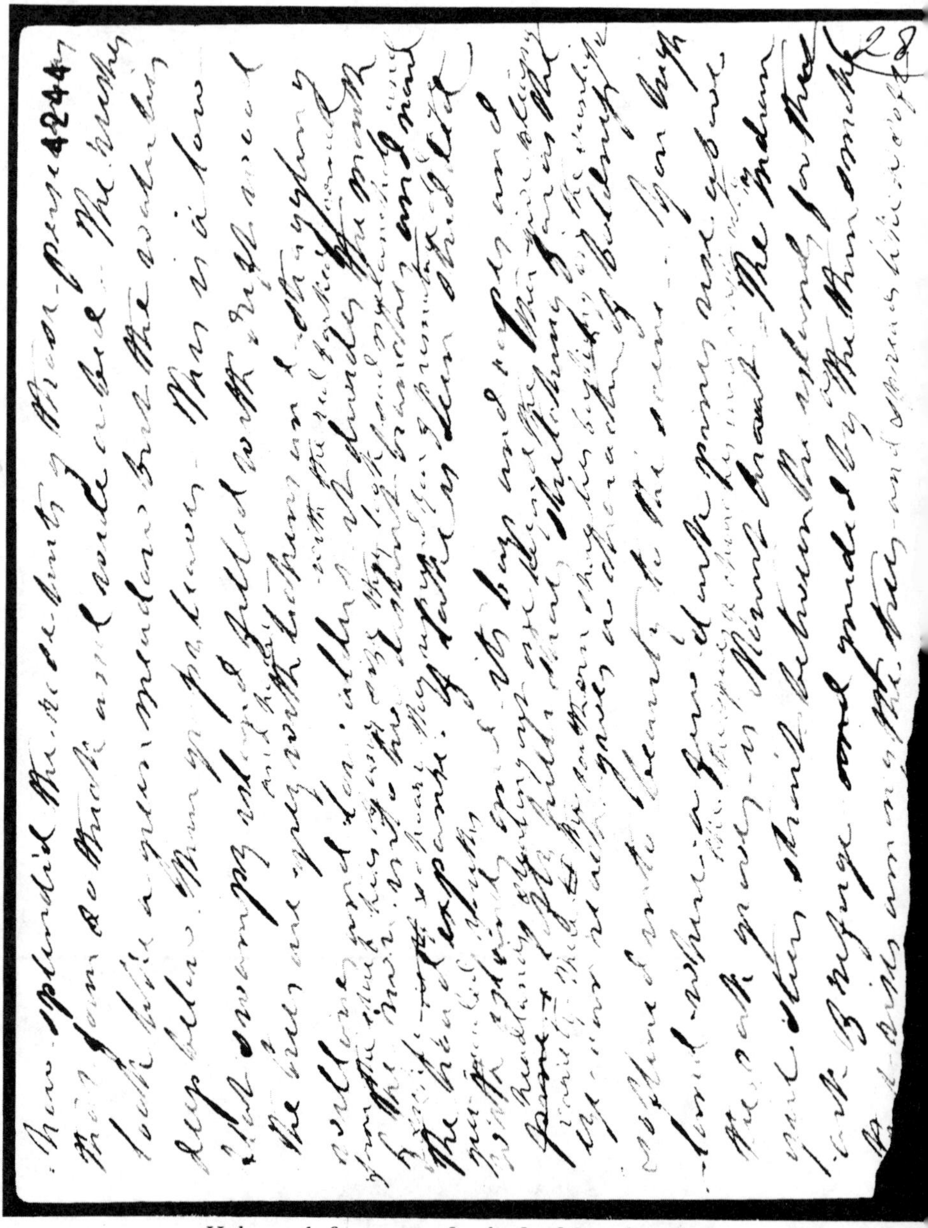

Holograph fragment of a draft of *Canadian Crusoes*

Canadian Crusoes
A Tale of The Rice Lake Plains

Catharine Parr Traill

Edited by
Rupert Schieder

Carleton University Press
1986

© Carleton University Press Inc., 1986

ISBN 0-88629-033-3 (casebound)
       0-88629-035-X (paperback)

Printed and bound in Canada by The Alger Press Limited,
Oshawa, Ontario

Canadian Cataloguing in Publication Data

Traill, Catharine Parr, 1802-1899
   Canadian Crusoes

(Centre for Editing Early Canadian Texts Series; 2)
First published: London: A. Hall, Virtue, 1852.
ISBN 0-88629-033-3 (casebound)
       0-88629-035-X (paperback)

I. Schieder, Rupert. 1915-   II. Title.
III. Series.

PS8439.R35C3 1986   jC813'.3   C85-0901685
PR9199.2.T73C3 1986

Distributed by:
   Oxford University Press Canada
   70 Wynford Drive
   DON MILLS, Ontario   M3C 1J9
   (416) 441-2941

ACKNOWLEDGEMENT

Carleton University Press and the Centre for Editing Early Canadian
Texts gratefully acknowledge the support of Carleton University and
the Social Sciences and Humanities Research Council of Canada in the
preparation and publication of this edition of *Canadian Crusoes*.

Cover of the paperback: Courtesy of the National Library of Canada

Contents

Abbreviations

ALS	Autograph letter signed
CEECT	Centre for Editing Early Canadian Texts
DCB	*Dictionary of Canadian Biography*
DNB	*Dictionary of National Biography*
NcD	Duke University Library, Durham, North Carolina
NSWA	Acadia University Library, Wolfville, Nova Scotia
OKQ	Queen's University Library, Kingston, Ontario
OOC	Ottawa Public Library, Ottawa, Ontario
OOCC	Carleton University Library, Ottawa, Ontario
OONL	National Library of Canada, Ottawa, Ontario
OPAL	Lakehead University Library, Thunder Bay, Ontario
OPET	Trent University Library, Peterborough, Ontario
OPETP	Peterborough Public Library, Peterborough, Ontario
OTAR	Archives of Ontario, Toronto, Ontario
OTMC	Massey College Library, Toronto, Ontario
OTMCL	Metropolitan Toronto Library, Toronto, Ontario
OTNY	North York Public Library, Willowdale, Ontario
OTP	Toronto Public Libraries, Toronto, Ontario
OTU	University of Toronto Library, Toronto, Ontario
PAC	Public Archives of Canada, Ottawa, Ontario
TFC	Traill Family Collection

Foreword

The Centre for Editing Early Canadian Texts (CEECT) was established to effect the publication of scholarly editions of major works of early English-Canadian prose that are now either out of print or available only in corrupt reprints. Begun by Carleton University in 1979, CEECT has been funded jointly by Carleton and by a Major Editorial Grant from the Social Sciences and Humanities Research Council of Canada since 1 July 1981. During this time six editions have been in preparation. Catharine Parr Traill's extremely popular narrative about children lost in the backwoods, *Canadian Crusoes. A Tale of the Rice Lake Plains*, first published in 1852, is the second work to be published in the CEECT series.

In preparing these editions, advice and guidance have been sought from a broad range of international scholarship, and contemporary principles and procedures for the scholarly editing of literary texts have been followed. These principles and procedures have been adapted, of course, to suit the special circumstances of Canadian literary scholarship and the particular needs of each of the works in the CEECT series.

The text of each scholarly edition in this series has been critically established after the history of its composition and first publication has been researched and its editions analysed and compared. The critical text is clear, with only authorial notes, if any, appearing in the body of the book. Each of these editions also has an editor's introduction with a separate section on the text, and, as concluding apparatus, explanatory notes, a bibliographical description of the copy-text and, when relevant, of other authoritative editions, a list of other versions of the text, a record of emendations made to the copy-text, a list of line-end hyphenated compounds in the copy-text as they are resolved in the CEECT edition, and a list of line-end hyphenated compounds in the CEECT edition as they should be resolved in quotations from this text. An historical collation is also included when more than one edition has authority, and, as necessary, appendices containing material directly relevant to the text.

In the preparation of all these CEECT editions for publication, identical procedures, in so far as the particular history of each work allowed, have been followed. An attempt has been made to find and analyse every pre-publication version of the work known to exist. In the absence of a manuscript or proof, at least five copies of each edition that was a candidate for copy-text have been examined, and at least three copies of each of the other editions that the author might have revised. Every edition of the work has been subjected to as thorough a bibliographical study as possible. In addition to gathering all the known information about their printing and publication, these texts have been collated using oral and ocular collation, devices such as the light-table and the Hinman collator, and the computer. Specialists from the University's Computing Services have developed several programs to help in the proofreading and comparison of texts, to perform word-searches, and to compile and store much of the information for the concluding apparatus. The edited text, printed from a magnetic tape prepared at Carleton, is proofread against its copy-text at all appropriate stages.

Editor's Preface

Quite by chance, some sixty years ago, I discovered Catharine Parr Traill. My one-room school in a small railroad town in northwestern Ontario had a "library" that could be fitted into one shelf behind the wood stove. There, one day after school had been dismissed, I stumbled upon a much-thumbed copy of what I now recognize was the cheap reprint of *Canadian Crusoes* issued by Nelson's in 1923 as *Lost in the Backwoods*. My childish mind was bothered at first; for I couldn't see how a book with "Lost" in the title could be written by someone named "Traill." I soon overcame that block, however. I read it so often then that I've never forgotten, over all these decades, the grey-green cover, the four coloured illustrations, and the way the fate of the three lost children gripped my interest. When it was suggested that I undertake the preparation of a CEECT edition of the original *Canadian Crusoes*, I had a feeling that I had come almost full circle. I began, just 130 years after Mrs. Traill finished her book, the quest for *Crusoes* that has taken over, almost obsessed, some of my friends would say, my life for the last five years.

The search, which began close at hand in the libraries and archives in Toronto, soon took me to the sites of the narrative, the shores of Rice Lake and the Otonabee and Trent Rivers. In Ottawa the Public Archives provided papers of the Traill and Strickland families. In the summer of 1981 I searched through the British Library, the Stationers' Hall, the Public Record Office, and farther afield, the Record Offices of Norfolk and Suffolk, the Bodleian Library, the Cambridge University Library, the National Library of Scotland, and the Nelson archives in Edinburgh University Library.

Since then, through visits to the United States and through the resources of the libraries in Toronto and interlibrary loan, I have inspected the complete works, published and unpublished, of Catharine Parr Traill and all the editions and impressions of *Canadian Crusoes* and *Lost in the Backwoods* that appear to exist. I've had a long correspondence with the surviving descendants of the firms that published the work in Great Britain and the United States. To supplement the material collected, I have looked into the history of publishing, printing, and distribution, and the practices of reviewers on both sides of the Atlantic.

I soon found that obstacles block the path of anyone who sets out to trace the history of the writing and publishing of *Canadian Crusoes*. A fire that consumed the Traills' log house on the south shore of Rice Lake in 1857 destroyed all but a few sheets of manuscript related to the work. Among the letters and journals in the Record Offices of Norfolk and Suffolk and the Public Archives of Canada, there are few from the period when the work was being written and published. The firms that produced the different editions of the book have either been dissolved or gone through complicated changes of ownership or partnership. Having finally tracked down, by a circuitous route, the descendants of the first British publisher, I was frustrated to find that they had lost all their records during the Blitz in 1941. Although the original printers are still in business — now in a town that Catharine Parr Traill knew well as a child — they destroyed their nineteenth-century records. No descendants of the first American publishers have been located. The later publishers appear to have no pertinent papers. By adding to the documents that were relevant, however, details gleaned — to use one of Mrs. Traill's favourite words — from newspapers and from publishers' trade journals, I have been able to piece together a chronological account of the growth and publication of this 1852 work and its successors, up to the Nelson's impression that I first read so long ago.

To this search for *Crusoes*, a number of institutions and individuals have contributed. Carleton University and the Social Sciences and Humanities Research Council of Canada, through their support of CEECT, have provided me with a good deal of money for travel, subsistence, and research assistance in the last four years. I am grateful to both these institutions and to those that lent CEECT rare editions of *Canadian Crusoes* and *Lost in the Backwoods* for microfilming or collating. These are Acadia University; The University of Alberta; Carleton University; Lakehead University; Massey College, University of Toronto; Mount Allison University; the National Library of Canada; North York Public Library; the Osborne Collection of Early Children's Books, Toronto Public Libraries; the Ottawa Public Library; Queen's University; the University of Toronto; the University of Western Ontario; and York University. I also wish to express my appreciation to the Public Archives of Canada for permitting CEECT to use their Central Microfilming Unit in Ottawa; the Buffalo and Erie County Public Library for microfilming their uniquely misdated copy of *Lost in the Backwoods* for CEECT; and the Dunn family and Professor Michael Gnarowski for lending CEECT their copies of Mrs. Traill's popular work.

In addition, the Public Archives of Canada made accessible to me the large Traill Family Collection, without which no professional work can be done; I wish to acknowledge as well their permission to quote from this material, and to reproduce as the frontispiece of this edition a manuscript page from this magnificent collection. The Archives of Ontario afforded records relevant to the Rice Lake-Peterborough-Lakefield area in the mid-nineteenth century. Museums and libraries, both private and public, provided me with copies of the different editions of Catharine Parr Traill's works. To the staffs of five libraries I am particularly indebted: the Metropolitan Toronto Library, the Osborne Collection of the Toronto Public Libraries, the Thomas Fisher Rare Book Library in the University of Toronto, and those of Massey College and Trinity College. I am even more deeply in debt to Robert Nikirk of the Grolier Club of New York, Desmond Neill at Massey College, and Linda Corman and Elsie Del Bianco at Trinity College; all these librarians were constantly responsive to my need for advice and help.

The members of the editorial board of CEECT, chaired by the indefatigable Mary Jane Edwards, have constantly been available for advice and gentle correction. I am especially grateful to Mary Jane and to Rob McDougall who never failed to share their experience as editors. Past and present members of the CEECT staff, including Heather Avery, Mary Comfort, Jennifer Fremlin, Marion Phillips, and John Thurston, have always been ready to help in any way they could; they have been particularly willing to undertake additional research for me.

No one can now work on Catharine Parr Traill without being indebted to Carl Ballstadt, Elizabeth Hopkins, and Michael Peterman for their labours on her letters. With three eager researchers on the history of the Rice Lake area, Norma Martin, Catherine Milne, and Donna McGillis, I have enjoyed excursions to the sites Mrs. Traill used in her narrative. And to so many friends I am grateful for their patience during the long process of this quest for *Crusoes*.

Rupert M. Schieder
Toronto
September 1985

Editor's Introduction

In October 1850, when Catharine Parr Traill (1802-99) wrote the dedication for the novel she had entitled *Canadian Crusoes*, she put the final touch to the narrative about children lost in the backwoods on which she had been working for more than three years. From "Oaklands," a farm on the south shore of Rice Lake, in what was then Canada West, she sent the manuscript off to her sisters in England. Almost two years later, *Canadian Crusoes. A Tale of the Rice Lake Plains* was published in London.

The history of Mrs. Traill's story about lost children, written primarily for the young readers addressed in her dedication, begins in 1837. On 2 August of that year Mrs. Traill, who had been living on the Otonabee River near Lakefield, Upper Canada, since her emigration from England almost five years earlier, copied into her journal an advertisement from the *Cobourg Star* offering a reward for information about a child "about six years of age" lost on the Rice Lake Plains, and an appended announcement that the child had been found "near Cold Springs alive and well after having wandered in the woods five days and nights."[1] To illustrate the dangers of "the wilderness in which we live," Mrs. Traill added other accounts of similar losses. One of these told how three children from two neighbouring families were lost in the forest when they went in search of strayed cattle. It traced the anguish of the two mothers over five years and broke off with a suggestion of a rescue or return.[2] The subject was obviously important to Mrs. Traill, not only because of her own young children but also because of the possibilities for a writer in constant need of marketable material that might bring some relief from the financial burdens of her family. Mrs. Traill made the entries dramatic by giving names to the mothers, exploring their feelings and motives, and inventing appropriate dialogue.

xvii

This material is expanded and elaborated in another journal entry, undated, but probably made a few years later. Entitled "The Bereaved Mothers," the story was "written down from memory" by a young lady "who had heard the history . . . from an old American major and his wife."[3] The narrative possibilities of this "history" have been developed. The locality is specified as "the end of hunters creek"; the time is given as "close to the old American wars," presumably 1812-14; both sets of parents and the children are named; and the character of a vain, frivolous child is firmly established by the time the entry breaks off.

In 1838 Mrs. Traill made use of the subject of lost children in "The Mill of the Rapids: A Canadian Sketch," published in *Chambers's Edinburgh Journal*.[4] The writer, almost as if it were a weakness, confesses her keen interest: "Now, I have almost as great a love for a story about being lost in the woods, as I had when a child on the knee for the pitiful story of the Babes in the Wood." The story anticipates *Canadian Crusoes* in several ways. Aware of the value of immediacy, Mrs. Traill shifted the point of view from the parents to the lost brother and sister, who, like the children in *Crusoes*, confuse two lakes and are "nearly all the time — never more than a mile" from home. She also stressed the industry and self-sufficiency of the two children, including their ingenuity in kindling a fire with birch bark "dried" in the "bosom."

Five years later, in 1843, in "A Canadian Scene," which also appeared in *Chambers's*,[5] Mrs. Traill described her own experience during a three-day hunt for a neighbour's child and gave a detailed account of the techniques of the search that ended with the discovery of the child unharmed, near a deserted house.

In 1849, now living at "Oaklands," she sent to her sister Agnes Strickland in London a long short story, "The Two Widows of Hunter's Creek. A True Story of the Canadas," which was printed in *Home Circle*.[6] Mrs. Traill had obviously reworked and elaborated yet again the material on lost children in her journals. A number of details were repeated: the location; the names of the two families, although the roles of the two mothers have been reversed; the vain frivolous daughter; the search for strayed cattle; the point of view of the bereaved mothers; and the narration by an old American major. New in the extended narrative are the stress on authenticity, the adventures of the three lost children with Indians, and the reappearance of the children at the end.

Evidently Mrs. Traill then decided to write an even longer narrative that combined her theme of lost children, and its accumulated factual and fictional details, with the Crusoe figure that Catharine and her sisters had already used in their early writings.[7] On 22 Mar. 1850 she wrote from "Oaklands" to Ellen Dunlop, the daughter of her close friend and neighbour Frances Stewart: "I have been writing a little now every night at my Canadian Crusoes, and hope if I keep tolerably well to have the volume ready by the middle of May. I think more of the copying than of the composition. I am in good hope of winning fifty pounds when it is ready and that cheers me up to persevere in my work."[8]

Mrs. Traill apparently wrote several drafts of *Canadian Crusoes*. Among manuscript sheets that survived the fire that consumed "Oaklands" in 1857 was a remnant of a quite early draft of the introductory section of the narrative.[9] In this draft the setting is still Hunter's Creek, a location that she was to change to Cold Creek. The cousins Hector and Louis are thirteen and twelve instead of fourteen. The younger brothers of Hector and Catharine are named Duncan and Dugald rather than Kenneth and Duncan. Events that are later developed in detail are merely sketched. Missing from these four manuscript sheets, which were expanded to twelve pages in the first edition, are many topographical details and much botanical, zoological, and ornithological information that Mrs. Traill added at a later time.

A portion of what appears to be a later draft of *Canadian Crusoes* is also to be found among these surviving sheets.[10] Covering five sheets, the remnant includes a description of some flowers; the details of the process of drying wild rice; a graphic hunting scene involving Indiana, Catharine, and a French-Canadian lumberer; a section of their journey down the Otonabee River; and their arrival back at Rice Lake. The details and the wording on these five sheets are close to those on four pages of Chapter XVI in the first edition. In all nine sheets the copy is very rough. Rather than periods, semicolons, and commas, the dash is constantly used. Obviously, even the later draft still needed detailed revision.

On 23 Apr. 1850 Mrs. Traill was still composing: "I have been very busy writing and am not far from the end of my book but the copying has to be done and this is to me the worst part."[11] On 28 September she could at last write: "I have yesterday finished my arduous . . . task of copying the MS of the Canadian Crusoes — 354 pages besides some notes. . . . I wrote latterly some 20 close pages a day." In a kind of postscript, she added, "I must trust however that some good may attend my Crusoes."[12] Just over two weeks later, the dedication written, the manuscript that was to become *Canadian Crusoes* was ready to be sent to her sisters in London.

In this last version of her narrative Mrs. Traill traces the adventures of three children of two related neighbouring families in the Cold Springs area between Lake Ontario and Rice Lake in the last quarter of the eighteenth century. Hector, solid and dependable, and Louis, giddy but ingenious, both fourteen years old, and Catharine, Hector's sister, sensitive and responsible, twelve, set out to find strayed cattle, but they lose their way and reach the Plains on the south shore of Rice Lake. During the next two years, they manage to survive the hardships of the wilderness, a spectacular forest fire, and the menace of rival Indian bands. They rescue Indiana, a Mohawk girl, from a cruel death, and Catharine, captured by the Ojibwas, contrives to escape. Finally, an old French-Canadian lumberer, who turns out to be a friend of their families, leads them back to their grieving parents. They discover that, all the while, they have been no more than eight miles from home.

Although Mrs. Traill realized that her tale "would be too adventurous and romantic" for some readers, she defended its authenticity. In a letter written on 19 June 1853, she said that "the Indian portion was founded on facts that were related to me," and added ". . . though improbable in these days, the circumstances are not impossible that life should have been supported as there stated. The union of the young people would make them more easily sustained."[13] That *Canadian Crusoes* is based on fact is quite clear. The plot is anchored in a specific historical period by the importance of "the famous battle of Quebec"[14] to the subsequent events. Although about nine decades are actually spanned, from 1759 to the time of writing, the reader is constantly kept aware of two contrasted periods, the time of the events during the days of pioneer settlement in Upper Canada and the time of the narration in the mid-nineteenth century, the "then" and the "now" of the region. Both in the text and in footnotes and appendices, Mrs. Traill assumes the role of local historian, pointing out the changes that have taken place.

The different sites of the action, such as the Valley of the Big Stone and the Upper Race Course, are so accurately described that each can be recognized today on the shores and islands of Rice Lake and in the area of the Otonabee River. When a specific property is mentioned, she adds the name and history of past and present occupants, some of whom are her neighbours and friends. These are also so precisely identified that most can be found in the census rolls of the district for 1850.

She is equally authentic in her attention to the details of plant life. Nature seldom functions solely as a background, because, in the struggle for survival in the forest, certain plants are important for their practical, culinary, or medicinal value. Flowers, plants, and trees are identified formally by their botanical classifications, usually by their Latin names.

Paradoxically, although the Indians play the menacing roles of romance, through them Mrs. Traill contributes to the historical record of Indian life in Canada, in particular the life of the Mohawks and the Ojibwas from early days to the time of their conversion to Christianity. The authenticity of her record is emphasized by the footnotes and the lengthy appendices supported by material from an autobiography of George Copway, an Indian missionary,[15] and by the extension of the narrative to include detailed accounts of Indian customs and crafts.

Canadian Crusoes takes, most of all, its authenticity from different aspects of Mrs. Traill's life: her family traditions and background, her early education and reading, her religious beliefs, her first writings, and her experiences as a pioneer settler raising her family in the backwoods of Upper Canada. Catharine Parr Traill, the fifth of eight surviving children of Thomas and Elizabeth Strickland, was born in London on 9 Jan. 1802.[16] The Stricklands had a strong sense of family tradition. They claimed to be related to the aristocratic Stricklands of Sizergh, Westmorland,[17] but the connection appears to have been either remote or apocryphal.[18] Catharine was evidently named after Catherine Parr, the sixth wife of Henry VIII, with whom the family also claimed a connection, although the spelling of the queen's Christian name was not adopted.

When she was quite young, her father, Thomas Strickland, retired as "manager of the Greenland docks"[19] on the River Thames to take up business in East Anglia. Although the family occupied three different houses, the most important was Reydon Hall, a large red-brick manor house, "built in the Tudor style,"[20] near the town of Southwold on the Suffolk coast.[21] It was Reydon and the surrounding countryside and the local history and legends associated with this setting that remained fixed in Catharine's mind for the rest of her long life and affected her writing. In her old age she recalled the "old ruined Abbeys," the castles they explored,[22] the tales of adventurers, smugglers, and the contests and battles of the sixteenth and seventeenth centuries, especially those that involved the Stuarts.

The peculiar position of their parents and the form of the children's early education fostered a family interdependence and strengthened the young Stricklands' interests in nature and in the historical and legendary past. At Reydon Hall, they were quite isolated socially. Looking back many years later, Catharine wrote: "There was little social intercourse took place between us and the neighbours. We were not one of themselves."[23] Their ambiguous position has been noted by Una Pope-Hennessy: "socially they fell between two stools, being neither of the county nor yet connected with a business. It is evident that though their circumstances were genteel, their upbringing gentle, and their residence a Hall, they were not at this time accepted by the county families who avoided all suspicion of contact with trade or the middle-class."[24] Catharine observed the effects on the Strickland children: "Brought up as we were without any companionship apart from strangers in our own family we formed a little world for ourselves."[25]

This early interdependence was intensified by the form of the children's education. Instead of sending the six young girls to schools, Thomas and Elizabeth Strickland taught them at home. To supplement the parents' teaching, the older children, Elizabeth, Agnes, Sarah, and Jane Margaret, in turn taught the younger, Catharine and Susanna, and Samuel and Thomas until they were sent to school. Their interest in tales and legends was fostered by their mother and her old nurse Betty Holt, who entertained them with stories such as "The Babes in the Woods." This story, to which Catharine often referred in her works, is an obvious source of the theme of lost children.[26]

The range of subjects covered was wide. It included history, geography, mathematics, botany, the natural sciences, and some languages, certainly French and Italian,[27] and perhaps German. It was not, however, the range of the subjects as much as the method of teaching that remained foremost in Catharine's mind: "My father would never tell us anything we wanted to know, without first endeavouring to make us exercise our own reason."[28] The object of the children's education was "to render them independent and to call forth their talents, and to form industrious habits."[29] The children were schooled in the importance of independence, self-reliance, discipline, and responsibility,[30] characteristics that make for survival in *Canadian Crusoes*. The study of natural objects was central, including the collecting, identifying, and labelling of botanical specimens, occupations and interests evident in Catharine Parr Traill's writing throughout her life.

This study was important in a more fundamental way. Catharine points out the moral aspect of nature study, which teaches readers to "look through nature up to nature's God" and "elevates the mind and awakens feelings of devotion"[31] to God, "that Almighty Being, whose piercing eye is abroad all over his works."[32] Catharine recalled later the religious observances in their evangelical Anglican family, with "catechisms and collects" to be learned and "the text to be duly remembered, and repeated and all the forms of the church carefully observed," with regular reading of "the Bible or rather a chapter in the Old Testament" and paraphrases of the Psalms.[33] Despite what she called "the doubts and infidelity of modern sceptics,"[34] Catharine's trust in an ever-present omnipotent God, evident throughout *Canadian Crusoes*, and her devotion to evangelical Christian principles, which she identified as "our low views,"[35] remained unshaken to the end of her life. The pages of her writing are marked by quotations, or paraphrased passages from the Bible, either consciously or unconsciously introduced, comprising words and phrases that had become, through daily contact, such an inherent part of her thought and vocabulary that it would not occur to her to check their accuracy.

The children were encouraged to pursue their reading interests. Fortunately, what her sister Susanna later described as "the good old-fashioned library"[36] had many books among which they could browse. Catharine recalled that they "ransacked the library for books. . . . We even tried 'Locke on the human understanding' but as may be imagined we made small progress in that direction."[37] Their reading was wide, given the proprieties and customs of the day: history, Pope's translation of Homer,[38] the English classics in poetry, fiction, and drama, and natural history, including in the last category Gilbert White's *Natural History of Selborne* (1789),[39] so important for Catharine's books. The large number of quotations and references in Catharine's writing shows how indelible were the impressions made by this early reading. In addition to the ever-present Biblical quotations, there are constant references to passages in the plays of Shakespeare. Of the history books Catharine recalled particularly Paul de Rapin's *History of England* (tr. Nicholas Tindal, 1743) and Catharine Macaulay's *History of England from the Accession of James I to that of the Brunswick Line* (1763-83). These books "had the effect of awaking" in Agnes, who achieved fame later as a biographer and historian, "an undying interest in the unfortunate Charles the 1st and his descendants."[40] That this enthusiasm was shared by Catharine is evident in the references to the Stuarts throughout *Canadian Crusoes*. Catharine speaks, too, of the sisters' reading Defoe's *Robinson Crusoe* (1719)[41] and being "well acquainted" with Thomas Day's pedagogic *Sandford and Merton* (1783-89).[42] Their taste for fiction could have been further served by the "city library" in Norwich, of which both Catharine and Jane Margaret speak,[43] and by the circulating library that Agnes sometimes encountered when visiting friends.[44] It is significant that, in addition to Thomas Day's moral fiction, it is the novels of Anna Maria and Jane Porter, Maria Edgeworth, and Mrs. Inchbald that Jane Margaret lists;[45] for here, when the sisters came to write themselves, they had models of the most influential kinds of popular fiction.

The isolation that made the children "form a little world for themselves" had an important practical consequence. Catharine recalled that it was their "lonely and isolated" life that spurred them on to their "first attempt at writing," which led to "important after results."[46] Catharine and her younger sister took the first step: "To break the tedium of the dull winter Susanna and myself formed the notion that we would try and write something of a novel, or tale ourselves — The idea was, just to amuse ourselves by reading at night to our elder sister, what we had written during the day."[47] Catharine chose for her subject the "domestic life in Alpine regions, in the days of William Tell."[48] "For the MS. rough copy of this little tale," Catharine "received the sum of ten guineas,"[49] although it was never published. The direct comment by an omniscient narrator that came to be an integral part of all Catharine's work is already prominent in this moral tale. The "Swiss" virtues of industry, ingenuity, so important in *Canadian Crusoes*, and frugality are lauded, and at the end, "truth and honesty . . . rewarded."[50]

Catharine was the first of the sisters to have a manuscript published. In May 1818, when she was sixteen, Thomas Strickland, who had recently lost the greater part of his fortune, died suddenly.[51] An executor took one of Catharine's manuscripts to London, where it was published as *The Tell-Tale; An Original Collection of Moral and Amusing Stories* (1818).[52] The possibility of supporting themselves now gave the Strickland sisters an additional reason for writing.

During the 1820s both Elizabeth, the eldest, and Agnes established useful editorial connections in the publishing world of London, particularly with periodicals that provided markets for the young writers.[53] Living and writing at home, Catharine had remarkable success during the next fourteen years. Several lists, compiled by Catharine in later life and sometimes conflicting, suggest that she had published, between the ages of fifteen and thirty, some eight books. To these can be added seven or eight that she did not include, perhaps because of failing memory.[54] On one of her lists she observed: "These books were all popular and were paid for readily — I never had a MS. rejected."[55]

Eager to succeed, Catharine as a young girl took her materials from her omnivorous reading, but also, occasionally, from her own limited experience at Reydon and in Norwich, and moulded them into the accepted popular patterns of the historical narrative, the moral fairy tale, the fable, and the brief expository essay. Some of this early writing foreshadows the concerns of the later, more mature Catharine. *Reformation; or,*

The Cousins (1819) makes some attempt to deal with the "Occurrences of Real Life" of its subtitle. The titles of two early works *Sketches from Nature; or, Hints to Juvenile Naturalists* (1830) and *The Young Emigrants; or, Pictures of Canada. Calculated to Amuse and Instruct the Minds of Youth* (1826) indicate interests that would be central to Catharine's most important later writing. In *Sketches from Nature*, abandoning the fable conventions, she examines the characteristics and habits of birds and animals in precise detail. In *The Young Emigrants*, again breaking away from traditional patterns, Catharine combines the letters of Suffolk acquaintances who had emigrated with facts she found in two accounts by travellers.[56] Some details of the description of a forest fire appear again in *Canadian Crusoes*. The subtitle, "Calculated to Amuse and Instruct," indicates the didactic aim embodied in *The Young Emigrants*, an inherent part of the constant practice of Catharine Parr Traill, the evangelical Christian. Titles such as *Reformation* and *Prejudice Reproved; or, The History of the Negro Toy-seller* (1826) are likewise indicators of her natural bent towards didactic fiction. All of her narratives, often peopled by contrasted characters, end happily; for no problem is so serious that it cannot be solved, no individual so base or evil that he cannot be reformed.

Of her general disposition and her view of life, she wrote in 1836: "It has ever been my way to extract the sweet rather than the bitter in the cup of life, and surely it is best and wisest so to do. . . . I believe that one of the chief ingredients in human happiness is a capacity for enjoying the blessings we possess."[57] For her, "the doubts and infidelity of modern sceptics" only serve to "taint" beliefs.[58] Looking back, the older Catharine wrote: "I was young and hopeful. . . . To me there was *always* [her emphasis] a silver lining to the cloud — and surely it was a gift from God, that it has ever been thus, in days of trouble and sorrow, often in after years, I could look upwards and say — Lord, Thy will be done."[59] Although not blindly optimistic, she sees the individual and the world in terms of "blessings." Her unquestioned belief in the positive capabilities of the individual

in a world watched over by an omnipresent, omnipotent being,
which makes itself felt in all her writing, is particularly evident in
Canadian Crusoes.

During these years of prolific production, the Strickland
sisters succeeded in breaking out of their "little world,"[60] and
new relationships were formed that permanently disrupted the
family life of the Stricklands. Catharine much later recalled the
sequence of events that began in 1831 with her visits to the
London home of "the Poet Thomas Pringle," the Secretary of
the Anti-Slavery League:

> Susanna . . . there met . . . Lieut. Moodie. . . . It was
> there I met Mr. Traill who was a friend and fellow officer
> in the 21st Royal Scotch Fusiliers. He was a widower, with
> two sons, a mutual attachment sprang up, and we were
> married. It was the year of the great emigration, and both
> my husband and Mr. Moodie determined to go to Canada.
> It was on the *13th of May, 1832* that I was married in our
> parish church at Reydon.[61]

Catharine's husband, Thomas Traill, from an upper-class
Orkney background, with an Oxford degree and Scottish
literary associations,[62] subject to "nervous irritability"[63] and
repeated periods of paralyzing depression, whose disposition
would make his relations with his sons and neighbours
difficult,[64] was hardly an ideal settler for the new world.
Catharine, however, recounts their setting out, a week after their
marriage, "young and hopeful," bidding "a sad farewell to
Home, country and my beloved mere and sisters, whom I was
destined never to see again."[65] Catharine later described the
voyage in detail, from London to Edinburgh, and from there to
Thomas Traill's family home "Westove" in the Orkneys, "to take
leave of his friends and relatives and to see his two sons."[66] At
Inverness she renewed an early fascination: "It was charming
. . . to hear talk of the young Chevalier — the hero of my

girlhood, by the grandsons and granddaughters, of those devoted men, who had striven to the death for the cause of the Stuarts."[67]

On 7 July 1832, the Traills sailed from Greenock.[68] That fall they settled near Catharine's brother, Samuel Strickland, who, having emigrated in 1825, was farming on the Otonabee River near Lakefield. Once more Catharine, though now in radically different circumstances, was a member of a circumscribed "little world." Although she lived in a number of different houses, they were all located within the same region: on the Otonabee, in Peterborough, and on the south shore of Rice Lake. There were few literary or social contacts. Two of the most prized were Frances Stewart and her daughter Ellen Dunlop, who often provided a much-needed refuge and served as sympathetic recipients of Mrs. Traill's frequent letters.

From the time the Traills established themselves in their small log house in their clearing in the backwoods, their lives were consumed with hard labour, constant sickness, and crop failures in a continuous struggle for subsistence. With nine children arriving within fourteen years and with her husband's inability to deal with constant crises, the load of responsibility fell on Mrs. Traill. Fortunately, she remained energetic, confident, and optimistic, the product of the Strickland training in self-reliance and responsibility.

Although her life was taken up with the fundamental occupations necessary for survival, the need for extra income was even greater here than it had been at Reydon after the death of her father, and Mrs. Traill alone was capable of earning money. As a result, from the time she arrived in Upper Canada, Mrs. Traill wrote continually. By the spring of 1835, she had finished *The Backwoods of Canada: Being Letters from the Wife of an Emigrant Officer, Illustrative of the Domestic Economy of British America*, the publication of which by Charles Knight in London in 1836 was probably arranged through the useful connections of her older sisters.[69] The letters give a meticulous and graphic account of the family's pioneering trials. As in *Canadian Crusoes*,

Mrs. Traill's documentation in her informative introduction, in the numerous footnotes, which include botanical identifications, in her observations on the changes that have taken place since her arrival in 1832, and in the series of appendices on practical questions lends authenticity to the book. And almost every year pieces appeared in periodicals in Great Britain, the United States, and Canada: poems, anecdotes, short essays, graphic accounts of the life around her, and a series of fictional narratives.[70] These included the narratives written and published during the 1830s and 1840s that were to become *Canadian Crusoes*.

The manuscript that Mrs. Traill sent to her sisters in England in the late fall of 1850 has apparently not survived; so its condition cannot be ascertained. Between the time of their receiving it and its publication in 1852, however, Agnes edited the manuscript and added a preface. If the condition of this manuscript resembled that of Catharine's later book *Lady Mary and Her Nurse* (1856), Agnes' editing may have included clarification of Catharine's handwriting, correction of her style, and possibly more substantial revisions. About *Lady Mary and Her Nurse*, Jane Margaret complained to Catharine: "I rallied all my fainting energy to finish my task — not indeed a light one dear Kate for though the work is a very interesting one you had left it very imperfect in construction and there was an immensity to do, to fit it for an English public — Agnes who looked over it sometimes was as puzzled as myself and it required to be corrected not only in proof but two revises."[71]

Catharine hoped that the connections of Elizabeth and Agnes with London publishers would lead to profitable negotiations and speedy publication. She was disappointed to learn, therefore, that the parcel of manuscripts had not even been opened until July 1851 and that the current obsession with the "Catholic question" in Britain made literary negotiations impossible.[72] By early 1852, however, she could at last write to Ellen Dunlop: "I am sure you were all glad about my selling the Canadian Crusoes."[73] The sisters by then had sold the right to an edition of two thousand copies to Hall, Virtue of London for fifty pounds.[74]

Having bought the copyright to Mrs. Traill's book, Hall, Virtue organized its publication. In the spring and early summer of 1852, Richard Clay of London printed the text; the popular wood-engraver and illustrator, William Harvey, produced twelve engravings for it; and the well-known designer, John Leighton, prepared the design for the casing. The book was ready for publication by the end of July. On 30 July an advertisement appeared in the London *Times*: "Published this day, with Harvey's designs. fcp. cloth, gilt edges, price 6s., The Canadian Crusoes. By Mrs. Traill, Author of the 'Backwoods of Canada.' Edited by Agnes Strickland. Arthur Hall, Virtue and Co., 25 Paternoster-row."[75] This advertisement was repeated five times in the next eleven days.

Over the next few months *Canadian Crusoes* was reviewed in several publications by anonymous reviewers. Most discussed it as a book for young readers. On 15 August in the *Observer*, the reviewer devoted most of his long notice to a detailed summary of the plot and quoted at length from Agnes' preface. He recognized the "freshness" of the text, and praised the "truth and gracefulness" of "its description of American backwood scenery, animal and vegetable productions."[76] On 28 August the writer of a one-paragraph review in *John Bull*, employing a number of the clichés of Victorian reviewing, spoke of this "prettily conceived tale," "elegantly illustrated," that sets out to amuse and to instruct with "interesting pictures of American scenery and of Indian life."[77] The reviewer in the *Daily News* on 4 September, noting the large amount of description of American scenery and "traits of Indian manners," stressed the "useful information," and the "practical lessons of self-reliance," "ingenuity," and "readiness of resource," characteristics needed in the bush where "the losing in the woods" appears to be "one of the commonest perils."[78] In the September issue of *Tait's Edinburgh Magazine*, the reviewer pointed out that the moral purpose of the writer was "to inculcate the virtues of energy and self-reliance." He added: "The story is made the vehicle of a good deal of instruction besides that of a moral kind — the phenomena of the uncultured forest, its botanical treasures and its living occupants, furnishing the text." While labelling the book a "little romance," he stressed the realistic aspects. "The scenes in the Indian camp and settlement are very different from the delineations of the American novelists, and are probably nearer to the truth."[79]

The reviewer in *Sharpe's London Magazine* took a different approach. The writer devoted half of a one-paragraph review to the careers of the Strickland sisters. The comments on *Canadian Crusoes*, "a charming book," "a very pretty book ... full of interest and information," are vague. Those on the illustrations, however, are definite. Whereas the reviewers in the *Observer*, *John Bull*, and *Tait's* had nothing but praise for the illustrator, this reviewer had specific objections. Although *Sharpe's London Magazine* was owned by the publisher of *Canadian Crusoes*, the reviewer felt free to criticize the firm's illustrator: "The illustrations are drawn with Mr. Harvey's well-known taste and spirit, but why will he persist in putting 'old heads on young shoulders,' an operation declared to be 'impossible,' and which, when Mr. Harvey makes it possible, is anything but pleasant."[80]

In April 1852, while waiting for payment from Hall, Virtue, Mrs. Traill had been exploring the North American market.[81] Two of her earlier works, *Fables for the Nursery* (1825) and *The Juvenile Forget-Me-Not* (1827), had already been published in the United States, probably in pirated editions, the *Fables* by C. S. Francis of Boston and New York. One of the people to whom Mrs. Traill wrote was George Putnam, who had issued a pirated edition of Susanna Moodie's *Roughing It in the Bush* in July 1852.[82] She had evidently received an answer before 11 Oct. 1852; for she wrote Putnam that day regretting that she had been "too late in my application to you respecting the re-issue of the 'Canadian'," and thanking him for "trying to interest Mr. Francis in my behalf — from that gentleman I have not received any communication."[83]

On 15 Oct. 1852 Francis announced that the firm would "shortly publish" the novel, the English edition of which had been available in New York since September.[84] On 15 December, despite the 1853 date on the title-page, it was listed among "New Works/American," that were "Published During the Month of November . . . reprints from English Editions."[85] *The Canadian Crusoes. A Tale of the Rice Lake Plains*, reset from the English edition and stereotyped by Billin and Brothers of New York, was published with the imprint of C. S. Francis of New York and Crosby, Nichols and Co. of Boston. John William Orr, the celebrated American wood-engraver, copied five of Harvey's illustrations for reproduction in this edition. On 18 December this *Crusoes* was advertised for sale in the *Pilot* by B. Dawson, a Montreal bookseller.[86]

Some time between 11 Oct. and 27 Dec. 1852, Mrs. Traill had received what she called "promises" from C. S. Francis. On the 27th her son James wrote to his aunt Susanna Moodie: "The Canadian Crusoes is just published [in] New York by Francis, a person of respectability and . . . if he does as he promises that is . . . if [the] book sells well he will give Mamma something handsome. Perhaps you may have seen it though we have not as yet. The English edition is [beautifully ?] illustrated, so say the papers."[87] Shortly after James wrote this letter, Mrs. Traill received at last both the British and the American editions.[88] By 5 Apr. 1853, she had what she called a "present" of fifty dollars from Francis who evidently had decided to send her the not unusual conscience money.[89] On 19 June 1853 she wrote to Ellen Dunlop: "You will be pleased to hear . . . that my little work is getting very popular in the States where it was republished. Francis sent me a nice present, and promised me more next year, and highly praised my book which he said is likely to be of great advantage to author and publisher."[90]

This American edition of *The Canadian Crusoes* certainly proved to be "of great advantage" to the publisher; for it went through at least nine more impressions. Three appeared, in 1854, 1856, and 1859, with the combined imprint of C. S.

Francis of New York and Crosby, Nichols and Co. of Boston. From this time the name of C. S. Francis disappeared from the title-page. Subsequent impressions were issued from Boston, each by a different company as the original Crosby, Nichols and Co. experienced changes in ownership.[91] There is, however, no indication that this American edition was of any "advantage" at all to the author; for the letter of 19 June to Ellen Dunlop is the last record of Mrs. Traill's dealing with an American publisher.

In the early 1850s Mrs. Traill was writing steadily. Some of her most graphic, first-hand observations of life around her in the backwoods appeared as the "Forest Gleanings" series in the Toronto *Anglo-American Magazine* in 1852-53.[92] In 1854 her detailed account of the domestic economy of mid-nineteenth-century life in the backwoods, *The Female Emigrant's Guide, and Hints on Canadian Housekeeping*, was published; it was republished as *The Canadian Settler's Guide* from 1855 on.[93] In 1856 *Lady Mary and Her Nurse; or, A Peep Into the Canadian Forest*, which had already appeared in serial form in Canada, was published in London.[94] It was issued by the same firm as *Canadian Crusoes*, and printed by the same printer, with illustrations by the same artist. It has many of the same features as *Canadian Crusoes*: direct comment, piety, numerous footnotes, factual details and Latin botanical identifications, and the "then-now" theme. It went through many editions and impressions in both Great Britain and the United States where it was republished, like *Canadian Crusoes*, by Francis of New York and Crosby, Nichols of Boston and their various successors.[95]

After the appearance of *Lady Mary* in 1856, no new work by Mrs. Traill was published for twelve years; for her life was disturbed by a series of blows. "Oaklands" burned down so swiftly on 26 Aug. 1857 and with such suddenness that its contents were almost completely lost. "The only things saved in the confusion of that midnight fire," she wrote late in her life, "were a few books that lay on my writing table with the MSS papers" that were used ten years later in a book on Canadian wild flowers.[96] Mrs. Traill never mentions in her letters or journals the manuscript sheets related to different stages in the composition of *Canadian Crusoes* that also survived. After the disaster Frances Stewart gave the Traills shelter; for it was more than two years before they could afford a place of their own.[97] All Mrs. Traill's letters attest to her desperate need for money to pay daily expenses and to settle accumulating debts. In September 1857 she is reduced to hoping "to redeem the losses . . . by writing, by needlework and knitting, pressing flowers and other matters."[98]

As a possible source of money, Mrs. Traill still had the rights to *Canadian Crusoes*. She had known for some time that the book was a success. Writing to her sister Susanna on 6 Jan. 1854, she quoted her sister Elizabeth: "Your Crusoes are very much admired."[99] On 21 Jan. 1855, Agnes, probably in response to a request by Catharine to investigate the possibility of a new edition, wrote that "the 'Crusoes' " had "sold well," but that Hall, Virtue still had some of the two thousand copies of the 1852 edition left. They hoped, however, "ere long to come to a reprint," if business conditions improved in Britain.[100] On 12 August, probably in 1858, Jane Margaret wrote her: "If Agnes has not found time to apprise you of it I have some good news to tell — She has corrected the second edition of your Crusoes and torn the promise of fifty pounds from Virtue who said five like the rogue he was."[101]

At this point Catharine, impatient, began to deal directly with Hall, Virtue, and agreed to his terms for a new edition. Agnes, who only discovered that Catharine had invalidated her agency on a visit to the publisher, was furious at her sister's thoughtless, naive interference and at her having "fallen into the toils of a designing knave,"[102] as she called Arthur Hall. Despite Agnes' subsequent attempts to secure better conditions, the second edition appeared in 1859 on the terms Hall, Virtue had arranged with Catharine. She may have received that year twenty-five pounds, half the sum Agnes fought for. This 1859 edition, based on the first edition but with minor revisions to the text, was also printed by Clay of London.

Some four years later Agnes wrote to Catharine that "Hall is out of the business having proved himself a great rogue."[103] In 1862 the name of J. S. Virtue had appeared alone on the title-page of the second issue of the 1859 edition of *Crusoes*. Sheets from the 1859 edition were also issued as a new American edition by Virtue and Yorston of New York some time between 1864 and 1872, when J. S. Virtue and John C. Yorston, an American, were business associates in New York.[104]

In the early sixties Mrs. Traill attempted once more to obtain money from her works. With the death of her husband on 21 June 1859, both her responsibilities and financial difficulties had increased. It was only with a special grant from the British Government, evidently arranged by Lady Charlotte Greville, who admired her botanical specimens, and some financial help from her sister Agnes and her brother Samuel that she made her last move, in the spring of 1860, to "Westove," the house named after her husband's Orkney home that she had had built for her in Lakefield.[105] On 16 May 1863 she wrote to her daughter Katharine from Toronto that she had been making daily calls on James Campbell, the publisher and wholesale bookseller, in the hope of seeing William Nelson, of the Edinburgh firm of Thomas Nelson, who regularly visited Campbell, their Toronto agent, to promote sales.[106] After several fruitless attempts to get in touch with the Scottish publisher through Campbell, Mrs. Traill wrote, according to her journal entry for 12 Feb. 1866, directly to "Nelson the Publisher."[107] After long anxious waiting, on 2 Feb. 1867 she had news indirectly through her niece, a daughter of Susanna Moodie. She wrote to her own daughter Katharine: "Mr. Campbell told Agnes Fitz[gibbon] that Nelson had bought the copy right of the C. Crusoes from Virtue and wants me to revise it for him — Now it is not Virtues property to sell so I must write Mr. Nelson and say so."[108] Mrs. Traill's letter has not survived, but by 8 May 1867 she had received an offer from Nelson and Sons that she considered "shabby," but, pressed for money, she decided that she must accept.[109] By 20 June an agreement had been reached. She wrote to her daughter Anne: "I must tell you that I got a letter from Nelson offering me £40 for the copyrights of the C. Crusoes and 'Little Mary' if I corrected, and made some additions. It was little enough, but I consented and have sent off the corrections etc, last week."[110]

Some of the corrections and additions in *Canadian Crusoes* were concerned with the book's botanical material. Just at this time Mrs. Traill was putting the final touches to *Canadian Wild Flowers. Painted and Lithographed by Agnes Fitzgibbon, with Botanical Descriptions by C. P. Traill*, which was published in 1868 by John Lovell of Montreal. This was the first of two works[111] that represented the culmination of years of study begun under her father's guidance. She had been collecting notes for a projected work on Canadian botany for some time before the 1857 fire. Some of these had been published in 1853 as "Canadian Flower Gatherer" in the *Anglo-American Magazine*[112] and in 1863 as "Flowers and their Moral Teaching" in the Toronto periodical *British American Magazine*.[113] In her journal in 1863 and in her letters in 1864 and 1865, she keeps referring to her manuscript on plant life.[114] By 1867, when she came to make her corrections for Nelson's, she had already sent the publisher sections of *Canadian Wild Flowers*. In this book Mrs. Traill gave detailed descriptions of each plant, stressed its culinary or medicinal value, and supplied the Latin name from *North American Flora* (1814), by Frederick Pursh, whom she names as her only precursor in this field.[115] In 1867, then, Mrs. Traill could easily and quickly correct, expand, and make definitive the botanical material that she had included in the 1852 edition of *Canadian Crusoes*. These 1867 corrections and additions were Mrs. Traill's final touches to her book.

According to a letter written to her daughter Anne, probably in December 1867, she was at that time still waiting for her money "from that old humbug Nelson."[116] Although *Lady Mary and Her Nurse* was published as *Afar in the Forest; or, Pictures of Life and Scenery in the Wilds of Canada* in 1869, Nelson's edition of *Canadian Crusoes* did not appear until 1882. It was then published as *Lost in the Backwoods. A Tale of the Canadian Forest*, and it differed substantially from its predecessors. One of the most striking differences was the addition of twenty illustrations to the original twelve by Harvey.

Five later impressions of this edition, which can only be distinguished by their title-pages and by the casings of the various Nelson series in which they appeared, were published in 1884, 1886, 1890, 1892, and 1896.[117] Nelson's put out another impression of the 1882 edition in 1901, two years after Mrs. Traill's death on 29 Aug. 1899. In 1909 a new printing of the 1882 edition was published in "Nelson's Travel Series." In this version the illustrations that had appeared on the pages in the earlier impressions were removed and therefore type was rearranged to fill in the resulting spaces. Lines were excised to make chapter endings coincide with page endings. Four coloured plates were tipped in to replace the thirty-two illustrations in the 1882 edition. A second impression of this printing was published in 1923 in the "Blue Star Series."[118]

In Mrs. Traill's letters there is one reference to the Nelson edition. She wrote to her son William on 21 Oct. 1890: "It is well got up, with many new illustrations — as '*Lost in the Backwoods*' — I do not approve of the change of title."[119] In some notes written late in her life listing her publications, she called the new title "*very stupid* and as I think illegal."[120] In 1923 Mrs. Traill's book completed a circle; for after being published in London, New York, and Edinburgh, it was then published in Toronto, some ninety miles from the scene of its events and its composition, as *Canadian Crusoes. A Tale of the Rice Lake Plains* by McClelland and Stewart. This new edition, based on the 1852 text, had on the verso of its title-leaf McClelland and Stewart's claim to copyright. It was this claim that prompted Nelson's Toronto agent to write to the Edinburgh office on 17 Dec. 1923 to ask about his firm's rights. The book was obviously still a valuable property; for he suggested their issuing a "cheaper school edition" for which "a sale of something between five and ten thousand copies" could be found "within the year."[121] The Edinburgh firm replied that their copyright to the book bought in October 1867 had now expired, and promised to consider the suggestion of a cheap school edition,[122] but such an edition never materialized. This CEECT edition of *Canadian Crusoes* is the first since 1923.

Although Catharine Parr Traill has received a great deal of attention,[123] there have been few studies of *Canadian Crusoes*. Most of the books and articles have emphasized Catharine Parr Traill the settler, the cultural phenomenon. When the concern has shifted from the woman to the works, it has lighted on the botanical writings, especially *Canadian Wild Flowers* and *Studies of Plant Life in Canada*, and those recording the details of pioneer life, *The Backwoods of Canada* and *The Canadian Settler's Guide*.

During the last fifteen years several writers have discussed *Canadian Crusoes*, either in a section of a general study or in relation to other works by Mrs. Traill. In 1973 in *Notable Canadian Children's Books*, Sheila Egoff and Alvine Bélisle call it her "first genuine Canadian children's book" and stress its following "every ploy of the didactic school of writing for children then dominant in England."[124] Three years later in the *Literary History of Canada*, Sheila Egoff singled out the theme and the centrality of landscape for comment. Despite its "flowery nineteenth-century language," she found that "as a piece of Canadiana it retains elements of interest." She judged its popularity to be "well deserved, even though the scarcity of Canadian children's books probably accounted for some of its staying power."[125] In 1976, Clara Thomas discussed it in some detail in relation to *The Young Emigrants*. She points out Mrs. Traill's conception of man's role as an "ordering agent" in the world of nature, the use of racial stereotypes, and Mrs. Traill's optimistic view of the possibilities of a "melding" of the different racial strains, the French, the Scottish, and the Indian.[126] In his comprehensive study of Catharine Parr Traill published in 1983, Carl Ballstadt includes the most detailed examination of *Canadian Crusoes* to date. Although he makes some suggestions about its technical aspects, he is chiefly concerned with the book as "fable," as "manual of elemental pioneering and survival," as "microcosm of the society Traill envisions," and as "a book of wisdom literature containing maxims on conduct and expressions of Christian faith."[127] So far *Canadian Crusoes* has not been inspected in detail either from the point of view of narrative technique or as a single work in its own right. Despite this scarcity of critical comment, Catharine Parr Traill's book about children lost in the backwoods has helped shape the literary imagination of many adult Canadians.

THE TEXT

The intention of this CEECT edition of Catharine Parr Traill's *Canadian Crusoes* is to provide the contemporary reader with a reliable text as close as possible to the author's intentions. Apart from the nine sheets of early draft fragments no manuscript of the work has been located. Only the editions published during Mrs. Traill's lifetime can be considered for copy-text and as sources of authorial emendations. These are the first English edition of 1852, the American edition of 1853, the second English edition of 1859, and the Nelson edition of 1882. Since the 1853 American edition was printed from the 1852 English edition and since Mrs. Traill had nothing to do with the minor changes that were introduced, it has been rejected both as a copy-text and a source of emendation. Only the three British editions, then, have been used to establish the text of this CEECT edition.

Although Agnes undoubtedly made changes to the manuscript that Mrs. Traill sent to her sisters in 1850 and added a preface before sending it to the publisher, the 1852 Hall, Virtue edition is the version closest to Mrs. Traill's original work. It presents her title, her dedication, the text most similar to the one she wrote, and her footnotes and appendices. It is, furthermore, the parent edition for all subsequent versions of the text. It is, accordingly, the choice as the copy-text.

Although neither the 1859 nor the 1882 edition is eligible as copy-text, both, unlike the 1853 American, have been considered as sources of emendation in the preparation of the CEECT edition.

The 1859 edition was printed from the 1852. In this new edition compositorial and other obvious errors in the 1852 were corrected. More substantial revisions were also made. Some of the most extensive and detailed of these occur in Agnes' preface. Other changes seem to result from a wish to avoid what might not be considered "proper." A graphic description of Indian intertribal slaughter (p. 212)[128] is softened; a suggestion of possible infidelity (pp. 4-5) and a jocular reference to a lumberer's fondness for the bottle (pp. 56-57) are cut. This acute sense of propriety, noticeable enough in Catharine, is particularly characteristic of Agnes. It is probable, then, that Agnes made these changes to the text. There is no evidence that the changes were cleared with Catharine. This edition, therefore, is not a source of authorial emendations.

Since, however, in 1867 Catharine used a copy of the 1859 edition to make the corrections and additions that were a condition of the offer from Nelson's, the 1859 is the link between the 1852 edition and the 1882, the only other edition of the work known to contain revisions by Catharine.

In the absence of the actual copy of the 1859 edition that Mrs. Traill sent to "old Nelson," the 1882 provides the only evidence of the 1867 corrections and additions. The 1882 edition, however, is a shortened and substantially altered version of Mrs. Traill's original work. Its reliability as a source of authorial revisions is, therefore, open to question. The 1882 has been altered in a variety of ways not likely to have had their source in Mrs. Traill. Not only is the title changed, but there are also changes in the text. For example, consistently throughout the text the North American "the fall" has been changed to "autumn," more usual in Great Britain (p. 64; 1882, p. 63). As well, words, phrases, sentences, paragraphs, and one block of four pages are deleted. Mrs. Traill's dedication, her sister's preface, one-quarter of the footnotes, and all sixteen pages of appendices have disappeared. A new preface and twenty additional illustrations are included, and a different style of casing is used.

As a result of the changes in the text of *Canadian Crusoes*, its effect is substantially altered. Passages of direct comment by the omniscient author, in which Mrs. Traill characteristically addresses the reader in generalizing, often moralizing terms, have been lost. The most commonly deleted direct addresses to the reader are those that embody the "then-now" theme, to which Mrs. Traill returned so often. These contrast the early pioneer settlements with the cultivated properties of her neighbours, and the primitive wilderness with the bridges, mills, court-houses, and churches that are the marks of courage, perseverance, order, and Christian civilization. This material too is an integral part of Catharine Parr Traill's thinking and writing.

In the most extended of the deleted "then-now" passages Mrs. Traill, with mixed feelings, addresses the effects of these changes on the Indians (pp. 314-17). What is obvious is her concern and sympathy for them. In the narrative of the 1882 edition, with its deletions, the Indian men, in contrast to the women, are presented as proud, cruel, vengeful warriors. It is only in the original text and in the material provided at that time by the footnotes and appendices that other aspects are evident: their suffering and stoicism, their customs and art, their own religion, and their conversion to Christianity, subjects of importance to Catharine Parr Traill.

The effect of these changes is intensified by practical decisions made by Nelson's about the book. The changes in title and the supplying of a new preface are typical. Evidently Nelson's did not consider Mrs. Traill's title attractive enough for the international audience they sought; so they substituted the more ominous *Lost in the Backwoods* and added a subtitle that evoked the lure of the unknown, *A Tale of the Canadian Forest*. Earlier, Mrs. Traill's *Lady Mary and Her Nurse; or, A Peep Into the Canadian*

Forest, with its delicate original title, had been transformed by Nelson's into the more forbidding *Afar in the Forest; or, Pictures of Life and Scenery in the Wilds of Canada*. The new preface dated "Edinburgh, 1882," written by a member of the Nelson firm, gives an inaccurate version of the first title and stresses the "attractive" and "romantic" aspects of this "interesting tale." This preface, obviously written to tempt buyers, runs counter to the author's purposes and her conception of the book.

The change in the illustrations demonstrates this same concentration on sales. Nelson's obviously decided that additional illustrations would make the work more attractive to buyers; for the title-page announces "With Thirty-Two Engravings." These include the twelve original engravings by William Harvey, reduced in size, and twenty others by a variety of illustrators, almost all unidentified, that vary from small cuts of insects, animals, birds, and Indian objects, to seven full-page illustrations. While some of the latter could be seen as having a tenuous connection with the text, others are not merely irrelevant but quite misleading.

The casing is similarly transformed. The gilt decorations on the casings of the 1852 and 1859 editions are chiefly limited to the spine. The 1882 displays on the front cover five Indian warriors around a campfire and on the spine a trapper lighting his pipe. The decorations on both the front cover and the spine are gilt. It is a move towards the flamboyant that was exploited extravagantly in Nelson's later impressions.

Nelson's was an aggressively practical firm. *Lady Mary* and *Canadian Crusoes*, portraying the life of the settlers, offered readers the lure of the unknown. Already published on both sides of the Atlantic, welcomed by warm reviews, the two books had proved themselves profitable by the number of editions and impressions required in both Great Britain and the United States. Nelson's knew that they had acquired property with marketable potential, particularly for the young people's market to which they directed so much of their publishing and distributing energies. They obviously intended to make changes to enhance that potential. Since they had acquired the copyright to Mrs. Traill's work, they could alter it to suit their marketing schemes.

Mrs. Traill was powerless now. When the 1852 and the 1859 editions had appeared, Agnes and Jane Margaret were present in London to edit and correct copy and to protect their sister's interests. In 1882 none of the family had control over the edition. Agnes Strickland had died in 1874. Mrs. Traill wrote, late in her life, "Since the death of my beloved sister Agnes Strickland . . . I have had no one to act as my agent in literary business . . . with publishers."[129] One must conclude, therefore, that despite its being based on a text corrected by Mrs. Traill, the 1882 edition is primarily Nelson's.

In view of Mrs. Traill's total lack of involvement in the changes in the 1859 and her minimal role in the preparation of the 1882, it is obvious that both these editions are suspect as sources of authorial emendation to the 1852 copy-text. In this CEECT edition, therefore, no changes in the 1859 have been accepted as authorial, and only revisions to botanical details and one ornithological identification have been accepted from the 1882 as having their source in Mrs. Traill's 1867 "corrections" and "additions." The botanical changes are of two kinds. Botanical terminology including Latin names has been added. In the 1882 edition "May-apples" (p. 48), for example, are further identified as "*Podophyllum peltatum.*" In the identification of "bitter-sweet," "*Solanum dulcamara*" (p. 40) becomes "*Celastrus scandens*" (1882, p. 44). These more precise labels can, with confidence, be attributed to Catharine Parr Traill, the authority on botanical lore and the author of *Canadian Wild Flowers*.

The CEECT text, however, does follow the example of the 1859 in correcting compositorial and other obvious errors in the 1852 copy-text that were first caught in this edition. For example, "redar" (p. 228) has been replaced by "cedar" (CEECT, p. 149), "Catherine" (p. 123) by "Catharine" (CEECT, p. 81), and "religions" in the phrase "her religions notions"

(p. 219) by "religious" (CEECT, p. 144). A few words and phrases changed in the 1859 edition to make sense of the 1852 have also been accepted in the CEECT text. Thus "I shall not go single-handed" (p. 312), denoting the speaker's intention to carry gifts with him, becomes "I shall not go empty-handed" (CEECT, p. 207).

The CEECT text also follows the 1882 in correcting other errors not caught in 1859. In the phrase "the tender caresses of living mothers" (p. 291), "living" has been changed to "loving" (CEECT, p. 193). Other changes incorporated into the CEECT text from the 1882 edition prevent misreadings and provide accurate place names. The 1882 substitution of "forlornness" (1882, p. 255) corrects the use of "friendliness" (p. 274) to describe Catharine's state during captivity. Similarly, the 1882 corrects the reference to Hector and Louis as Catharine's "brothers" (p. 277) to "brother and cousin" (1882, p. 257). The 1882 also corrects the spelling of place names, such as Gore's Landing (p. 338; 1882, p. 308).

Other errors in the 1852 that were not caught in either 1859 or 1882 have been corrected in the CEECT edition. Perhaps the most interesting is the change part-way through the first edition from "Duncan" to "Donald"; in the CEECT edition the father and brother of Hector and Catharine have been consistently named Duncan. "Cambelltown" (p. 288) has been replaced by "Campbelltown" (CEECT, p. 191). In addition to accepting the changes in botanical terms in the 1882, the editor has compared all these terms in both the 1852 and 1882 editions with those used by Mrs. Traill in her works on Canadian wild flowers and plant life and with those in standard authorities. Three errors, which might be attributed to a printer, have been corrected. "Persicaria" (CEECT, p. 224) replaces "perseicarias" (p. 337; 1882, p. 307); "*euchroma*" (CEECT, p. 45), "*erichroma*" (p. 68; 1882, p. 66); and "*castilleja*" (CEECT, pp. 7, 61), "*castilegia*" (1882, pp. 17, 87).

The treatment of the appendices in the CEECT edition is modified by the fact that they were not included in 1882. A few corrections made in 1859 have been incorporated into the CEECT edition. In both the 1852 and the 1859 a number of proper names used in the appendices stand in incorrect or unusual forms. These may at the outset have been the result of Mrs. Traill's handwriting, which is frequently difficult to read, and the unfamiliarity of these names to both Agnes and an English printer. In addition, some of the material in the appendices has been copied inaccurately or paraphrased from the work of George Copway, the Indian missionary. None of the following forms can be located on maps of that period: Samcoe, Sangeeny (p. 362; 1859, p. 356), Elome (p. 365; 1859, p. 359), Quintè, Colburn, and Gannoyne (p. 366; 1859, p. 360). They have, therefore, been changed to their more usual forms. The "Sangeenys" (p. 362; 1859, p. 356), the name of an Indian group, has also been changed to the "Saugeens" (CEECT, p. 244), and "Pondash" (p. 367; 1859, p. 361) to "Poudash" (CEECT, p. 250). Page references in the appendices to passages in the text have been adjusted to fit the pagination of the CEECT edition.[130] This last change has been silently made, as have the changes in the chapter numbers from Roman to Arabic and the removal of the period after these. All other changes made to the copy-text are included in the list of emendations in the concluding apparatus.

The 1852 preface written by Agnes has been preserved in the CEECT edition, not in its former place of prominence, but in the concluding apparatus. Changes to the preface made for the 1859 edition have not been included. Nelson's 1882 preface has also been consigned to the concluding apparatus. The illustrations, whether those supplied by Hall, Virtue in 1852 or those added by Nelson's in 1882, have no relation to Mrs. Traill's original manuscript. They have therefore been excluded.

The choice of the 1852 *Canadian Crusoes* as copy-text, the acceptance as authorial emendations of only those revisions that can be confidently attributed to Mrs. Traill, and the limitation of other emendations to the correction of obvious errors result in a text that reflects as accurately as can be ascertained the author's intentions for her narrative freed from the interfering hands of

Agnes and her successors. This minimal intervention in the copy-text has the added advantage of preserving a style characteristic of Mrs. Traill. Its inconsistencies of spelling and punctuation, its grammatical idiosyncracies, and its idiom that represents earlier usage all help reveal the authentic voice of Catharine Parr Traill.

In the preparation of this scholarly edition, a bibliographical analysis of each edition that included, when relevant, its subsequent issues or impressions was undertaken, and as many copies as possible of each version examined.[131] Five copies of the first English edition, one copy of the first American, one copy of the 1859, one copy of the 1882, and one copy of its 1886 impression were microfilmed. Photocopies made from these microfilms of the 1852, 1853, 1859, and 1882 were used to enter these texts on the computer. Microfilms, photocopies, and original copies were compared through various kinds of collation. To establish an ideal copy of the 1852 edition and to identify its states, five photocopies were collated on a light-table. Two members of staff, working independently, performed this collation. Three copies of the 1853 American edition, including an 1854 and an 1856 impression, were collated orally, as were three copies of the 1859 edition, including one copy of its second issue in 1862. The 1882 Nelson edition was also collated orally; in this collation a copy of the 1882 was compared with one copy of each of its 1884 and 1901 impressions and with two copies of the 1886 impression.[132] Selected pages of the 1909 and 1923 Nelson reprints were also collated orally to help establish their relation to the 1882. Finally, by means of specially written programs, two computer collations were performed. The first compared the 1852 edition with the 1853, the 1859, and the 1882. As a result of this collation, it became clear that the 1853 American edition was printed from the 1852 English and contained no authorial revisions. The second computer collation, therefore, compared the 1852, 1859, and 1882 editions. The results of these collations are available at the Centre for Editing Early Canadian Texts.

To prepare the text of the CEECT edition, the photocopy

made from CEECT's microfilm copy of the 1852 edition held by the Osborne Collection of Early Children's Books at the Toronto Public Libraries (no call number) was entered twice, each time by a different typist, on a computer. These versions were proofread by means of a computer program designed to compare one typist's version with the other's. When differences showed up in the running of the program, the typists' versions were corrected to make them conform with each other and with the copy of the Osborne original. Oral and ocular proofreadings were performed to compare the version of the 1852 on the computer with other copies of this edition. Before the magnetic tape of the CEECT edition was sent to the printer, its contents were proofread orally, and the CEECT text of *Canadian Crusoes* compared to the 1852 copy-text so that all the emendations made to this text could be verified. The CEECT text was also proofread at each stage in its progress from magnetic tape to van dykes.

ENDNOTES TO INTRODUCTION

1   PAC, TFC, MG 29 D 81, Vol. 3, p. 3456. When no page number is supplied, the item is identified as "additional material," found at the end of the "Finding Guide," followed by the number of the sheet there. Approximate dates are added in square brackets. In this, and in all other quotations included in the introduction, the grammar, punctuation, and spelling of the original have been retained.

2   PAC, TFC, Vol. 3, pp. 3456-59.

3   PAC, TFC, Vol. 2, pp. 3213-14.

4   *Chambers's Edinburgh Journal*, 7 (1838), 322-23.

5   Ibid., 12 (1843), 79.

6   *Home Circle*, 1 (1849), 33-35.

7   See, for example, Agnes and Elizabeth Strickland, *The Rival Crusoes* (London: Harris, 1823).

8   PAC, TFC, additional material, sheet #47, ALS, Catharine Parr Traill to Ellen Dunlop, 22 Mar. 1850.

9   PAC, TFC, Vol. 2, pp. 3259-62.

10   PAC, TFC, Vol. 3, pp. 4239-44.

11   PAC, TFC, additional material, sheet #47, ALS, Catharine Parr Traill to Ellen Dunlop, 23 Apr. 1850.

12 PAC, TFC, additional material, sheet #47, ALS, Catharine Parr Traill to Ellen Dunlop, 28 Sept. 1850.
13 PAC, TFC, additional material, sheet #47, ALS, Catharine Parr Traill to Ellen Dunlop, 19 June 1853.
14 *Canadian Crusoes. A Tale of the Rice Lake Plains*, ed. Rupert Schieder (Ottawa: Carleton University Press, 1986), p. 2. All subsequent references to this edition are included in the text as (CEECT, p. 000).
15 See Appendices D, F, G, and K, and explanatory note on George Copway in concluding apparatus.
16 PAC, TFC, Vol. 6, p. 8857. Biographical material on the Traill and Strickland families is derived chiefly from articles that Catharine Parr Traill wrote late in her life; they are found in the following sections: TFC, Vol. 5, pp. 8185-8467; Vol. 6, pp. 8468-8893; Vol. 7, pp. 10841-66; Vol. 8, pp. 12693-12703.
17 PAC, TFC, Vol. 8, pp. 12693 ff.
18 Una Pope-Hennessy, *Agnes Strickland, Biographer of the Queens of England, 1796-1874* (London: Chatto and Windus, 1940), p. 7.
19 Mary Agnes Fitzgibbon, "Biographical Sketch," in *Pearls and Pebbles; or, Notes of an Old Naturalist*, by Catharine Parr Traill (Toronto: Briggs, 1894), p. iv.
20 PAC, TFC, Vol. 7, p. 10877.
21 PAC, TFC, Vol. 6, p. 8862.
22 PAC, TFC, Vol. 6, p. 8861.
23 PAC, TFC, Vol. 7, p. 10881.
24 Pope-Hennessy, *Agnes Strickland*, pp. 20-21.
25 PAC, TFC, Vol. 7, p. 10867.
26 PAC, TFC, Vol. 6, p. 8861; *Cot and Cradle Stories*, ed. Mary Agnes Fitzgibbon (Toronto: Briggs; Montreal: Coates; Halifax: Huestis, 1895), p. 48.
27 Catharine Parr Traill, *The Backwoods of Canada: Being Letters from the Wife of an Emigrant Officer, Illustrative of the Domestic Economy of British America* (London: Knight, 1836), pp. 15, 233.
28 Catharine Parr Traill, *Sketches from Nature; or, Hints to Juvenile Naturalists* (London: Harvey and Darton, 1830), p. 33.
29 PAC, TFC, Vol. 6, p. 8860. See also Catharine Parr Traill, "Preface," *Sketch Book of a Young Naturalist; or, Hints to Students of Nature* (London: Harvey and Darton, 1831), pp. iii-viii.
30 PAC, TFC, Vol. 6, pp. 8854, 8860.
31 *Sketches from Nature*, p. viii; *Sketch Book of a Young Naturalist*, p. vii.
32 *Sketches from Nature*, p. xix. See also *Pearls and Pebbles*, passim.
33 PAC, TFC, Vol. 7, pp. 10861-62.
34 *The Backwoods of Canada*, p. 168.
35 PAC, TFC, Vol. 15, additional material, sheet #54, ALS, Catharine Parr Traill to William Edward Traill, 26 July 1891.
36 Susanna Moodie, "The Late Agnes Strickland," *Globe* (Toronto), 25 July 1874, p. 2.
37 PAC, TFC, Vol. 6, p. 8865.

38 Jane Margaret Strickland, *Life of Agnes Strickland* (Edinburgh/London: Blackwood, 1887), p. 3.

39 Catharine Parr Traill, *Studies of Plant Life in Canada; or, Gleanings from the Forest, Lake and Plain*, illus. Mrs. Chamberlin (Ottawa: Woodburn, 1885), p. 3.

40 PAC, TFC, Vol. 7, pp. 10854-55.

41 There is no evidence that the Stricklands read Johann Wyss' *Swiss Family Robinson* (1812), translated and published by William Godwin, 1814.

42 *Sketch Book of a Young Naturalist*, p. 193.

43 *Pearls and Pebbles*, p. xiii; Jane Margaret Strickland, *Life of Agnes Strickland*, p. 8.

44 *Life of Agnes Strickland*, p. 6.

45 Ibid., p. 6.

46 PAC, TFC, Vol. 6, p. 8864.

47 PAC, TFC, Vol. 6, p. 8865.

48 PAC, TFC, Vol. 6, p. 8867.

49 PAC, TFC, Vol. 6, p. 8868; Judith St. John, comp., *The Osborne Collection of Early Children's Books, 1566-1910* (Toronto: Toronto Public Library, 1966), p. 312; OTP, Osborne Collection of Early Children's Books, Holograph List of the Works of Catharine Parr Traill, p. [1].

50 OTP, Osborne Collection, Holograph copy of "The Swiss Herdboy and His Alpine Mouse," p. 80.

51 PAC, TFC, Vol. 6, p. 8870; Pope-Hennessy, *Agnes Strickland*, p. 18; Jane Margaret Strickland, *Life of Agnes Strickland*, pp. 13-14.

52 PAC, TFC, Vol. 3, p. 4066; Osborne Collection, Holograph List, p. [2]; Catharine Parr Traill, *The Tell-Tale; An Original Collection of Moral and Amusing Stories* (London: Harris, 1818); *Pearls and Pebbles*, pp. xiii-xiv.

53 Pope-Hennessy, *Agnes Strickland*, pp. 21-24, 33-34; Susanna Moodie, "To the Editor of the *Literary Garland*," *Literary Garland*, 4 (1842), 319.

54 PAC, TFC, Vol. 3, pp. 4065-70; Vol. 6, pp. 8948-57; OTMCL, Frances Stewart papers, Note on the publication of her books by Catharine Parr Traill. Those listed include: *The Tell-Tale: An Original Collection of Moral and Amusing Stories* [1818]; *Little Downy; or, The History of a Field-Mouse. A Moral Tale* (1822); *Prejudice Reproved; or, The History of the Negro Toy-seller* (1826); *The Young Emigrants; or, Pictures of Canada. Calculated to Amuse and Instruct the Minds of Youth* (1826); *The Keepsake Guineas; or, The Best Use of Money* (1828); *The Step-Brothers. A Tale* (1828); *Sketches from Nature; or, Hints to Juvenile Naturalists* (1830); *Sketch Book of a Young Naturalist; or Hints to the Students of Nature* (1831). To these can be added *Reformation; or,The Cousins; From Occurrences in Real Life* (1819); part of *The Juvenile Forget-Me-Not; or, Cabinet of Entertainment and Instruction* (1827), with Agnes and Elizabeth; *The Flower Basket, or Original Nursery Rhymes and Tales*, or *The Flower Basket; or, Poetical*

Blossoms: Original Nursery Rhymes and Tales [1830]; *Amendment; or, Charles Grant and His Sister*, published with *The Little Prisoner; or, Passion and Patience* by Susanna (1828); *Fables for the Nursery; Original and Select* (1825), unless it is a version of *Nursery Fables* or *Nursery Tales*; perhaps *Narratives of Nature, and History Book for Young Naturalists*, an odd expanded combination of *Sketches from Nature* and *Sketch Book of a Young Naturalist*; and apparently, *Happy Because Good; The Tame Pheasant, and the Blind Brother and Kind Sister* (Judith St. John, comp., *The Osborne Collection of Early Children's Books, 1476-1910* (Toronto: Toronto Public Library, 1975), p. 951).

55 OTP, Osborne Collection, Holograph List, p. [3].

56 Carl Ballstadt, "Catharine Parr Traill (1802-1899)," in *Canadian Writers and Their Works*, eds. Robert Lecker, Jack David, and Ellen Quigley (Toronto: ECW Press, 1983), Fiction Series, Vol. 1, pp. 156, 163.

57 *The Backwoods of Canada*, p. 310.

58 Ibid., p. 168.

59 PAC, TFC, Vol. 6, p. 8875.

60 PAC, TFC, Vol. 7, p. 10867.

61 PAC, TFC, Vol. 6, p. 8872.

62 PAC, TFC, Vol. 6, p. 8875.

63 PAC, TFC, Vol. 2, p. 2955, journal entry, 23 June 1859.

64 PAC, TFC, Vol. 2, p. 2316, ALS, Catharine Parr Traill to Susanna Moodie, 16 Apr. 1846; Vol. 2, p. 2424, ALS, Catharine Parr Traill to Frances Stewart, 17 Jan. 1851; OTMCL, Frances Stewart papers, ALS, Catharine Parr Traill to Frances Stewart, n.d.; PAC, TFC, Vol. 2, p. 2953, Thomas Traill, journal entry, 24 Sept. 1858; PAC, TFC, Vol. 2, p. 2333, ALS, Catharine Parr Traill to Susanna Moodie, 2 Nov. 1851; OTMCL, Frances Stewart papers, ALS, Catharine Parr Traill to Frances Stewart, n.d.

65 PAC, TFC, Vol. 6, pp. 8875, 8872.

66 PAC, TFC, Vol. 6, p. 8872.

67 PAC, TFC, Vol. 6, pp. 8878-79.

68 PAC, TFC, Vol. 6, p. 8883.

69 Ballstadt, "Catharine Parr Traill (1802-1899)," p. 155.

70 These appeared in Great Britain in *New Year's Gift, Chambers's Edinburgh Journal, Sharpe's London Magazine*, and *Home Circle*; in New York in *Albion or British, Colonial and Foreign Weekly Gazette*; in Belleville in the *Victoria Magazine*, edited by the Moodies; in Montreal in the *Literary Garland*.

71 PAC, TFC, Vol. 14, additional material, sheet #51, ALS, Jane Margaret Strickland to Catharine Parr Traill, 27 Mar. [1855].

72 PAC, TFC, Vol. 2, pp. 2333-34, ALS, Catharine Parr Traill to Susanna Moodie, 2 Nov. 1851; OTMCL, Frances Stewart papers, ALS, Catharine Parr Traill to Frances Stewart, n.d. "The Catholic Question" refers to the general outcry in reaction to the bull issued by Pius IX in

1850 establishing territorial dioceses in Great Britain. See Llewellyn Woodward, *The Age of Reform 1815-1870*, 2nd ed. (Oxford: Clarendon Press, 1962), pp. 521-22.

73 PAC, TFC, Vol. 2, pp. 1922-27, ALS, Catharine Parr Traill to Ellen Dunlop, 12 Feb. 1852.

74 PAC, TFC, Vol. 6, p. 8967.

75 *Times, Supplement to the Times* (London), 30 July 1852, p. 11.

76 *Observer* (London), 15 Aug. 1852, p. 7.

77 *John Bull*, 32 (28 Aug. 1852), 557.

78 *Daily News* (London), 4 Sept. 1852, p. 2.

79 *Tait's Edinburgh Magazine*, 19 (1852), 572.

80 *Sharpe's London Magazine*, NS 1 (1852), 191. Jane Margaret Strickland wrote even more tartly about the pictures by the same illustrator in *Lady Mary and Her Nurse* (1856): "frights they are and frights must remain as Hall and Virtue never alter theirs. . . . I suppose they employ a cheap artist for illustrating their books." PAC, TFC, Vol. 14, additional material, sheet #51, ALS, Jane Margaret Strickland to Catharine Parr Traill, 27 Mar. 1855.

81 PAC, TFC, Vol. 14, additional material, sheet #47, ALS, Catharine Parr Traill to Ellen Dunlop, 1 Apr. 1852.

82 Center for Research Libraries (Chicago), University of Illinois, Publishers' Archives MF-3882, Archives of Richard Bentley and Son 1829-98, "Incoming Correspondence 1839-58," Reel 44, n. pag., ALS, Susanna Moodie to Richard Bentley, 20 July 1852.

83 PAC, Lande Collection, MG53 B45, ALS, Catharine Parr Traill to George Putnam, 11 Oct. 1852.

84 *Norton's Literary Gazette and Publishers' Circular*, 2 (15 Sept. 1852), 172; 2 (15 Oct. 1852), 202.

85 Ibid., 2 (15 Dec. 1852), 242.

86 *Pilot* (Montreal), 18 Dec. 1852, p. [3].

87 PAC, TFC, Vol. 2, pp. 2335-38, ALS, Catharine Parr Traill and James Traill to Susanna Moodie, 27 Dec. 1852. James' handwriting is difficult to decipher here, particularly as this section has been crossed. The adverb may be either "bountifully" or "beautifully"; the latter has been accepted.

88 OTMCL, Frances Stewart papers, ALS, Catharine Parr Traill to Frances Stewart [early January 1853], letter continued 8 Jan. 1853.

89 PAC, TFC, Vol. 2, p. 3263, journal entry, 5 Apr. 1853.

90 PAC, TFC, Vol. 14, additional material, sheet #47, ALS, Catharine Parr Traill to Ellen Dunlop, 19 June 1853.

91 Crosby, Nichols, Lee, 1861; Crosby, Nichols, 1862; Crosby, Nichols, n.d., probably between 1861 and 1864; Crosby and Ainsworth, with Felt of New York, 1866; Woolworth, Ainsworth, n.d., probably after 1864; and Hall and Whiting, 1881. These publishers have been traced in the journal that began in 1851 as *Norton's Literary Gazette and Publishers' Circular*, 1851-53, continued as *Norton's Literary Advertiser*, *American Publishers' Circular and Literary Gazette*, *American Literary Gazette* *and Publishers' Circular*, 1855-72, and became *Publishers' Weekly* in 1872.

92 These appeared in *Anglo-American Magazine*, 1 (1852), 318-20, 353-54, 417-20, 513-18; 2 (1853), 33-39, 182-84, 426-30, 603-10; and 3 (1853), 82-83, 83-85, 276-78, 401-04, 493-98.

93 Toronto: Maclear, 1854; Toronto: Old Countryman Office, 1855.

94 "The Governor's Daughter: or, Rambles in the Canadian Forest," *Maple Leaf*, 1 (1853), 1-10, 33-39, 84-91, 113-20, 146-51, 172-76; 2 (1853), 12-16, 44-50, 71-75, 111-17, 137-42, 165-67; *Lady Mary and Her Nurse; or, A Peep Into the Canadian Forest* (London: Hall, Virtue, 1856).

95 Catharine Parr Traill, *Stories of the Canadian Forest: or, Little Mary and Her Nurse*, New York/Boston: Francis, 1857; New York: Francis, 1859; Boston: Crosby, Nichols, Lee, 1861; Boston: Crosby and Nichols, 1862; Boston: Hall and Whiting, 1881; Boston: Crosby and Nichols, n.d.; Boston: Woolworth, n.d.

96 OTMCL, Frances Stewart papers, Catharine Parr Traill late notes; PAC, TFC, Vol. 2, p. 2952, journal entry.

97 Ballstadt, "Catharine Parr Traill (1802-1899)," p. 152.

98 PAC, TFC, Vol. 14, additional material, sheet #48, ALS, Catharine Parr Traill to Ellen Dunlop, 10 Sept. 1857.

99 PAC, TFC, Vol. 2, p. 2341, ALS, Catharine Parr Traill to Susanna Moodie, 6 Jan. 1854.

100 PAC, TFC, Vol. 1, p. 561, ALS, Agnes Strickland to Catharine Parr Traill, 21 Jan. 1855.

101 PAC, TFC, Vol. 14, additional material, sheet #51, ALS, Jane Margaret Strickland to Catharine Parr Traill, 12 Aug. [1858].

102 PAC, TFC, Vol. 1, pp. 608-28, ALS, Agnes Strickland to Catharine Parr Traill, 11 Jan., 5 Mar., 21 Mar. 1859. The quotation is from Vol. 1, p. 613, 11 Jan. 1859.

103 PAC, TFC, Vol. 1, p. 685, ALS, Agnes Strickland to Catharine Parr Traill, [September or October 1863].

104 *Norton's Literary Gazette and Publishers' Weekly*, 2 (1 Feb. 1864), 260; *Publishers' Weekly*, No. 1375 (4 July 1898), p. 909.

105 PAC, TFC, Vol. 6, p. 8889; *Pearls and Pebbles*, p. xxxi.

106 PAC, TFC, Vol. 2, p. 2567, ALS, Catharine Parr Traill to Katharine Agnes Strickland Traill, 16 May 1863.

107 PAC, TFC, Vol. 3, p. 3818, journal entry, 12 Feb. 1866.

108 PAC, TFC, Vol. 2, p. 2632, ALS, Catharine Parr Traill to Katharine Agnes Strickland Traill, 2 Feb. 1867.

109 PAC, TFC, Vol. 15, additional material, sheet #53, ALS, Catharine Parr Traill to William Edward Traill, 8 May 1867.

110 PAC, TFC, Vol. 1, p. 1513, ALS, Catharine Parr Traill to Anne T. F. Atwood, 20 June 1867.

111 *Canadian Wild Flowers* was supplemented in 1885 by another work, published by Woodburn in Ottawa, covering a wider field, *Studies of Plant Life in Canada; or, Gleanings from Forest, Lake, and Plain, by Mrs. C. P. Traill, Illustrated with Chromo-Lithographs from Drawings by Mrs. Chamberlin*. Mrs. Chamberlin was her niece Agnes who had remarried.

112 *Anglo-American Magazine*, 3 (1853), 219.
113 *British American Magazine*, 1 (1863), 55-59.
114 PAC, TFC, Vol. 2, p. 2970, 1863 journal entry, 29 Nov. 1863; OTMCL, Frances Stewart papers, ALS, Catharine Parr Traill to Frances Stewart, 17 Mar. 1864; PAC, TFC, Vol. 14, additional material, sheet #52, ALS, Catharine Parr Traill to Katharine Agnes Strickland Traill, 2 Feb. 1865; Vol. 2, pp. 2608-13, ALS, Catharine Parr Traill to Katharine Agnes Strickland Traill, 2 Mar. 1865; Vol. 2, pp. 2614-17, ALS, Catharine Parr Traill to Katharine Agnes Strickland Traill, 17 Mar. 1865.
115 Catharine Parr Traill, *Canadian Wild Flowers, Painted and Lithographed by Agnes Fitzgibbon, with Botanical Descriptions by C. P. Traill* (Montreal: Lovell, 1868), p. [5].
116 PAC, TFC, Vol. 1, p. 1523, ALS, Catharine Parr Traill to Anne T. F. Atwood, [December 1867].
117 There is one copy held in the Buffalo and Erie County Public Library that appears to be dated 1880. The date is wrong. On the title-page Mrs. Traill is identified as the "Author of 'In the Forest,'" a version of the title of *Lady Mary and Her Nurse* that first appeared in 1881. The preface is dated 1882. On close inspection, the "0" appears to have been "6," possibly subjected, for some reason, to alteration. That it is a copy of the 1886 impression was confirmed by the CEECT collation.
118 *Bookseller* (London), OS 53/NS 2 (8 Oct. 1909), 1444, and *Bookseller*, 10 May 1923, p. 14.
119 PAC, TFC, Vol. 15, additional material, sheet #54, ALS, Catharine Parr Traill to W. E. Traill, 21 Oct. 1890.
120 PAC, TFC, Vol. 3, p. 4068, late notes on publications.
121 Edinburgh University Library, Nelson Archives File, Dept. 11, ALS, S. B. Watson to [?] Graham, 17 Dec. 1923.
122 Ibid., ALS, [?] Graham to S. B. Watson, 8 Jan. 1924.
123 Ballstadt, "Catharine Parr Traill (1802-1899)," pp. 158-62, 191-93.
124 *Notable Canadian Children's Books / Un choix de livres canadiens pour la jeunesse* (Ottawa: National Library of Canada, 1973), p. 4.
125 *Literary History of Canada*, ed. Carl F. Klinck, 2nd ed. (Toronto: University of Toronto Press, 1976), Vol. 2, p. 136.
126 "Traill's Canadian Settlers," *Canadian Children's Literature*, Nos. 5-6 (1976), pp. 35, 36, 37.
127 Ballstadt, "Catharine Parr Traill (1802-1899)," pp. 173-74.
128 In this and subsequent references the numbers in parentheses refer to pages in the 1852 edition. In the references to the 1859 and the 1882 Nelson, the date will precede the page number.
129 PAC, TFC, Vol. 6, p. 8954, late notes.
130 The one exception to this adjustment is that Appendix A, paginated in the copy-text to Agnes Strickland's "Preface," appears without a page reference in the CEECT edition.

131 The provenance of the copies of each version examined and of those microfilmed is included in the "Bibliographical Description" and the list of "Published Versions" in the concluding apparatus.

132 The copy of *Lost in the Backwoods* held by the Buffalo and Erie County Public Library and listed as published in 1880 proved to be a copy of the 1886 impression. See also Note 117.

CANADIAN CRUSOES.

A Tale

OF

THE RICE LAKE PLAINS.

BY

CATHARINE PARR TRAILL,

AUTHORESS OF "THE BACKWOODS OF CANADA," ETC.

EDITED BY AGNES STRICKLAND.

ILLUSTRATED BY HARVEY,

LONDON:

ARTHUR HALL, VIRTUE, & CO.

25, PATERNOSTER ROW.

1852.

DEDICATED

TO THE CHILDREN OF THE SETTLERS

ON

THE RICE LAKE PLAINS,

BY THEIR

FAITHFUL FRIEND AND WELL-WISHER

THE AUTHORESS.

OAKLANDS, RICE LAKE,

15*th Oct*. 1850.

CHAPTER 1

"The morning had shot her bright streamers on high,
O'er Canada, opening all pale to the sky;
Still dazzling and white was the robe that she wore,
Except where the ocean wave lash'd on the shore."

Jacobite Song.

THERE lies between the Rice Lake and the Ontario, a
deep and fertile valley, surrounded by lofty wood-crowned
hills, the heights of which were clothed chiefly with
groves of oak and pine, though the sides of the hills and
the alluvial bottoms gave a variety of noble timber trees
of various kinds, as the maple, beech, hemlock, and
others. This beautiful and highly picturesque valley is
watered by many clear streams of pure refreshing water,
from whence the spot has derived its appropriate
appellation of "Cold Springs."

At the time my little history commences, this now
highly cultivated spot was an unbroken wilderness,—all
but two small farms, where dwelt the only occupiers of
the soil,—which owned no other possessors than the
wandering hunting tribes of wild Indians, to whom the
right of the hunting grounds north of Rice Lake
appertained, according to their forest laws.

To those who travel over beaten roads, now partially
planted, among cultivated fields and flowery orchards,
and see cleared farms and herds of cattle and flocks of
sheep, the change would be a striking one. I speak of the
time when the neat and flourishing town of Cobourg, now
an important port on the Ontario, was but a village in

embryo—if it contained even a log-house or a block-house it was all that it did, and the wild and picturesque ground upon which the fast increasing village of Port Hope is situated, had not yielded one forest tree to the axe of the settler. No gallant vessel spread her sails to waft the abundant produce of grain and Canadian stores along the waters of that noble sheet of water; no steamer had then furrowed its bosom with her iron wheels, bearing the stream of emigration towards the wilds of our Northern and Western forests, there to render a lonely trackless desert a fruitful garden. What will not time and the industry of man, assisted by the blessing of a merciful God, effect? To him be the glory and honour; for we are taught, that "without the Lord build the city, their labour is but lost that build it; without the Lord keep the city, the watchman waketh but in vain."

But to my tale. And first it will be necessary to introduce to the acquaintance of my young readers the founders of our little settlement at Cold Springs.

Duncan Maxwell was a young Highland soldier, a youth of eighteen, at the famous battle of Quebec, where, though only a private, he received the praise of his colonel for his brave conduct. At the close of the battle Duncan was wounded, and as the hospital was full at the time with sick and disabled men, he was lodged in the house of a poor French Canadian widow in the Quebec suburb; here, though a foreigner and an enemy, he received much kind attention from his excellent hostess and her family, which consisted of a young man about his own age, and a pretty black-eyed lass not more than sixteen. The widow Perron was so much occupied with other lodgers—for she kept a sort of boarding-house—that she had not much time to give to Duncan, so that he was left a great deal to her son Pierre, and a little to Catharine, her daughter.

Duncan Maxwell was a fine, open-tempered, frank lad, and he soon won the regard of Pierre and his little sister.

In spite of the prejudices of country, and the difference of language and national customs, a steady and increasing friendship grew up between the young Highlander and the children of his hostess; therefore it was not without feelings of deep regret that they heard the news, that the corps to which Duncan belonged was ordered for embarkation to England, and Duncan was so far convalescent as to be pronounced quite well enough to join them. Alas for poor Catharine! she now found that parting with her patient was a source of the deepest sorrow to her young and guileless heart; nor was Duncan less moved at the separation from his gentle nurse. It might be for years, and it might be for ever, he could not tell; but he could not tear himself away without telling the object of his affections how dear she was to him, and to whisper a hope that he might yet return one day to claim her as his bride; and Catharine, weeping and blushing, promised to wait for that happy day, or to remain single for his sake, while Pierre promised to watch over his friend's interests and keep alive Catharine's love; for, said he, artlessly, "la belle Catrine is pretty and lively, and may have many suitors before she sees you again, mon ami."

They say the course of true love never did run smooth; but, with the exception of this great sorrow, the sorrow of separation, the love of our young Highland soldier and his betrothed knew no other interruption, for absence served only to strengthen the affection which was founded on gratitude and esteem.

Two long years passed, however, and the prospect of re-union was yet distant, when an accident, which disabled Duncan from serving his country, enabled him to retire with the usual little pension, and return to Quebec to seek his affianced. Some changes had taken place during that short period: the widow Perron was dead; Pierre, the gay, lively-hearted Pierre, was married to the daughter of a lumberer; and Catharine, who had no relatives in Quebec, had gone up the country with her brother and his wife, and was living in some little settlement above Montreal with them.

Thither Duncan, with the constancy of his nature, followed, and shortly afterwards was married to his faithful Catharine. On one point they had never differed, both being of the same religion.

Pierre had seen a good deal of the fine country on the shores of the Ontario; he had been hunting with some friendly Indians between the great waters and the Rice Lake, and he now thought if Duncan and himself could make up their minds to a quiet life in the woods, there was not a better spot than the hill pass between the plains and the big lake to fix themselves upon. Duncan was of the same opinion when he saw the spot. It was not rugged and bare like his own Highlands, but softer in character, yet his heart yearned for the hill country. In those days there was no obstacle to taking possession of any tract of land in the unsurveyed forests, therefore Duncan agreed with his brother-in-law to pioneer the way with him, get a dwelling put up and some ground prepared and "seeded down," and then to return for their wives and settle themselves down at once as farmers. Others had succeeded, had formed little colonies, and become the heads of villages in due time; why should not they? And now behold our two backwoodsmen fairly commencing their arduous life; but it was nothing, after all, to Pierre, by previous occupation a hardy lumberer, or the Scottish soldier, accustomed to brave all sorts of hardships in a wild country, himself a mountaineer, inured to a stormy climate, and scanty fare, from his earliest youth. But it is not my intention to dwell upon the trials and difficulties courageously met and battled with by our settlers and their young wives.

There was in those days a spirit of resistance among the first settlers on the soil, a spirit to do and bear, that is less commonly met with now. The spirit of civilization is now so widely diffused, that her comforts are felt even in the depths of the forest, so that the newly come emigrant feels comparatively few of the physical evils that were endured by the older inhabitants.

The first seed-wheat that was cast into the ground by Duncan and Pierre, was brought with infinite trouble a distance of fifty miles in a little skiff, navigated along the shores of the Ontario by the adventurous Pierre, and from the nearest landing-place transported on the shoulders of himself and Duncan to their homestead:—a day of great labour but great joy it was when they deposited their precious freight in safety on the shanty floor. They were obliged to make two journeys for the contents of the little craft. What toil, what privation they endured for the first two years! and now the fruits of it began slowly to appear. No two creatures could be more unlike than Pierre and Duncan. The Highlander, stern, steady, persevering, cautious, always giving ample reasons for his doing or his not doing. The Canadian, hopeful, lively, fertile in expedients, and gay as a lark; if one scheme failed another was sure to present itself. Pierre and Duncan were admirably suited to be friends and neighbours. The steady perseverance of the Scot helped to temper the volatile temperament of the Frenchman. They generally contrived to compass the same end by different means, as two streams descending from opposite hills will meet in one broad river in the same valley.

Years passed on; the farm, carefully cultivated, began to yield its increase, and food and warm clothing were not wanting in the homesteads. Catharine had become, in course of time, the happy mother of four healthy children; her sister-in-law had even exceeded her in these wel-come contributions to the population of a new colony.

Between the children of Pierre and Catharine the most charming harmony prevailed; they grew up as one family,

a pattern of affection and early friendship. Though
different in tempers and dispositions, Hector Maxwell, the
eldest son of the Scottish soldier, and his cousin, young
Louis Perron, were greatly attached; they, with the
young Catharine and Mathilde, formed a little coterie of
inseparables; their amusements, tastes, pursuits,
occupations, all blended and harmonized delightfully;
there were none of those little envyings and bickerings
among them that pave the way to strife and disunion in
after life.

Catharine Maxwell and her cousin Louis were more like
brother and sister than Hector and Catharine, but
Mathilde was gentle and dove-like, and formed a contrast
to the gravity of Hector and the vivacity of Louis and
Catharine.

Hector and Louis were fourteen—strong, vigorous,
industrious and hardy, both in constitution and habits.
The girls were turned of twelve. It is not with Mathilde
that our story is connected, but with the two lads and
Catharine. With the gaiety and naïveté of the
Frenchwoman, Catharine possessed, when occasion
called it into action, a thoughtful and well-regulated
mind, abilities which would well have repaid the care of
mental cultivation; but of book-learning she knew nothing
beyond a little reading, and that but imperfectly, acquired
from her father's teaching. It was an accomplishment
which he had gained when in the army, having been
taught by his colonel's son, a lad of twelve years of age,
who had taken a great fancy to him, and had at parting
given him a few of his school-books, among which was a
Testament, without cover or title-page. At parting, the
young gentleman recommended its daily perusal to
Duncan. Had the gift been a Bible, perhaps the soldier's
obedience to his priest might have rendered it a dead letter
to him, but as it fortunately happened, he was unconscious
of any prohibition to deter him from becoming acquainted

with the truths of the Gospel. He communicated the power of perusing his books to his children Hector and Catharine, Duncan and Kenneth, in succession, with a feeling of intense reverence; even the labour of teaching was regarded as a holy duty in itself, and was not undertaken without deeply impressing the obligation he was conferring upon them whenever they were brought to the task. It was indeed a precious boon, and the children learned to consider it as the pearl beyond all price in the trials that awaited them in their eventful career. To her knowledge of religious truths young Catharine added an intimate acquaintance with the songs and legends of her father's romantic country, which was to her even as fairyland; often would her plaintive ballads and old tales, related in the hut or the wigwam to her attentive auditors, wile away heavy thoughts; Louis and Mathilde, her cousins, sometimes wondered how Catharine had acquired such a store of ballads and wild tales as she could tell.

It was a lovely sunny day in the flowery month of June; Canada had not only doffed that "dazzling white robe" mentioned in the songs of her Jacobite emigrants, but had assumed the beauties of her loveliest season, the last week in May and the first three of June being parallel to the English May, full of buds and flowers and fair promise of ripening fruits. The high sloping hills surrounding the fertile vale of Cold Springs were clothed with the blossoms of the gorgeous scarlet castilleja coccinea, or painted-cup; the large pure white blossoms of the lily-like trillium grandiflorum; the delicate and fragile lilac geranium, whose graceful flowers woo the hand of the flower-gatherer only to fade almost within his grasp; the golden cypripedium, or mocassin flower, so singular, so lovely in its colour and formation, waved heavily its yellow blossoms as the breeze shook the stems; and there, mingling with a thousand various floral beauties, the azure lupine claimed its place, shedding almost a heavenly tint upon the earth. Thousands of roses were blooming on the more level ground, sending forth their rich fragrance, mixed with the delicate scent of the feathery ceanothus, (New Jersey tea.) The vivid greenness of the young leaves of the forest, the tender tint of the springing corn, were contrasted with the deep dark fringe of waving pines on the hills, and the yet darker shade of the spruce and balsams on the borders of the creeks, for so our Canadian forest rills are universally termed. The bright glancing wings of the summer red-bird, the crimson-headed woodpecker, the gay blue-bird, and noisy but splendid plumed jay, might be seen among the branches; the air was filled with beauteous sights and soft murmuring melodies. Under the shade of the luxuriant hop-vines, that covered the rustic porch in front of the little dwelling, the light step of Catharine Maxwell might be heard mixed with the drowsy whirring of the big wheel, as she passed to and fro guiding the thread of yarn in its course: and now she sang snatches of old mountain songs, such as she had learned from her father; and now, with livelier air, hummed some gay French tune to the household melody of her spinning wheel, as she advanced and retreated with her thread, unconscious of the laughing black eye that was watching her movements from among the embowering foliage that shielded her from the morning sun.

"Come, ma belle cousine," for so Louis delighted to call her. "Hector and I are waiting for you to go with us to the 'Beaver Meadow.' The cattle have strayed, and we think we shall find them there. The day is delicious, the very flowers look as if they wanted to be admired and plucked, and we shall find early strawberries on the old Indian clearing."

Catharine cast a longing look abroad, but said, "I fear, Louis, I cannot go to-day, for see, I have all these rolls of wool to spin up, and my yarn to wind off the reel and twist; and then, my mother is away."

"Yes, I left her with mamma," replied Louis, "and she said she would be home shortly, so her absence need not stay you. She said you could take a basket and try and bring home some berries for sick Louise. Hector is sure he knows a spot where we shall get some fine ones, ripe and red." As he spoke Louis whisked away the big wheel to one end of the porch, gathered up the hanks of yarn and tossed them into the open wicker basket, and the next minute the large, coarse, flapped straw hat, that hung upon the peg in the porch, was stuck not very gracefully on the top of Catharine's head and tied beneath her chin, with a merry rattling laugh, which drowned effectually the small lecture that Catharine began to utter, by way of reproving the light-hearted boy.

"But where is Mathilde?"

"Sitting like a dear good girl, as she is, with sick Louise's head on her lap, and would not disturb the poor sick thing for all the fruit and flowers in Canada. Marie cried sadly to go with us, but I promised her and petite Louise lots of flowers and berries if we get them, and the dear children were as happy as queens when I left them."

"But stay, cousin, you are sure my mother gave her consent to my going? We shall be away chief part of the day. You know it is a long walk to the Beaver Meadow and back again," said Catharine, hesitating as Louis took her hand to lead her out from the porch.

"Yes, yes, ma belle," said the giddy boy, quickly; "so come along, for Hector is waiting at the barn; but stay, we shall be hungry before we return, so let us have some cakes and butter, and do not forget a tin-cup for water."

Nothing doubting, Catharine, with buoyant spirits, set about her little preparations, which were soon completed; but just as she was leaving the little garden enclosure, she ran back to kiss Kenneth and Duncan, her young brothers. In the farm yard she found Hector with his axe on his shoulder. "What are you taking the axe for, Hector? you will find it heavy to carry," said his sister.

"In the first place, I have to cut a stick of blue-beech to make a broom for sweeping the house, sister of mine; and that is for your use, Miss Kate; and in the next place, I have to find, if possible, a piece of rock elm or hiccory for axe handles; so now you have the reason why I take the axe with me."

The children now left the clearing, and struck into one of the deep defiles that lay between the hills, and cheerfully they laughed and sung and chattered, as they sped on their pleasant path; nor were they loth to exchange the glowing sunshine for the sober gloom of the forest shade. What handfuls of flowers of all hues, red, blue, yellow and white, were gathered only to be gazed at, carried for a while, then cast aside for others fresher and fairer. And now they came to cool rills that flowed, softly murmuring, among mossy limestone, or blocks of red or grey granite, wending their way beneath twisted roots and fallen trees; and often Catharine lingered to watch the eddying dimples of the clear water, to note the tiny bright fragments of quartz or crystallized limestone that formed a shining pavement below the stream; and often she paused to watch the angry movements of the red squirrel, as, with feathery tail erect, and sharp scolding note, he crossed their woodland path, and swiftly darting up the rugged bark of some neighbouring pine or hemlock, bade the intruders on his quiet haunts defiance; yet so bold in his indignation, he scarcely condescended to ascend beyond their reach.

The long-continued hollow tapping of the large red-headed woodpecker, or the singular subterranean sound caused by the drumming of the partridge, striking his wings upon his breast to woo his gentle mate, and the soft whispering note of the little tree-creeper, as it flitted from one hemlock to another, collecting its food between the fissures of the bark, were among the few sounds that broke the noontide stillness of the woods; but to all such sights and sounds the lively Catharine and her cousin were not indifferent. And often they wondered that Hector gravely pursued his onward way, and seldom lingered as they did to mark the bright colours of the flowers, or the bright sparkling of the forest rill.

"What makes Hec so grave?" said Catharine to her companion, as they seated themselves upon a mossy trunk, to await his coming up, for they had giddily chased each other till they had far outrun him.

"Hector, sweet coz, is thinking perhaps of how many bushels of corn or wheat this land would grow if cleared, or he may be examining the soil or the trees, or is looking for his stick of blue-beech for your broom, or the hiccory for his axe handle, and never heeding such nonsense as woodpeckers and squirrels, and lilies and moss and ferns, for Hector is not a giddy thing like his cousin Louis, or—"

"His sister Kate," interrupted Catharine, merrily; "but when shall we come to the Beaver Meadow?"

"Patience, ma belle, all in good time. Hark, was not that the ox-bell? No; Hector whistling." And soon they heard the heavy stroke of his axe ringing among the trees, for he had found the blue-beech, and was cutting it to leave on the path, that he might take it home on their return; he had also marked some hiccory of a nice size for his axe handles, to bring home at some future time.

The children had walked several miles, and were not sorry to sit down and rest till Hector joined them. He was well pleased with his success, and declared he felt no fatigue. "As soon as we reach the old Indian clearing, we shall find strawberries," he said, "and a fresh cold spring, and then we will have our dinners."

"Come, Hector,—come, Louis," said Catharine, jumping up, "I long to be gathering the strawberries; and see, my flowers are faded, so I will throw them away, and the basket shall be filled with fresh fruit instead, and we must not forget petite Marie and sick Louise, or dear Mathilde. Ah, how I wish she were here at this minute! But here is the opening to the Beaver Meadow."

And the sunlight was seen streaming through the opening trees as they approached the cleared space, which some called the "Indian clearing," but is now more generally known as the little Beaver Meadow. It was a pleasant spot, green, and surrounded with light bowery trees and flowering shrubs, of a different growth from those that belong to the dense forest. Here the children found, on the hilly ground above, fine ripe strawberries, the earliest they had seen that year, and soon all weariness was forgotten while pursuing the delightful occupation of gathering the tempting fruit; and when they had refreshed themselves, and filled the basket with leaves and fruit, they slaked their thirst from the stream, which wound its way among the bushes. Catharine neglected not to reach down flowery bunches of the fragrant white-thorn and of the high-bush cranberry, then radiant with nodding umbels of snowy blossoms, or to wreath the handle of the little basket with the graceful trailing runners of the lovely twin-flowered plant, the Linnæa borealis, which she always said reminded her of the twins, Louise and Marie, her little cousins. And now the day began to wear away, for they had lingered long in the little clearing; they had wandered from the path by which they entered it; and had neglected, in their eagerness to look for the strawberries, to notice any particular mark by which they might regain it. Just when they began to think of returning, Louis noticed a beaten path, where there seemed recent prints of cattle hoofs on a soft spongy soil beyond the creek.

"Come, Hector," said he gaily, "this is lucky; we are on the cattle path; no fear but it will lead us directly home, and that by a nearer track."

Hector was undecided about following it, he fancied it bent too much towards the setting sun; but his cousin overruled his objection. "And is not this our own creek?" he said; "I have often heard my father say it had its rise somewhere about this old clearing."

Hector now thought Louis might be right, and they boldly followed the path among the poplars and thorns and bushes that clothed its banks, surprised to see how open the ground became, and how swift and clear the stream swept onward.

"Oh, this dear creek," cried the delighted Catharine, "how pretty it is! I shall often follow its course after this; no doubt it has its source from our own Cold Springs."

And so they cheerfully pursued their way, till the sun, sinking behind the range of westerly hills, soon left them in gloom; but they anxiously hurried forward when the stream wound its noisy way among steep stony banks, clothed scantily with pines and a few scattered silver-barked poplars. And now they became bewildered by two paths leading in opposite directions; one upward among the rocky hills, the other through the opening gorge of a deep ravine.

Here, overcome with fatigue, Catharine seated herself on a large block of granite, near a great bushy pine that grew beside the path by the ravine, unable to proceed; and Hector, with a grave and troubled countenance, stood beside her, looking round with an air of great perplexity. Louis, seating himself at Catharine's feet, surveyed the deep gloomy valley before them, and sighed heavily. The conviction had now forcibly struck him that they had mistaken the path altogether. The very aspect of the country was different; the growth of the trees, the flow of the stream, all indicated a change of soil and scene. Darkness was fast drawing its impenetrable veil around them; a few stars were stealing out, and gleaming down as if with pitying glance upon the young wanderers; but they could not light up their pathway, or point their homeward track. The only sounds, save the lulling murmur of the rippling stream below, were the plaintive note of the whip-poor-will, from a gnarled oak that grew near them, and the harsh grating scream of the night hawk, darting about in the higher regions of the air, pursuing its noisy congeners, or swooping down with that peculiar hollow rushing sound, as of a person blowing into some empty vessel, when it seizes with wide-extended bill its insect prey.

Hector was the first to break the silence. "Cousin Louis, we were wrong in following the course of the stream; I fear we shall never find our way back to-night."

Louis made no reply; his sad and subdued air failed not to attract the attention of his cousins.

"Why, Louis, how is this? you are not used to be cast down by difficulties," said Hector, as he marked something like tears glistening in the dark eyes of his cousin.

Louis's heart was full, he did not reply, but cast a troubled glance upon the weary Catharine, who leaned heavily against the tree beneath which she sat.

"It is not," resumed Hector, "that I mind passing a summer's night under such a sky as this, and with such a dry grassy bed below me; but I do not think it is good for Catharine to sleep on the bare ground in the night dews,— and then they will be so anxious at home about our absence."

Louis burst into tears, and sobbed out,—"And it is all my doing that she came out with us; I deceived her, and my aunt will be angry and much alarmed, for she did not know of her going at all. Dear Catharine, good cousin Hector, pray forgive me!" But Catharine was weeping too much to reply to his passionate entreaties, and Hector, who never swerved from the truth, for which he had almost a stern reverence, hardly repressed his indignation at what appeared to him a most culpable act of deceit on the part of Louis.

The sight of her cousin's grief and self-abasement touched the tender heart of Catharine, for she was kind and dove-like in her disposition, and loved Louis, with all his faults. Had it not been for the painful consciousness of the grief their unusual absence would occasion at home, Catharine would have thought nothing of their present adventure; but she could not endure the idea of her high-principled father taxing her with deceiving her kind indulgent mother and him: it was this humiliating thought which wounded the proud heart of Hector, causing him to upbraid his cousin in somewhat harsh terms for his want of truthfulness, and steeled him against the bitter grief that wrung the heart of the penitent Louis, who, leaning his wet cheek on the shoulder of the kinder Catharine, sobbed as if his heart would break, heedless of her soothing words and affectionate endeavours to console him.

"Dear Hector," she said, turning her soft, pleading eyes on the stern face of her brother, "you must not be so very angry with poor Louis; remember it was to please me, and give me the enjoyment of a day of liberty with you and himself in the woods, among the flowers and trees and birds, that he committed this fault."

"Catharine, Louis spoke an untruth and acted deceitfully, and look at the consequences,—we shall have forfeited our parents' confidence, and may have some days of painful privation to endure before we regain our home, if we ever do find our way back to Cold Springs," replied Hector.

"It is the grief and anxiety our dear parents will endure this night," answered Catharine, "that distresses my mind; but," she added in more cheerful tones, "let us not despair, no doubt to-morrow we shall be able to retrace our steps."

With the young there is ever a magical spell in that little word *to-morrow*,—it is a point which they pursue as fast as it recedes from them; sad indeed is the young heart that does not look forward with hope to the morrow!

The cloud still hung on Hector's brow, till Catharine gaily exclaimed, "Come, Hector! come, Louis! we must not stand idling thus; we must think of providing some shelter for the night; it is not good to rest upon the bare ground exposed to the night dews.—See, here is a nice hut, half made," pointing to a large upturned root which some fierce whirlwind had hurled from the lofty bank into the gorge of the dark glen.

"Now you must make haste, and lop off a few pine boughs, and stick them into the ground, or even lean them against the roots of this old oak, and there, you see, will be a capital house to shelter us. To work, to work, you idle boys, or poor wee Katty must turn squaw and build her own wigwam," she playfully added, taking up the axe which rested against the feathery pine beneath which Hector was leaning. Now, Catharine cared as little as her brother and cousin about passing a warm summer's night under the shade of the forest trees, for she was both hardy and healthy; but her woman's heart taught her that the surest means of reconciling the cousins would be by mutually interesting them in the same object,—and she was right. In endeavouring to provide for the comfort of their dear companion, all angry feelings were forgotten by Hector, while active employment chased away Louis's melancholy.

Unlike the tall, straight, naked trunks of the pines of the forest, those of the plains are adorned with branches often to the very ground, varying in form and height, and often presenting most picturesque groups, or rising singly among scattered groves of the silver-barked poplar or graceful birch-trees; the dark, mossy greenness of the stately pine contrasting finely with the light waving foliage of its slender graceful companions.

Hector, with his axe, soon lopped boughs from one of the adjacent pines, which Louis sharpened with his knife, and with Catharine's assistance drove into the ground, arranging them in such a way as to make the upturned oak, with its roots and the earth which adhered to them, form the back part of the hut, which, when completed, formed by no means a contemptible shelter. Catharine then cut fern and deer grass with Louis's *couteau-de-chasse*, which he always carried in a sheath at his girdle, and spread two beds, one, parted off by dry boughs and bark, for herself in the interior of the wigwam, and one for her brother and cousin nearer the entrance. When all was finished to her satisfaction, she called the two boys, and, according to the custom of her parents, joined them in the lifting up of their hands as an evening sacrifice of praise and thanksgiving. Nor were these simple-hearted children backward in imploring help and protection from the Most High. They earnestly prayed that no dangerous creature might come near to molest them during the hours of darkness and helplessness, no evil spirit visit them, no unholy or wicked thoughts intrude into their minds; but that holy angels and heavenly thoughts might hover over them, and fill their hearts with the peace of God which passeth all understanding.—And the prayer of the poor wanderers was heard, for they slept that night in peace, unharmed in the vast solitude. So passed their first night on the Plains.

CHAPTER 2

"Fear not, ye are of more value than many sparrows."

THE sun had risen in all the splendour of a Canadian summer morning, when the sleepers arose from their leafy beds. In spite of the novelty of their situation, they had slept as soundly and tranquilly as if they had been under the protecting care of their beloved parents, on their little paillasses of corn straw; but they had been cared for by Him who neither slumbereth nor sleepeth, and they waked full of youthful hope, and in fulness of faith in His mercy into whose hands they had commended their souls and bodies before they retired to rest.

While the children slept in peace and safety, what terrors had filled the minds of their distracted parents! what a night of anguish and sorrow had they passed!

When night had closed in without bringing back the absent children, the two fathers, lighting torches of fat pine, went forth in search of the wanderers. How often did they raise their voices in hopes their loud halloos might reach the hearing of the lost ones! How often did they check their hurried steps to listen for some replying call! But the sighing breeze in the pine tops, or sudden rustling of the leaves caused by the flight of the birds, startled by the unusual glare of the torches, and the echoes of their own voices, were the only sounds that met their anxious ears. At daybreak they returned, sad and dispirited, to their homes, to snatch a morsel of food, endeavour to cheer the drooping hearts of the weeping mothers, and hurry off, taking different directions. But, unfortunately, they had little clue to the route which Hector and Louis had taken, there being many cattle paths through the woods. Louis's want of truthfulness had caused this uncertainty, as he had left no intimation of the path he purposed taking when he quitted his mother's house: he had merely said he was going with Hector in search of the cattle, giving no hint of his intention of asking Catharine to accompany them: he had but told his sick sister, that he would bring home strawberries and flowers, and that he would soon return. Alas, poor thoughtless Louis, how little did you think of the web of woe you were then weaving for yourself, and all those to whom you and your giddy companions were so dear! Children, think twice, ere ye deceive once!

Catharine's absence would have been quite unaccountable but for the testimony of Duncan and Kenneth, who had received her sisterly caresses before she joined Hector at the barn; and much her mother marvelled what could have induced her good dutiful Catharine to have left her work and forsaken her household duties to go rambling away with the boys, for she never left the house when her mother was absent from it, without her express permission, and now she was gone— lost to them, perhaps for ever. There stood the wheel she had been turning, there hung the untwisted hanks of yarn, her morning task,—and there they remained week after week and month after month, untouched, a melancholy memorial to the hearts of the bereaved parents of their beloved.

It were indeed a fruitless task to follow the agonized fathers in their vain search for their children, or to paint the bitter anguish that filled their hearts as day passed after day, and still no tidings of the lost ones. As hope faded, a deep and settled gloom stole over the sorrowing parents, and reigned throughout the once cheerful and gladsome homes. At the end of a week the only idea that remained was, that one of these three casualties had befallen the lost children:—death, a lingering death by famine; death, cruel and horrible, by wolves or bears; or yet more terrible, with tortures by the hands of the dreaded Indians, who occasionally held their councils and hunting parties on the hills about the Rice Lake, which was known only by the elder Perron as the scene of many bloody encounters between the rival tribes of the Mohawks and Chippewas: its localities were scarcely ever visited by our settlers, lest haply they should fall into the hands of the bloody Mohawks, whose merciless dispositions made them in those days a by-word even to the less cruel Chippewas and other Indian nations.

It was not in the direction of the Rice Lake that Maxwell and his brother-in-law sought their lost children; and even if they had done so, among the deep glens and hill passes of what is now commonly called the Plains, they would have stood little chance of discovering the poor wanderers. After many days of fatigue of body and distress of mind, the sorrowing parents sadly relinquished the search as utterly hopeless, and mourned in bitterness of spirit over the disastrous fate of their first-born and beloved children. —"There was a voice of woe, and lamentation, and great mourning; Rachel weeping for her children, and refusing to be comforted, because they were not."

The miserable uncertainty that involved the fate of the lost ones was an aggravation to the sufferings of the mourners: could they but have been certified of the manner of their deaths, they fancied they should be more contented; but, alas! this fearful satisfaction was withheld.

"Oh, were their tale of sorrow known,
  'Twere something to the breaking heart,
  The pangs of doubt would then be gone,
  And fancy's endless dreams depart."

But let us quit the now mournful settlement of the Cold Springs, and see how it really fared with the young wanderers.

When they awoke the valley was filled with a white creamy mist, that arose from the bed of the stream, (now known as Cold Creek,) and gave an indistinctness to the whole landscape, investing it with an appearance perfectly different to that which it had worn by the bright, clear light of the moon. No trace of their footsteps remained to guide them in retracing their path; so hard and dry was the stony ground that it left no impression on its surface. It was with some difficulty they found the creek, which was concealed from sight by a lofty screen of gigantic hawthorns, high-bush cranberries, poplars, and birch-trees. The hawthorn was in blossom, and gave out a sweet perfume, not less fragrant than the "May" which makes the lanes and hedgerows of "merrie old England" so sweet and fair in May and June, as chanted in many a genuine pastoral of our olden time; but when our simple Catharine drew down the flowery branches to wreathe about her hat, she loved the flowers for their own native sweetness and beauty, not because poets had sung of them;—but young minds have a natural poetry in themselves, unfettered by rule or rhyme.

At length their path began to grow more difficult. A tangled mass of cedars, balsams, birch, black ash, alders, and *tamarack* (Indian name for the larch), with a dense thicket of bushes and shrubs, such as love the cool, damp soil of marshy ground, warned our travellers that they must quit the banks of the friendly stream, or they might become entangled in a trackless swamp. Having taken copious and refreshing draughts from the bright waters, and bathed their hands and faces, they ascended the grassy bank, and again descending, found themselves in one of those long valleys, enclosed between lofty sloping banks, clothed with shrubs and oaks, with here and there a stately pine. Through this second valley they pursued their way, till emerging into a wider space, they came among those singularly picturesque groups of rounded gravel hills, where the Cold Creek once more met their view, winding its way towards a grove of evergreens, where it was again lost to the eye.

This lovely spot is now known as Sackville's Mill-dike. The hand of man has curbed the free course of the wild forest stream, and made it subservient to his will, but could not destroy the natural beauties of the scene.[1]

Fearing to entangle themselves in the swamp, they kept the hilly ground, winding their way up to the summit of the lofty ridge of the oak hills, the highest ground they had yet attained; and here it was that the silver waters of the Rice Lake in all its beauty burst upon the eyes of the wondering and delighted travellers. There it lay, a sheet of liquid silver just emerging from the blue veil of mist that hung upon its surface, and concealed its wooded shores on either side. All feeling of dread and doubt and danger was lost, for the time, in one rapturous glow of admiration at a scene so unexpected and so beautiful as that which they now gazed upon from the elevation they had gained. From this ridge they looked down the lake, and the eye could take in an extent of many miles, with its verdant wooded islands, which stole into view one by one as the rays of the morning sun drew up the moving curtain of mist that enveloped them; and soon both northern and southern shores became distinctly visible, with all their bays and capes and swelling oak and pine-crowned hills.

And now arose the question, "Where are we? What lake is this? Can it be the Ontario, or is it the Rice Lake? Can yonder shores be those of the Americans, or are they the hunting-grounds of the dreaded Indians?" Hector remembered having often heard his father say that the

[1] This place was originally owned by a man of taste, who resided for some time upon the spot, till finding it convenient to return to his native country, the saw-mill passed into other hands. The old log-house on the green bank above the mill-stream is still standing, though deserted; the garden-fence, broken and dilapidated, no longer protects the enclosure, where the wild rose mingles with that of Provence,—the Canadian creeper with the hop.

Ontario was like an inland sea, and the opposite shores not visible unless in some remarkable state of the atmosphere, when they had been occasionally discerned by the naked eye, while here they could distinctly see objects on the other side, the peculiar growth of the trees, and even flights of wild fowl winging their way among the rice and low bushes on its margin. The breadth of the lake from shore to shore could not, they thought, exceed three or four miles; while its length, in an easterly direction, seemed far greater beyond what the eye could take in.[1]

They now quitted the lofty ridge, and bent their steps towards the lake. Wearied with their walk, they seated themselves beneath the shade of a beautiful feathery pine, on a high promontory that commanded a magnificent view down the lake.

"How pleasant it would be to have a house on this delightful bank, overlooking the lake," said Louis; "only think of the fish we could take, and the ducks and wild fowl we could shoot! and it would be no very hard matter to hollow out a log canoe, such a one as I have heard my father say he has rowed in across many a lake and broad river below, when he was lumbering."

"Yes, it would, indeed, be a pleasant spot to live upon,"[2] said Hector, "though I am not quite sure that the land is as good just here as it is at Cold Springs; but all these flats and rich valleys would make fine pastures, and produce plenty of grain, too, if cultivated."

"You always look to the main chance, Hec," said Louis, laughing; "well, it was worth a few hours' walking this morning to look upon so lovely a sheet of water as this. I

[1] The length of the Rice Lake, from its headwaters near Black's Landing to the mouth of the Trent, is said to be twenty-five miles; its breadth from north to south varies from three to six.

[2] Now the site of a pleasant cottage, erected by an enterprising gentleman from Devonshire, who has cleared and cultivated a considerable portion of the ground described above; a spot almost unequalled in the plains for its natural beauties and extent of prospect.

would spend two nights in a wigwam,—would not you, ma belle?—to enjoy such a sight."

"Yes, Louis," replied his cousin, hesitating as she spoke; "it is very pretty, and I did not mind sleeping in the little hut; but then I cannot enjoy myself as much as I should have done had my father and mother been aware of my intention of accompanying you. Ah, my dear, dear parents!" she added, as the thought of the anguish the absence of her companions and herself would cause at home came over her. "How I wish I had remained at home! Selfish Catharine! foolish idle girl!"

Poor Louis was overwhelmed with grief at the sight of his cousin's tears, and as the kind-hearted but thoughtless boy bent over her to soothe and console her, his own tears fell upon the fair locks of the weeping girl, and bedewed the hand he held between his own.

"If you cry thus, cousin," he whispered, "you will break poor Louis's heart, already sore enough with thinking of his foolish conduct."

"Be not cast down, Catharine," said her brother, cheeringly; "we may not be so far from home as you think. As soon as you are rested we will set out again, and we may find something to eat; there must be strawberries on these sunny banks."

Catharine soon yielded to the voice of her brother, and drying her eyes, proceeded to descend the sides of the steep valley that lay to one side of the high ground where they had been sitting.

Suddenly darting down the bank, she exclaimed, "Come, Hector; come, Louis: here indeed is provision to keep us from starving;"—for her eye had caught the bright red strawberries among the flowers and herbage on the slope; large ripe strawberries, the very finest she had ever seen.

"There is indeed, ma belle," said Louis, stooping as he spoke to gather up, not the fruit, but a dozen fresh partridge eggs from the inner shade of a thick tuft of grass and herbs that grew beside a fallen tree. Catharine's voice and sudden movements had startled the partridge[1] from her nest, and the eggs were soon transferred to Louis's straw hat, while a stone flung by the steady hand of Hector stunned the parent bird. The boys laughed exultingly as they displayed their prizes to the astonished Catharine, who, in spite of hunger, could not help regretting the death of the mother bird. Girls and women rarely sympathise with men and boys in their field sports, and Hector laughed at his sister's doleful looks as he handed over the bird to her.

"It was a lucky chance," said he, "and the stone was well aimed, but it is not the first partridge that I have killed in this way. They are so stupid you may even run them down at times; I hope to get another before the day is over. Well, there is no fear of starving to-day, at all events," he added, as he inspected the contents of his cousin's hat; "twelve nice fresh eggs, a bird, and plenty of fruit."

"But how shall we cook the bird and the eggs? We have no means of getting a fire made," said Catharine.

"As to the eggs," said Louis, "we can eat them raw; it is not for hungry wanderers like us to be over nice about our food."

"They would satisfy us much better were they boiled, or roasted in the ashes," observed Hector.

"True. Well, a fire, I think, can be got with a little trouble."

"But how?" asked Hector.

"Oh, there are many ways, but the readiest would be a flint with the help of my knife."

"A flint?"

[1] The Canadian partridge is a species of grouse, larger than the English or French partridge. We refer our young readers to the finely arranged specimens in the British Museum, (open to the public,) where they may discover "Louis's partridge."

"Yes, if we could get one—but I see nothing but granite, which crumbles and shivers when struck—we could not get a spark. However, I think it's very likely that one of the round pebbles I see on the beach yonder may be found hard enough for the purpose."

To the shore they bent their steps as soon as the little basket had been well filled with strawberries, and descending the precipitous bank, fringed with young saplings, birch, ash, and poplars, they quickly found themselves beside the bright waters of the lake. A flint was soon found among the water-worn stones that lay thickly strewn upon the shore, and a handful of dry sedge, almost as inflammable as tinder, was collected without trouble; though Louis, with the recklessness of his nature, had coolly proposed to tear a strip from his cousin's apron as a substitute for tinder,—a proposal that somewhat raised the indignation of the tidy Catharine, whose ideas of economy and neatness were greatly outraged, especially as she had no sewing implements to assist in mending the rent. Louis thought nothing of that; it was a part of his character to think only of the present, little of the past, and to let the future provide for itself. Such was Louis's great failing, which had proved a fruitful source of trouble both to himself and others. In this respect he bore a striking contrast to his more cautious companion, who possessed much of the gravity of his father. Hector was as heedful and steady in his decisions as Louis was rash and impetuous.

After many futile attempts, and some skin knocked off their knuckles through awkward handling of the knife and flint, a good fire was at last kindled, as there was no lack of dry wood on the shore; Catharine then triumphantly produced her tin pot, and the eggs were boiled, greatly to the satisfaction of all parties, who were by this time sufficiently hungry, having eaten nothing since the previous evening more substantial than the strawberries they had taken during the time they were gathering them in the morning.

Catharine had selected a pretty, cool, shady recess, a natural bower, under the overhanging growth of cedars, poplars, and birch, which were wreathed together by the flexile branches of the wild grape vine and bitter-sweet, which climbed to a height of fifteen feet[1] among the branches of the trees, which it covered as with a mantle. A pure spring of cold, delicious water welled out from beneath the twisted roots of an old hoary-barked cedar, and found its way among the shingles on the beach to the lake, a humble but constant tributary to its waters. Some large blocks of water-worn stone formed convenient seats and a natural table, on which the little maiden arranged the forest fare; and never was a meal made with greater appetite or taken with more thankfulness than that which our wanderers ate that morning. The eggs (part of which they reserved for another time) were declared to be better than those that were daily produced from the little hen-house at Cold Springs. The strawberries, set out in little pottles made with the shining leaves of the oak, ingeniously pinned together by Catharine with the long spurs of the hawthorn,[2] were voted delicious, and the pure water most refreshing, that they drank, for lack of better cups, from a large mussel-shell which Catharine had picked up among the weeds and pebbles on the beach.

Many children would have wandered about weeping and disconsolate, lamenting their sad fate, or have embittered the time by useless repining, or, perhaps, by

[1] *Celastrus scandens*,—Bitter-sweet or Woody nightshade. This plant, like the red-berried briony of England, is highly ornamental. It possesses powerful properties as a medicine, and is in high reputation among the Indians.

[2] The long-spurred American hawthorn may be observed by our young readers among that beautiful collection of the hawthorn family and its affinities, which flourish on the north side of Kensington Gardens.

venting their uneasiness in reviling the principal author of their calamity—poor, thoughtless Louis; but such were not the dispositions of our young Canadians. Early accustomed to the hardships incidental to the lives of the settlers in the bush, these young people had learned to bear with patience and cheerfulness privations that would have crushed the spirits of children more delicately nurtured. They had known every degree of hunger and nakedness; during the first few years of their lives they had often been compelled to subsist for days and weeks upon roots and herbs, wild fruits, and game which their fathers had learned to entrap, to decoy, and to shoot. Thus Louis and Hector had early been initiated into the mysteries of the chase. They could make dead-falls, and pits, and traps, and snares,—they were as expert as Indians in the use of the bow,—they could pitch a stone, or fling a wooden dart at partridge, hare, and squirrel, with almost unerring aim; and were as swift of foot as young fawns. Now it was that they learned to value in its fullest extent this useful and practical knowledge, which enabled them to face with fortitude the privations of a life so precarious as that to which they were now exposed.

It was one of the elder Maxwell's maxims,—Never let difficulties overcome you, but rather strive to conquer them; let the head direct the hand, and the hand, like a well-disciplined soldier, obey the head as chief. When his children expressed any doubts of not being able to accomplish any work they had begun, he would say, "Have you not hands, have you not a head, have you not eyes to see, and reason to guide you? As for impossibilities, they do not belong to the trade of a soldier,—he dare not see them." Thus were energy and perseverance early instilled into the minds of his children; they were now called upon to give practical proofs of the precepts that had been taught them in childhood. Hector trusted to his axe, and Louis to his *couteau-de-chasse* and pocket-knife; the latter was a present from an old forest friend of his father's, who had visited them the previous winter, and which, by good luck, Louis had in his pocket,—a capacious pouch, in which were stored many precious things, such as coils of twine and string, strips of leather, with odds and ends of various kinds; nails, bits of iron, leather, and such miscellaneous articles as find their way most mysteriously into boys' pockets in general, and Louis Perron's in particular, who was a wonderful collector of such small matters.

The children were not easily daunted by the prospect of passing a few days abroad on so charming a spot, and at such a lovely season, where fruits were so abundant; and when they had finished their morning meal, so providentially placed within their reach, they gratefully acknowledged the mercy of God in this thing.

Having refreshed themselves by bathing their hands and faces in the lake, they cheerfully renewed their wanderings, though something loth to leave the cool shade and the spring for an untrodden path among the hills and deep ravines that furrow the shores of the Rice Lake in so remarkable a manner; and often did our weary wanderers pause to look upon the wild glens and precipitous hills, where the fawn and the shy deer found safe retreats, unharmed by the rifle of the hunter,—where the osprey and white-headed eagle built their nests, unheeded and unharmed. Twice that day, misled by following the track of the deer, had they returned to the same spot,—a deep and lovely glen, which had once been a water-course, but was now a green and shady valley. This they named the Valley of the Rock, from a remarkable block of red granite that occupied a central position in the narrow defile; and here they prepared to pass the second night on the Plains. A few boughs cut down and interlaced with the shrubs round a small space cleared with Hector's axe, formed shelter, and leaves and grass, strewed on the

ground, formed a bed, though not so smooth, perhaps, as
the bark and cedar-boughs that the Indians spread within
their summer wigwams for carpets and couches, or the
fresh heather that the Highlanders gather on the wild
Scottish hills.

While Hector and Louis were preparing the sleeping-
chamber, Catharine busied herself in preparing the
partridge for their supper. Having collected some thin
peelings from the rugged bark of a birch-tree, that grew
on the side of the steep bank to which she gave the
appropriate name of the "Birken shaw," she dried it in her
bosom, and then beat it fine upon a big stone, till it
resembled the finest white paper. This proved excellent
tinder, the aromatic oil contained in the bark of the birch
being highly inflammable. Hector had prudently retained
the flint that they had used in the morning, and a fire was
now lighted in front of the rocky stone, and a forked stick,
stuck in the ground, and bent over the coals, served as a
spit, on which, gipsy-fashion, the partridge was
suspended,—a scanty meal, but thankfully partaken of,
though they knew not how they should breakfast next
morning. The children felt they were pensioners on God's
providence not less than the wild denizens of the
wilderness around them.

When Hector—who by nature was less sanguine than his
sister or cousin—expressed some anxiety for their provi-
sions for the morrow, Catharine, who had early listened
with trusting piety of heart to the teaching of her father,
when he read portions from the holy word of God, gently
laid her hand upon her brother's head, which rested on
her knees, as he sat upon the grass beside her, and said, in
a low and earnest tone, " 'Consider the fowls of the air;
they sow not, neither do they reap, nor gather into barns,
yet your heavenly Father feedeth them. Are ye not much
better than they?' Surely, my brother, God careth for us as
much as for the wild creatures, that have no sense to praise

and glorify his holy name. God cares for the creatures He has made, and supplies them with knowledge where they shall find food when they hunger and thirst. So I have heard my father say; and surely our father knows, for is he not a wise man, Hector?"

"I remember," said Louis, thoughtfully, "hearing my mother repeat the words of a good old man she knew when she lived in Quebec;—'When you are in trouble, Mathilde,' he used to say to her, 'kneel down, and ask God's help, nothing doubting but that He has the power as well as the will to serve you, if it be for your good; for He is able to bring all things to pass. It is our own want of faith that prevents our prayers from being heard.' And, truly, I think the wise old man was right," he added.

It was strange to hear grave words like these from the lips of the giddy Louis. Possibly they had the greater weight on that account. And Hector, looking up with a serious air, replied, "Your mother's friend was a good man, Louis. Our want of trust in God's power must displease Him. And when we think of all the great and glorious things He has made,—that blue sky, those sparkling stars, the beautiful moon that is now shining down upon us, and the hills and waters, the mighty forest, and little creeping plants and flowers that grow at our feet, —it must, indeed, seem foolish in his eyes that we should doubt his power to help us, who not only made all these things, but ourselves also."

"True," said Catharine; "but then, Hector, we are not as God made us; for the wicked one cast bad seed in the field where God had sown the good."

"Let us, however, consider what we shall do for food; for, you know, God helps those that help themselves," said Louis. "Let us consider a little. There must be plenty of fish in the lake, both small and great."

"But how are we to get them out of it?" rejoined Catharine. "I doubt the fish will swim at their ease there, while we go hungry."

"Do not interrupt me, ma chère. Then, we see the track of deer, and the holes of the woodchuck; we hear the cry of squirrels and chitmunks, and there are plenty of partridges, and ducks, and quails, and snipes; of course, we have to contrive some way to kill them. Fruits there are in abundance, and plenty of nuts of different kinds. At present we have plenty of fine strawberries, and huckleberries will be ripe soon in profusion, and bilberries too, and you know how pleasant they are; as for raspberries, I see none; but by-and-by there will be May-apples (*Podophyllum peltatum*)—I see great quantities of them in the low grounds; grapes, high-bush-cranberries, haws as large as cherries, and sweet too; squaw-berries, wild plums, choke-cherries, and bird-cherries. As to sweet acorns, there will be bushels and bushels of them for the roasting, as good as chestnuts, to my taste; and butter-nuts, and hickory-nuts,—with many other good things." And here Louis stopped for want of breath to continue his catalogue of forest dainties.

"Yes; and there are bears, and wolves, and racoons, too, that will eat us for want of better food," interrupted Hector, slyly. "Nay, Katty, do not shudder, as if you were already in the clutches of a big bear. Neither bear nor wolf shall make mincemeat of thee, my girl, while Louis and thy brother are near, to wield an axe or a knife in thy defence."

"Nor catamount spring upon thee, ma belle cousine," added Louis, gallantly, "while thy bold cousin Louis can scare him away."

"Well, now that we know our resources, the next thing is to consider how we are to obtain them, my dears," said Catharine. "For fishing, you know, we must have a hook and line, a rod, or a net. Now, where are these to be met with?"

Louis nodded his head sagaciously. "The line I think I can provide; the hook is more difficult, but I do not despair even of that. As to the rod, it can be cut from any slender sapling on the shore. A net, ma chere, I could make with very little trouble, if I had but a piece of cloth to sew over a hoop."

Catharine laughed. "You are very ingenious, no doubt, Monsieur Louis, but where are you to get the cloth and the hoop, and the means of sewing it on?"

Louis took up the corner of his cousin's apron with a provoking look.

"My apron, sir, is not to be appropriated for any such purpose. You seem to covet it for everything."

"Indeed, ma petite, I think it very unbecoming and very ugly, and never could see any good reason why you and Mamma and Mathilde should wear such frightful things."

"It is to keep our gowns clean, Louis, when we are milking and scrubbing, and doing all sorts of household duties," said Catharine.

"Well, ma belle, you have neither cows to milk, nor house to clean," replied the annoying boy; "so there can be little want of the apron. I could turn it to fifty useful purposes."

"Pooh, nonsense," said Hector, impatiently, "let the child alone, and do not tease her about her apron."

"Well, then, there is another good thing I did not think of before, water mussels. I have heard my father and old Jacob the lumberer say, that, roasted in their shells in the ashes, with a seasoning of salt and pepper, they are good eating when nothing better is to be got."

"No doubt, if the seasoning can be procured," said Hector, "but, alas for the salt and the pepper!"

"Well, we can eat them with the best of all sauces— hunger; and then, no doubt, there are crayfish in the gravel under the stones, but we must not mind a pinch to our fingers in taking them."

"To-morrow then let us breakfast on fish," said Hector. "You and I will try our luck, while Kate gathers strawberries; and if our line should break, we can easily cut

those long locks from Catharine's head, and twist them
into lines,"—and Hector laid his hands upon the long
fair hair that hung in shining curls about his sister's neck.

"Cut my curls! This is even worse than cousin Louis's
proposal of making tinder and fishing-nets of my apron,"
said Catharine, shaking back the bright tresses, which,
escaping from the snood that bound them, fell in golden
waves over her shoulders.

"In truth, Hec, it were a sin and a shame to cut her
pretty curls, that become her so well," said Louis. "But we
have no scissors, ma belle, so you need fear no injury to
your precious locks."

"For the matter of that, Louis, we could cut them with
your *couteau-de-chasse*. I could tell you a story that my
father told me, not long since, of Charles Stuart, the
second king of that name in England. You know he was
the grand-uncle of the young Chevalier Charles Edward,
that my father talks of, and loves so much."

"I know all about him," said Catharine, nodding
sagaciously; "let us hear the story of his grand-uncle. But I
should like to know what my hair and Louis's knife can
have to do with King Charles."

"Wait a bit, Kate, and you shall hear, that is, if you have
patience," said her brother. "Well then, you must know,
that after some great battle, the name of which I forget,[1] in
which the King and his handful of brave soldiers were
defeated by the forces of the Parliament, (the
Roundheads, as they were called,) the poor young king
was hunted like a partridge upon the mountains; a large
price was set on his head, to be given to any traitor who
should slay him, or bring him prisoner to Oliver Cromwell.
He was obliged to dress himself in all sorts of queer
clothes, and hide in all manner of strange, out of the way
places, and keep company with rude and humble men, the

[1] Battle of Worcester.

better to hide his real rank from the cruel enemies that sought his life. Once he hid along with a gallant gentleman,[1] one of his own brave officers, in the branches of a great oak. Once he was hid in a mill; and another time he was in the house of one Pendril, a woodman. The soldiers of the Parliament, who were always prowling about, and popping in unawares wherever they suspected the poor king to be hidden, were, at one time, in the very room where he was standing beside the fire."

"Oh!" exclaimed Catharine, "that was frightful. And did they take him prisoner?"

"No; for the wise woodman and his brothers, fearing lest the soldiers should discover that he was a cavalier and a gentleman, by the long curls that the king's men all wore in those days, and called *lovelocks*, begged of his majesty to let his hair be cropped close to his head."

"That was very hard, to lose his nice curls."

"I dare say the young king thought so too, but it was better to lose his hair than his head. So, I suppose, the men told him, for he suffered them to cut it all close to his head, laying down his head on a rough deal table, or a chopping-block, while his faithful friends with a large knife trimmed off the curls."

"I wonder if the young king thought at that minute of his poor father, who, you know, was forced by wicked men to lay down his head upon a block to have it cut from his shoulders, because Cromwell, and others as hard-hearted as himself, willed that he should die."

"Poor king!" said Catharine, sighing, "I see that it is better to be poor children, wandering on these plains under God's own care, than to be kings and princes at the mercy of bad and sinful men."

"Who told your father all these things, Hec?" said Louis.

"It was the son of his brave colonel, who knew a great

[1] Colonel Careless.

deal about the history of the Stuart kings, for our colonel
had been with Prince Charles, the young chevalier, and
fought by his side when he was in Scotland; he loved him
dearly, and, after the battle of Culloden, where the Prince
lost all, and was driven from place to place, and had not
where to lay his head, he went abroad in hopes of better
times; but those times did not come for the poor Prince;
and our colonel, after a while, through the friendship of
General Wolfe, got a commission in the army that was
embarking for Quebec, and, at last, commanded the
regiment to which my father belonged. He was a kind
man, and my father loved both him and his son, and
grieved not a little when he parted from him."

"Well," said Catharine, "as you have told me such a nice
story, Mister Hec, I shall forgive the affront about my
curls."

"Well, then, to-morrow we are to try our luck at fishing,
and if we fail, we will make us bows and arrows to kill deer
or small game; I fancy we shall not be over particular as to
its quality. Why should not we be able to find subsistence as
well as the wild Indians?"

"True," said Hector, "the wild men of the wilderness,
and the animals and birds, all are fed by the things that He
provideth; then, wherefore should His white children
fear?"

"I have often heard my father tell of the privations of
the lumberers, when they have fallen short of provisions,
and of the contrivances of himself and old Jacob Morelle,
when they were lost for several days, nay, weeks I believe it
was. Like the Indians, they made themselves bows and
arrows, using the sinews of the deer, or fresh thongs of
leather, for bow-strings; and when they could not get
game to eat, they boiled the inner bark of the slippery elm
to jelly, or birch bark, and drank the sap of the sugar
maple when they could get no water but melted snow only,
which is unwholesome; at last, they even boiled their own
mocassins."

"Indeed, Louis, that must have been a very unsavoury dish," said Catharine.

"That old buckskin vest would have made a famous pot of soup of itself," added Hector, "or the deer-skin hunting shirt."

"Well, they might have been reduced even to that," said Louis, laughing, "but for the good fortune that befel them in the way of a half-roasted bear."

"Nonsense, cousin Louis, bears do not run about ready roasted in the forest, like the lambs in the old nursery tale."

"Well now, Kate, this was a fact; at least, it was told as one by old Jacob, and my father did not deny it; shall I tell you about it? After passing several hungry days with no better food to keep them alive than the scrapings of the inner bark of the poplars and elms, which was not very substantial for hearty men, they encamped one night in a thick dark swamp,—not the sort of place they would have chosen, but they could not help themselves, having been enticed into it by the tracks of a deer or a moose,—and night came upon them unawares, so they set to work to kindle up a fire with spunk, and a flint and knife; rifle they had none, or maybe they would have had game to eat. Old Jacob fixed upon a huge hollow pine, that lay across their path, against which he soon piled a glorious heap of boughs and arms of trees, and whatever wood he could collect, and lighted up a fine fire. You know what a noble hand old Jacob used to be at making up a roaring fire; he thought, I suppose, if he could not have warmth within, he would have plenty of it without. The wood was dry pine and cedar and birch, and it blazed away, and crackled and burnt like a pine-torch. By-and-by they heard a most awful growling close to them. 'That's a big bear, as I live,' said old Jacob, looking all about, thinking to see one come out from the thick bush; but Bruin was nearer to him than he thought, for presently a great black bear burst out from the but-end of the great burning log, and made towards

Jacob; just then the wind blew the flame outward, and it caught the bear's thick coat, and he was all in a blaze in a moment. No doubt the heat of the fire had penetrated to the hollow of the log, where he had lain himself snugly up for the winter, and wakened him; but Jacob seeing the huge black brute all in a flame of fire, began to think it was Satan's own self come to carry him off, and he roared with fright, and the bear roared with pain and rage, and my father roared with laughing to see Jacob's terror; but he did not let the bear laugh at him, for he seized a thick pole that he had used for closing in the brands and logs, and soon demolished the bear, who was so blinded with the fire and smoke that he made no fight; and they feasted on roast bear's flesh for many days, and got a capital skin to cover them beside."

"What, Louis, after the fur was all singed?" said Catharine.

"Kate, you are too particular," said Louis; "a story never loses, you know."

Hector laughed heartily at the adventure, and enjoyed the dilemma of the bear in his winter quarter; but Catharine was somewhat shocked at the levity displayed by her cousin and brother, when recounting the terror of old Jacob and the sufferings of the poor bear.

"You boys are always so unfeeling," she said, gravely.

"Indeed, Kate," said her brother, "the day may come when the sight of a good piece of roast bear's flesh will be no unwelcome sight. If we do not find our way back to Cold Springs before the winter sets in, we may be reduced to as bad a state as poor Jacob and my uncle were in the pine swamps, on the banks of the St. John."

"Ah!" said Catharine, trembling, "that would be too bad to happen."

"Courage, ma belle, let us not despair for the morrow. Let us see what to-morrow will do for us; meantime, we will not neglect the blessings we still possess; see, our partridge is ready, let us eat our supper, and be thankful; and for grace let us say, 'Sufficient unto the day is the evil thereof.'"

Long exposure to the air had sharpened their appetites —the hungry wanderers needed no further invitation, the scanty meal, equally divided, was soon despatched.

It is a common saying, but excellent to be remembered by any wanderers in our forest wilds, that those who travel by the sun travel in a circle, and usually find themselves at night in the same place from whence they started in the morning; so it was with our wanderers. At sunset, they found themselves once more in the ravine, beside the big stone, in which they had rested at noon. They had imagined themselves miles and miles distant from it; they were grievously disappointed. They had encouraged each other with the confident hope that they were drawing near to the end of their bewildering journey; they were as far from their home as ever, without the slightest clue to guide them to the right path. Despair is not a feeling which takes deep root in the youthful breast. The young are always so hopeful; so confident in their own wisdom and skill in averting or conquering danger; so trusting; so willing to believe that there is a peculiar Providence watching over them. Poor children! they had indeed need of such a belief to strengthen their minds and encourage them to fresh exertions, for new trials were at hand.

The broad moon had already flooded the recesses of the glen with light, and all looked fresh and lovely in the dew, which glittered on tree and leaf, on herb and flower. Catharine, who, though weary with her fatiguing wanderings, could not sleep, left the little hut of boughs which her companions had put up near the granite rock in the valley for her accommodation, and ascended the western bank, where the last jutting spur of its steep side formed a lofty cliff-like promontory, at the extreme verge of which the roots of one tall spreading oak formed a most inviting seat, from whence the traveller looked down into a level track, which stretched away to the edge of the lake. This flat had been the estuary of the mountain stream, which had once rushed down between the hills, forming a narrow gorge; but now, all was changed; the waters had ceased to flow, the granite bed was overgrown, and carpeted with deer-grass and flowers of many hues, wild fruits and bushes, below; while majestic oaks and pines towered above. A sea of glittering foliage lay beneath Catharine's feet; in the distance the eye of the young girl rested on a belt of shining waters, which girt in the shores like a silver zone; beyond, yet more remote to the northward, stretched the illimitable forest.

Never had Catharine looked upon a scene so still or so fair to the eye; a holy calm seemed to shed its influence over her young mind, and peaceful tears stole down her cheeks. Not a sound was there abroad, scarcely a leaf stirred; she could have stayed for hours there gazing on the calm beauty of nature, and communing with her own heart, when suddenly a stirring rustling sound caught her ear; it came from a hollow channel on one side of the promontory, which was thickly overgrown with the shrubby dogwood, wild roses and bilberry bushes. Imagine the terror which seized the poor girl, on perceiving a grisly beast breaking through the covert of the bushes. With a scream and a bound, which the most deadly fear alone could have inspired, Catharine sprung from the supporting trunk of the oak, dashed down the precipitous side of the ravine; now clinging to the bending sprays of the flexile dogwood—now to some fragile birch or poplar—now trusting to the yielding heads of the sweet-scented *ceanothus*, or filling her hands with sharp thorns from the roses that clothed the bank; flowers, grass, all were alike clutched at in her rapid and fearful descent.

A loose fragment of granite on which she had unwittingly placed her foot rolled from under her; unable to regain her balance she fell forwards, and was precipitated through the bushes into the ravine below, conscious only of unspeakable terror and an agonising pain in one of her ancles, which rendered her quite powerless. The noise of the stones she had dislodged in her fall and her piteous cries, brought Louis and Hector to her side, and they bore her in their arms to the hut of boughs and laid her down upon her bed of leaves and grass and young pine boughs. When Catharine was able to speak, she related to Louis and Hector the cause of her fright. She was sure it must have been a wolf by his sharp teeth, long jaws, and grizzly coat. The last glance she had had of him had filled her with terror, he was standing on a fallen tree with his eyes fixed upon her—she could tell them no more that happened, she never felt the ground she was on, so great was her fright.

Hector was half disposed to scold his sister for rambling over the hills alone, but Louis was full of tender compassion for *la belle cousine*, and would not suffer her to be chidden. Fortunately, no bones had been fractured, though the sinews of her ankle were severely sprained; but the pain was intense, and after a sleepless night, the boys found to their grief and dismay, that Catharine was unable to put her foot to the ground. This was an unlooked-for aggravation of their misfortunes; to pursue their wandering was for the present impossible; rest was their only remedy, excepting the application of such cooling medicaments as circumstances would supply them with. Cold water constantly applied to the swollen joint, was the first thing that was suggested; but, simple as was the lotion, it was not easy to obtain it in sufficient quantities. They were a full quarter of a mile from the lake shore, and the cold springs near it were yet further off; and then the only vessel they had was the tin-pot, which hardly contained a pint; at the same time the thirst of the fevered sufferer was intolerable, and had also to be provided for. Poor

Catharine, what unexpected misery she now endured!

The valley and its neighbouring hills abounded in strawberries; they were now ripening in abundance; the ground was scarlet in places with this delicious fruit; they proved a blessed relief to the poor sufferer's burning thirst. Hector and Louis were unwearied in supplying her with them.

Louis, ever fertile in expedients, crushed the cooling fruit and applied them to the sprained foot; rendering the application still more grateful by spreading them upon the large smooth leaves of the sapling oak; these he bound on with strips of the leathery bark of the moose-wood,[1] which he had found growing in great abundance near the entrance of the ravine. Hector, in the meantime, was not idle. After having collected a good supply of ripe strawberries, he climbed the hills in search of birds' eggs and small game. About noon he returned with the good news of having discovered a spring of fine water in an adjoining ravine, beneath a clump of bass-wood and black cherry-trees; he had also been so fortunate as to kill a woodchuck, having met with many of their burrows in the gravelly sides of the hills. The woodchuck seems to be a link between the rabbit and badger; its colour is that of a leveret; it climbs like the racoon and burrows like the rabbit; its eyes are large, full, and dark, the lip cleft, the soles of the feet naked, claws sharp, ears short; it feeds on grasses, grain, fruit, and berries. The flesh is white, oily, and, in the summer, rank, but is eaten in the fall by the Indians and woodsmen; the skin is not much valued. They are easily killed by dogs, though, being expert climbers, they often baffle their enemies, clinging to the bark beyond their reach; a stone or stick well-aimed soon kills them, but they often bite sharply.

[1] "*Dirca palustris*,"—Moose-wood. American mezereon, leather-wood. From the Greek, *dirka*, a fountain or wet place, its usual place of growth.

The woodchuck proved a providential supply, and Hector cheered his companions with the assurance that they could not starve, as there were plenty of these creatures to be found. They had seen one or two about the Cold Springs, but they are less common in the deep forest lands than on the drier, more open plains.

"It is a great pity we have no larger vessel to bring our water from the spring in," said Hector, looking at the tin-pot, "one is so apt to stumble among stones and tangled underwood. If we had only one of our old bark dishes we could get a good supply at once."

"There is a fallen birch not far from this," said Louis; "I have here my trusty knife; what is there to hinder us from manufacturing a vessel capable of holding water, a gallon if you like?"

"How can you sew it together, cousin?" asked Catharine; "you have neither deer sinews, nor war-tap."[1]

"I have a substitute at hand, ma belle," and Louis pointed to the strips of leatherwood that he had collected for binding the dressings on his cousin's foot.

When an idea once struck Louis, he never rested till he worked it out in some way. In a few minutes he was busily employed, stripping sheets of the ever-useful birch-bark from the trunk that had fallen at the foot of the "Wolf's Crag," for so the children had named the memorable spot where poor Catharine's accident had occurred.

The rough outside coatings of the bark, which are of silvery whiteness, but are ragged from exposure to the action of the weather in the larger and older trees, he peeled off, and then cutting the bark so that the sides lapped well over, and the corners were secured from cracks, he proceeded to pierce holes opposite to each other, and with some trouble managed to stitch them tightly together, by drawing strips of the moose or leather-

---

[1] The Indian name for the flexible roots of the *tamarack*, or swamp larch, which they make use of in manufacturing the birch baskets and canoes.

wood through and through. The first attempt, of course, was but rude and ill-shaped, but it answered the purpose, and only leaked a little at the corners for want of a sort of flap, which he had forgotten to allow in cutting out the bark; this flap in the Indian baskets and dishes turns up, and keeps all tight and close. The defect he remedied in his subsequent attempts. In spite of its deficiencies, Louis's water-jar was looked upon with great admiration, and highly commended by Catharine, who almost forgot her sufferings while watching her cousin's proceedings.

Louis was elated by his own successful ingenuity, and was for running off directly to the spring. "Catharine shall now have cold water to bathe her poor ancle with, and to quench her thirst," he said, joyfully springing to his feet, ready for a start up the steep bank; but Hector quietly restrained his lively cousin, by suggesting the possibility of his not finding the "fountain in the wilderness," as Louis termed the spring, or losing himself altogether.

"Let us both go together, then," cried Louis. Catharine cast on her cousin an imploring glance.

"Do not leave me, dear Louis; Hector, do not let me be left alone." Her sorrowful appeal stayed the steps of the volatile Louis.

"Go you, Hector, as you know the way; I will not leave you, Kate, since I was the cause of all you have suffered; I will abide by you in joy or in sorrow till I see you once more safe in your own dear mother's arms."

Comforted by this assurance, Catharine quickly dashed away the gathering tears from her cheeks, and chid her own foolish fears.

"But you know, dear cousin," she said, "I am so helpless, and then the dread of that horrible wolf makes a coward of me."

After some little time had elapsed, Hector returned; the bark vessel had done its duty to admiration, it only wanted a very little improvement to make it complete. The water was cold and pure. Hector had spent a little time in deepening the mouth of the spring, and placing some stones about it. He described the ravine as being much deeper and wider, and more gloomy than the one they occupied. The sides and bottom were clothed with magnificent oaks. It was a grand sight, he said, to stand on the jutting spurs of this great ravine, and look down upon the tops of the trees that lay below, tossing their rounded heads like the waves of a big sea. There were many lovely flowers, vetches of several kinds, blue, white, and pencilled, twining among the grass. A beautiful white-belled flower, that was like the "Morning glory," (*Convolvulus major*,) and scarlet-cups[1] in abundance, with roses in profusion. The bottom of this ravine was strewed in places with huge blocks of black granite, cushioned with thick green moss; it opened out into a wide flat, similar to the one at the mouth of the valley of the Big Stone.[2]

These children were not insensible to the beauties of nature, and both Hector and his sister had insensibly imbibed a love of the grand and the picturesque, by listening with untiring interest to their father's animated and enthusiastic descriptions of his Highland home, and the wild mountainous scenery that surrounded it. Though brought up in solitude and uneducated, yet there was nothing vulgar or rude in the minds or manners of these young people. Simple and untaught they were, but they were guileless, earnest, and unsophisticated; and if they lacked the knowledge that is learned from books, they possessed much that was useful and practical, which had been taught by experience and observation in the school of necessity.

[1] *Euchroma*, or painted-cup.
[2] The mouth of this ravine is now under the plough, and waving fields of golden grain and verdant pastures have taken place of the wild shrubs and flowers that formerly adorned it. The lot belongs to G. Ley, Esq.

For several days the pain and fever arising from her sprain rendered any attempt at removing Catharine from the valley of the "Big Stone" impracticable. The ripe fruit began to grow less abundant in their immediate vicinity, and neither woodchuck, partridge, nor squirrel had been killed; and our poor wanderers now endured the agonising pains of hunger. Continual exposure to the air by night and by day contributed not a little to increase the desire for food. It is true, there was the yet untried lake, "bright, boundless, and free," gleaming in silvery splendour, but in practice they knew nothing of the fisher's craft, though, as a matter of report, they were well acquainted with all the mysteries of it, and had often listened with delight to the feats performed by their respective fathers in the art of angling, spearing and netting.

"I have heard my father say, that so bold and numerous were the fish in the lakes and rivers he was used to fish in, that they could be taken by the hand, with a crooked pin and coarse thread, or wooden spear; but that was in the lower province; and oh, what glorious tales I have heard him tell of spearing fish by torch-light!"

"The fish may be wiser or not so numerous in this lake," said Hector; "however, if Kate can bear to be moved, we will go down to the shore and try our luck; but what can we do? we have neither hook nor line provided."

Louis nodded his head, and sitting down on a projecting root of a scrub oak, produced from the depths of his capacious pocket a bit of tin, which he carefully selected from among a miscellaneous hoard of treasures. "Here," said he, holding it up to the view as he spoke; "here is the slide of an old powder-flask, which I picked up from among some rubbish that my sister had thrown out the other day."

"I fear you will make nothing of that," said Hector, "a bit of bone would be better. If you had a file now, you might do something."

"Stay a moment, Monsieur Hec., what do you call this?" and Louis triumphantly handed out of his pocket the very instrument in question, a few inches of a broken, rusty file; very rusty, indeed, it was, but still it might be made to answer in such ingenious hands as those of our young French Canadian. "I well remember, Katty, how you and Mathilde laughed at me for treasuring up this old thing months ago. Ah, Louis, Louis, you little knew the use it was to be put to then," he added thoughtfully, apostrophising himself; "how little do we know what is to befal us in our young days!"

"God knows it all," said Hector, gravely, "we are under His good guidance."

"You are right, Hec., let us trust in His mercy and He will take good care of us. Come, let us go to the lake," Catharine added, and sprung to her feet, but as quickly sunk down upon the grass, and regarded her companions with a piteous look, saying, "I cannot walk one step; alas, alas! what is to become of me; I am only a useless burden to you. If you leave me here, I shall fall a prey to some savage beast, and you cannot carry me with you in your search for food."

"Dry your tears, sweet cousin, you shall go with us. Do you think that Hector or Louis would abandon you in your helpless state, to die of hunger or thirst, or to be torn by wolves or bears? We will carry you by turns; the distance to the lake is nothing, and you are not so very heavy, ma belle cousine; see, I could dance with you in my arms, you are so light a burden,"—and Louis gaily caught the suffering girl up in his arms, and with rapid steps struck into the deer path that wound through the ravine towards the lake, but when they reached a pretty rounded knoll, (where Wolf Tower[1] now stands,) Louis was fain to place his cousin on a flat stone beneath a big oak that grew beside the bank, and fling himself on the flowery ground at her feet, while

[1] See account of the "Wolf Tower," in the Appendix.

he drew a long breath, and gathered the fruit that grew among the long grass to refresh himself after his fatigue; and then, while resting on the "Elfin Knowe," as Catharine called the hill, he employed himself with manufacturing a rude sort of fish-hook with the aid of his knife, the bit of tin, and the rusty file; a bit of twine was next produced,— boys have always a bit of string in their pockets, and Louis, as I have before hinted, was a provident hoarder of such small matters. The string was soon attached to the hook, and Hector was not long in cutting a sapling that answered well the purpose of a fishing-rod, and thus equipped they proceeded to the lake shore, Hector and Louis carrying the crippled Catharine by turns. When there, they selected a sheltered spot beneath a grove of over-hanging cedars and birches, festooned with wild vines, which, closely woven, formed a natural bower, quite impervious to the rays of the sun. A clear spring flowing from the upper part of the bank among the hanging network of loose fibres and twisted roots, fell tinkling over a mossy log at her feet, and quietly spread itself among the round shingly pebbles that formed the beach of the lake. Beneath this pleasant bower Catharine could repose, and watch her companions at their novel employment, or bathe her feet and infirm ancle in the cool streamlet that rippled in tiny wavelets over its stony bed.

If the amusement of fishing prove pleasant and exciting when pursued for pastime only, it may readily be conceived that its interest must be greatly heightened when its object is satisfying a craving degree of hunger. Among the sunny spots on the shore, innumerable swarms of the flying grasshopper or field crickets were sporting, and one of these proved an attractive bait. The line was no sooner cast into the water, than the hook was seized, and many were the brilliant specimens of sun-fish that our eager fishermen cast at Catharine's feet, all gleaming with gold and azure scales. Nor was there any lack of perch, or that delicate fish commonly known in these waters as the pink roach.

Tired at last with their easy sport, the hungry boys next proceeded to the grateful task of scaling and dressing their fish, and this they did very expeditiously, as soon as the more difficult part, that of kindling up a fire on the beach, had been accomplished with the help of the flint, knife, and dried rushes. The fish were then suspended, Indian fashion, on forked sticks stuck in the ground and inclined at a suitable angle towards the glowing embers,—a few minutes sufficed to cook them.

"Truly," said Catharine, when the plentiful repast was set before her, "God hath, indeed, spread a table for us here in the wilderness;" so miraculous did this ample supply of delicious food seem in the eyes of this simple child of nature.

They had often heard tell of the facility with which the fish could be caught, but they had known nothing of it from their own experience, as the streams and creeks about Cold Springs afforded them but little opportunity for exercising their skill as anglers; so that, with the rude implements with which they were furnished, the result of their morning success seemed little short of divine interference in their behalf. Happy and contented in the belief that they were not forgotten by their heavenly Father, these poor "children in the wood" looked up with gratitude to that beneficent Being who suffereth not even a sparrow to fall unheeded.

Upon Catharine, in particular, these things made a deep impression, and there as she sat in the green shade, soothed by the lulling sound of the flowing waters, and the soft murmuring of the many-coloured insects that hovered among the fragrant leaves which thatched her sylvan bower, her young heart was raised in humble and holy aspirations to the great Creator of all things living. A peaceful calm diffused itself over her mind, as with hands meekly folded across her breast, the young girl prayed with the guileless fervour of a trusting and faithful heart.

The sun was just sinking in a flood of glory behind the dark pine-woods at the head of the lake, when Hector and Louis, who had been carefully providing fish for the morrow, (which was the Sabbath,) came loaded with their finny prey carefully strung upon a willow wand, and found Catharine sleeping in her bower. Louis was loth to break her tranquil slumbers, but her careful brother reminded him of the danger to which she was exposed, sleeping in the dew by the water side; "Moreover," he added, "we have some distance to go, and we have left the precious axe and the birch-bark vessel in the valley."

These things were too valuable to be lost, and so they roused the sleeper, and slowly recommenced their toilsome way, following the same path that they had made in the morning. Fortunately, Hector had taken the precaution to bend down the flexile branches of the dogwood and break the tops of the young trees that they had passed between on their route to the lake, and by this clue they were enabled with tolerable certainty to retrace their way, nothing doubting of arriving in time at the wigwam of boughs by the rock in the valley.

Their progress was, however, slow, burdened with the care of the lame girl, and heavily laden with the fish. The purple shades of twilight soon clouded the scene, deepened by the heavy masses of foliage, which cast a greater degree of obscurity upon their narrow path; for they had now left the oak-flat and entered the gorge of the valley. The utter loneliness of the path, the grotesque shadows of the trees, that stretched in long array across the steep banks on either side, taking, now this, now that wild and fanciful shape, awakened strange feelings of dread in the mind of these poor forlorn wanderers; like most persons bred up in solitude, their imaginations were strongly tinctured with superstitious fears. Here then, in the lonely wilderness, far from their beloved parents and social hearth, with no visible arm to protect them from danger, none to encourage or to cheer them, can it be matter of surprise if they started with terror-blanched cheeks at every fitful breeze that rustled the leaves or waved the branches above them?

The gay and lively Louis, blithe as any wild bird in the bright sunlight, was the most easily oppressed by this strange superstitious fear, when the shades of evening were closing round, and he would start with ill-disguised terror at every sound or shape that met his ear or eye, though the next minute he was the first to laugh at his own weakness. In Hector, the feeling was of a graver, more solemn cast, recalling to his mind all the wild and wondrous tales with which his father was wont to entertain the children, as they crouched round the huge log-fire of an evening. It is strange the charm these marvellous tales possess for the youthful mind, no matter how improbable, or how often told; year after year they will be listened to with the same ardour, with an interest that appears to grow with repetition. And still, as they slowly wandered along, Hector would repeat to his breathless auditors those Highland legends that were as familiar to their ears as household words, and still they listened with fear and wonder, and deep awe, till at each pause he made, the deep-drawn breath and half-repressed shudder might be heard. And now the little party paused irresolutely, fearing to proceed,—they had omitted to notice some landmark in their progress; the moon had not long been up, and her light was as yet indistinct; so they sat them down on a little grassy spot on the bank, and rested till the moon should lighten their path.

Louis was confident they were not far from "the big stone," but careful Hector had his doubts, and Catharine was weary. The children had already conceived a sort of home feeling for the valley and the mass of stone that had sheltered them for so many nights, and soon the dark mass came in sight, as the broad full light of the now risen moon fell upon its rugged sides; they were nearer to it than they had imagined.

"Forward for 'the big stone' and the wigwam," cried Louis.

"Hush!" said Catharine, "look there," raising her hand with a warning gesture.

"Where? what?"

"The wolf! the wolf!" gasped out the terrified girl. There indeed, upon the summit of the block, in the attitude of a sentinel or watcher, stood the gaunt-figured animal, and as she spoke, a long wild cry, the sound of which seemed as if it came midway between the earth and the tops of the tall pines on the lofty ridge above them, struck terror into their hearts, as with speechless horror they gazed upon the dark outline of the terrible beast. There it stood, with its head raised, its neck stretched outward, and ears erect, as if to catch the echo that gave back those dismal sounds; another minute and he was gone, and the crushing of branches and the rush of many feet on the high bank above, was followed by the prolonged cry of some poor fugitive animal,—a doe, or fawn, perhaps,—in the very climax of mortal agony; and then the lonely recesses of the forest took up that fearful death-cry, the far-off shores of the lake and the distant islands prolonged it, and the terrified children clung together in fear and trembling.

A few minutes over, and all was still. The chase had turned across the hills to some distant ravine; the wolves were all gone—not even the watcher was left, and the little valley lay once more in silence, with all its dewy roses and sweet blossoms glittering in the moonlight; but though around them all was peace and loveliness, it was long ere confidence was restored to the hearts of the panic-stricken and trembling children. They beheld a savage enemy in every mass of leafy shade, and every rustling bough struck fresh terrors into their excited minds. They might have exclaimed with the patriarch Jacob, "How dreadful is this place!"

With hand clasped in hand, they sat them down among the thick covert of the bushes, for now they feared to move forward, lest the wolves should return; sleep was long a stranger to their watchful eyes, each fearing to be the only one left awake, and long and painful was their vigil. Yet nature, overtasked, at length gave way, and sleep came down upon their eyelids; deep, unbroken sleep, which lasted till the broad sunlight breaking through the leafy curtains of their forest-bed, and the sound of waving boughs and twittering birds, once more wakened them to life and light; recalling them from happy dreams of home and friends, to an aching sense of loneliness and desolation. This day they did not wander far from the valley, but took the precaution, as evening drew on, to light a large fire, the blaze of which they thought would keep away any beast of prey. They had no want of food, as the fish they had caught the day before proved an ample supply. The huckle-berries were ripening too, and soon afforded them a never-failing source of food; there were also an abundance of bilberries, the sweet rich berries of which proved a great treat, besides being very nourishing.

CHAPTER 3

"Oh for a lodge in the vast wilderness,
The boundless contiguity of shade!"

A FORTNIGHT had now passed, and Catharine still suffered so much from pain and fever, that they were unable to continue their wanderings; all that Hector and his cousin could do, was to carry her to the bower by the lake, where she reclined whilst they caught fish. The painful longing to regain their lost home had lost nothing of its intensity; and often would the poor sufferer start from her bed of leaves and boughs, to wring her hands and weep, and call in piteous tones upon that dear father and mother, who would have given worlds had they been at their command, to have heard but one accent of her beloved voice, to have felt one loving pressure from that fevered hand. Hope, the consoler, hovered over the path of the young wanderers, long after she had ceased to whisper comfort to the desolate hearts of the mournful parents.

Of all that suffered by this sad calamity, no one was more to be pitied than Louis Perron; deeply did the poor boy lament the thoughtless folly which had involved his cousin Catharine in so terrible a misfortune. "If Kate had not been with me," he would say, "we should not have been lost; for Hector is so cautious and so careful, he would not have left the cattle-path; but we were so heedless, we thought only of flowers and insects, of birds, and such trifles, and paid no heed to our way." Louis Perron, such is life. The young press gaily onward, gathering the flowers, and following the gay butterflies that attract them in the form of pleasure and amusement; they forget the grave counsels of the thoughtful, till they find the path they have followed is beset with briers and thorns; and a thousand painful difficulties that were unseen, unexpected, overwhelm and bring them to a sad sense of their own folly; and perhaps the punishment of their errors does not fall upon themselves alone, but upon the innocent, who have unknowingly been made participators in their fault.

By the kindest and tenderest attention to all her comforts, Louis endeavoured to alleviate his cousin's sufferings, and soften her regrets; nay, he would often speak cheerfully and even gaily to her, when his own heart was heavy, and his eyes ready to overflow with tears.

"If it were not for our dear parents and the dear children at home," he would say, "we might spend our time most happily upon these charming plains; it is much more delightful here than in the dark thick woods; see how brightly the sunbeams come down and gladden the ground, and cover the earth with fruit and flowers. It is pleasant to be able to fish and hunt, and trap the game. Yes, if they were all here, we would build us a nice log-house, and clear up these bushes on the flat near the lake. This "Elfin Knowe," as you call it, Kate, would be a nice spot to build upon. See these glorious old oaks; not one should be cut down, and we would have a boat and a canoe, and voyage across to yonder islands. Would it not be charming, ma belle?" and Catharine, smiling at the picture drawn so eloquently, would enter into the spirit of the project, and say,—

"Ah! Louis, that would be pleasant."

"If we had but my father's rifle now," said Hector, "and old Wolfe."

"Yes, and Fanchette, dear little Fanchette, that trees the partridges and black squirrels," said Louis.

"I saw a doe and a half-grown fawn beside her this very morning, at break of day," said Hector. "The fawn was so little fearful, that if I had had a stick in my hand, I could have killed it. I came within ten yards of the spot where it stood. I know it would be easy to catch one by making a dead-fall."[1]

"If we had but a dear fawn to frolic about us, like Mignon, dear innocent Mignon," cried Catharine, "I should never feel lonely then."

"And we should never want for meat, if we could catch a fine fawn from time to time, ma belle."

"Hec., what are you thinking of?"

"I was thinking, Louis, that if we were doomed to remain here all our lives, we must build a house for ourselves; we could not live in the open air without shelter as we have done. The summer will soon pass, and the rainy season will come, and the bitter frosts and snows of winter will have to be provided against."

"But, Hector, do you really think there is no chance of finding our way back to Cold Springs? We know it must be behind this lake," said Louis.

"True, but whether east, west, or south, we cannot tell; and whichever way we take now is but a chance, and if once we leave the lake and get involved in the mazes of that dark forest, we should perish, for we know there is neither water nor berries, nor game to be had as there is here, and we might be soon starved to death. God was good who led us beside this fine lake, and upon these fruitful plains."

"It is a good thing that I had my axe when we started from home," said Hector. "We should not have been so well off without it; we shall find the use of it if we have to build a house. We must look out for some spot where there is a spring of good water, and—"

"No horrible wolves," interrupted Catharine: "though I love this pretty ravine, and the banks and braes about us, I

[1] A sort of trap in which game is taken in the woods, or on the banks of creeks.

do not think I shall like to stay here. I heard the wolves only last night, when you and Louis were asleep."

"We must not forget to keep watch-fires."

"What shall we do for clothes?" said Catharine, glancing at her home-spun frock of wool and cotton plaid.

"A weighty consideration, indeed," sighed Hector; "clothes must be provided before ours are worn out, and the winter comes on."

"We must save all the skins of the woodchucks and squirrels," suggested Louis; "and fawns when we catch them."

"Yes, and fawns when we get them," added Hector; "but it is time enough to think of all these things; we must not give up all hope of home."

"I give up all hope? I shall hope on while I have life," said Catharine. "My dear, dear father, he will never forget his lost children; he will try and find us, alive or dead; he will never give up the search."

Poor child, how long did this hope burn like a living torch in thy guileless breast. How often, as they roamed those hills and valleys, were thine eyes sent into the gloomy recesses of the dark ravines and thick bushes, with the hope that they would meet the advancing form and outstretched arms of thy earthly parents: all in vain—yet the arms of thy heavenly Father were extended over thee, to guide, to guard, and to sustain thee.

How often were Catharine's hands filled with wild-flowers, to carry home, as she fondly said, to sick Louise, or her mother. Poor Catharine, how often did your bouquets fade; how often did the sad exile water them with her tears,—for hers was the hope that keeps alive despair.

When they roused them in the morning to recommence their fruitless wanderings, they would say to each other: "Perhaps we shall see our father, he may find us here to-day;" but evening came, and still he came not, and they were no nearer to their father's home than they had been the day previous.

"If we could but find our way back to the 'Cold Creek,' we might, by following its course, return to Cold Springs," said Hector.

"I doubt much the fact of the 'Cold Creek' having any connexion with our Spring," said Louis; "I think it has its rise in the 'Beaver Meadow,' and following its course would only entangle us among those wolfish balsam and cedar swamps, or lead us yet further astray into the thick recesses of the pine forest. For my part, I believe we are already fifty miles from Cold Springs."

It is one of the bewildering mistakes that all persons who lose their way in the pathless woods fall into, they have no idea of distance, or the points of the compass, unless they can see the sun rise and set, which is not possible to do when surrounded by the dense growth of forest-trees; they rather measure distance by the time they have been wandering, than by any other token.

The children knew that they had been a long time absent from home, wandering hither and thither, and they fancied their journey had been as long as it had been weary. They had indeed the comfort of seeing the sun in his course from east to west, but they knew not in what direction the home they had lost lay; it was this that troubled them in their choice of the course they should take each day, and at last determined them to lose no more time so fruitlessly, where the peril was so great, but seek for some pleasant spot where they might pass their time in safety, and provide for their present and future wants.

"The world was all before them, where to choose
    Their place of rest, and Providence their guide."

Catharine declared her ancle was so much stronger than it had been since the accident, and her health so much amended, that the day after the conversation just recorded, the little party bade farewell to the valley of the "big stone," and ascending the steep sides of the hills, bent their steps eastward, keeping the lake to their left hand; Hector led the way, loaded with their houshold utensils, which consisted only of the axe, which he would trust to no one but himself, the tin-pot, and the birch-basket. Louis had his cousin to assist up the steep banks, likewise some fish to carry, which had been caught early in the morning.

The wanderers thought at first to explore the ground near the lake shore, but soon abandoned this resolution, on finding the under-growth of trees and bushes become so thick, that they made little progress, and the fatigue of travelling was greatly increased by having continually to put aside the bushes or bend them down.

Hector advised trying the higher ground; and after following a deer-path through a small ravine that crossed the hills, they found themselves on a fine extent of table-land, richly, but not too densely wooded with white and black oaks (*Quercus alba* and *Quercus nigra*), diversified with here and there a solitary pine, which reared its straight and pillar-like trunk in stately grandeur above its leafy companions; a meet eyrie for the bald-eagle, that kept watch from its dark crest over the silent waters of the lake, spread below like a silver zone studded with emeralds.

In their progress, they passed the head of many small ravines, which divided the hilly shores of the lake into deep furrows; these furrows had once been channels, by which the waters of some upper lake (the site of which is now dry land) had at a former period poured down into the valley, filling the basin of what now is called the Rice Lake. These waters with resistless course had ploughed their way between the hills, bearing in their course those blocks of granite and limestone which are so widely scattered both on the hill-tops and the plains, or form a rocky pavement at the bottom of the narrow defiles. What a sight of sublime desolation must that outpouring of the waters have presented, when those steep banks were riven by the sweeping torrents that were loosened from their former bounds. The pleased eye rests upon these tranquil shores, now covered with oaks and pines, or waving with a flood of golden grain, or varied by neat dwellings and fruitful gardens; and the gazer on that peaceful scene scarcely pictures to himself what it must have been when no living eye was there to mark the rushing floods, when they scooped to themselves the deep bed in which they now repose.

Those lovely islands that sit like stately crowns upon the waters, were doubtless the wreck that remained of the valley; elevated spots, whose rocky bases withstood the force of the rushing waters, that carried away the lighter portions of the soil. The southern shore, seen from the lake, seems to lie in regular ridges running from south to north; some few are parallel with the lake-shore, possibly where some insurmountable impediment turned the current of the subsiding waters; but they all find an outlet through their connexion with ravines communicating with the lake.

There is a beautiful level tract of land, with only here and there a solitary oak growing upon it, or a few stately pines; it is commonly called the "upper Race-course," merely on account of the smoothness of the surface; it forms a high table-land, nearly three hundred feet above the lake, and is surrounded by high hills. This spot, though now dry and covered with turf and flowers, and low bushes, has evidently once been a broad sheet of water. To the eastward lies a still more lovely and attractive spot, known as the "lower Race-course;" it lies on a lower level than the former one, and, like it, is embanked by a ridge of distant hills; both have ravines leading down to the Rice Lake, and may have been the sources from whence its channel was filled. Some convulsion of nature at a remote period, by raising the waters above their natural level, might have caused a disruption of the banks, and drained their beds, as they now appear ready for the ploughshare or the spade. In the month of June these flats are brilliant with the splendid blossoms of the *castilleja coccinea*, or painted cup, the azure lupine (*Lupinus perennis*) and snowy *trillium*; dwarf roses (*Rosa blanda*) scent the evening air, and grow as if planted by the hand of taste.

A carpeting of the small downy saxifrage (*Saxifraga nivalis*) with its white silky leaves covers the ground in early spring. In the fall, it is red with the bright berries and dark box-shaped leaves of a species of creeping winter-green, that the Indians call spiceberry (*Gaultheria procumbens*); the leaves are highly aromatic, and it is medicinal as well as agreeable to the taste and smell. In the month of July a gorgeous assemblage of orange lilies (*Lilium Philadelphicum*) take the place of the lupine and trilliums; these splendid lilies vary from orange to the brightest scarlet; various species of sunflowers and *coreopsis* next appear, and elegant white *pyrolas*[1] scent the air and charm the eye. The delicate lilac and white shrubby asters next appear, and these are followed by the large deep blue gentian, and here and there by the elegant fringed gentian.[2] These are the latest and loveliest of the flowers that adorn this tract of land. It is indeed a garden of nature's own planting, but the wild garden is being converted into fields of grain, and the wild flowers give place to a new race of vegetables, less ornamental, but more useful to man and the races of domestic animals that depend upon him for their support.

Our travellers, after wandering over this lovely plain, found themselves, at the close of the day, at the head of a fine ravine,[3] where they had the good fortune to perceive a

[1] Indian bean, also called Indian potato (*Apios tuberosa*).
[2] Gentiana linearis, G. crenata.
[3] Kilvert's Ravine, above Pine-tree Point.

spring of pure water, oozing beneath some large moss-covered blocks of black waterworn granite; the ground was thickly covered with moss about the edges of the spring, and many varieties of flowering shrubs and fruits were scattered along the valley and up the steep sides of the surrounding hills. There were whortleberries, or huckleberries, as they are more usually called, in abundance; bilberries dead ripe, and falling from the bushes at a touch. The vines that wreathed the low bushes and climbed the trees were loaded with clusters of grapes, but these were yet hard and green; dwarf filberts grew on the dry gravelly sides of the hills, yet the rough prickly calyx that enclosed the nut, filled their fingers with minute thorns, that irritated the skin like the stings of the nettle; but as the kernel when ripe was sweet and good, they did not mind the consequences. The moist part of the valley was occupied by a large bed of May-apples,[1] the fruit of which was of unusual size, but they were not ripe, August being the month when they ripen; there were also wild plums still green, and wild cherries and blackberries ripening; there were great numbers of the woodchucks' burrows on the hills, while partridges and quails were seen under the thick covert of the blue-berried dog-wood,[2] that here grew in abundance at the mouth of the ravine where it opened to the lake. As this spot offered many advantages, our travellers halted for the night, and resolved to make it their head-quarters for a season, till they should meet with an eligible situation for building a winter shelter.

Here, then, at the head of the valley, sheltered by one of the rounded hills that formed its sides, our young people erected a summer hut, somewhat after the fashion of an

[1] *Podophyllum peltatum*,—Mandrake, or May-apple.

[2] *Cornus sericea*. The blue berries of this shrub are eaten by the partridge and wild-ducks; also by the pigeons and other birds. There are several species of this shrub common to the Rice Lake.

Indian wigwam, which was all the shelter that was requisite while the weather remained so warm. Through the opening at the gorge of this ravine they enjoyed a peep at the distant waters of the lake which terminated the vista, while they were quite removed from its unwholesome vapours.

The temperature of the air for some days had been hot and sultry, scarcely modified by the cool delicious breeze that usually sets in about nine o'clock, and blows most refreshingly till four or five in the afternoon. Hector and Louis had gone down to fish for supper, while Catharine busied herself in collecting leaves and dried deer-grass, moss and fern, of which there was abundance near the spring. The boys had promised to cut some fresh cedar boughs near the lake shore, and bring them up to form a foundation for their bed, and also to strew Indian-fashion over the floor of the hut by way of a carpet. This sort of carpeting reminds one of the times when the palaces of our English kings were strewed with rushes, and brings to mind the old song:—

"Oh! the golden days of good Queen Bess,
When the floors were strew'd with rushes,
And the doors went on the latch—"

Despise not then, you, my refined young readers, the rude expedients adopted by these simple children of the forest, who knew nothing of the luxuries that were to be met with in the houses of the great and the rich. The fragrant carpet of cedar or hemlock-spruce sprigs strewn lightly over the earthen floor, was to them a luxury as great as if it had been taken from the looms of Persia or Turkey, so happy and contented were they in their ignorance. Their bed of freshly gathered grass and leaves, raised from the earth by a heap of branches carefully arranged, was to them as pleasant as beds of down, and the rude hut of bark and poles, as curtains of silk or damask.

Having collected as much of these materials as she deemed sufficient for the purpose, Catharine next gathered up dry oak branches, plenty of which lay scattered here and there, to make a watch-fire for the night, and this done, weary and warm, she sat down on a little hillock, beneath the cooling shade of a grove of young aspens, that grew near the hut; pleased with the dancing of the leaves, which fluttered above her head, and fanned her warm cheek with their incessant motion, she thought, like her cousin Louise, that the aspen was the merriest tree in the forest, for it was always dancing, dancing, dancing, even when all the rest were still.

She watched the gathering of the distant thunder-clouds, which cast a deeper, more sombre shade upon the pines that girded the northern shores of the lake as with an ebon frame. Insensibly her thoughts wandered far away from the lonely spot whereon she sat, to the stoup[1] in front of her father's house, and in memory's eye she beheld it all exactly as she had left it. There stood the big spinning-wheel, just as she had set it aside; the hanks of dyed yarn suspended from the rafters, the basket filled with the carded wool ready for her work. She saw in fancy her father, with his fine athletic upright figure, his sunburnt cheeks and clustering sable hair, his clear energetic hazel eye ever beaming upon her, his favourite child, with looks of love and kindness as she moved to and fro at her wheel.[2] There, too, was her mother, with her light step and sweet cheerful voice, singing as she pursued her daily avocations; and Duncan and Kenneth driving up the cows to be milked, or chopping firewood. And as these images, like the figures of the magic lantern, passed in all their living colours before her mental vision, her head drooped heavier and lower till it sunk upon her arm, and then she

[1] The Dutch word for verandah, which is still in common use among the Canadians.

[2] Such is the method of working at the large wool wheel, unknown or obsolete in England.

started, looked round, and slept again, her face deeply buried in her young bosom; and long and peacefully the young girl slumbered.

A sound of hurrying feet approaches, a wild cry is heard and panting breath, and the sleeper with a startling scream sprang to her feet: she dreamed that she was struggling in the fangs of a wolf—its grisly paws were clasped about her throat; the feeling was agony and suffocation—her languid eyes open. Can it be?—what is it that she sees? Yes, it is Wolfe; not the fierce creature of her dreams by night and her fears by day, but her father's own brave devoted dog. What joy, what hope rushed to her heart! She threw herself upon the shaggy neck of the faithful beast, and wept from the fulness of heart.

"Yes," she joyfully cried, "I knew that I should see him again. My own dear, dear, loving father! Father! father! dear, dear father, here are your children. Come, come quickly!" and she hurried to the head of the valley, raising her voice, that the beloved parent, who she now confidently believed was approaching, might be guided to the spot by the well-known sound of her voice.

Poor child! the echoes of thy eager voice, prolonged by every projecting headland of the valley, replied in mocking tones, "Come quickly!"

Bewildered she paused, listened breathlessly, and again she called, "Father, come quickly, come!" and again the deceitful sounds were repeated, "Quickly come!"

The faithful dog, who had succeeded in tracking the steps of his lost mistress, raised his head and erected his ears, as she called on her father's name; but he gave no joyful bark of recognition as he was wont to do when he heard his master's step approaching. Still Catharine could not but think that Wolfe had only hurried on before, and that her father must be very near.

The sound of her voice had been heard by her brother and cousin, who, fearing some evil beast had made its way to the wigwam, hastily wound up their line, and left the fishing-ground to hurry to her assistance. They could hardly believe their eyes when they saw Wolfe, faithful old Wolfe, their earliest friend and playfellow, named by their father after the gallant hero of Quebec. And they too, like Catharine, thought that their friends were not far distant, and joyfully they climbed the hills and shouted aloud, and Wolfe was coaxed and caressed, and besought to follow them to point out the way they should take: but all their entreaties were in vain; worn out with fatigue and long fasting, the poor old dog refused to quit the embers of the fire, before which he stretched himself, and the boys now noticed his gaunt frame and wasted flesh—he looked almost starved. The fact now became evident that he was in a state of great exhaustion. Catharine thought he eyed the spring with wishful looks, and she soon supplied him with water in the bark dish, to his great relief.

Wolfe had been out for several days with his master, who would repeat, in tones of sad earnestness, to the faithful creature, "Lost, lost, lost!" It was his custom to do so when the cattle strayed, and Wolfe would travel in all directions till he found them, nor ceased his search till he discovered the objects he was ordered to bring home. The last night of the father's wanderings, when, sick and hopeless, he came back to his melancholy home, as he sat sleeplessly rocking himself to and fro, he involuntarily exclaimed, wringing his hands, "Lost, lost, lost!" Wolfe heard what to him was an imperative command; he rose, and stood at the door, and whined; mechanically his master rose, lifted the latch, and again exclaimed in passionate tones those magic words, that sent the faithful messenger forth into the dark forest path. Once on the trail he never left it, but with an instinct incomprehensible as it was powerful, he continued to track the woods, lingering long on spots where the wanderers had left any signs of their sojourn; he had for some time been baffled at the Beaver Meadow, and again where they had crossed Cold Creek, but had regained the scent and traced them to the valley of the "big stone," and then with the sagacity of the bloodhound and the affection of the terrier he had, at last, discovered the objects of his unwearied, though often baffled search.

What a state of excitement did the unexpected arrival of old Wolfe create! How many questions were put to the poor beast, as he lay with his head pillowed on the knees of his loving mistress! Catharine knew it was foolish, but she could not help talking to the dumb animal, as if he had been conversant with her own language. Ah, old Wolfe, if your home-sick nurse could but have interpreted those expressive looks, those eloquent waggings of your bushy tail, as it flapped upon the grass, or waved from side to side; those gentle lickings of the hand, and mute sorrowful glances, as though he would have said, "Dear mistress, I know all your troubles. I know all you say, but I cannot answer you!" There is something touching in the silent sympathy of the dog, to which only the hard-hearted and depraved can be quite insensible. I remember once hearing of a felon, who had shown the greatest obstinacy and callous indifference to the appeals of his relations, and the clergyman that attended him in prison, whose heart was softened by the sight of a little dog, that had been his companion in his days of comparative innocence, forcing its way through the crowd, till it gained the foot of the gallows; its mute look of anguish and affection unlocked the fount of human feeling, and the condemned man wept —perhaps the first tears he had shed since childhood's happy days.

The night closed in with a tempest of almost tropical violence. The inky darkness of the sky was relieved, at intervals, by sheets of lurid flame, which revealed, by its intense brightness, every object far off or near. The distant lake, just seen amid the screen of leaves through the gorge of the valley, gleamed like a sea of molten sulphur; the deep narrow defile, shut in by the steep and wooded hills, looked deeper, more wild and gloomy, when revealed by that vivid glare of light.

There was no stir among the trees, the heavy rounded masses of foliage remained unmoved; the very aspen, that tremulous sensitive tree, scarcely stirred; it seemed as if the very pulses of nature were at rest. The solemn murmur that preceded the thunder-peal might have been likened to the moaning of the dying. The children felt the loneliness of the spot. Seated at the entrance of their sylvan hut, in front of which their evening fire burned brightly, they looked out upon the storm in silence and in awe. Screened by the sheltering shrubs that grew near them, they felt comparatively safe from the dangers of the storm, which now burst in terrific violence above the valley. Cloud answered to cloud, and the echoes of the hills prolonged the sound, while shattered trunks and brittle branches filled the air, and shrieked and groaned in that wild war of elements.

Between the pauses of the tempest the long howl of the wolves, from their covert in some distant cedar swamp at the edge of the lake, might be heard from time to time,—a sound that always thrilled their hearts with fear. To the mighty thunder-peal that burst above their heads they listened with awe and wonder. It seemed, indeed, to them as if it were the voice of Him who "sendeth out his voice, yea, and that a mighty voice." And they bowed and adored his majesty; but they shrank with curdled blood from the cry of the *felon wolf*.

And now the storm was at its climax, and the hail and rain came down in a whitening flood upon that ocean of forest leaves; the old grey branches were lifted up and down, and the stout trunks rent, for they would not bow down before the fury of the whirlwind, and were scattered all abroad like chaff before the wind.

The children thought not of danger for themselves, but they feared for the safety of their fathers, whom they believed to be not far off from them. And often 'mid the raging of the elements, they fancied they could distinguish familiar voices calling upon their names. "If our father had not been near, Wolfe would not have come hither."

"Ah, if our father should have perished in this fearful storm," said Catharine, weeping, "or have been starved to death while seeking for us!" and Catharine covered her face and wept more bitterly.

But Louis would not listen to such melancholy forebodings. Their fathers were both brave hardy men, accustomed to every sort of danger and privation; they were able to take care of themselves. Yes, he was sure they were not far off; it was this unlucky storm coming on that had prevented them from meeting.

"To-morrow, ma chère, will be a glorious day after the storm; it will be a joyful one too, we shall go out with Wolfe, and he will find his master, and then—oh, yes! I dare say my dear father will be with yours. They will have taken good heed to the track, and we shall soon see our dear mothers and chère petite Louise."

The storm lasted till past midnight, when it gradually subsided, and the poor wanderers were glad to see the murky clouds roll off, and the stars peep forth among their broken masses; but they were reduced to a pitiful state, the hurricane having beaten down their little hut, and their garments were drenched with rain. However, the boys made a good fire with some bark and boughs they had in store; there were a few sparks in their back log unextinguished, and these they gladly fanned up into a blaze, with which they dried their wet clothes, and warmed themselves. The air was now cool almost to chilliness, and for some days the weather remained unsettled, and the sky overcast with clouds, while the lake presented a leaden hue, crested with white mimic waves.

They soon set to work to make another hut, and found close to the head of the ravine a great pine uprooted, affording them large pieces of bark, which proved very serviceable in thatching the sides of the hut. The boys employed themselves in this work, while Catharine cooked the fish they had caught the day before, with a share of which old Wolfe seemed to be mightily well pleased. After they had breakfasted, they all went up towards the high table-land above the ravine, with Wolfe, to look round in hope of getting sight of their friends from Cold Springs, but though they kept an anxious look out in every direction, they returned, towards evening, tired and hopeless. Hector had killed a red squirrel, and a partridge which Wolfe "treed,"—that is, stood barking at the foot of the tree in which it had perched,—and the supply of meat was a seasonable change. They also noticed, and marked with the axe, several trees where there were bee-hives, intending to come in the cold weather, and cut them down. Louis's father was a great and successful bee-hunter; and Louis rather prided himself on having learned something of his father's skill in that line. Here, where flowers were so abundant and water plentiful, the wild bees seemed to be abundant also; besides, the open space between the trees, admitting the warm sunbeam freely, was favourable both for the bees and the flowers on which they fed, and Louis talked joyfully of the fine stores of honey they should collect in the fall. He had taught little Fanchon, a small French spaniel of his father's, to find out the trees where the bees hived, and also the nests of the ground-bees, and she would bark at the foot of the tree, or scratch with her feet on the ground, as the other dogs barked at the squirrels or the woodchucks; but Fanchon was far away, and Wolfe was old, and would learn no new tricks, so Louis knew he had nothing but his own observation and the axe to depend upon for procuring honey.

The boys had been unsuccessful for some days past in fishing; neither perch nor sunfish, pink roach nor mud-pouts[1] were to be caught. However, they found water-mussels by groping in the sand, and cray-fish among the gravel at the edge of the water only; the latter pinched their fingers very spitefully. The mussels were not very palatable, for want of salt; but hungry folks must not be dainty, and Louis declared them very good when well roasted, covered up with hot embers. "The fish-hawks," said he, "set us a good example, for they eat them, and so do the eagles and herons. I watched one the other day with a mussel in his bill; he flew to a high tree, let his prey fall, and immediately darted down to secure it; but I drove him off, and, to my great amusement, perceived the wise fellow had just let it fall on a stone, which had cracked the shell for him just in the right place. I often see shells lying at the foot of trees, far up the hills, where these birds must have left them. There is one large thick-shelled mussel, that I have found several times with a round hole drilled through the shell, just as if it had been done with a small auger, doubtless the work of some bird with a strong beak."

"Do you remember," said Catharine, "the fine pink mussel-shell that Hec. picked up in the little corn-field last year; it had a hole in one of the shells too,[2] and when my uncle saw it, he said it must have been dropped by some large bird, a fish-hawk possibly, or a heron, and brought from the great lake, as it had been taken out of some deep water, the mussels in our creeks being quite thin-shelled and white."

"Do you remember what a quantity of large fish bones

[1] All these fish are indigenous to the fresh waters of Canada.

[2] This ingenious mode of cracking the shells of mussels is common to many birds. The crow (*Corvus corone*) has been long known by American naturalists to break the thick shells of the river mussels, by letting them fall from a height on to rocks and stones.

we found in the eagle's nest on the top of our hill, Louis?"
said Hector.

"I do; those fish must have been larger than our perch
and sun-fish; they were brought from this very lake, I dare
say."

"If we had a good canoe now, or a boat, and a strong
hook and line, we might become great fishermen."

"Louis," said Catharine, "is always thinking about
canoes, and boats, and skiffs; he ought to have been a
sailor."

Louis was confident that if they had a canoe he could
soon learn to manage her; he was an excellent sailor
already in theory. Louis never saw difficulties; he was
always hopeful, and had a very good opinion of his own
cleverness; he was quicker in most things, his ideas flowed
faster than Hector's, but Hector was more prudent, and
possessed one valuable quality—steady perseverance; he
was slow in adopting an opinion, but when once
convinced, he pushed on steadily till he mastered the
subject or overcame the obstacle.

"Catharine," said Louis, one day, "the huckleberries are
now very plentiful, and I think it would be a wise thing to
gather a good store of them, and dry them for the winter.
See, ma chère, wherever we turn our eyes, or place our
feet, they are to be found; the hill sides are purple with
them. We may, for aught we know, be obliged to pass the
rest of our lives here; it will be well to prepare for the
winter when no berries are to be found."

"It will be well, mon ami, but we must not dry them in
the sun; for let me tell you, Mr. Louis, that they will be
quite tasteless—mere dry husks."

"Why so, ma belle?"

"I do not know the reason, but I only know the fact, for
when our mothers dried the currants and raspberries in
the sun, such was the case, but when they dried them on
the oven floor, or on the hearth, they were quite nice."

"Well, Cath., I think I know of a flat thin stone that will make a good hearthstone, and we can get sheets of birch bark and sew into flat bags, to keep the dried fruit in."

They now turned all their attention to drying huckleberries (or whortleberries).[1] Catharine and Louis (who fancied nothing could be contrived without his help) attended to the preparing and making of the bags of birch bark; but Hector was soon tired of girl's work, as he termed it, and, after gathering some berries, would wander away over the hills in search of game, and to explore the neighbouring hills and valleys, and sometimes it was sunset before he made his appearance. Hector had made an excellent strong bow, like the Indian bow, out of a tough piece of hickory wood, which he found in one of his rambles, and he made arrows with wood that he seasoned in the smoke, sharpening the heads with great care with his knife, and hardening them by exposure to strong heat, at a certain distance from the fire. The entrails of the woodchucks, stretched, and scraped and dried, and rendered pliable by rubbing and drawing through the hands, answered for a bow-string; but afterwards, when they got the sinews and hide of the deer, they used them, properly dressed for the purpose.

Hector also made a cross-bow, which he used with great effect, being a true and steady marksman. Louis and he would often amuse themselves with shooting at a mark, which they would chip on the bark of a tree; even Catharine was a tolerable archeress with the long-bow, and the hut was now seldom without game of one kind or other. Hector seldom returned from his rambles without partridges, quails, or young pigeons, which are plentiful at

[1] From the abundance of this fruit, the Indians have given the name of Whortleberry Plain to the lands on the south shore. During the month of July and the early part of August, large parties come to the Rice Lake Plains to gather huckleberries, which they preserve by drying, for winter use. These berries make a delicious tart or pudding, mixed with bilberries and red-currants, requiring little sugar.

this season of the year; many of the old ones that pass over
in their migratory flight in the spring, stay to breed, or
return thither for the acorns and berries that are to be
found in great abundance. Squirrels, too, are very
plentiful at this season. Hector and Louis remarked that
the red and black squirrels never were to be found very
near each other. It is a common belief, that the red
squirrels make common cause with the grey, and beat the
larger enemy off the ground. The black squirrel, for a
succession of years, was very rarely to be met with on the
Plains, while there were plenty of the red and grey in the
"oak openings." [1] Deer, at the time our young Crusoes were
living on the Rice Lake Plains, were plentiful, and, of
course, so were those beasts that prey upon them,—wolves,
bears, and wolverines, besides the Canadian lynx, or
catamount, as it is here commonly called, a species of
wild-cat or panther. These wild animals are now no longer
to be seen; it is a rare thing to hear of bears or wolves, and
the wolverine and lynx are known only as matters of
history in this part of the country; these animals disappear
as civilization advances, while some others increase and
follow man, especially many species of birds, which seem
to pick up the crumbs that fall from the rich man's board,
and multiply about his dwelling; some adopt new habits
and modes of building and feeding, according to the
alteration and improvement in their circumstances.

While our young people seldom wanted for meat, they
felt the privation of the bread to which they had been
accustomed very sensibly. One day, while Hector and
Louis were busily engaged with their assistant, Wolfe, in
unearthing a woodchuck, that had taken refuge in his
burrow, on one of the gravelly hills above the lake,

[1] Within the last three years, however, the black squirrels have been
very numerous, and the red are less frequently to be seen. The flesh of
the black squirrel is tender, white, and delicate, like that of a young
rabbit.

Catharine amused herself by looking for flowers; she had filled her lap with ripe May-apples,[1] but finding them cumbersome in climbing the steep wooded hills, she deposited them at the foot of a tree near the boys, and pursued her search; and it was not long before she perceived some pretty grassy-looking plants, with heads of bright lilac flowers, and on plucking one pulled up the root also. The root was about the size and shape of a large crocus, and, on biting it, she found it far from disagreeable, sweet, and slightly astringent; it seemed to be a favourite root with the woodchucks, for she noticed that it grew about their burrows on dry gravelly soil, and many of the stems were bitten, and the roots eaten, a warrant in full of wholesomeness. Therefore, carrying home a parcel of the largest of the roots, she roasted them in the embers, and they proved almost as good as chestnuts, and more satisfying than the acorns of the white oak, which they had often roasted in the fire, when they were out working on the fallow, at the log heaps. Hector and Louis ate heartily of the roots, and commended Catharine for the discovery. Not many days afterwards, Louis accidentally found a much larger and more valuable root, near the lake shore. He saw a fine climbing shrub, with close bunches of dark reddish-purple pea-shaped flowers, which scented the air with a delicious perfume. The plant climbed to a great height over the young trees, with a profusion of dark

---

[1] *Podophyllum peltatum*—May-apple, or Mandrake. The fruit of the May-apple, in rich moist soil, will attain to the size of the magnum bonum, or egg-plum, which it resembles in colour and shape. It makes a delicious preserve, if seasoned with cloves or ginger; when eaten uncooked, the outer rind, which is thick and fleshy, and has a rank taste, should be thrown aside; the fine acid pulp in which the seeds are imbedded alone should be eaten. The root of the Podophyllum is used as a cathartic by the Indians. The root of this plant is reticulated, and when a large body of them are uncovered, they present a singular appearance, interlacing each other in large meshes, like an extensive net-work; these roots are white, as thick as a man's little finger, and fragrant, and spread horizontally along the surface. The blossom is like a small white rose.

green leaves and tendrils. Pleased with the bowery appearance of the plant, he tried to pull one up, that he might show it to his cousin, when the root displayed a number of large tubers, as big as good-sized potatoes, regular oval-shaped; the inside was quite white, tasting somewhat like a potato, only pleasanter, when in its raw state, than an uncooked potato. Louis gathered his pockets full, and hastened home with his prize, and, on being roasted, these new roots were decided to be little inferior to potatoes; at all events, they were a valuable addition to their slender stores, and they procured as many as they could find, carefully storing them in a hole, which they dug for that purpose in a corner of their hut.[1] Hector suggested that these roots would be far better late in the fall, or early in the spring, than during the time that the plant was in bloom, for he knew from observation and experience that at the flowering season the greater part of the nourishment derived from the soil goes to perfect the flower and the seeds. Upon scraping the cut tuber, there was a white floury powder produced, resembling the starchy substance of the potato.

"This flour," said Catharine, "would make good porridge with milk."

"Excellent, no doubt, my wise little cook and housekeeper," said Louis, laughing, "but, ma belle cousine, where is the milk, and where is the porridge-pot to come from?"

"Indeed," said Catharine, "I fear, Louis, we must wait long for both."

One fine day, Louis returned home from the lake shore in great haste, for the bows and arrows, with the interesting news that a herd of five deer were in the water, and making for Long Island.

---

[1] This plant appears to me to be a species of the *Psoralea esculenta*, or Indian bread-root, which it resembles in description, excepting that the root of the above is tuberous, oval, and connected by long filaments. The largest tubers are furthest from the stem of the plant.

"But, Louis, they will be gone out of sight and beyond the reach of the arrows," said Catharine, as she handed him down the bows and a sheaf of arrows, which she quickly slung round his shoulders by the belt of skin, which the young hunter had made for himself.

"No fear, ma chère; they will stop to feed on the beds of rice and lilies. We must have Wolfe. Here, Wolfe, Wolfe, Wolfe,—here, boy, here!"

Catharine caught a portion of the excitement that danced in the bright eyes of her cousin, and declaring that she too would go and witness the hunt, ran down the ravine by his side, while Wolfe, who evidently understood that they had some sport in view, trotted along by his mistress, wagging his great bushy tail, and looking in high good humour.

Hector was impatiently waiting the arrival of the bows and Wolfe. The herd of deer, consisting of a noble buck, two full-grown females, and two young half-grown males, were quietly feeding among the beds of rice and rushes, not more than fifteen or twenty yards from the shore, apparently quite unconcerned at the presence of Hector, who stood on a fallen trunk eagerly eyeing their motions; but the hurried steps of Louis and Catharine, with the deep sonorous baying of Wolfe, soon roused the timid creatures to a sense of danger, and the stag, raising his head and making, as the children thought, a signal for retreat, now struck boldly out for the nearest point of Long Island.

"We shall lose them," cried Louis, despairingly, eyeing the long bright track that cut the silvery waters, as the deer swam gallantly out.

"Hist, hist, Louis," said Hector, "all depends upon Wolfe. Turn them, Wolfe; hey, hey, seek them, boy!"

Wolfe dashed bravely into the lake.

"Head them! head them!" shouted Hector.

Wolfe knew what was meant; with the sagacity of a long-trained hunter, he made a desperate effort to gain the advantage by a circuitous route. Twice the stag turned irresolute, as if to face his foe, and Wolfe, taking the time, swam ahead, and then the race began. As soon as the boys saw the herd had turned, and that Wolfe was between them and the island, they separated, Louis making good his ambush to the right among the cedars, and Hector at the spring to the west, while Catharine was stationed at the solitary pine-tree, at the point which commanded the entrance of the ravine.

"Now, Cathy," said her brother, "when you see the herd making for the ravine, shout and clap your hands, and they will turn either to the right or to the left. Do not let them land, or we shall lose them. We must trust to Wolfe for their not escaping to the island. Wolfe is well trained, he knows what he is about."

Catharine proved a dutiful ally, she did as she was bid; she waited till the deer were within a few yards of the shore, then she shouted and clapped her hands. Frightened at the noise and clamour, the terrified creatures coasted along for some way, till within a little distance of the thicket where Hector lay concealed, the very spot from which they had emerged when they first took to the water; to this place they boldly steered. Louis, who had watched the direction the herd had taken with breathless interest, now noiselessly hurried to Hector's assistance, taking an advantageous post for aim, in case Hector's arrow missed, or only slightly wounded one of the deer.

Hector, crouched beneath the trees, waited cautiously till one of the does was within reach of his arrow, and so good and true was his aim, that it hit the animal in the throat a little above the chest; the stag now turned again, but Wolfe was behind, and pressed him forward, and again the noble animal strained every nerve for the shore. Louis now shot his arrow, but it swerved from the mark;

he was too eager, it glanced harmlessly along the water; but the cool, unimpassioned hand of Hector sent another arrow between the eyes of the doe, stunning her with its force, and then, another from Louis laid her on her side, dying, and staining the water with her blood.

The herd, abandoning their dying companion, dashed frantically to the shore, and the young hunters, elated by their success, suffered them to make good their landing without further molestation. Wolfe, at a signal from his master, ran in the quarry, and Louis declared exultingly, that as his last arrow had given the *coup de grace*, he was entitled to the honour of cutting the throat of the doe; but this the stern Highlander protested against, and Louis, with a careless laugh, yielded the point, contenting himself with saying, "Ah, well, I will get the first steak of the venison when it is roasted, and that is far more to my taste." Moreover, he privately recounted to Catharine the important share he had had in the exploit, giving her, at the same time, full credit for the worthy service she had performed, in withstanding the landing of the herd. Wolfe, too, came in for a large share of the honour and glory of the chase.

The boys were soon hard at work, skinning the animal, and cutting it up. This was the most valuable acquisition they had yet effected, for many uses were to be made of the deer, besides eating the flesh. It was a store of wealth in their eyes.

During the many years that their fathers had sojourned in the country, there had been occasional intercourse with the fur traders and trappers, and, sometimes, with friendly disposed Indians, who had called at the lodges of their white brothers for food and tobacco.

From all these men, rude as they were, some practical knowledge had been acquired, and their visits, though few and far between, had left good fruit behind them; something to think about and talk about, and turn to future advantage.

The boys had learned from the Indians how precious were the tough sinews of the deer for sewing. They knew how to prepare the skins of the deer for mocassins, which they could cut out and make as neatly as the squaws themselves. They could fashion arrow-heads, and knew how best to season the wood for making both the long and cross-bow; they had seen the fish-hooks these people manufactured from bone and hard wood; they knew that strips of fresh-cut skins would make bow-strings, or the entrails of animals dried and rendered pliable. They had watched the squaws making baskets of the inner bark of the oak, elm, and basswood, and mats of the inner bark of the cedar, with many other ingenious works that they now found would prove useful to them, after a little practice had perfected their inexperienced attempts. They also knew how to dry venison as the Indians and trappers prepare it, by cutting the thick fleshy portions of the meat into strips, from four to six inches in breadth, and two or more in thickness. These strips they strung upon poles supported on forked sticks, and exposed them to the drying action of the sun and wind. Fish they split open, and removed the back and head bones, and smoked them slightly, or dried them in the sun.

Their success in killing the doe greatly raised their spirits; in their joy they embraced each other, and bestowed the most affectionate caresses on Wolfe for his good conduct.

"But for this dear, wise old fellow, we should have had no venison for dinner to-day," said Louis; "and so, Wolfe, you shall have a choice piece for your own share."

Every part of the deer seemed valuable in the eyes of the young hunters; the skin they carefully stretched out upon sticks to dry gradually, and the entrails they also preserved for bow-strings. The sinews of the legs and back, they drew out, and laid carefully aside for future use.

"We shall be glad enough of these strings by-and-by," said careful Hector; "for the summer will soon be at an end, and then we must turn our attention to making ourselves winter clothes and mocassins."

"Yes, Hec., and a good warm shanty; these huts of bark and boughs will not do when once the cold weather sets in."

"A shanty would soon be put up," said Hector; "for even Kate, wee bit lassie as she is, could give us some help in trimming up the logs."

"That I could, indeed," replied Catharine; "for you may remember, Hec., that the last journey my father made to the Bay,[1] with the pack of furs, that you and I called a *Bee*[2] to put up a shed for the new cow that he was to drive back with him, and I am sure Mathilde and I did as much good as you and Louis. You know you said you could not have got on nearly so well without our help."

"Yes, and you cried because you got a fall off the shed when it was only four logs high."

"It was not for the fall that I cried," said Catharine, resentfully, "but because cousin Louis and you laughed at me, and said, 'Cats, you know, have nine lives, and seldom are hurt, because they light on their feet,' and I thought it was very cruel to laugh at me when I was in pain. Beside, you called me 'puss,' and 'poor pussie' all the rest of the *Bee*."

"I am sure, ma belle, I am very sorry if I was rude to you," said Louis, trying to look penitent for the offence.

[1] Bay of Quinté.

[2] A *Bee* is a practical instance of duty to a neighbour. We fear it is peculiar to Canada, although deserving of imitation in all Christian colonies. When any work which requires many hands is in the course of performance, as the building of log-houses, barns, or shanties, all the neighbours are summoned, and give their best assistance in the construction. Of course the assisted party is liable to be called upon by the community in turn, to repay in kind the help he has received.

"For my part, I had forgotten all about the fall; I only know that we passed a very merry day. Dear aunt made us a fine Johnny-cake for tea, with lots of maple molasses; and the shed was a capital shed, and the cow must have thought us fine builders, to have made such a comfortable shelter for her, with no better help."

"After all," said Hector, thoughtfully; "children can do a great many things if they only resolutely set to work, and use the wits and the strength that God has given them to work with. A few weeks ago, and we should have thought it utterly impossible to have supported ourselves in a lonely wilderness like this by our own exertions in fishing and hunting."

"If we had been lost in the forest, we must have died with hunger," said Catharine; "but let us be thankful to the good God who led us hither, and gave us health and strength to help ourselves."

CHAPTER 4

"Aye from the sultry heat,
   We to our cave retreat,
O'ercanopied by huge roots, intertwined,
Of wildest texture, blacken'd o'er with age,
Round them their mantle green the climbers twine.
   Beneath whose mantle—pale,
   Fann'd by the breathing gale,
We shield us from the fervid mid-day rage,
Thither, while the murmuring throng
Of wild bees hum their drowsy song."—

COLERIDGE.

"LOUIS, what are you cutting out of that bit of wood?" said Catharine, the very next day after the first ideas of the shanty had been started.

"Hollowing out a canoe."

"Out of that piece of stick?" said Catharine, laughing. "How many passengers is it to accommodate, my dear."

"Don't teaze, ma belle. I am only making a model. My canoe will be made out of a big pine log, and large enough to hold three."

"Is it to be like the big sap-trough in the sugar-bush at home?" Louis nodded assent.

"I long to go over to the island; I see lots of ducks popping in and out of the little bays beneath the cedars, and there are plenty of partridges, I am sure, and squirrels,—it is the very place for them."

"And shall we have a sail as well as oars?"

"Yes; set up your apron for a sail."

Catharine cast a rueful look upon the tattered remnant of the apron.

"It is worth nothing now," she said, sighing; "and what am I to do when my gown is worn out? It is a good thing it is so strong; if it had been cotton, now, it would have been torn to bits among the bushes."

"We must make clothes of skins as soon as we get enough," said Hector; "Louis, I think you can manufacture a bone needle; we can pierce the holes with the strong thorns, or a little round bone bodkin, that can be easily made."

"The first rainy day, we will see what we can do," replied Louis; "but I am full of my canoe just now."

"Indeed, Louis, I believe you never think of anything else; but even if we had a canoe to-morrow, I do not think that either you or I could manage one," said cautious Hector.

"I could soon learn, as others have done before me. I wonder who first taught the Indians to make canoes, and venture out on the lakes and streams. Why should we be more stupid than these untaught heathens? I have listened so often to my father's stories and adventures when he was out lumbering on the St. John river, that I am as familiar with the idea of a boat, as if I had been born in one. Only think now, ma belle," he said, turning to Catharine; "just think of the fish—the big ones we could get if we had but a canoe to push out from the shore beyond those rush-beds."

"It strikes me, Louis, that those rush-beds, as you call them, must be the Indian rice that we have seen the squaws make their soup of."

"Yes; and you remember old Jacob used to talk of a fine lake that he called Rice Lake, somewhere to the northward of the Cold Springs, where he said there was plenty of game of all kinds, and a fine open place, where people could see through the openings among the trees. He said it was a great hunting-place for the Indians in the fall of the year, and that they came there to gather in the harvest of wild rice."

"I hope the Indians will not come here and find us out," said Catharine, shuddering; "I think I should be more frightened at the Indians than at the wolves. Have we not heard fearful tales of their cruelty?"

"But we have never been harmed by them; they have always been civil enough when they came to the Springs."

"They came, you know, for food, or shelter, or something that they wanted from us; but it may be different when they find us alone and unprotected, encroaching upon their hunting grounds."

"The place is wide enough for us and them; we will try and make them our friends."

"The wolf and the lamb do not lie down in the fold together," observed Hector. "The Indian is treacherous. The wild man and the civilized man do not live well together, their habits and dispositions are so contrary the one to the other. We are open, and they are cunning, and they suspect our openness to be only a greater degree of cunning than their own—they do not understand us. They are taught to be revengeful, and we are taught to forgive our enemies. So you see that what is a virtue with the savage, is a crime with the Christian. If the Indian could be taught the word of God, he might be kind and true, and gentle as well as brave."

It was with conversations like this that our poor wanderers wiled away their weariness. The love of life, and the exertions necessary for self-preservation, occupied so large a portion of their thoughts and time, that they had hardly leisure for repining. They mutually cheered and animated each other to bear up against the sad fate that had thus severed them from every kindred tie, and shut them out from that home to which their young hearts were bound by every endearing remembrance from infancy upwards.

One bright September morning, our young people set

off on an exploring expedition, leaving the faithful Wolfe
to watch the wigwam, for they well knew he was too honest
to touch their store of dried fish and venison himself, and
too trusty and fierce to suffer wolf or wild cat near it.

They crossed several narrow deep ravines, and the low
wooded flat[1] along the lake shore, to the eastward of Pine-
tree Point. Finding it difficult to force their way through
the thick underwood that always impedes the progress of
the traveller on the low shores of the lake, they followed
the course of an ascending narrow ridge, which formed a
sort of natural causeway between two parallel hollows, the
top of this ridge being, in many places, not wider than a
cart or waggon could pass along. The sides were most
gracefully adorned with flowering shrubs, wild vines,
creepers of various species, wild cherries of several kinds,
hawthorns, bilberry bushes, high-bush cranberries, silver
birch, poplars, oaks and pines; while in the deep ravines
on either side grew trees of the largest growth, the heads
of which lay on a level with their path. Wild cliffy banks,
beset with huge boulders of red and grey granite and
water-worn limestone, showed that it had once formed the
boundary of the lake, though now it was almost a quarter
of a mile in its rear. Springs of pure water were in
abundance, trickling down the steep rugged sides of this
wooded glen. The children wandered onwards, delighted
with the wild picturesque path they had chosen, sometimes
resting on a huge block of moss-covered stone, or on the
twisted roots of some ancient grey old oak or pine, while
they gazed with curiosity and interest on the lonely but
lovely landscape before them. Across the lake, the dark
forest shut all else from their view, rising in gradual far-off
slopes, till it reached the utmost boundary of sight. Much

---

[1] Now the fertile farm of Joe Harris, a Yankee settler, whose pleasant
meadows and fields of grain form a pretty feature from the lake. It is
one of the oldest clearings on the shore, and speaks well for the
persevering industry of the settler and his family.

the children marvelled what country it might be that lay in the dim, blue, hazy distance,—to them, indeed, a *terra incognita*—a land of mystery; but neither of her companions laughed when Catharine gravely suggested the probability of this unknown shore to the northward being her father's beloved Highlands. Let not the youthful and more learned reader smile at the ignorance of the Canadian girl; she knew nothing of maps, and globes, and hemispheres,—her only book of study had been the Holy Scriptures, her only teacher a poor Highland soldier.

Following the elevated ground above this deep valley, the travellers at last halted on the extreme edge of a high and precipitous mound, that formed an abrupt termination to the deep glen. They found water not far from this spot fit for drinking, by following a deer-path a little to the southward. And there, on the borders of a little basin on a pleasant brae, where the bright silver birch waved gracefully over its sides, they decided upon building a winter house. They named the spot Mount Ararat: "For here," said they, "we will build us an ark of refuge, and wander no more." And Mount Ararat is the name which the spot still bears. Here they sat them down on a fallen tree, and ate a meal of dried venison, and drank of the cold spring that welled out from beneath the edge of the bank. Hector felled a tree to mark the site of their house near the birches, and they made a regular blaze on the trees as they returned home towards the wigwam, that they might not miss the place. They found less difficulty in retracing their path than they had formerly, as there were some striking peculiarities to mark it, and they had learned to be very minute in the marks they made as they travelled, so that they now seldom missed the way they came by. A few days after this, they removed all their household stores, viz. the axe, the tin pot, bows and arrows, baskets, and bags of dried fruit, the dried venison and fish, and the deer-skin; nor did they forget the deer scalp, which they bore away as a trophy, to be fastened up over the door of their new dwelling, for a memorial of their first hunt on the shores of the Rice Lake. The skin was given to Catharine to sleep on.

The boys were now busy from morning till night chopping down trees for house-logs. It was a work of time and labour, as the axe was blunt, and the oaks hard to cut; but they laboured on without grumbling, and Kate watched the fall of each tree with lively joy. They were no longer dull; there was something to look forward to from day to day—they were going to commence housekeeping in good earnest and they would be warm and well lodged before the bitter frosts of winter could come to chill their blood. It was a joyful day when the log walls of the little shanty were put up, and the door hewed out. Windows they had none, so they did not cut out the spaces for them;[1] they could do very well without, as hundreds of Irish and Highland emigrants have done before and since.

A pile of stones rudely cemented together with wet clay and ashes against the logs, and a hole cut in the roof, formed the chimney and hearth in this primitive dwelling. The chinks were filled with wedge-shaped pieces of wood, and plastered with clay: the trees, being chiefly oaks and pines, afforded no moss. This deficiency rather surprised the boys, for in the thick forest and close cedar swamps, moss grows in abundance on the north side of the trees, especially on the cedar, maple, beech, bass, and iron wood; but there were few of these, excepting a chance one or two in the little basin in front of the house. The roof was next put on, which consisted of split cedars; and when the little dwelling was thus far habitable, they were all very happy. While the boys had been putting on the roof, Catharine had collected the stones for the chimney, and cleared the earthen floor of the chips and rubbish with a broom of

[1] Many a shanty is put up in Canada without windows, and only an open space for a door, with a rude plank set up to close it in at night.

cedar boughs, bound together with a leathern thong. She had swept it all clean, carefully removing all unsightly objects, and strewing it over with fresh cedar sprigs, which gave out a pleasant odour, and formed a smooth and not unseemly carpet for their little dwelling. How cheerful was the first fire blazing up on their own hearth! It was so pleasant to sit by its gladdening light, and chat away of all they had done and all that they meant to do. Here was to be a set of split cedar shelves, to hold their provisions and baskets; there a set of stout pegs were to be inserted between the logs for hanging up strings of dried meat, bags of birch-bark, or the skins of the animals they were to shoot or trap. A table was to be fixed on posts in the centre of the floor. Louis was to carve wooden platters and dishes, and some stools were to be made with hewn blocks of wood, till something better could be devised. Their bedsteads were rough poles of iron-wood, supported by posts driven into the ground, and partly upheld by the projection of the logs at the angles of the wall. Nothing could be more simple. The framework was of split cedar; and a safe bed was made by pine boughs being first laid upon the frame, and then thickly covered with dried grass, moss, and withered leaves. Such were the lowly but healthy couches on which these children of the forest slept.

A dwelling so rudely framed and scantily furnished would be regarded with disdain by the poorest English peasant. Yet many a settler's family have I seen as roughly lodged, while a better house was being prepared for their reception; and many a gentleman's son has voluntarily submitted to privations as great as these, from the love of novelty and adventure, or to embark in the tempting expectation of realizing money in the lumbering trade, working hard, and sharing the rude log shanty and ruder society of those reckless and hardy men, the Canadian lumberers. During the spring and summer months, these men spread themselves through the trackless forests, and along the shores of nameless lakes and unknown streams, to cut the pine or oak lumber, such being the name they give to the felled stems of trees, which are then hewn, and in the winter dragged out upon the ice, where they are formed into rafts, and floated down the waters till they reach the great St. Lawrence, and are, after innumerable difficulties and casualties, finally shipped for England. I have likewise known European gentlemen voluntarily leave the comforts of a civilized home, and associate themselves with the Indian trappers and hunters, leading lives as wandering and as wild as the uncultivated children of the forest.

The nights and early mornings were already growing sensibly more chilly. The dews at this season fall heavily, and the mists fill the valleys, till the sun has risen with sufficient heat to draw up the vapours. It was a good thing that the shanty was finished so soon, or the exposure to the damp air might have been productive of ague and fever. Every hour almost they spent in making little additions to their household comforts, but some time was necessarily passed in trying to obtain provisions. One day Hector, who had been out from dawn till moonrise, returned with the welcome news that he had shot a young deer, and required the assistance of his cousin to bring it up the steep bank— (it was just at the entrance of the great ravine)—below the precipitous cliff near the lake; he had left old Wolfe to guard it in the meantime. They had now plenty of fresh broiled meat, and this store was very acceptable, as they were obliged to be very careful of the dried meat that they had.

This time Catharine adopted a new plan. Instead of cutting the meat in strips, and drying it, (or jerking it, as the lumberers term it,) she roasted it before the fire, and hung it up, wrapping it in thin sheets of birch bark. The juices, instead of being dried up, were preserved, and the meat was more palatable. Catharine found great store of wild plums in a beautiful valley, not far from the shanty; these she dried for the winter store, eating sparingly of them in their fresh state; she also found plenty of wild black currants, and high-bush cranberries, on the banks of a charming creek of bright water that flowed between a range of high pine hills, and finally emptied itself into the lake.[1] There were great quantities of water-cresses in this pretty brook; they grew in bright round cushion-like tufts at the bottom of the water, and were tender and wholesome. These formed an agreeable addition to their diet, which had hitherto been chiefly confined to animal food, for they could not always meet with a supply of the bread-roots, as they grew chiefly in damp, swampy thickets on the lake shore, which were sometimes very difficult of access; however, they never missed any opportunity of increasing their stores, and laying up for the winter such roots as they could procure.

As the cool weather and frosty nights drew on, the want of warm clothes and bed-covering became more sensibly felt: those they had were beginning to wear out. Catharine had managed to wash her clothes at the lake several times, and thus preserved them clean and wholesome; but she was often sorely puzzled how the want of her dress was to be supplied as time wore on, and many were the consultations she held with the boys on the important subject. With the aid of a needle she might be able to manufacture the skins of the small animals into some sort of jacket, and the doe-skin and deer-skin could be made into garments for the boys. Louis was always suppling and rubbing the skins to make them soft. They had taken off the hair by sprinkling it with wood ashes, and rolling it up with the hairy side inwards. Out of one of these skins he made excellent mocassins, piercing the holes with a

---

[1] This little stream flows through the green meadows of "Glenlynden," watering the grounds of Mr. Alfred Hayward, whose picturesque cottage forms a most attractive object to the eye of the traveller.

sharpened bone bodkin, and passing the sinews of the deer through, as he had seen his father do, by fixing a stout fish-bone to the deer-sinew thread; thus he had an excellent substitute for a needle, and with the aid of the old file he sharpened the point of the rusty nail, so that he was enabled, with a little trouble, to drill a hole in a bone needle, for his cousin Catharine's use. After several attempts, he succeeded in making some of tolerable fineness, hardening them by exposure to a slow steady degree of heat, till she was able to work with them, and even mend her clothes with tolerable expertness. By degrees, Catharine contrived to cover the whole outer surface of her homespun woollen frock with squirrel and mink, musk-rat and woodchuck skins. A curious piece of fur patchwork of many hues and textures it presented to the eye,—a coat of many colours, it is true; but it kept the wearer warm, and Catharine was not a little proud of her ingenuity and industry: every new patch that was added was a source of fresh satisfaction, and the mocassins, that Louis fitted so nicely to her feet, were great comforts. A fine skin that Hector brought triumphantly in one day, the spoil from a fox that had been caught in one of his deadfalls, was in due time converted into a dashing cap, the brush remaining as an ornament to hang down on one shoulder. Catharine might have passed for a small Diana, when she went out with her fur dress and bow and arrows to hunt with Hector and Louis.

Whenever game of any kind was killed, it was carefully skinned and the fur stretched upon bent sticks, being first turned, so as to present the inner part to the drying action of the air. The young hunters were most expert in this work, having been accustomed for many years to assist their fathers in preparing the furs which they disposed of to the fur traders, who visited them from time to time, and gave them various articles in exchange for their peltries; such as powder and shot, and cutlery of different kinds, as knives, scissors, needles, and pins, with gay calicoes and cotton handkerchiefs for the women.

As the evenings lengthened, the boys employed themselves with carving wooden platters: knives and forks and spoons they fashioned out of the larger bones of the deer, which they often found bleaching in the sun and wind, where they had been left by their enemies the wolves; baskets too they made, and birch dishes, which they could now finish so well, that they held water, or any liquid; but their great want was some vessel that would bear the heat of the fire. The tin pot was so small that it could be made little use of in the cooking way. Catharine had made an attempt at making tea, on a small scale, of the leaves of the sweet fern,—a graceful woody fern, with a fine aromatic scent like nutmegs;[1] this plant is highly esteemed among the Canadians as a beverage, and also as a remedy against the ague; it grows in great abundance on dry sandy lands and wastes, by waysides.

"If we could but make some sort of earthen pot that would stand the heat of the fire," said Louis, "we could get on nicely with cooking."

But nothing like the sort of clay used by potters had been seen, and they were obliged to give up that thought, and content themselves with roasting or broiling their food. Louis, however, who was fond of contrivances, made an oven, by hollowing out a place near the hearth, and lining it with stones, filling up the intervals with wood ashes and such clay as they could find, beaten into a smooth mortar. Such cement answered very well, and the oven was heated by filling it with hot embers; these were removed when it was sufficiently heated, and the meat or roots placed within, the oven being covered over with a flat stone previously heated before the fire, and covered with live coals. This sort of oven had often been described by

[1] *Comptonia asplenifolia*, a small shrub of the sweet-gale family.

old Jacob, as one in common use among some of the Indian tribes in the lower province, in which they cook small animals, and make excellent meat of them; they could bake bread also in this oven, if they had had flour to use.[1]

Since the finishing of the house and furnishing it, the young people were more reconciled to their lonely life, and even entertained decided home feelings for their little log cabin. They never ceased, it is true, to talk of their parents, and brothers, and sisters, and wonder if all were well, and whether they still hoped for their return, and to recal all their happy days spent in the home which they now feared they were destined never again to behold. About the same time they lost the anxious hope of meeting some one from home in search of them at every turn when they went out. Nevertheless they were becoming each day more cheerful and more active. Ardently attached to each other, they seemed bound together by a yet more sacred tie of brotherhood. They were now all the world to one another, and no cloud of disunion came to mar their happiness. Hector's habitual gravity and caution were tempered by Louis's lively vivacity and ardour of temper, and they both loved Catharine, and strove to smoothe, as much as possible, the hard life to which she was exposed, by the most affectionate consideration for her comfort, and she in return endeavoured to repay them by cheerfully enduring all privations, and making light of all their trials, and taking a lively interest in all their plans and contrivances.

Louis had gone out to fish at the lake one autumn morning. During his absence, a sudden squall of wind came on, accompanied with heavy rain. As he stayed longer than usual, Hector began to feel uneasy, lest some accident had befallen him, knowing his adventurous spirit,

[1] This primitive oven is much like what voyagers have described as in use among the natives of many of the South Sea islands.

and that he had for some days previous been busy constructing a raft of cedar logs, which he had fastened together with wooden pins. This raft he had nearly finished, and was even talking of adventuring over to the nearest island to explore it, and see what game, and roots, and fruits it afforded.

Bidding Catharine stay quietly within-doors till his return, Hector ran off, not without some misgivings of evil having befallen his rash cousin, which fears he carefully concealed from his sister, as he did not wish to make her needlessly anxious. When he reached the shore, his mind was somewhat relieved by seeing the raft on the beach, just as it had been left the night before, but neither Louis nor the axe was to be seen, nor the fishing-rod and line.

"Perhaps," thought he, "Louis has gone further down to the mouth of the little creek, in the flat east of this, where we caught our last fish; or maybe he has gone up to the old place at Pine-tree Point."

While he yet stood hesitating within himself which way to turn, he heard steps as of some one running, and perceived his cousin hurrying through the bushes in the direction of the shanty. It was evident by his disordered air, and the hurried glances that he cast over his shoulder from time to time, that something unusual had occurred to disturb him.

"Halloo! Louis, is it bear, wolf, or catamount that is on your trail?" cried Hector, almost amused by the speed with which his cousin hurried onward. "Why, Louis, whither away?"

Louis now turned and held up his hand, as if to enjoin silence, till Hector came up to him.

"Why, man, what ails you? what makes you run as if you were hunted down by a pack of wolves?"

"It is not wolves, or bears either," said Louis, as soon as he could get breath to speak, "but the Indians are all on Bare-hill, holding a war council, I suppose, for there are several canoe-loads of them."

"How came you to see them?"

"I must tell you that when I parted from you and Cathy, instead of going down to my raft, as I thought at first I would do, I followed the deer path through the little ravine, and then ascending the side of the valley, I crossed the birch grove, and kept down the slope within sight of the creek. While I was looking out upon the lake, and thinking how pretty the islands were, rising so green from the blue water, I was surprised by seeing several dark spots dotting the lake. At first, you may be sure, I thought they must be a herd of deer, only they kept too far apart, so I sat down on a log to watch, thinking if they turned out to be deer, I would race off for you and Wolfe, and the bows and arrows, that we might try our chance for some venison; but as the black specks came nearer and nearer, I perceived they were canoes with Indians in them, three in each. They made for the mouth of the creek, and ran ashore among the thick bushes. I watched them with a beating heart, and lay down flat, lest they should spy me out; for those fellows have eyes like catamounts, so keen and wild—they see everything without seeming to cast a glance on it. Well, I saw them wind up the ridge till they reached the Bare-hill.[1] You remember that spot; we called it so from its barren appearance. In a few minutes a column of smoke rose and curled among the pine-trees, and then another and another, till I counted five fires burning brightly; and, as I stood on the high ground, I could distinguish the figures of many naked savages moving about, running to and fro like a parcel of black ants on a cedar log; and by-and-by I heard them raise a yell like a pack of ravenous wolves on a deer track. It made my

---

[1] Supposed to be a council hill. It is known by the name of Bare-hill, from the singular want of verdure on its surface. It is one of the steepest on the ridge above the little creek; being a picturesque object, with its fine pine-trees, seen from Mr. Hayward's grounds, and forms, I believe, a part of his property.

heart leap up in my breast. I forgot all the schemes that had just got into my wise head, of slipping quietly down, and taking off one of the empty birch canoes, which you must own would have been a glorious thing for us; but when I heard the noise these wild wretches raised, I darted off, and ran as if the whole set were at my heels. I think I just saved my scalp." And Louis put his hand to his head, and tugged his thick black curls, as if to ascertain that they were still safe from the scalping knives of his Indian enemies.

"And now, Hec, what is to be done? We must hide ourselves from the Indians; they will kill us, or take us away with them if they find us."

"Let us go home and talk over our plans with Cathy."

"Yes; for I have heard my father say two heads are better than one, and so three of course must be still better than two."

"Why," said Hector, laughing, "it depends upon the stock of practical wisdom in the heads, for two fools, you know, Louis, will hardly form one rational plan."

Various were the schemes devised for their security. Hector proposed pulling down the shanty, and dispersing the logs, so as to leave no trace of the little dwelling; but to this neither his cousin nor his sister would agree. To pull down the new house that had cost them so much labour, and which had proved such a comfort to them, they could not endure even in idea.

"Let us put out the fire, and hide ourselves in the big ravine below Mount Ararat, dig a cave in one of the hills, and convey our household goods thither." Such was Louis's plan.

"The ravines would be searched directly," suggested Hector; "besides, the Indians know they are famous coverts for deer and game of all sorts; they might chance to pop upon us, and catch us like woodchucks in a burrow."

"Yes, and burn us," said Catharine, with a shudder. "I know the path that leads direct to the 'Happy Valley,' (the name she had given to the low flat, now known as the 'lower Race-course,') and it is not far from here, only ten minutes' walk in a straight line. We can conceal ourselves below the steep bank that we descended the other day; and there are several springs of fresh water, and plenty of nuts and berries; and the trees, though few, are so thickly covered with close spreading branches that touch the very ground, that we might hide ourselves from a hundred eyes were they ever so cunning and prying."

Catharine's counsel was deemed the most prudent, and the boys immediately busied themselves with hiding under the broken branches of a prostrate tree such articles as they could not conveniently carry away, leaving the rest to chance; with the most valuable they loaded themselves, and guided by Catharine, who, with her dear old dog, marched forward along the narrow footpath that had been made by some wild animals, probably deer, in their passage from the lake to their feeding-place, or favourite covert, on the low sheltered plain; where, being quite open, and almost, in parts, free from trees, the grass and herbage were sweeter and more abundant, and the springs of water fresh and cool.

Catharine cast many a fearful glance through the brushwood as they moved onward, but saw no living thing, excepting a family of chitminks gaily chasing each other along a fallen branch, and a covey of quails, that were feeding quietly on the red berries of the *Mitchella repens*, or twinberry,[1] as it is commonly called, of which the partridges and quails are extremely fond; for Nature, with liberal hand, has spread abroad her bounties for the small denizens, furred or feathered, that haunt the Rice Lake and its flowery shores.

[1] Also partridge-berry and checker-berry, a lovely creeping winter-green, with white fragrant flowers, and double scarlet berry.

After a continued but gentle ascent through the oak opening, they halted at the foot of a majestic pine, and looked round them. It was a lovely spot as any they had seen; from west to east, the lake, bending like a silver crescent, lay between the boundary hills of forest trees; in front, the long lines of undulating wood-covered heights faded away into mist, and blended with the horizon. To the east, a deep and fertile valley lay between the high lands, on which they rested, and the far ridge of oak hills. From their vantage height, they could distinguish the outline of the Bare-hill, made more distinct by its flickering fires and the smoke wreaths that hung like a pearly-tinted robe among the dark pines that grew upon its crest. Not long tarrying did our fugitives make, though perfectly safe from detection by the distance and their shaded position, for many a winding vale and wood-crowned height lay between them and the encampment.

But fear is not subject to the control of reason, and in the present instance it invested the dreaded Indians with superhuman powers of sight and of motion. A few minutes' hasty flight brought our travellers to the brow of a precipitous bank, nearly a hundred feet above the level open plain which they sought. Here, then, they felt comparatively safe: they were out of sight of the camp fires, the spot they had chosen was open, and flight, in case of the approach of the Indians, not difficult, while hiding-places were easy of access. They found a deep, sheltered hollow in the bank, where two mighty pines had been torn up by the roots, and prostrated headlong down the steep, forming a regular cave, roofed by the earth and fibres that had been uplifted in their fall. Pendent from these roots hung a luxuriant curtain of wild grape-vines and other creepers, which formed a leafy screen, through which the most curious eye could scarcely penetrate. This friendly vegetable veil seemed as if provided for their concealment, and they carefully abstained from disturbing the pendent foliage, lest they should, by so doing, betray their hiding-place to their enemies. They found plenty of long grass, and abundance of long soft green moss and ferns near a small grove of poplars, which surrounded a spring of fine water. They ate some dried fruit and smoked fish, and drank of the clear spring; and after they had said their evening prayers, they laid down to sleep, Catharine's head pillowed on the neck of her faithful guardian, Wolfe. In the middle of the night a startling sound, as of some heavy body falling, wakened them all simultaneously. The night was so dark they could see nothing, and terror-struck, they sat gazing into the impenetrable darkness of their cave, not even daring to speak to each other, hardly even to breathe. Wolfe gave a low grumbling bark, and resumed his couchant posture as if nothing worthy of his attention was near to cause the disturbance. Catharine trembled and wept, and prayed for safety against the Indians and beasts of prey, and Hector and Louis listened, till they fell asleep in spite of their fears. In the morning, it seemed as if they had dreamed some terrible dream, so vague were their recollections of the fright they had had, but the cause was soon perceived. A large stone that had been heaved up with the clay that adhered to the roots and fibres, had been loosened, and had fallen on the ground, close to the spot where Catharine lay. So ponderous was the mass, that had it struck her, death must have been the consequence of the blow; and Hector and Louis beheld it with fear and amazement, while Catharine regarded it as a proof of Divine mercy and protection from Him in whose hand her safety lay. The boys, warned by this accident, carefully removed several large stones from the roof, and tried the safety of their clay walls with a stout staff, to ascertain that all was secure, before they again ventured to sleep beneath this rugged canopy.

CHAPTER 5

"The soul of the wicked desireth evil; his neighbour findeth no favour in his eyes."—

Proverbs.

FOR several days, they abstained from lighting a fire, lest the smoke should be seen; but this, the great height of the bank would have effectually prevented. They suffered much cold at night from the copious dews, which, even on sultry summer's evenings, is productive of much chilling. They could not account for the fact that the air, at night, was much warmer on the high hills than in the low valleys; they were even sensible of a rush of heat as they ascended to the higher ground. These simple children had not been taught that it is the nature of the heated air to ascend, and its place to be supplied by the colder and denser particles. They noticed the effects, but understood nothing of the causes that ruled them.

The following days they procured several partridges, but feared to cook them; however, they plucked them, split them open, and dried the flesh for a future day. A fox or racoon, attracted by the smell of the birds, came one night, and carried them off, for in the morning they were gone. They saw several herd of deer crossing the plain, and one day Wolfe tracked a wounded doe to a covert under the poplars, near a hidden spring, where she had lain herself down to die in peace, far from the haunts of her fellows. The arrow was in her throat; it was of white flint, and had evidently been sent from an Indian bow. It was almost with fear and trembling that they availed themselves of the venison thus providentially thrown in their way, lest the Indians should track the blood of the doe, and take vengeance on them for appropriating it for their own use. Not having seen anything of the Indians, who seemed to confine themselves to the neighbourhood of the lake, after many days had passed, they began to take courage, and even lighted an evening fire, at which they cooked as much venison as would last them for several days, and hung the remaining portions above the smoke to preserve it from injury.

One morning, Hector proclaimed his intention of ascending the hills, in the direction of the Indian camp. "I am tired of remaining shut up in this dull place, where we can see nothing but this dead flat, bounded by those melancholy pines in the distance that seem to shut us in."

Little did Hector know that beyond that dark ridge of pine hills lay the home of their childhood, and but a few miles of forest intervened to hide it from their sight. Had he known it, how eagerly would his feet have pressed onward in the direction of that dark barrier of evergreens!

Thus is it often in this life: we wander on, sad and perplexed, our path beset with thorns and briars. We cannot see our way clear; doubts and apprehensions assail us. We know not how near we are to the fulfilment of our wishes; we see only the insurmountable barriers, the dark thickets and thorns of our way; and we know not how near we are to our Father's home, where he is waiting to welcome the wanderers of the flock back to the everlasting home, the fold of the Good Shepherd.

Hector became impatient of the restraint that the dread of the Indians imposed upon his movements; he wanted to see the lake again, and to roam abroad free and uncontrolled.

"After all," said he; "we never met with any ill treatment from the Indians that used to visit us at Cold Springs; we may even find old friends and acquaintances among them."

"The thing is possible, but not very likely," replied Louis. "Nevertheless, Hector, I would not willingly put myself in their power. The Indian has his own notion of things, and might think himself quite justified in killing us, if he found us on his hunting-grounds.[1] I have heard my father say,—and he knows a great deal about these people, —that their chiefs are very strict in punishing any strangers that they find killing game on their bounds uninvited. They are both merciless and treacherous when angered, and we could not even speak to them in their own language, to explain by what chance we came here."

This was very prudent of Louis, uncommonly so, for one who was naturally rash and headstrong, but unfortunately Hector was inflexible and wilful: when once he had made up his mind upon any point, he had too good an opinion of his own judgment to give it up. At last, he declared his intention, rather than remain a slave to such cowardly fears as he now deemed them, to go forth boldly, and endeavour to ascertain what the Indians were about, how many there were of them, and what real danger was to be apprehended from facing them.

"Depend upon it," he added, "cowards are never safer than brave men. The Indians despise cowards, and would be more likely to kill us if they found us cowering here in this hole like a parcel of wolf-cubs, than if we openly faced them and showed that we neither feared them, nor cared for them."

"Hector, dear Hector, be not so rash!" cried his sister,

[1] George Copway, an intelligent Rice Lake Indian, says the Indian hunting-grounds are parcelled out, and secured by right of law and custom among themselves, no one being allowed to hunt upon another's grounds uninvited. If any one belonging to another family or tribe is found trespassing, all his goods are taken from him; a handful of powder and shot, as much as he would need to shoot game for his sustenance in returning straight home, and his gun, knife, and tomahawk only are left, but all his game and furs are taken from him: a message is sent to his chief, and if he transgresses a third time, he is banished and outlawed.—*Life of G. Copway, Missionary, written by himself*.

passionately weeping. "Ah! if we were to lose you, what would become of us?"

"Never fear, Kate; I will run into no needless danger. I know how to take care of myself. I am of opinion that the Indian camp is broken up; they seldom stay long in one place. I will go over the hills and examine the camp at a distance and the lake shore. You and Louis may keep watch for my return from the big pine that we halted under on our way hither."

"But, Hector, if the savages should see you, and take you prisoner," said Catharine, "what would you do?"

"I will tell you what I would do. Instead of running away, I would boldly walk up to them, and by signs make them understand that I am no scout, but a friend in need of nothing but kindness and friendship. I never yet heard of the Indian that would tomahawk the defenceless stranger that sought his camp openly in peace and goodwill."

"If you do not return by sunset, Hector, we shall believe that you have fallen into the hands of the savages," said Catharine, mournfully regarding her brother.

"If it were not for Catharine," said Louis, "you should not go alone, but, if evil befel this helpless one, her blood would be upon my head, who led her out with us, tempting her with false words."

"Never mind that now, dearest cousin," said Catharine, tenderly laying her hand on his arm. "It is much better that we should have been all three together; I should never have been happy again if I had lost both Hec and you. It is better as it is; you and Hec would not have been so well off if I had not been with you to help you, and keep up your spirits by my songs and stories."

"It is true, ma chère; but that is the reason that I am bound to take care of my little cousin, and I could not consent to exposing you to danger, or leaving you alone; so, if Hec will be so headstrong, I will abide by you."

Hector was so confident that he should return in safety, that at last Louis and Catharine became more reconciled to his leaving them, and soon busied themselves in preparing some squirrels that Louis had brought in that morning.

The day wore away slowly, and many were the anxious glances that Catharine cast over the crest of the high bank to watch for her brother's return; at last, unable to endure the suspense, she with Louis left the shelter of the valley; they ascended the high ground, and bent their steps to the trysting tree, which commanded all the country within a wide sweep.

A painful and oppressive sense of loneliness and desolation came over the minds of the cousins as they sat together at the foot of the pine, which cast its lengthened shadow upon the ground before them. The shades of evening were shrouding them, wrapping the lonely forest in gloom. The full moon had not yet risen, and they watched for the first gleam that should break above the eastern hills to cheer them, as for the coming of a friend.

Sadly these two poor lonely ones sat hand in hand, talking of the happy days of childhood, of the perplexing present and the uncertain future. At last, wearied out with watching and anxiety, Catharine leaned her head upon the neck of old Wolfe and fell asleep, while Louis restlessly paced to and fro in front of the sleeper; now straining his eye to penetrate the surrounding gloom, now straining his ear to catch the first sound that might indicate the approach of his absent cousin.

It was almost with a feeling of irritability that he heard the quick sharp note of the wakeful "Whip-poor-will," as she flew from bough to bough of an old withered tree beside him. Another, and again another of these midnight watchers took up the monotonous never-varying cry of "Whip-poor-will, Whip-poor-will;" and then came forth, from many a hollow oak and birch, the spectral night-hawk from hidden dens, where it had lain hushed in silence all day, from dawn till sunset. Sometimes their sharp hard wings almost swept his cheek, as they wheeled round and round in circles, first narrow, then wide, and wider extending, till at last they soared far above the tallest tree-tops, and launching out in the high regions of the air, uttered from time to time a wild shrill scream, or hollow booming sound, as they suddenly descended to pounce with wide-extended throat upon some hapless moth or insect, that sported all unheeding in mid air, happily unconscious of the approach of so unerring a foe.

Petulantly Louis chid these discordant minstrels of the night, and joyfully he hailed the first gush of moonlight that rose broad and full and red, over the Oak-hills to the eastward.

Louis envied the condition of the unconscious sleeper, who lay in happy forgetfulness of all her sorrows, her fair curls spread in unbound luxuriance over the dark shaggy neck of the faithful Wolfe, who seemed as if proud of the beloved burden that rested so trustingly upon him. Sometimes the careful dog just unclosed his large eyes, raised his nose from his shaggy paws, snuffed the night air, growled in a sort of under tone, and dosed again, but watchfully.

It would be no easy task to tell the painful feelings that agitated young Louis's breast. He was angry with Hector, for having thus madly, as he thought, rushed into danger. "It was wilful and almost cruel," he thought "to leave them the prey of such tormenting fears on his account;" and then the most painful fears for the safety of his beloved companion took the place of less kindly thoughts, and sorrow filled his heart. The broad moon now flooded the hills and vales with light, casting broad checkering shadows of the old oaks' grey branches and now reddened foliage across the ground.

Suddenly the old dog raises his head, and utters a short half angry note: slowly and carefully he rises, disengaging himself gently from the form of the sleeping girl, and stands forth in the full light of the moon. It is an open cleared space, that mound beneath the pine-tree; a few low shrubs and seedling pines, with the slender waving branches of the late-flowering pearly tinted asters, the elegant fringed gentian, with open bells of azure blue, the last and loveliest of the fall flowers and winter-greens, brighten the ground with wreaths of shining leaves and red berries.

Louis is on the alert, though as yet he sees nothing. It is not a full free note of welcome, that Wolfe gives; there is something uneasy and half angry in his tone. Yet it is not fierce, like the bark of angry defiance he gives, when wolf, or bear, or wolverine is near.

Louis steps forward from the shadow of the pine branches, to the edge of the inclined plane in the foreground. The slow tread of approaching steps is now distinctly heard advancing—it may be a deer. Two figures approach, and Louis moves a little within the shadow again. A clear shrill whistle meets his ear. It is Hector's whistle, he knows that, and assured by its cheerful tone, he springs forward and in an instant is at his side, but starts at the strange companion that he half leads, half carries. The moonlight streams broad and bright upon the shrinking figure of an Indian girl, apparently about the same age as Catharine: her ashy face is concealed by the long masses of raven black hair, which falls like a dark veil over her features; her step is weak and unsteady, and she seems ready to sink to the earth with sickness or fatigue. Hector, too, seems weary. The first words that Hector said were, "Help me, Louis, to lead this poor girl to the foot of the pine; I am so tired I can hardly walk another step."

Louis and his cousin together carried the Indian girl to the foot of the pine. Catharine was just rousing herself from sleep, and she gazed with a bewildered air on the strange companion that Hector had brought with him.

The stranger lay down, and in a few minutes sank into a sleep so profound it seemed to resemble that of death itself. Pity and deep interest soon took the place of curiosity and dread in the heart of the gentle Catharine, and she watched the young stranger's slumber as tenderly as though she had been a sister, or beloved friend, while Hector proceeded to relate in what manner he had encountered the Indian girl.

"When I struck the high slope near the little birch grove we called the '*birken shaw*,' I paused to examine if the council-fires were still burning on Bare-hill, but there was no smoke visible, neither was there a canoe to be seen at the lake shore where Louis had described their landing-place at the mouth of the creek. All seemed as silent and still as if no human footstep had trodden the shore. I sat down and watched for nearly an hour till my attention was attracted by a noble eagle, which was sailing in wide circles over the tall pine-trees on Bare-hill. Assured that the Indian camp was broken up, and feeling some curiosity to examine the spot more closely, I crossed the thicket of cranberries and cedars and small underwood that fringed the borders of the little stream, and found myself, after a little pushing and scrambling, among the bushes at the foot of the hill.

"I thought it not impossible I might find something to repay me for my trouble—flint arrow-heads, a knife, or a tomahawk—but I little thought of what these cruel savages had left there,—a miserable wounded captive, bound by the long locks of her hair to the stem of a small tree, her hands, tied by thongs of hide to branches which they had bent down to fasten them to her feet, bound fast to the same tree as that against which her head was fastened; her position was one that must have been most painful: she had evidently been thus left to perish by a miserable death, of hunger and thirst; for these savages, with a fiendish cruelty, had placed within sight of their victim an earthen jar of water, some dried deers' flesh, and a cob[1] of Indian corn. I have the corn here," he added, putting his hand in his breast, and displaying it to view.

"Wounded she was, for I drew this arrow from her shoulder," and he showed the flint head as he spoke, "and fettered; with food and drink in sight, the poor girl was to perish, perhaps to become a living prey to the wolf, and the eagle that I saw wheeling above the hill top. The poor thing's lips were black and parched with pain and thirst; she turned her eyes piteously from my face to the water jar as if to implore a draught. This I gave her, and then having cooled the festering wound, and cut the thongs that bound her, I wondered that she still kept the same immoveable attitude, and thinking she was stiff and cramped with remaining so long bound in one position, I took her two hands and tried to induce her to move. I then for the first time noticed that she was tied by the hair of her head to the tree against which her back was placed; I was obliged to cut the hair with my knife, and this I did not do without giving her pain, as she moaned impatiently. She sunk her head on her breast, and large tears fell over my hands, as I bathed her face and neck with the water from the jar; she then seated herself on the ground, and remained silent and still for the space of an hour, nor could I prevail upon her to speak, or quit the seat she had taken. Fearing that the Indians might return, I watched in all directions, and at last I began to think it would be best to carry her in my arms; but this I found no easy task, for she seemed greatly distressed at any attempt I made to lift her, and by her gestures I fancied she thought I was going to kill her. At last my patience began to be exhausted, but I did not like to annoy her. I spoke to her as gently and soothingly as I could. By degrees she seemed to listen with more composure to me, though she evidently

[1] A head of the Maize, or Indian corn, is called a "cob."

knew not a word of what I said to her. She rose at last, and taking my hands, placed them above her head, stooping low as she did so, and this seemed to mean, she was willing at last to submit to my wishes; I lifted her from the ground, and carried her for some little way, but she was too heavy for me,—she then suffered me to lead her along whithersoever I would take her, but her steps were so slow and feeble, through weakness, that many times I was compelled to rest while she recovered herself. She seems quite subdued now, and as quiet as a lamb."

Catharine listened, not without tears of genuine sympathy, to the recital of her brother's adventures. She seemed to think he had been inspired by God to go forth that day to the Indian camp, to rescue the poor forlorn one from so dreadful a death.

Louis's sympathy was also warmly aroused for the young savage, and he commended Hector for his bravery and humanity.

He then set to work to light a good fire, which was a great addition to their comfort as well as cheerfulness. They did not go back to their cave beneath the upturned trees, to sleep, preferring lying, with their feet to the fire, under the shade of the pine. Louis, however, was despatched for water and venison for supper.

The following morning, by break of day, they collected their stores, and conveyed them back to the shanty. The boys were thus employed, while Catharine watched beside the wounded Indian girl, whom she tended with the greatest care. She bathed the inflamed arm with water, and bound the cool healing leaves of the *tacamahac* [1] about it with the last fragment of her apron, she steeped dried berries in water, and gave the cooling drink to quench the fever-thirst that burned in her veins, and glittered in her full soft melancholy dark eyes, which were raised at

[1] Indian balsam.

intervals to the face of her youthful nurse, with a timid hurried glance, as if she longed, yet feared to say, "Who are you that thus tenderly bathe my aching head, and strive to soothe my wounded limbs, and cool my fevered blood? Are you a creature like myself, or a being sent by the Great Spirit, from the far-off happy land to which my fathers have gone, to smooth my path of pain, and lead me to those blessed fields of sunbeams and flowers where the cruelty of the enemies of my people will no more have power to torment me?"

CHAPTER 6

"Here the wren of softest note
Builds its nest and warbles well;
Here the blackbird strains his throat;
Welcome, welcome to our cell."—

COLERIDGE.

THE day was far advanced, before the sick Indian girl could be brought home to their sylvan lodge, where Catharine made up a comfortable couch for her, with boughs and grass, and spread one of the deer-skins over it, and laid her down as tenderly and carefully as if she had been a dear sister. This good girl was overjoyed at having found a companion of her own age and sex. "Now," said she, "I shall no more be lonely, I shall have a companion and friend to talk to and assist me;" but when she turned in the fulness of her heart to address herself to the young stranger, she felt herself embarrassed in what way to make her comprehend the words she used to express the kindness that she felt for her, and her sorrow for her sufferings.

The young stranger would raise her head, look intently at her, as if striving to interpret her words, then sadly shake her head, and utter her words in her own plaintive language, but, alas! Catharine felt it was to her as a sealed book.

She tried to recal some Indian words of familiar import, that she had heard from the Indians when they came to her father's house, but in vain; not the simplest phrase occurred to her, and she almost cried with vexation at her

own stupidity; neither was Hector or Louis more fortunate
in attempts at conversing with their guest.

At the end of three days, the fever began to abate; the
restless eye grew more steady in its gaze, the dark flush
faded from the cheek, leaving it of a grey ashy tint, not the
hue of health, such as even the swarthy Indian shows, but
wan and pallid, her eyes bent mournfully on the ground.

She would sit quiet and passive while Catharine bound
up the long tresses of her hair, and smoothed them with
her hands and the small wooden comb that Louis had cut
for her use. Sometimes she would raise her eyes to her new
friend's face, with a quiet sad smile, and once she took her
hands within her own, and gently pressed them to her
breast and lips and forehead in token of gratitude, but she
seldom gave utterance to any words, and would remain
with her eyes fixed vacantly on some object which seemed
unseen or to awaken no idea in her mind. At such times
the face of the young squaw wore a dreamy apathy of
expression, or rather it might with more propriety have
been said, the absence of all expression, almost as blank as
that of an infant of a few weeks old.

How intently did Catharine study that face, and strive to
read what was passing within her mind! how did the lively
intelligent Canadian girl, the offspring of a more
intellectual race, long to instruct her Indian friend, to
enlarge her mind by pointing out such things to her
attention as she herself took interest in! She would then
repeat the name of the object that she showed her several
times over, and by degrees the young squaw learned the
names of all the familiar household articles about the
shanty, and could repeat them in her own soft plaintive
tone; and when she had learned a new word, and could
pronounce it distinctly, she would laugh, and a gleam of
innocent joy and pleasure would lighten up her fine dark
eyes, generally so fixed and sad-looking.

It was Catharine's delight to teach her pupil to speak a

language familiar to her own ears; she would lead her out among the trees, and name to her all the natural objects that presented themselves to view. And she in her turn made "Indiana" (for so they named the young squaw, after a negress that she had heard her father tell of, a nurse to one of his Colonel's infant children,) tell her the Indian names for each object they saw. Indiana soon began to enjoy in her turn the amusement arising from instructing Catharine and the boys, and often seemed to enjoy the blunders they made in pronouncing the words she taught them. When really interested in anything that was going on, her eyes would beam out, and her smile gave an inexpressible charm to her face, for her lips were red and her teeth even and brilliantly white, so purely white that Catharine thought she had never seen any so beautiful in her life before; at such times her face was joyous and innocent as a little child's, but there were also hours of gloom, that transformed it into an expression of sullen apathy; then a dull glassy look took possession of her eye, the full lip drooped and the form seemed rigid and stiff; obstinate determination neither to move nor speak characterised her in what Louis used to call the young squaw's "*dark hour.*" Then it was that the savage nature seemed predominant, and her gentle nurse almost feared to look at her protegée or approach her.

"Hector," said Louis, "you spoke about a jar of water being left at the camp; the jar would be a great treasure to us, let us go over for it." Hector assented to the proposal. "And we may possibly pick up a few grains of Indian corn, to add to what you showed us."

"If we are here in the spring," said Hector, "you and I will prepare a small patch of ground and plant it with this corn;" and he sat down on the end of a log and began carefully to count the rows of grain on the cob, and then each corn grain by grain. "Three hundred and ten sound grains. Now if every one of these produces a strong plant, we shall have a great increase, and beside seed for another year, there will be, if it is a good year, several bushels to eat."

"We shall have a glorious summer, mon ami, no doubt, and a fine flourishing crop, and Kate is a good hand at making supporne." [1]

"You forget we have no porridge pot."

"I was thinking of that Indian jar all the time. You will see what fine cookery we will make when we get it, if it will but stand fire. Come, let us be off, I am impatient till we get it home;" and Louis, who had now a new crotchet at work in his fertile and vivacious brain, was quite on the *qui vive*, and walked and danced along at a rate which proved a great disturbance to his graver companion, who tried to keep down his cousin's lively spirits, by suggesting the probability of the jar being cracked, or that the Indians might have returned for it; but Louis was not one of the doubting sort, and Louis was right in not damping the ardour of his mind by causeless fears. The jar was there at the deserted camp, and though it had been knocked over by some animal, it was sound and strong, and excited great speculation in the two cousins, as to the particular material of which it was made, as it was unlike any sort of pottery they had ever before seen. It seemed to have been manufactured from some very dark red earth, or clay mixed up with pounded granite, as it presented the appearance of some coarse crystals; it was very hard and ponderous, and the surface was marked over in a rude sort of pattern as if punctured and scratched with some pointed instrument. It seemed to have been hardened by fire, and, from the smoked hue of one side, had evidently done good service as a cooking utensil. Subsequently they

[1] Supporne, probably an Indian word for a stir-about, or porridge, made of Indian meal, a common dish in every Canadian or Yankee farmer's house.

learned the way in which it was used:[1] the jar being placed
near but not on the fire, was surrounded by hot embers,
and the water made to boil by stones being made red hot
and plunged into it: in this way soup and other food were
prepared, and kept stewing, with no further trouble after
once the simmering began, than adding a few fresh
embers at the side furthest from the fire; a hot stone also
placed on the top, facilitated the cooking process.

Louis, who like all French people was addicted to
cookery,—indeed it was an accomplishment he prided
himself on,—was enchanted with the improvement made
in their diet by the acquisition of the said earthen jar, or
pipkin, and gave Indiana some praise for initiating his
cousin in the use of it. Catharine and Hector declared that
he went out with his bow and arrows, and visited his dead-
falls and snares, ten times oftener than he used to do, just
for the sake of proving the admirable properties of this
precious utensil, and finding out some new way of
dressing his game.

At all events there was a valuable increase of furs, for
making up into clothing, caps, leggings, mitts, and other
articles.

From the Indian girl Catharine learned the value of
many of the herbs and shrubs that grew in her path, the
bark and leaves of various trees, and many dyes she could
extract, with which she stained the quills of the porcupine
and the strips of the wood of which she made baskets and
mats. The little creeping winter-green,[2] with its scarlet
berries, that grows on the dry flats, or sandy hills, which
the Canadians call spice-berry, she showed them was good
to eat, and she would crush the leaves, draw forth their

---

[1] Pieces of this rude pottery are often found along the shores of the
inland lakes, but I have never met with any of the perfect vessels in use
with the Indians, who probably find it now easier to supply themselves
with iron pots and crockery from the towns of the European settlers.

[2] *Gaultheria procumbens*,—Spice Winter-green.

fine aromatic flavour in her hands, and then inhale their fragrance with delight. She made an infusion of the leaves, and drank it as a tonic. The inner bark of the wild black cherry, she said was good to cure ague and fever. The root of the *dulçamara*, or bitter-sweet, she scraped down and boiled in the deer-fat, or the fat of any other animal, and made an ointment that possessed very healing qualities, especially as an immediate application to fresh burns.

Sometimes she showed a disposition to mystery, and would conceal the knowledge of the particular herbs she made use of; and Catharine several times noticed that she would go out and sprinkle a portion of the food she had assisted her in preparing, on the earth, or under some of the trees or bushes. When she was more familiar with their language, she told Catharine this was done in token of gratitude to the Good Spirit, who had given them success in hunting or trapping; or else it was to appease the malice of the Evil Spirit, who might bring mischief or loss to them, or sickness or death, unless his forbearance was purchased by some particular mark of attention.[1]

Attention, memory, and imitation, appeared to form the three most remarkable of the mental faculties developed by the Indian girl. She examined (when once her attention was roused) any object with critical minuteness. Any knowledge she had once acquired, she retained; her memory was great, she never missed a path she had once trodden; she seemed even to single out particular birds in a flock, to know them from their congeners. Her powers of imitation were also great; she brought patience and

---

[1] By the testimony of many of the Indians themselves, they appear to entertain a certain Polytheism in their belief. "We believed in one great wise benevolent being, Thesha-mon-e-doo, whose dwelling was in the sun. We believed also in many other lesser spirits—gods of the elements, and in one bad unappeasable spirit, Mah-je-mah-ne-doo, to whom we attributed bad luck, evil accidents, and sickness and death. This bad spirit has to be conciliated with meat and drink offerings."—*Life of George Copway, Native Missionary.*

perseverance to assist her, and when once thoroughly interested in any work she began, she would toil on untiringly till it was completed; and then what triumph shone in her eyes! At such times they became darkly brilliant with the joy that filled her heart. But she possessed little talent for invention; what she had seen done, after a few imperfect attempts, she could do again, but she rarely struck out any new path for herself.

At times she was docile and even playful, and appeared grateful for the kindness with which she was treated; each day seemed to increase her fondness for Catharine, and she appeared to delight in doing any little service to please and gratify her, but it was towards Hector that she displayed the deepest feeling of affection and respect. It was to him her first tribute of fruit or flowers, furs, mocassins, or ornamental plumage of rare birds was offered. She seemed to turn to him as to a master and protector. He was in her eyes the "*Chief*," the head of his tribe. His bow was strung by her, and stained with quaint figures and devices; his arrows were carved by her; the sheath of deer-skin was made and ornamented by her hands, that he carried his knife in; and the case for his arrows, of birch-bark, was wrought with especial neatness, and suspended by thongs to his neck, when he was preparing to go out in search of game. She gave him the name of the "Young Eagle." While she called Louis, "Nee-chee," or friend; to Catharine she gave the poetical name of, "Music of the Winds,"—Ma-wah-osh.

When they asked her to tell them her own name, she would bend down her head in sorrow and refuse to pronounce it. She soon answered to the name of Indiana, and seemed pleased with the sound.

But of all the household, next to Hector, old Wolfe was her greatest favourite. At first, it is true, the old dog regarded the new inmate with a jealous eye, and seemed uneasy when he saw her approach to caress him, but

Indiana soon reconciled him to her person, and a mutual friendly feeling became established between them, which seemed daily and hourly to increase, greatly to the delight of the young stranger. She would seat herself Eastern fashion, cross-legged on the floor of the shanty, with the capacious head of the old dog in her lap, and address herself to this mute companion, in wailing tones, as if she would unburthen her heart by pouring into his unconscious ear her tale of desolation and woe.

Catharine was always very particular and punctual in performing her personal ablutions, and she intimated to Indiana that it was good for her to do the same; but the young girl seemed reluctant to follow her example, till daily custom had reconciled her to what she evidently at first regarded as an unnecessary ceremony; but she soon took pleasure in dressing her dark hair, and suffering Catharine to braid it, and polish it till it looked glossy and soft. Indiana in her turn would adorn Catharine with the wings of the blue-bird or red-bird, the crest of the wood-duck, or quill feathers of the golden-winged flicker, which is called in the Indian tongue the shot-bird, in allusion to the round spots on its cream-coloured breast:[1] but it was not in these things alone she showed her grateful sense of the sisterly kindness that her young hostess showed to her; she soon learned to lighten her labours in every household work, and above all, she spent her time most usefully in manufacturing clothing from the skins of the wild animals, and in teaching Catharine how to fit and prepare them; but these were the occupation of the winter months. I must not forestall my narrative.

[1] The Golden-winged Flicker belongs to a sub-genus of woodpeckers; it is very handsome, and is said to be eatable; it lives on fruits and insects.

CHAPTER 7

"Go to the ant."—

Proverbs.

IT was now the middle of September; the weather, which had continued serene and beautiful for some time, with dewy nights and misty mornings, began to show symptoms of the change of season usual at the approach of the equinox. Sudden squalls of wind, with hasty showers, would come sweeping over the lake; the nights and mornings were damp and chilly. Already the tints of autumn were beginning to crimson the foliage of the oaks, and where the islands were visible, the splendid colours of the maple shone out in gorgeous contrast with the deep verdure of the evergreens and light golden-yellow of the poplar; but lovely as they now looked, they had not yet reached the meridian of their beauty, which a few frosty nights at the close of the month was destined to bring to perfection—a glow of splendour to gladden the eye for a brief space, before the rushing winds and rains of the following month were to sweep them away, and scatter them abroad upon the earth.

One morning, just after a night of heavy rain and wind, the two boys went down to see if the lake was calm enough for trying the raft, which Louis had finished before the coming on of the bad weather. The water was rough and crested with mimic waves, and they felt not disposed to launch the raft on so stormy a surface, but they stood looking out over the lake and admiring the changing foliage, when Hector pointed out to his cousin a dark speck dancing on the waters, between the two nearest islands. The wind, which blew very strong still from the north-east, brought the object nearer every minute. At first they thought it might be a pine-branch that was floating on the surface, when as it came bounding over the waves, they perceived that it was a birch-canoe, but impelled by no visible arm. It was a strange sight upon that lonely lake to see a vessel of any kind afloat, and, on first deciding that it was a canoe, the boys were inclined to hide themselves among the bushes, for fear of the Indians, but curiosity got the better of their fears.

"The owner of yonder little craft is either asleep or absent from her; for I see no paddle, and it is evidently drifting without any one to guide it," said Hector, after intently watching the progress of the tempest-driven vessel; assured as it approached nearer that such was the case, they hurried to the beach just as a fresh gust had lodged the canoe among the branches of a fallen cedar which projected out some way into the water.

By creeping along the trunk of the tree, and trusting at times to the projecting boughs, Louis, who was the most active and the lightest of weight, succeeded in getting within reach of the canoe, and with some trouble and the help of a stout branch that Hector handed to him, he contrived to moor her in safety on the shore, taking the precaution of hauling her well up on the shingle, lest the wind and water should set her afloat again. "Hec, there is something in this canoe, the sight of which will gladden your heart," cried Louis with a joyful look. "Come quickly, and see my treasures."

"Treasures! You may well call them treasures," exclaimed Hector, as he helped Louis to examine the contents of the canoe, and place them on the shore, side by side.

The boys could hardly find words to express their joy and surprise at the discovery of a large jar of parched rice, a tomahawk, an Indian blanket almost as good as new, a large mat rolled up with a bass bark rope several yards in length wound round it, and what was more precious than all, an iron three-legged pot in which was a quantity of Indian corn. These articles had evidently constituted the stores of some Indian hunter or trapper; possibly the canoe had been imperfectly secured and had drifted from its moorings during the gale of the previous night, unless by some accident the owner had fallen into the lake and been drowned; this was of course only a matter of conjecture on which it was useless to speculate, and the boys joyfully took possession of the good fortune that had so providentially been wafted, as it were, to their very feet.

"It was a capital chance for us, that old cedar having been blown down last night just where it was," said Louis; "for if the canoe had not been drawn into the eddy, and stopped by the branches, we might have lost it. I trembled when I saw the wind driving it on so rapidly that it would founder in the deep water, or go off to Long Island."

"I think we should have got it at Pine-tree Point," said Hector, "but I am glad it was lodged so cleverly among the cedar boughs. I was half afraid you would have fallen in once or twice, when you were trying to draw it nearer to the shore."

"Never fear for me, my friend; I can cling like a wild cat when I climb. But what a grand pot! What delightful soups, and stews, and boils, Catharine will make! Hurrah!" and Louis tossed up his new fur cap, that he had made with great skill from an entire fox skin, in the air, and cut sundry fantastic capers which Hector gravely condemned as unbecoming his mature age; (Louis was turned of fifteen;) but with the joyous spirit of a little child he sung, and danced, and laughed, and shouted, till the lonely echoes of the islands and far-off hills returned the unusual sound, and even his more steady cousin caught the infection, and laughed to see Louis so elated.

Leaving Hector to guard the prize, Louis ran gaily off to fetch Catharine to share his joy, and come and admire the canoe, and the blanket, and the tripod, and the corn, and the tomahawk. Indiana accompanied them to the lake shore, and long and carefully she examined the canoe and its contents, and many were the plaintive exclamations she uttered as she surveyed the things piece by piece, till she took notice of the broken handle of an Indian paddle which lay at the bottom of the vessel; this seemed to afford some solution to her of the mystery, and by broken words and signs she intimated that the paddle had possibly broken in the hand of the Indian, and that in endeavouring to regain the other part, he had lost his balance and been drowned. She showed Hector a rude figure of a bird engraved with some sharp instrument, and rubbed in with a blue colour. This, she said, was the totem or crest of the chief of the tribe, and was meant to represent a *crow*. The canoe had belonged to a chief of that name. While they were dividing the contents of the canoe among them to be carried to the shanty, Indiana, taking up the bass-rope and the blanket, bundled up the most of the things, and adjusting the broad thick part of the rope to the front of her head, she bore off the burden with great apparent ease, as a London or Edinburgh porter would his trunks and packages, turning round with a merry glance and repeating some Indian words with a lively air as she climbed with apparent ease the steep bank, and soon distanced her companions, to her great enjoyment. That night, Indiana cooked some of the parched rice, Indian fashion, with venison, and they enjoyed the novelty very much—it made an excellent substitute for bread, of which they had been so long deprived.

Indiana gave them to understand that the rice harvest would soon be ready on the lake, and that now they had got a canoe, they would go out and gather it, and so lay by a store to last them for many months.

This little incident furnished the inhabitants of the shanty with frequent themes for discussion. Hector declared that the Indian corn was the most valuable of their acquisitions. "It will insure us a crop, and bread and seed-corn for many years," he said; he also highly valued the tomahawk, as his axe was worn and blunt.

Louis was divided between the iron pot and the canoe. Hector seemed to think the raft, after all, might have formed a substitute for the latter; besides, Indiana had signified her intention of helping him to make a canoe. Catharine declared in favour of the blanket, as it would make, after thorough ablutions, warm petticoats with tight bodices for herself and Indiana. With deer-skin leggings, and a fur jacket, they should be comfortably clad. Indiana thought the canoe the most precious, and was charmed with the good jar and the store of rice: nor did she despise the packing rope, which she soon showed was of use in carrying burdens from place to place, Indian fashion: by placing a pad of soft fur in front of the head, she could carry heavy loads with great ease. The mat, she said, was useful for drying the rice she meant to store.

The very next day after this adventure, the two girls set to work, and with the help of Louis's large knife, which was called into requisition as a substitute for scissors, they cut out the blanket dresses, and in a short time made two comfortable and not very unsightly garments: the full, short, plaited skirts reached a little below the knee; light vests bordered with fur completed the upper part, and leggings, terminated at the ankles by knotted fringes of the doe-skin, with mocassins turned over with a band of squirrel fur, completed the novel but not very unbecoming costume; and many a glance of innocent satisfaction did our young damsels cast upon each other, when they walked forth in the pride of girlish vanity to display their dresses to Hector and Louis, who, for their parts, regarded them as most skilful dress-makers, and were never tired of admiring and commending their ingenuity in the cutting, making and fitting, considering what rude implements they were obliged to use in the cutting out and sewing of the garments.

The extensive rice beds on the lake had now begun to assume a golden tinge which contrasted very delightfully with the deep blue waters—looking, when lighted up by the sunbeams, like islands of golden-coloured sand. The ears, heavy laden with the ripe grain, drooped towards the water. The time of the rice-harvest was at hand, and with light and joyous hearts our young adventurers launched the canoe, and, guided in their movements by the little squaw, paddled to the extensive aquatic fields to gather it in, leaving Catharine and Wolfe to watch their proceedings from the raft, which Louis had fastened to a young tree that projected out over the lake, and which made a good landing-place, likewise a wharf where they could stand and fish very comfortably. As the canoe could not be overloaded on account of the rice-gathering, Catharine very readily consented to employ herself with fishing from the raft till their return.

The manner of procuring the rice was very simple. One person steered the canoe with the aid of the paddle along the edge of the rice beds, and another with a stick in one hand, and a curved sharp-edged paddle in the other, struck the heads off as they bent them over the edge of the stick; the chief art was in letting the heads fall into the canoe, which a little practice soon enabled them to do as expertly as the mower lets the grass fall in ridges beneath his scythe.

Many bushels of wild rice were thus collected. Nothing could be more delightful than this sort of work to our young people, and merrily they worked, and laughed, and sung, as they came home each day with their light bark, laden with a store of grain that they knew would preserve them from starving through the long, dreary winter that was coming on.

The canoe was a source of great comfort and pleasure to them; they were now able to paddle out into the deep water, and fish for masquinonjé and black bass, which they caught in great numbers.

Indiana seemed quite another creature when, armed with a paddle of her own carving, she knelt at the head of the canoe and sent it flying over the water; then her dark eyes, often so vacant and glassy, sparkled with delight, and her teeth gleamed with ivory whiteness as her face broke into smiles and dimples.

It was delightful then to watch this child of nature, and see how innocently happy she could be when rejoicing in the excitement of healthy exercise, and elated by a consciousness of the power she possessed of excelling her companions in feats of strength and skill which they had yet to acquire by imitating her.

Even Louis was obliged to confess that the young savage knew more of the management of a canoe, and the use of the bow and arrow, and the fishing-line, than either himself or his cousin. Hector was lost in admiration of her skill in all these things; and Indiana rose highly in his estimation, the more he saw of her usefulness.

"Every one to his craft," said Louis, laughing; "the little squaw has been brought up in the knowledge and practice of such matters from her babyhood; perhaps if we were to set her to knitting, and spinning, and milking of cows, and house-work, and learning to read, I doubt if she would prove half as quick as Catharine or Mathilde."

"I wonder if she knows anything of God or our Saviour," said Hector, thoughtfully.

"Who should have taught her? for the Indians are all heathens;" replied Louis.

"I have heard my dear mother say, the Missionaries have taken great pains to teach the Indian children down about Quebec and Montreal, and that so far from being stupid, they learn very readily," said Catharine.

"We must try and make Indiana learn to say her prayers; she sits quite still, and seems to take no notice of what we are doing when we kneel down, before we go to bed," observed Hector.

"She cannot understand what we say," said Catharine; "for she knows so little of our language yet, that of course she cannot comprehend the prayers, which are in other sort of words than what we use in speaking of hunting, and fishing, and cooking, and such matters."

"Well, when she knows more of our way of speaking, then we must teach her; it is a sad thing for Christian children to live with an untaught pagan," said Louis, who, being rather bigoted in his creed, felt a sort of uneasiness in his own mind at the poor girl's total want of the rites of his church; but Hector and Catharine regarded her ignorance with feelings of compassionate interest, and lost no opportunity that offered, of trying to enlighten her darkened mind on the subject of belief in the God who made, and the Lord who saved them. Simply and earnestly they entered into the task as a labour of love, and though for a long time Indiana seemed to pay little attention to what they said, by slow degrees the good seed took root and brought forth fruit worthy of Him whose Spirit poured the beams of spiritual light into her heart: but my young readers must not imagine these things were the work of a day—the process was slow, and so were the results, but they were good in the end.

And Catharine was glad when, after many months of patient teaching, the Indian girl asked permission to kneel down with her white friend, and pray to the Great Spirit and His Son in the same words that Christ Jesus gave to his disciples; and if the full meaning of that holy prayer, so full of humility and love, and moral justice, was not fully understood by her whose lips repeated it, yet even the act of worship and the desire to do that which she had been told was right, was, doubtless, a sacrifice better than the pagan rites which that young girl had witnessed among her father's people, who, blindly following the natural impulse of man in his depraved nature, regarded deeds of blood and cruelty as among the highest of human virtues, and gloried in those deeds of vengeance at which the Christian mind revolts with horror.

Indiana took upon herself the management of the rice, drying, husking and storing it, the two lads working under her direction. She caused several forked stakes to be cut and sharpened and driven into the ground; on these were laid four poles, so as to form a frame, over which she then stretched the bass-mat, which she secured by means of forked pegs to the frame; on the mat she then spread out the rice thinly, and lighted a fire beneath, taking good care not to let the flame set fire to the mat, the object being rather to keep up a strong, slow heat, by means of the red embers. She next directed the boys to supply her with pine or cedar boughs, which she stuck in close together, so as to enclose the fire within the area of the stakes. This was done to concentrate the heat and cause it to bear upwards with more power; the rice being frequently stirred with a sort of long-handled, flat shovel. After the rice was sufficiently dried, the next thing to be done was separating it from the husk, and this was effected by putting it by small quantities into the iron pot, and with a sort of wooden pestle or beetle, rubbing it round and round against the sides.[1] If they had not had the iron pot, a wooden trough must have been substituted in its stead.

When the rice was husked, the loose chaff was winnowed from it in a flat basket like a sieve, and it was then put by in coarse birch baskets, roughly sewed with leather-wood bark, or bags made of matting, woven by the little squaw from the cedar-bark. A portion was also

[1] The Indians often make use of a very rude, primitive sort of mortar, by hollowing out a bass-wood stump, and rubbing the rice with a wooden pounder.

parched, which was simply done by putting the rice dry into the iron pot, and setting it on hot embers, stirring the grain till it burst: it was then stored by for use. Rice thus prepared is eaten dry, as a substitute for bread, by the Indians.

The lake was now swarming with wild fowl of various kinds; crowds of ducks were winging their way across it from morning till night, floating in vast flocks upon its surface, or rising in noisy groups if an eagle or fish-hawk appeared sailing with slow, majestic circles above them, then settling down with noisy splash upon the calm water. The shores, too, were covered with these birds, feeding on the fallen acorns which fell ripe and brown with every passing breeze; the berries of the dogwood also furnished them with food; but the wild rice seemed the great attraction, and small shell-fish and the larvæ of many insects that had been dropped into the waters, there to come to perfection in due season, or to form a provision for myriads of wild fowl that had come from the far north-west to feed upon them, guided by that instinct which has so beautifully been termed by one of our modern poetesses,

"God's gift to the weak." [1]

[1] Mrs. Southey.

CHAPTER 8

"Oh, come and hear what cruel wrongs
Befel the Dark Ladye."—

COLERIDGE.

THE Mohawk girl was in high spirits at the coming of the wild fowl to the lake; she would clap her hands and laugh with almost childish glee as she looked at them darkening the lake like clouds resting on its surface.

"If I had but my father's gun, his good old gun, now!" would Hector say, as he eyed the timorous flocks as they rose and fell upon the lake; "but these foolish birds are so shy, that they are away before an arrow can reach them."

Indiana smiled in her quiet way; she was busy filling the canoe with green boughs, which she arranged so as completely to transform the little vessel into the semblance of a floating island of evergreen; within this bower she motioned Hector to crouch down, leaving a small space for the free use of his bow, while concealed at the prow she gently and noiselessly paddled the canoe from the shore among the rice-beds, letting it remain stationary or merely rocking to and fro with the undulatory motion of the waters.

The unsuspecting birds, deceived into full security, eagerly pursued their pastime or their prey, and it was no difficult matter for the hidden archer to hit many a black duck or teal or whistlewing, as it floated securely on the placid water, or rose to shift its place a few yards up or down the stream. Soon the lake around was strewed with the feathered game, which Wolfe, cheered on by Louis, who was stationed on the shore, brought to land.

Indiana told Hector that this was the season when the Indians made great gatherings on the lake for duck-shooting, which they pursued much after the same fashion as that which has been described, only instead of one, a dozen or more canoes would be thus disguised with boughs, with others stationed at different parts of the lake, or under the shelter of the island, to collect the birds. This sport was generally finished by a great feast.

The Indians offered the first of the birds as an oblation to the Great Spirit, as a grateful acknowledgment of his bounty in having allowed them to gather food thus plentifully for their families; sometimes distant tribes with whom they were on terms of friendship were invited to share the sport and partake of the spoils.

Indiana could not understand why Hector did not follow the custom of her Indian fathers, and offer the first duck or the best fish to propitiate the Great Spirit. Hector told her that the God he worshipped desired no sacrifice; that his holy Son, when he came down from heaven and gave himself as a sacrifice for the sins of the world, had satisfied his Father, the Great Spirit, an hundred-fold.

They feasted now continually upon the water-fowl, and Catharine learned from Indiana how to skin them, and so preserve the feathers for making tippets, and bonnets, and ornamental trimmings, which are not only warm, but light and very becoming. They split open any of the birds that they did not require for present consumption, and these they dried for winter store, smoking some after the manner that the Shetlanders and Orkney people smoke the solan geese: their shanty displayed an abundant store of provisions, fish, flesh, and fowl, besides baskets of wild rice, and bags of dried fruit.

One day Indiana came in from the brow of the hill, and told the boys that the lake eastward was covered with canoes; she showed, by holding up her two hands and then three fingers, that she had counted thirteen. The tribes had met for the annual duck-feast, and for the rice harvest. She advised them to put out the fire, so that no smoke might be seen to attract them; but said they would not leave the lake for hunting over the plains just then, as the camp was lower down on the point[1] east of the mouth of a big river, which she called "Otonabee."

Hector asked Indiana if she would go away and leave them, in the event of meeting with any of her own tribe. The girl cast her eyes on the earth in silence; a dark cloud seemed to gather over her face.

"If they should prove to be any of your father's people, or a friendly tribe, would you go away with them?" he again repeated, to which she solemnly replied,

"Indiana has no father, no tribe, no people; no blood of her father's warms the heart of any man, woman or child, saving herself alone; but Indiana is a brave, and the daughter of a brave, and will not shrink from danger: her heart is warm; red blood flows warm here," and she laid her hand on her heart. Then lifting up her hand, she said with slow but impassioned tone, "They left not one drop of living blood to flow in any veins but these," and her eyes were raised, and her arms stretched upwards towards heaven, as though calling down vengeance on the murderers of her father's house.

"My father was a Mohawk, the son of a great chief, who owned these hunting-grounds far as your eye can see to the rising and setting sun, along the big waters of the big lakes; but the Ojebwas, a portion of the Chippewa nation, by treachery cut off my father's people by hundreds in cold blood, when they were defenceless and at rest. It was a bloody day and a bloody deed."

Instead of hiding herself, as Hector and Louis strongly

[1] This point, commonly known as *Anderson's Point*, now the seat of the Indian village, used in former times to be a great place of rendezvous for the Indians, and was the site of a murderous carnage or massacre that took place about eighty years ago; the war-weapons and bones of the Indians are often turned up with the plough at this day.

advised the young Mohawk to do, she preferred remaining as a scout, she said, under the cover of the bushes on the edge of the steep that overlooked the lake, to watch their movements. She told Hector to be under no apprehension if the Indians came to the hut; not to attempt to conceal themselves, but offer them food to eat and water to drink. "If they come to the house and find you away, they will take your stores and burn your roof, suspecting that you are afraid to meet them openly; but they will not harm you if you meet them with open hand and fearless brow: if they eat of your bread, they will not harm you; me they would kill by a cruel death—the war-knife is in their heart against the daughter of the *brave*."

The boys thought Indiana's advice good, and they felt no fear for themselves, only for Catharine, whom they counselled to remain in the shanty with Wolfe.

The Indians seemed intent only on the sport which they had come to enjoy, seeming in high glee, and as far as they could see quite peaceably disposed; every night they returned to the camp on the north side, and the boys could see their fires gleaming among the trees on the opposite shore, and now and then in the stillness of the evening their wild shouts of revelry would come faintly to their ears, borne by the breeze over the waters of the lake.

The allusion that Indiana had made to her own history, though conveyed in broken and hardly intelligible language, had awakened feelings of deep interest for her in the breasts of her faithful friends. Many months after this she related to her wondering auditors the fearful story of the massacre of her kindred, and which I may as well relate, as I have raised the curiosity of my youthful readers, though to do so I must render it in my own language, as the broken half-formed sentences in which its facts were conveyed to the ears of my Canadian Crusoes would be unintelligible to my young friends.[1]

There had been for some time a jealous feeling existing between the chiefs of two principal tribes of the Ojebwas and the Mohawks, which like a smothered fire had burnt in the heart of each, without having burst into a decided blaze—for each strove to compass his ends and obtain the advantage over the other by covert means. The tribe of the Mohawks of which I now speak, claimed the southern shores of the Rice Lake for their hunting grounds, and certain islands and parts of the lake for fishing, while that of the Ojebwas considered themselves masters of the northern shores and certain rights of water beside. Possibly it was about these rights that the quarrel originated, but if so, it was not openly avowed between the "Black Snake," (that was the totem borne by the Mohawk chief,) and the "Bald Eagle" (the totem of the Ojebwa).

These chiefs had each a son, and the Bald Eagle had also a daughter of great and rare beauty, called by her people, "The Beam of the Morning;" she was the admiration of Mohawks as well as Ojebwas, and many of the young men of both the tribes had sought her hand, but hitherto in vain. Among her numerous suitors, the son of the Black Snake seemed to be the most enamoured of her beauty; and it was probably with some intention of winning the favour of the young Ojebwa squaw for his son, that the Black Snake accepted the formal invitation of the Bald Eagle to come to his hunting grounds during the rice harvest, and shoot deer and ducks on the lake, and to ratify a truce which had been for some time set on foot between them; but while outwardly professing friendship and a desire for peace, inwardly the fire of hatred burned fiercely in the breast of the Black Snake against the Ojebwa

---

[1] The facts of this narrative were gathered from the lips of the eldest son of a Rice Lake chief. I have preferred giving it in the present form, rather than as the story of the Indian girl. Simple as it is, it is matter of history.

chief and his only son, a young man of great promise, renowned among his tribe as a great hunter and warrior, but who had once offended the Mohawk chief by declining a matrimonial alliance with one of the daughters of a chief of inferior rank, who was closely connected to him by marriage. This affront rankled in the heart of the Black Snake, though outwardly he affected to have forgiven and forgotten the slight that had been put upon his relative.

The hunting had been carried on for some days very amicably, when one day the Bald Eagle was requested, with all due attention to Indian etiquette, to go to the wigwam of the Black Snake. On entering the lodge, he perceived the Mohawk strangely disordered; he rose from his mat, on which he had been sleeping, with a countenance fearfully distorted, his eyes glaring hideously, his whole frame convulsed, and writhing as in fearful bodily anguish, and casting himself upon the ground, he rolled and grovelled on the earth, uttering frightful yells and groans.

The Bald Eagle was moved at the distressing state in which he found his guest, and asked the cause of his disorder, but this the other refused to tell. After some hours the fit appeared to subside, but the chief remained moody and silent. The following day the same scene was repeated, and on the third, when the fit seemed to have increased in bodily agony, with great apparent reluctance, wrung seemingly from him by the importunity of his host, he consented to reveal the cause, which was, that the Bad Spirit had told him that these bodily tortures could not cease till the only son of his friend, the Ojebwa chief, had been sacrificed to appease his anger—neither could peace long continue between the two nations until this deed had been done; and not only must the chief's son be slain, but he must be pierced by his own father's hand, and his flesh served up at a feast at which the father must preside. The Black Snake affected the utmost horror and aversion at so bloody and unnatural a deed being committed to save his life and the happiness of his tribe, but the peace was to be ratified for ever if the sacrifice were made,—if not, war to the knife was to be ever between the Mohawks and Ojebwas.

The Bald Eagle seeing that his treacherous guest would make this an occasion of renewing a deadly warfare, for which possibly he was not at the time well prepared, assumed a stoical calmness, and replied,

"Be it so; great is the power of the Bad Spirit to cause evil to the tribes of the chiefs that rebel against his will. My son shall be sacrificed by my hand, that the evil one may be appeased, and that the Black Snake's body may have ease, and his people rest beside the fires of their lodges in peace."

"The Bald Eagle has spoken like a chief with a large heart," was the specious response of the wily Mohawk; "moreover, the Good Spirit also appeared, and said, 'Let the Black Snake's son and the Bald Eagle's daughter become man and wife, that peace may be found to dwell among the lodges, and the war-hatchet be buried for ever.' "

"The Beam of the Morning shall become the wife of the Young Pine," was the courteous answer; but stern revenge lay deep hidden beneath the unmoved brow and passionless lip.

The fatal day arrived; the Bald Eagle, with unflinching hand and eye that dropped no human tear of sorrow for the son of his love, plunged the weapon into his heart with Spartan-like firmness. The fearful feast of human flesh was prepared, and that old chief, pale but unmoved, presided over the ceremonies. The war-dance was danced round the sacrifice, and all went off well, as if no such fearful rite had been enacted: but a fearful retribution was at hand. The Young Pine sought the tent of the Bald Eagle's daughter that evening, and was received with all due deference, as a son of so great a chief as the Black Snake merited; he was regarded now as a successful suitor, and intoxicated with the beauty of the Beam of the Morning, pressed her to allow the marriage to take place in a few days. The bride consented, and a day was named for the wedding feast to be celebrated, and that due honour might be given to so great an event, invitations were sent out to the principal families of the Mohawk tribe, and these amounted to several hundreds of souls, while the young Ojebwa hunters were despatched up the river and to different parts of the country, avowedly to collect venison, beaver, and other delicacies to regale their guests, but in reality to summon by means of trusty scouts a large war party from the small lakes, to be in readiness to take part in the deadly revenge that was preparing for their enemies.

Meantime the squaws pitched the nuptial tent, and prepared the bridal ornaments. A large wigwam capable of containing all the expected guests was then constructed, adorned with the thick branches of evergreens so artfully contrived as to be capable of concealing the armed Ojebwas and their allies, who in due time were introduced beneath this leafy screen, armed with the murderous tomahawk and scalping-knife with which to spring upon their defenceless and unsuspecting guests. According to the etiquette always observed upon such occasions, all deadly weapons were left outside the tent. The bridegroom had been conducted with songs and dancing to the tent of the bride. The guests, to the number of several hundred naked and painted warriors, were assembled. The feast was declared to be ready; a great iron pot or kettle occupied the centre of the tent. According to the custom of the Indians, the father of the bridegroom was invited to lift the most important dish from the pot, whilst the warriors commenced their war-dance around him. This dish was usually a bear's head, which was fastened to a string left for the purpose of raising it from the pot.

"Let the Black Snake, the great chief of the Mohawks, draw up the head and set it on the table, that his people may eat and make merry, and that his wise heart may be glad;" were the scornful words of the Bald Eagle.

A yell of horror burst from the lips of the horror-stricken father, as he lifted to view the fresh and gory head of his only son, the *happy* bridegroom of the lovely daughter of the Ojebwa chief.

"Ha!" shouted the Bald Eagle, "is the great chief of the Mohawks a squaw, that his blood grows white and his heart trembles at the sight of his son, the bridegroom of the Beam of the Morning? The Bald Eagle gave neither sigh nor groan when he plunged the knife into the heart of his child. Come, brother, take the knife; taste the flesh and drink the blood of thy son: the Bald Eagle shrank not when you bade him partake of the feast that was prepared from his young warrior's body."

The wretched father dashed himself upon the earth, while his cries and howlings rent the air; those cries were answered by the war-whoop of the ambushed Ojebwas, as they sprang to their feet, and with deafening yells attacked the guests, who, panic-stricken, naked and defenceless, fell an easy prey to their infuriated enemies. Not one living foe escaped to tell the tale of that fearful marriage feast. A second Judith had the Indian girl proved. It was her plighted hand that had severed the head of her unsuspecting bridegroom to complete the fearful vengeance that had been devised in return for the merciless and horrible murder of her brother.

Nor was the sacrifice yet finished, for with fearful cries the Indians seized upon the canoes of their enemies, and with the utmost speed, urged by unsatisfied revenge, hurried down the lake to an island where the women and children and such of the aged or young men as were not

included among the wedding guests, were encamped in
unsuspecting security. Panic-stricken, the Mohawks
offered no resistance, but fell like sheep appointed for the
slaughter: the Ojebwas slew there the grey-head with the
infant of days. But while the youths and old men tamely
yielded to their enemies, there was one who, her spirit
roused to fury by the murder of her father, armed herself
with the war club and knife, and boldly withstood the
successful warriors. At the door of the tent of the
slaughtered chief the Amazon defended her children:
while the war lightning kindled in her dark eye, she
called aloud in scornful tones to her people to hide
themselves in the tents of their women, who alone were
braves, and would fight their battles. Fiercely she taunted
the men, but they shrank from the unequal contest, and
she alone was found to deal the death-blow upon the foe,
till overpowered with numbers, and pierced with frightful
wounds, she fell singing her own death-song and raising
the wail for the dead who lay around her. Night closed in,
but the work of blood still continued, till not a victim was
found, and again they went forth on their exterminating
work. Lower down they found another encampment, and
there also they slew all the inhabitants of the lodges; they
then returned back to the island, to gather together their
dead and collect the spoils of the tents. They were
weary with the fatigue of the slaughter of that fearful day;
they were tired of blood-shedding; the retribution had
satisfied even their love of blood: and when they found, on
returning to the spot where the heroine had stood at bay,
one young solitary female sitting beside the corpse of that
dauntless woman, her mother, they led her away, and did
all that their savage nature could suggest to soften her
anguish and dry her tears. They brought her to the tents
of their women, and clothed and fed her, and bade her
be comforted; but her young heart burned within her, and
she refused consolation. She could not forget the wrongs

of her people: she was the only living creature left of the
Mohawks on that island. The young girl was Indiana, the
same whom Hector Maxwell had found, wounded and
bound, and ready to perish with hunger and thirst on
Bare-hill.

Brooding with revenge in her heart, the young girl told
them that she had stolen unperceived into the tent of the
Bald Eagle, and aimed a knife at his throat, but the fatal
blow was arrested by one of the young men, who had
watched her enter the old chief's tent. A council was
called, and she was taken to Bare-hill, bound, and left in
the sad state already described.

It was with feelings of horror and terror that the
Christian children listened to this fearful tale, and Indiana
read in their averted eyes and pale faces the feelings with
which the recital of the tale of blood had inspired them.
And then it was as they sat beneath the shade of the
trees, in the soft misty light of an Indian summer moon,
that Catharine, with simple earnestness, taught her young
disciple those heavenly lessons of mercy and forgiveness
which her Redeemer had set forth by his life, his doctrines,
and his death.

And she told her, that if she would see that Saviour's
face in Heaven, and dwell with him in joy and peace for
ever, she must learn to pray for those dreadful men who
had made her fatherless and motherless, and her home a
desolation; that the fire of revenge must be quenched
within her heart, and the spirit of love alone find place
within it, or she could not become the child of God and
an inheritor of the kingdom of Heaven. How hard were
these conditions to the young heathen,—how contrary to
her nature, to all that she had been taught in the tents of
her fathers, where revenge was virtue, and to take the
scalp of an enemy a glorious thing!

Yet when she contrasted the gentle, kind, and dovelike
characters of her Christian friends, with the fierce bloody

people of her tribe and of her Ojebwa enemies, she could not but own they were more worthy of love and admiration: had they not found her a poor miserable trembling captive, unbound her, fed and cherished her, pouring the balm of consolation into her wounded heart, and leading her in bands of tenderest love to forsake those wild and fearful passions that warred in her soul, and bringing her to the feet of the Saviour, to become his meek and holy child, a lamb of his "extended fold?" [1]

[1] The Indian who related this narrative to me was a son of a Rice Lake chief, Mosang Poudash by name, who vouched for its truth as an historic fact remembered by his father, whose grandsire had been one of the actors in the massacre. Mosang Poudash promised to write down the legend, and did so in part, but made such confusion between his imperfect English and Indian language, that the MS. was unavailable for copying.

CHAPTER 9

"The horn of the hunter is heard on the hill."

Irish Song.

WHILE the Indians were actively pursuing their sports on the lake, shooting wild fowl, and hunting and fishing by torch-light, so exciting was the amusement of watching them, that the two lads, Hector and Louis, quite forgot all sense of danger, in the enjoyment of lying or sitting on the brow of the mount near the great ravine, and looking at their proceedings. Once or twice the lads were near betraying themselves to the Indians, by raising a shout of delight, at some skilful manœuvre that excited their unqualified admiration and applause.

At night, when the canoes had all retired to the camp on the north shore, and all fear of detection had ceased for the time, they lighted up their shanty fire, and cooked a good supper, and also prepared sufficiency of food for the following day. The Indians remained for a fortnight; at the end of that time Indiana, who was a watchful spy on their movements, told Hector and Louis that the camp was broken up, and that the Indians had gone up the river, and would not return again for some weeks. The departure of the Indians was a matter of great rejoicing to Catharine, whose dread of these savages had greatly increased since she had been made acquainted with the fearful deeds which Indiana had described; and what reliance could she feel in people who regarded deeds of blood and vengeance as acts of virtuous heroism?

Once, and only once during their stay, the Indians had passed within a short distance of their dwelling; but they were in full chase of a bear, which had been seen crossing the deep ravine near Mount Ararat, and they had been too intent upon their game to notice the shanty, or had taken it for the shelter of some trapper if it had been seen, for they never turned out of their path, and Catharine, who was alone at the time, drawing water from the spring, was so completely concealed by the high bank above her, that she had quite escaped their notice. Fortunately, Indiana gave the two boys a signal to conceal themselves when she saw them enter the ravine; and effectually hidden among the thick grey mossy trunks of the cedars at the lake shore, they remained secure from molestation, while the Indian girl dropped noiselessly down among the tangled thicket of wild vines and brushwood, which she drew cautiously over her, and closed her eyes, lest, as she naively remarked, their glitter should be seen and betray her to her enemies.

It was a moment of intense anxiety to our poor wanderers, whose terrors were more excited on behalf of the young Mohawk than for themselves, and they congratulated her on her escape with affectionate warmth.

"Are my white brothers afraid to die?" was the young squaw's half-scornful reply. "Indiana is the daughter of a brave; she fears not to die!"

The latter end of September, and the first week in October, had been stormy and even cold. The rainy season, however, was now over; the nights were often illuminated by the Aurora borealis, which might be seen forming an arch of soft and lovely brightness over the lake, to the north and north-eastern portions of the horizon, or shooting upwards, in ever-varying shafts of greenish light, now hiding, now revealing, the stars, which shone with softened radiance through the silvery veil that dimmed their beauty. Sometimes for many nights together the same appearance might be seen, and was usually the forerunner of frosty weather, though occasionally it was the precursor of cold winds, and heavy rains.

The Indian girl regarded it with superstitious feelings, but whether as an omen for good or ill, she would not tell. On all matters connected with her religious notions she was shy and reserved, though occasionally she unconsciously revealed them. Thus the warnings of death or misfortunes were revealed to her by certain ominous sounds in the woods, the appearance of strange birds or animals, or the moanings of others. The screeching of the owl, the bleating of the doe, or barking of the fox, were evil auguries, while the flight of the eagle and the croaking of the raven were omens of good. She put faith in dreams, and would foretel good or evil fortune from them; she could read the morning and evening clouds, and knew from various appearances of the sky, or the coming or departing of certain birds or insects, changes in the atmosphere. Her ear was quick in distinguishing the changes in the voices of the birds or animals; she knew the times of their coming and going, and her eye was quick to see as her ear to detect sounds. Her voice was soft, and low, and plaintive, and she delighted in imitating the little ballads or hymns that Catharine sung; though she knew nothing of their meaning, she would catch the tunes, and sing the song with Catharine, touching the hearts of her delighted auditors by the melody and pathos of her voice.

The season called Indian summer had now arrived: the air was soft and mild, almost oppressively warm; the sun looked red as though seen through the smoke clouds of a populous city. A soft blue haze hung on the bosom of the glassy lake, which reflected on its waveless surface every passing shadow, and the gorgeous tints of its changing woods on shore and island. Sometimes the stillness of the air was relieved by a soft sighing wind, which rustled the dying foliage as it swept by.

The Indian summer is the harvest of the Indian tribes. It is during this season that they hunt and shoot the wild fowl that come in their annual flights to visit the waters of the American lakes and rivers; it is then that they gather in their rice, and prepare their winter stores of meat, and fish, and furs. The Indian girl knew the season they would resort to certain hunting grounds. They were constant, and altered not their customs; as it was with their fathers, so it was with them.

Louis had heard so much of the Otonabee river from Indiana, that he was impatient to go and explore the entrance, and the shores of the lake on that side, which hitherto they had not ventured to do for fear of being surprised by the Indians. "Some fine day," said Louis, "we will go out in the canoe, explore the distant islands, and go up the river a little way."

Hector advised visiting all the islands by turns, beginning at the little islet which looks in the distance like a boat in full sail; it is level with the water, and has only three or four trees upon it. The name they had given to it was "Ship Island." The Indians have some name for it which I have forgotten; but it means, I have been told, "Witch Island." Hector's plan met with general approbation, and they resolved to take provisions with them for several days, and visit the islands and go up the river, passing the night under the shelter of the thick trees on the shore wherever they found a pleasant halting-place.

The weather was mild and warm, the lake was as clear and calm as a mirror, and in joyous mood our little party embarked and paddled up the lake, first to Ship Island, but this did not detain them many minutes; they then went to Grape Island, which they so named from the abundance of wild vines, now rich with purple clusters of the ripe grapes,—tart, but still not to be despised by our young adventurers; and they brought away a large birch basket heaped up with the fruit. "Ah, if we had but a good cake of maple sugar, now, to preserve our grapes with, and make such grape jelly as my mother makes!" said Louis.

"If we find out a sugar-bush we will manage to make

plenty of sugar," said Catharine; "there are maples not two hundred yards from the shanty, near the side of the steep bank to the east. You remember the pleasant spot which we named the Happy Valley,[1] where the bright creek runs, dancing along so merrily, below the pine-ridge?"

"Oh, yes, the same that winds along near the foot of Bare-hill, where the water-cresses grow."

"Yes, where I gathered the milk-weed the other day."

"What a beautiful pasture-field that will make, when it is cleared!" said Hector, thoughtfully.

"Hector is always planning about fields, and clearing great farms," said Louis, laughing. "We shall see Hec a great man one of these days; I think he has in his own mind brushed, and burned, and logged up all the fine flats and table-land on the plains before now, ay, and cropped it all with wheat, and peas, and Indian corn."

"We will have a clearing and a nice field of corn next year, if we live," replied Hector; "that corn that we found in the canoe will be a treasure."

"Yes, and the corn-cob you got on Bare-hill," said Catharine. "How lucky we have been! We shall be so happy whe   ur little field of corn flourishing round the s   as a good thing, Hec, that you went to the India   t day, though both Louis and I were very miser   ou were absent; but you see, God must have   , that the life of this poor girl might be saved, t   rt to us. Everything has prospered well with u   ame to us. Perhaps it is because we try to mak   of her, and so God blesses all our endeavour

"We are   Hector, "that there is joy with the angels of C   sinner that repenteth; doubtless, it is a joyful   ie heathen that knew not the name of God ar   orify his holy name."

[1] A lovely   t of Mount Ararat, now belonging to a worthy an   ily of the name of Brown. I wish Hector could see i   ultivated fertile farm.

Indiana, while exploring, had captured a porcupine; she declared that she should have plenty of quills for edging baskets and mocassins; beside, she said, the meat was white and good to eat. Hector looked with a suspicious eye upon the little animal, doubting the propriety of eating its flesh, though he had learned to eat musk rats, and consider them good meat, baked in Louis's Indian oven, or roasted on a forked stick, before the fire. The Indian porcupine is a small animal, not a very great deal larger than the common British hedgehog; the quills, however, are longer and stronger, and varied with alternate clouded marks of pure white and dark brownish grey; they are minutely barbed, so that if one enters the flesh it is with difficulty extracted, but will work through of itself in an opposite direction, and can then be easily pulled out. Dogs and cattle often suffer great inconvenience from getting their muzzles filled with the quills of the porcupine, the former when worrying the poor little animal, and the latter by accidentally meeting a dead one among the herbage; great inflammation will sometimes attend the extraction. Indians often lose valuable hounds from this cause. Beside porcupines, Indiana told her companions, there were some fine butter-nut-trees (*Juglans cinerea*) on the island, and they could collect a bagful of nuts in a very short time. This was good news, for the butter-nut is sweet and pleasant, almost equal to the walnut, of which it is a species.

The day was passed pleasantly enough in collecting nuts and grapes; but as this island did not afford any good cleared spot for passing the night, and, moreover, was tenanted by black snakes, several of which made their appearance among the stones near the edge of the water, they agreed by common council to go to Long Island, where Indiana said there was an old log-house, the walls of which were still standing, and where there was dry moss in plenty, which would make them a comfortable bed for the night. This old log-house she said had been built, she heard the Indians say, by a French Canadian trapper, who used to visit the lake some years ago; he was on friendly terms with the chiefs, who allowed him many privileges, and he bought their furs, and took them down the lake, through the river Trent, to some station-house on the great lake. They found they should have time enough to land and deposit their nuts and grapes and paddle to Long Island before sunset. Upon the western part of this fine island they had several times landed and passed some hours, exploring its shores; but Indiana told them, to reach the old log-house they must enter the low swampy bay to the east, at an opening which she called Indian Cove. To do this required some skill in the management of the canoe, which was rather over-loaded for so light a vessel; and the trees grew so close and thick that they had some difficulty in pushing their way through them without injuring its frail sides. These trees or bushes were chiefly black alder (*Alnus incuna*), high-bush cranberries (*Viburnum opulus*), dogwood, willows, and, as they proceeded further, and there was ground of a more solid nature, cedar, poplar, swamp oak, and soft maple, with silver birch and wild cherries. Long strings of silvery-grey tree-moss hung dangling over their heads, the bark and roots of the birch and cedars were covered with a luxuriant growth of green moss, but there was a dampness and closeness in this place that made it far from wholesome, and the little band of voyagers were not very sorry when the water became too shallow to admit of the canoe making its way through the swampy channel, and they landed on the banks of a small circular pond, as round as a ring, and nearly surrounded by tall trees, hoary with moss and lichens; large water-lilies floated on the surface of this miniature lake, and the brilliant red berries of the high-bush cranberry, and the purple clusters of grapes, festooned the trees.

"A famous breeding place this must be for ducks," observed Louis.

"And for flowers," said Catharine, "and for grapes and cranberries. There is always some beauty or some usefulness to be found, however lonely the spot."

"A fine place for musk-rats, and minks, and fishes," said Hector, looking round. "The old trapper knew what he was about when he made his lodge near this pond. And there, sure enough, is the log-hut, and not so bad a one either," and scrambling up the bank he entered the deserted little tenement, well pleased to find it in tolerable repair. There were the ashes on the stone hearth, just as it had been left years back by the old trapper; some rough hewn shelves, a rude bedstead of cedar poles still occupied a corner of the little dwelling; heaps of old dry moss and grass lay upon the ground; and the little squaw pointed with one of her silent laughs to a collection of broken egg-shells, where some wild duck had sat and hatched her downy brood among the soft materials which she had found and appropriated to her own purpose. The only things pertaining to the former possessor of the log-hut were an old, rusty, battered tin pannikin, now, alas! unfit for holding water; a bit of a broken earthen whisky jar; a rusty nail, which Louis pounced upon, and pocketed, or rather pouched,—for he had substituted a fine pouch of deer-skin for his worn-out pocket; and a fishing-line of good stout cord, which was wound on a splinter of red cedar, and carefully stuck between one of the rafters and the roof of the shanty. A rusty but efficient hook was attached to the line, and Louis, who was the finder, was quite overjoyed at his good fortune in making so valuable an addition to his fishing-tackle. Hector got only an odd worn-out mocassin, which he chucked into the little pond in disdain; while Catharine declared she would keep the old tin pot as a relic, and carefully deposited it in the canoe.

As they made their way into the interior of the island, they found that there were a great many fine sugar maples which had been tapped by some one, as the boys thought, by the old trapper; but Indiana, on examining the incisions in the trees, and the remnants of birch-bark vessels that lay mouldering on the earth below them, declared them to have been the work of her own people; and long and sadly did the young girl look upon these simple memorials of a race of whom she was the last living remnant. The young girl stood there in melancholy mood, a solitary, isolated being, with no kindred tie upon the earth to make life dear to her; a stranger in the land of her fathers, associating with those whose ways were not her ways, nor their thoughts her thoughts; whose language was scarcely known to her, whose God was not the God of her fathers. Yet the dark eyes of the Indian girl were not dimmed with tears as she thought of these things; she had learned of her people to suffer, and be still.

Silent and patient she stood, with her melancholy gaze bent on the earth, when she felt the gentle hand of Catharine laid upon her arm, and then kindly and lovingly passed round her neck, as she whispered,—

"Indiana, I will be to you as a sister, and will love you and cherish you, because you are an orphan girl, and alone in the world; but God loves you, and will make you happy. He is a Father to the fatherless, and the Friend of the destitute, and to them that have no helper."

The words of kindness and love need no interpretation; no book-learning is necessary to make them understood. The young, the old, the deaf, the dumb, the blind, can read this universal language; its very silence is often more eloquent than words—the gentle pressure of the hand, the half-echoed sigh, the look of sympathy will penetrate to the very heart, and unlock its hidden stores of human tenderness and love. The rock is smitten and the waters gush forth, a bright and living stream, to refresh and fertilize the thirsty soul.

The heart of the poor mourner was touched; she bowed down her head upon the hand that held her so kindly in its sisterly grasp, and wept soft sweet human tears full of grateful love, while she whispered, in her own low plaintive voice, "My white sister, I kiss you in my heart; I will love the God of my white brothers, and be his child."

The two friends now busied themselves in preparing the evening meal: they found Louis and Hector had lighted up a charming blaze on the desolate hearth. A few branches of cedar twisted together by Catharine, made a serviceable broom, with which she swept the floor, giving to the deserted dwelling a neat and comfortable aspect; some big stones were quickly rolled in, and made to answer for seats in the chimney corner. The new-found fishing-line was soon put into requisition by Louis, and with very little delay a fine dish of black bass, broiled on the coals, was added to their store of dried venison and roasted bread-roots, which they found in abundance on a low spot on the island. Grapes and butternuts which Hector cracked with stones by way of nut-crackers, finished their sylvan meal. The boys stretched themselves to sleep on the ground, with their feet, Indian fashion, to the fire; while the two girls occupied the mossy couch which they had newly spread with fragrant cedar and hemlock boughs.

The next island that claimed their attention was Sugar-Maple Island,[1] a fine, thickly-wooded island, rising with steep rocky banks from the water. A beautiful object, but too densely wooded to admit of our party penetrating beyond a few yards of its shores.

[1] Sugar Island, a charming object from the picturesque cottage of Alfred Hayward, Esq.

The next island they named the Beaver,[1] from its resemblance in shape to that animal. A fine, high, oval island beyond this they named Black Island,[2] from its dark evergreens; the next was that which seemed most to excite the interest of their Indian guide, although but a small stony island, scantily clothed with trees, lower down the lake. This place she called Spooke Island,[3] which means in the Indian tongue, a place for the dead; it is sometimes called Spirit Island, and here, in times past, used the Indian people to bury their dead. The island is now often the resort of parties of pleasure, who, from its being grassy and open, find it more available than those which are densely wooded. The young Mohawk regarded it with feelings of superstitious awe, and would not suffer Hector to land the canoe on its rocky shores.

"It is a place of spirits," she said; "the ghosts of my fathers will be angry if we go there." Even her young companions felt that they were upon sacred ground, and gazed with silent reverence upon the burial isle.

Strongly imbued with a love of the marvellous, which they had derived from their Highland origin, Indiana's respect for the spirits of her ancestors was regarded as most natural, and in silence, as if fearing to disturb the

[1] The Beaver, commonly called Sheep Island, from some person having pastured a few sheep upon it some few years ago. I have taken the liberty of preserving the name, to which it bears an obvious resemblance; the nose of the Beaver lies towards the west, the tail to the east. This island is nearly opposite to Gore's Landing, and forms a pleasing object from the windows and verandah of Claverton, the house of my esteemed friend, William Falkner, Esq., the Patriarch of the Plains, as he has often been termed; one of the only residents on the Rice Lake plains for many years; one of the few gentlemen who had taste enough to be charmed with this lovely tract of country, and to appreciate its agricultural resources, which, of late, have been so fully developed.

[2] Black Island, the sixth from the head of the lake; an oval island, remarkable for its evergreens.

[3] Appendix H.

solemnity of the spot, they resumed their paddles, and after awhile reached the mouth of the river Otonabee, which was divided into two separate channels by a long, low point of swampy land covered with stunted, mossy bushes and trees, rushes, drift-wood, and aquatic plants. Indiana told them this river flowed from the north, and that it was many days' journey up to the lakes; to illustrate its course, she drew with her paddle a long line with sundry curves and broader spaces, some longer, some smaller, with bays and inlets, which she gave them to understand were the chain of lakes that she spoke of. There were beautiful hunting grounds on the borders of these lakes, and many fine water-falls and rocky islands; she had been taken up to these waters during the time of her captivity. The Ojebwas, she said, were a branch of the great Chippewa nation, who owned much land and great waters thereabouts.

Compared with the creeks and streams that they had seen hitherto, the Otonabee appeared a majestic river, d an object of great admiration and curiosity, for it seen to them as if it were the high road leading up to unknown far-off land—a land of dark, mysteriou impenetrable forests,—flowing on, flowing on, in lonel, majesty, reflecting on its tranquil bosom the blue sky, the dark pines, and grey cedars,—the pure ivory water-lily, and every passing shadow of bird or leaf that flitted across its surface—so quiet was the onward flow of its waters.

A few brilliant leaves yet lingered on the soft maples and crimson-tinted oaks, but the glory of the forest had departed; the silent fall of many a sear and yellow leaf told of the death of summer and of winter's coming reign. Yet the air was wrapt in a deceitful stillness; no breath of wind moved the trees or dimpled the water. Bright wreaths of scarlet berries and wild grapes hung in festoons among the faded foliage. The silence of the forest was unbroken, save by the quick tapping of the little midland wood-pecker, or

the shrill scream of the blue jay; the whirring sound of the
large white and grey duck, (called by the frequenters of
these lonely waters the whistle-wing,) as its wings swept the
waters in its flight; or the light dripping of the paddle;—so
still, so quiet was the scene.

As the day was now far advanced, the Indian girl
advised them either to encamp for the night on the river
bank, or to use all speed in returning. She seemed to view
the aspect of the heavens with some anxiety. Vast volumes
of light copper-tinted clouds were rising, the sun seen
through its hazy veil looked red and dim, and a hot sultry
air unrelieved by a breath of refreshing wind oppressed
our young voyagers; and though the same coppery clouds
and red sun had been seen for several successive days, a
sort of instinctive feeling prompted the desire in all to
return; and after a few minutes' rest and refreshment,
they turned their little bark towards the lake; and it was
well that they did so: by the time they had reached the
middle of the lake, the stillness of the air was rapidly
changing. The rose-tinted clouds that had lain so long
piled upon each other in mountainous ridges, began to
move upwards, at first slowly, then with rapidly
accelerated motion. There was a hollow moaning in the
pine tops, and by fits a gusty breeze swept the surface of
the water, raising it into rough, short, white-crested ridges.

These signs were pointed out by Indiana as the
harbinger of a rising hurricane; and now a swift spark of
light like a falling star glanced on the water, as if there to
quench its fiery light. Again the Indian girl raised her dark
hand and pointed to the rolling storm-clouds, to the
crested waters and the moving pine tops; then to the head
of the Beaver Island—it was the one nearest to them. With
an arm of energy she wielded the paddle, with an eye of
fire she directed the course of their little vessel, for well
she knew their danger and the need for straining every
nerve to reach the nearest point of land. Low muttering

peals of thunder were now heard, the wind was rising with electric speed. Away flew the light bark, with the swiftness of a bird, over the water; the tempest was above, around and beneath. The hollow crash of the forest trees as they bowed to the earth could be heard, sullenly sounding from shore to shore. And now the Indian girl, flinging back her black streaming hair from her brow, knelt at the head of the canoe, and with renewed vigour plied the paddle. The waters, lashed into a state of turbulence by the violence of the storm, lifted the canoe up and down, but no word was spoken—they each felt the greatness of the peril, but they also knew that they were in the hands of Him who can say to the tempest-tossed waves, "Peace, be still," and they obey Him.

Every effort was made to gain the nearest island; to reach the mainland was impossible, for the rain poured down a blinding deluge; it was with difficulty the little craft was kept afloat, by baling out the water; to do this, Louis was fain to use his cap, and Catharine assisted with the old tin-pot which she had fortunately brought from the trapper's shanty.

The tempest was at its height when they reached the nearest point of the Beaver, and joyful was the grating sound of the canoe as it was vigorously pushed up on the shingly beach, beneath the friendly shelter of the overhanging trees, where, perfectly exhausted by the exertions they had made, dripping with rain and overpowered by the terrors of the storm, they threw themselves on the ground, and in safety watched its progress—thankful for an escape from such imminent peril.

Thus ended the Indian summer—so deceitful in its calmness and its beauty. The next day saw the ground white with snow, and hardened into stone by a premature frost. Our poor voyagers were not long in quitting the shelter of the Beaver Island, and betaking them once more to their ark of refuge—the log-house on Mount Ararat.

The winter, that year, set in with unusual severity some weeks sooner than usual, so that from the beginning of November to the middle of April the snow never entirely left the ground. The lake was soon covered with ice, and by the month of December it was one compact solid sheet from shore to shore.

CHAPTER 10

"Scared by the red and noisy light."—

COLERIDGE.

HECTOR and Louis had now little employment, excepting chopping fire-wood, which was no very arduous task for two stout healthy lads, used from childhood to handling the axe. Trapping, and hunting, and snaring hares, were occupations which they pursued more for the excitement and exercise than from hunger, as they had laid by abundance of dried venison, fish, and birds, besides a plentiful store of rice. They now visited those trees that they had marked in the summer, where they had noticed the bees hiving, and cut them down; in one they got more than a pailful of rich honey-comb, and others yielded some more, some less; this afforded them a delicious addition to their boiled rice, and dried acid fruits. They might have melted the wax, and burned candles of it; but this was a refinement of luxury that never once occurred to our young house-keepers: the dry pine knots that are found in the woods are the settlers' candles; but Catharine made some very good vinegar with the refuse of the honey and combs, by pouring water on it, and leaving it to ferment in a warm nook of the chimney, in one of the birch-bark vessels, and this was an excellent substitute for salt as a seasoning to the fresh meat and fish. Like the Indians, they were now reconciled to the want of this seasonable article.

Indiana seemed to enjoy the cold weather; the lake, though locked up to every one else, was open to her; with

the aid of the tomahawk she patiently made an opening in
the ice, and over this she built a little shelter of pine
boughs stuck into the ice. Armed with a sharp spear carved
out of hardened wood, she would lie upon the ice and
patiently await the rising of some large fish to the air-hole,
when dexterously plunging it into the unwary creature,
she dragged it to the surface. Many a noble fish did the
young squaw bring home, and cast at the feet of him whom
she had tacitly elected as her lord and master; to him she
offered the voluntary service of a faithful and devoted
servant—I might almost have said, slave.

During the middle of December there were some days
of such intense cold, that even our young Crusoes, hardy
as they were, preferred the blazing log-fire and warm ingle
nook, to the frozen lake and cutting north-west wind
which blew the loose snow in blinding drifts over its bleak,
unsheltered surface. Clad in the warm tunic and petticoat
of Indian blanket with fur-lined mocassins, Catharine and
her Indian friend felt little cold excepting to the face when
they went abroad, unless the wind was high, and then
experience taught them to keep at home. And these cold
gloomy days they employed in many useful works. Indiana
had succeeded in dyeing the quills of the porcupine that
she had captured on Grape Island; with these she worked
a pair of beautiful mocassins and an arrow case for Hector,
besides making a sheath for Louis's *couteau-de-chasse*, of
which the young hunter was very proud, bestowing great
praise on the workmanship.

Indiana appeared to be deeply engrossed with some
work that she was engaged in, but preserved a provoking
degree of mystery about it, to the no small annoyance of
Louis, who, among his other traits of character, was
remarkably inquisitive, wanting to know the why and
wherefore of everything he saw.

Indiana first prepared a frame of some tough wood, it
might be the inner bark of the oak or elm or hiccory; this

was pointed at either end, and wide in the middle—not very much unlike the form of some broad, flat fish; over this she wove an open network of narrow thongs of deer-hide, wetted to make it more pliable, and securely fastened to the frame: when dry, it became quite tight, and resembled a sort of coarse bamboo-work such as you see on cane-bottomed chairs and sofas.

"And now, Indiana, tell us what sort of fish you are going to catch in your ingenious little net," said Louis, who had watched her proceedings with great interest. The girl shook her head, and laughed till she showed all her white teeth, but quietly proceeded to commence a second frame like the first.

Louis put it on his head. No: it could not be meant to be worn there, that was plain. He turned it round and round. It must be intended for some kind of bird-trap: yes, that must be it; and he cast an inquiring glance at Indiana. She blushed, shook her head, and gave another of her silent laughs.

"Some game like battledore and shuttle-cock,"—and snatching up a light bass-wood chip, he began tossing the chip up and catching it on the netted frame. The little squaw was highly amused, but rapidly went on with her work. Louis was now almost angry at the perverse little savage persevering in keeping him in suspense. She would not tell him till the other was done: then there were to be a pair of these curious articles: and he was forced at last to sit quietly down to watch the proceeding of the work. It was night before the two were completed, and furnished with straps and loops. When the last stroke was put to them, the Indian girl knelt down at Hector's feet, and binding them on, pointed to them with a joyous laugh, and said, "Snow-shoe—for walk on snow—good!"

The boys had heard of snow-shoes, but had never seen them, and now seemed to understand little of the benefit to be derived from the use of them. The young Mohawk quickly transferred the snow-shoes to her own feet, and soon proved to them that the broad surface prevented those who wore them from sinking into the deep snow. After many trials Hector began to acknowledge the advantage of walking with the snow-shoes, especially on the frozen snow on the ice-covered lake. Indiana was well pleased with the approbation that her manufactures met with, and very soon manufactured for "Nee-chee," as they all now called Louis, a similar present. As to Catharine, she declared the snow-shoes made her ancles ache, and that she preferred the mocassins that her cousin Louis made for her.

During the long bright days of February they made several excursions on the lake, and likewise explored some of the high hills to the eastward. On this ridge there were few large trees; but it was thickly clothed with scrub oaks, slender poplars, and here and there fine pines, and picturesque free-growing oaks of considerable size and great age—patriarchs, they might be termed, among the forest growth.[1] Over this romantic range of hill and dale, free as the air they breathed, roamed many a gallant herd of deer, unmolested unless during certain seasons when the Indians came to hunt over these hills. Surprised at the different growth of the oaks on this side the plains, Hector could not help expressing his astonishment to Indiana, who told him that it was caused by the custom that her people had had from time immemorial of setting fire to the bushes in the early part of spring. This practice, she said, promoted the growth of the deer-grass, made good cover for the deer themselves, and effectually prevented the increase of the large timbers. This circumstance gives a singular aspect to this high ridge of hills when contrasted with the more wooded portions to the

[1] One of these hoary monarchs of the Oak-hills still stands at the head of the lawn at Oaklands, formerly the property of Mr. W. Falkner, now the residence of the Authoress.

westward. From the lake these eastern hills look verdant, and as if covered with tall green fern. In the month of October a rich rosy tint is cast upon the leaves of the scrub oaks by the autumnal frosts, and they present a glowing unvaried crimson of the most glorious hue, only variegated in spots by a dark feathery evergreen, or a patch of light waving poplars turned by the same wizard's wand to golden yellow.

There were many lovely spots,—lofty rounded hills, and deep shady dells, with extended table-land, and fine lake views; but on the whole our young folks preferred the oak openings and the beautiful wooded glens of the western side, where they had fixed their home.

There was one amusement that they used greatly to enjoy during the cold bright days and moonlight nights of midwinter. This was gliding down the frozen snow on the steep side of the dell near the spring, seated on small hand-sleighs, which carried them down with great velocity. Wrapped in their warm furs, with caps fastened closely over their ears, what cared they for the cold? Warm and glowing from head to foot, with cheeks brightened by the delightful exercise, they would remain for hours enjoying the amusement of the snow-slide; the bright frost gemming the ground with myriads of diamonds, sparkling in their hair, or whitening it till it rivalled the snow beneath their feet. Then, when tired out with the exercise, they returned to the shanty, stirred up a blazing fire, till the smoked rafters glowed in the red light; spread their simple fare of stewed rice sweetened with honey, or maybe a savoury soup of hare or other game; and then, when warmed and fed, they kneeled together, side by side, and offered up a prayer of gratitude to their Maker, and besought his care over them during the dark and silent hours of night.

Had these young people been idle in their habits and desponding in their tempers, they must have perished with cold and hunger, instead of enjoying many necessaries and even some little luxuries in their lonely forest home. Fortunately they had been brought up in the early practice of every sort of usefulness, to endure every privation with cheerful fortitude; not, indeed, quietly to sit down and wait for better times, but vigorously to create those better times by every possible exertion that could be brought into action to assist and ameliorate their condition.

To be up and doing, is the maxim of a Canadian; and it is this that nerves his arm to do and bear. The Canadian settler, following in the steps of the old Americans, learns to supply all his wants by the exercise of his own energy. He brings up his family to rely upon their own resources, instead of depending upon his neighbours.

The children of the modern emigrant, though enjoying a higher degree of civilization and intelligence, arising from a liberal education, might not have fared so well under similar circumstances as did our Canadian Crusoes, because, unused to battle with the hardships incidental to a life of such privation as they had known, they could not have brought so much experience, or courage, or ingenuity to their aid. It requires courage to yield to circumstances, as well as to overcome them.

Many little useful additions to the interior of their dwelling were made by Hector and Louis during the long winter. They made a smoother and better table than the first rough one that they put together. They also made a rough partition of split cedars, to form a distinct and separate sleeping-room for the two girls; but as this division greatly circumscribed their sitting and cooking apartment, they resolved, as soon as the spring came, to cut and draw in logs for putting up a better and larger room to be used as a summer parlour. Indiana and Louis made a complete set of wooden trenchers out of butternut, a fine hard wood of excellent grain, and less liable to warp or crack than many others.

Louis's skill as a carpenter was much greater than that of his cousin. He not only possessed more judgment and was more handy, but he had a certain taste and neatness in finishing his work, however rough his materials and rude his tools. He inherited some of that skill in mechanism for which the French have always been remarked. With his knife and a nail he would carve a plum-stone into a miniature basket, with handle across it, all delicately wrought with flowers and checker-work. The shell of a butter-nut would be transformed into a boat, with thwarts, and seats, and rudder; with sails of bass-wood or birch-bark. Combs he could cut out of wood or bone, so that Catharine could dress her hair, or confine it in braids or bands at will. This was a source of great comfort to her; and Louis was always pleased when he could in any way contribute to his cousin's happiness. These little arts Louis had been taught by his father. Indeed, the great distance that their little settlement was from any town or village had necessarily forced their families to depend on their own ingenuity and invention to supply many of their wants. Once or twice a-year they saw a trading fur-merchant, as I before observed; and those were glorious days for Hector and Louis, who were always on the alert to render the strangers any service in their power, as by that means they sometimes received little gifts from them, and gleaned up valuable information as to their craft as hunters and trappers. And then there were wonderful tales of marvellous feats and hair-breadth escapes to listen to, as they sat with eager looks and open ears round the blazing log-fire in the old log-house. Now they would in their turns have tales to tell of strange adventures, and all that had befallen them since the first day of their wanderings on the Rice Lake Plains.

The long winter passed away unmarked by any very stirring event. The Indians had revisited the hunting-grounds; but they confined themselves chiefly to the eastern side of the plains, the lake, and the islands, and did not come near their little dwelling to molest them. The latter end of the month of March presented fine sugar-making weather; and as they had the use of the big iron pot, they resolved to make maple sugar and some molasses. Long Island was decided upon as the most eligible place: it had the advantage over Maple Island of having a shanty ready built for a shelter during the time they might see fit to remain, and a good boiling-place, which would be a comfort to the girls, as they need not be exposed to the weather during the process of sugaring. The two boys soon cut down some small pines and bass-woods, which they hewed out into sugar-troughs; Indiana manufactured some rough pails of birch-bark; and the first favourable day for the work they loaded up a hand-sleigh with their vessels, and marched forth over the ice to the island, and tapped the trees they thought could yield sap for their purpose. And many pleasant days they passed during the sugar-making season. They did not leave the sugar-bush for good till the commencement of April, when the sun and wind beginning to unlock the springs that fed the lake, and to act upon its surface, taught them that it would not long be prudent to remain on the island. The loud booming sounds that were now frequently heard of the pent-up air beneath striving to break forth from its icy prison, were warnings not to be neglected. Openings began to appear, especially at the entrance of the river, and between the islands, and opposite to some of the larger creeks; blue streams that attracted the water-fowl, ducks, and wild geese, that came, guided by that instinct that never errs, from their abiding-places in far-off lands; and Indiana knew the signs of the wild birds coming and going with a certainty that seemed almost marvellous to her simple-minded companions.

How delightful were the first indications of the coming spring! How joyously our young Crusoes heard the first tapping of the red-headed woodpecker, the low, sweet, warbling note of the early song-sparrow, and twittering chirp of the snow-bird, or that neat quakerly-looking bird, that comes to cheer us with the news of sunny days and green buds, the low, tender, whispering note of the chiccadee, flitting among the pines or in the thick branches of the shore-side trees! The chattering note of the little striped chitmunk, as it pursued its fellows over the fallen trees, and the hollow sound of the male partridge heavily striking his wings against his sides to attract the notice of the female birds—were among the early spring melodies, for such they seemed to our forest dwellers, and for such they listened with eager ears, for they told them—

"That winter, cold winter, was past,
And that spring, lovely spring, was approaching at last."

They watched for the first song of the robin,[1] and the full melody of the red wood-thrush;[2] the rushing sound of the passenger-pigeon, as flocks of these birds darted above their heads, sometimes pausing to rest on the dry limb of some withered oak, or darting down to feed upon the scarlet berries of the spicy winter-green, the acorns that still lay upon the now uncovered ground, or the berries of hawthorn and dogwood that still hung on the bare bushes. The pines were now putting on their rich, mossy, green spring dresses; the skies were deep blue; nature, weary of her long state of inaction, seemed waking into life and light.

On the Plains the snow soon disappears, for the sun and air has access to the earth much easier than in the close, dense forest; and Hector and Louis were soon able to move about with axe in hand, to cut the logs for the

[1] *Turdus migratorius*, or American robin.
[2] *Turdus melodus*, or wood-thrush.

addition to the house which they proposed making. They also set to work as soon as the frost was out of the ground, to prepare their little field for the Indian corn. This kept them quite busy. Catharine attended to the house, and Indiana went out fishing and hunting, bringing in plenty of small game and fish every day. After they had piled and burned up the loose boughs and trunks that encumbered the space which they had marked out, they proceeded to enclose it with a brush fence, which was done by felling the trees that stood in the line of the field, and letting them fall so as to form the bottom log of the fence, which they then made of sufficient height by piling up arms of trees and brush-wood. Perhaps in this matter they were too particular, as there was no fear of "breachy cattle," or any cattle, intruding on the crop; but Hector maintained that deer and bears were as much to be guarded against as oxen and cows.

The little enclosure was made secure from any such depredators, and was as clean as hands could make it, and the two cousins were sitting on a log, contentedly surveying their work, and talking of the time when the grain was to be put in. It was about the beginning of the second week in May, as near as they could guess from the bursting of the forest buds and the blooming of such of the flowers as they were acquainted with. Hector's eyes had followed the flight of a large eagle that now, turning from the lake, soared away majestically towards the east or Oakhills. But soon his eye was attracted to another object. The loftiest part of the ridge was enveloped in smoke. At first he thought it must be some mist-wreath hovering over its brow; but soon the dense rolling clouds rapidly spread on each side, and he felt certain that it was from fire, and nothing but fire, [1] that those dark volumes arose.

"Louis, look yonder! the hills to the east are on fire."

"On fire, Hector? you are dreaming!"

[1] Appendix I.

"Nay, but look there!"

The hills were now shrouded in one dense, rolling cloud; it moved on with fearful rapidity down the shrubby side of the hill, supplied by the dry, withered foliage and deer-grass, which was like stubble to the flames.

"It is two miles off, or more," said Louis; "and the creek will stop its progress long before it comes near us—and the swamp there, beyond Bare Hill."

"The cedars are as dry as tinder; and as to the creek, it is so narrow, a burning tree falling across would convey the fire to this side; besides, when the wind rises, as it always does when the bush is on fire, you know how far the burning leaves will fly. Do you remember when the forest was on fire last spring, how long it continued to burn, and how fiercely it raged! It was lighted by the ashes of your father's pipe, when he was out in the new fallow; the leaves were dry, and kindled; and before night the woods were burning for miles."

"It was a grand spectacle, those pine-hills, when the fire got in among them," said Louis. "See, see how fast the fires kindle; that must be some fallen pine that they have got hold of; now, look at the lighting up of that hill—is it not grand?"

"If the wind would but change, and blow in the opposite direction!" said Hector, anxiously.

"The wind, mon ami, seems to have little influence; for as long as the fire finds fuel from the dry bushes and grass, it drives on, even against the wind."

As they spoke the wind freshened, and they could plainly see a long line of wicked, bright flames, in advance of the dense mass of vapour which hung in its rear. On it came, that rolling sea of flame, with inconceivable rapidity, gathering strength as it advanced. The demon of destruction spread its red wings to the blast, rushing on with fiery speed; and soon hill and valley were wrapped in one sheet of flame.

"It must have been the work of the Indians," said Louis. "We had better make a retreat to the island, in case of the fire crossing the valley. We must not neglect the canoe; if the fire sweeps round by the swamp, it may come upon us unawares, and then the loss of the canoe would prevent escape by the lake. But here are the girls; let us consult them."

"It is the Indian burning," said Indiana; "that is the reason there are so few big trees on that hill; they burn it to make the grass better for the deer."

Hector had often pointed out to Louis the appearance of fire having scorched the bark of the trees, where they were at work, but it seemed to have been many years back; and when they were digging for the site of the root-house[1] below the bank, which they had just finished, they had met with charred wood, at the depth of six feet below the soil, which must have lain there till the earth had accumulated over it; a period of many years must necessarily have passed since the wood had been burned, as it was so much decomposed as to crumble beneath the wooden shovel which they were digging with.

All day they watched the progress of that fiery sea whose waves were flame—red, rolling flame. Onward it came, with resistless speed, overpowering every obstacle, widening its sphere of action, till it formed a perfect semicircle about them. As the night drew on, the splendour of the scene became more apparent, and the path of the fire better defined; but there was no fear of the conflagration spreading as it had done in the daytime. The wind had sunk, and the copious dews of evening effectually put a stop to the progress of the fire. The children could now gaze in security upon the magnificent spectacle before them, without the excitement produced by its rapid spread during the daytime. They lay down to

[1] Root-houses are built over deep excavations below the reach of the frost, or the roots stored would be spoiled.

sleep in perfect security that night, but with the consciousness that, as the breeze sprung up in the morning, they must be on the alert to secure their little dwelling and its contents from the devastation that threatened it. They knew that they had no power to stop its onward course, as they possessed no implement better than a rough wood-shovel, which would be found very ineffectual in opening a trench or turning the ground up, so as to cut off the communication with the dry grass, leaves, and branches, which are the fuel for supplying the fires on the Plains. The little clearing on one side the house they thought would be its safeguard, but the fire was advancing on three sides of them.

"Let us hold a council, as the Indians do, to consider what is to be done."

"I propose," said Louis, "retreating, bag and baggage, to the nearest point of Long Island."

"My French cousin has well spoken," said Hector, mimicking the Indian mode of speaking; "but listen to the words of the wise. I propose to take all our household stores that are of the most value, to the island, and lodge the rest safely in our new root-house, first removing from its neighbourhood all such light, loose matter as is likely to take fire; the earthen roof will save it from destruction; as to the shanty, it must take its chance to stand or fall."

"The fence of the little clearing will be burned, no doubt. Well, never mind, better that than our precious selves; and the corn, fortunately, is not yet sown," said Louis.

Hector's advice met with general applause, and the girls soon set to work to secure the property they meant to leave.

It was a fortunate thing that the root-house had been finished, as it formed a secure store-house for their goods, and would also be made available as a hiding-place from the Indians, in time of need. The boys carefully scraped away all the combustible matter from its vicinity, and also from the house; but the rapid increase of the fire now warned them to hurry down to join Catharine and the young Mohawk, who had gone off to the lake shore, with such things as they required to take with them.

CHAPTER 11

"I know a lake where the cool waves break,
And softly fall on the silver sand,
And no stranger intrudes on that solitude,
And no voices but ours disturb the strand."

IRISH SONG.

THE breeze had sprung up, and had already brought the fire down as far as the creek. The swamp had long been on fire, and now the flames were leaping among the decayed timbers, roaring and crackling among the pines, and rushing to the tops of the cedars, springing from heap to heap of the fallen branches, and filling the air with dense volumes of black and suffocating smoke. So quickly did the flames advance that Hector and Louis had only time to push off the canoe before the heights along the shore were wrapped in smoke and fire. Many a giant oak and noble pine fell crashing to the earth, sending up showers of red sparks, as its burning trunk shivered in its fall. Glad to escape from the suffocating vapour, the boys quickly paddled out to the island, enjoying the cool, fresh air of the lake. Reposing on the grass beneath the trees, they passed the day, sheltered from the noonday sun, and watched the progress of the fires upon the shore. At night the girls slept securely under the canoe, which they raised on one side by means of forked sticks stuck in the ground.

It was a grand sight to see the burning plains at night, reflected on the water. A thousand flaming torches flickered upon its still surface, to which the glare of a gas-lighted city would have been dim and dull by contrast.

Louis and Hector would speculate on the probable chances of the shanty escaping from the fire, and of the fence remaining untouched. Of the safety of the root-house they entertained no fear, as the grass was already springing green on the earthen roof; and below they had taken every precaution to secure its safety, by scraping up the earth near it.[1]

Catharine lamented for the lovely spring-flowers that would be destroyed by the fire.

"We shall have neither huckleberries nor strawberries this summer," she said, mournfully; "and the pretty roses and bushes will be scorched, and the ground black and dreary."

"The fire passes so rapidly over that it does not destroy many of the forest trees, only the dead ones are destroyed; and that, you know, leaves more space for the living ones to grow and thrive in," said Hector. "I have seen, the year after a fire has run in the bush, a new and fresh set of plants spring up, and even some that looked withered recover; the earth is renewed and manured by the ashes; and it is not so great a misfortune as it at first appears."

"But how black and dismal the burnt pine-woods look for years!" said Louis; "I do not think there is a more melancholy sight in life than one of those burnt pine-woods. There it stands, year after year, the black, branchless trees pointing up to the blue sky, as if crying for vengeance against those that kindled the fires."

[1] Many a crop of grain and comfortable homestead has been saved by turning a furrow round the field; and great conflagrations have been effectually stopped by men beating the fire out with spades, and hoeing up the fresh earth so as to cut off all communication with the dry roots, grass, and leaves that feed its onward progress. Water, even could it be got, which is often impossible, is not near so effectual in stopping the progress of fire; even women and little children can assist in such emergencies.

"They do, indeed, look ugly," said Catharine; "yet the girdled ones look very nearly as ill." [1]

At the end of two days the fires had ceased to rage, though the dim smoke-wreaths to the westward showed where the work of destruction was still going on.

As there was no appearance of any Indians on the lake, nor yet at the point (Anderson's Point, as it is now called), on the other side, they concluded the fires had possibly originated by accident,—some casual hunter or trapper having left his camp-fire unextinguished; but as they were not very likely to come across the scene of the conflagration, they decided on returning back to their old home without delay; and it was with some feeling of anxiety that they hastened to see what evil had befallen their shanty.

"The shanty is burned!" was the simultaneous exclamation of both Louis and Hector, as they reached the rising ground that should have commanded a view of its roof. "It is well for us that we secured our things in the root-house," said Hector.

"Well, if that is safe, who cares? we can soon build up a new house, larger and better than the old one," said Louis. "The chief part of our fence is gone, too, I see; but that we can renew at our leisure; no hurry, if we get it done a month hence, say I. Come, *ma belle*, do not look so sorrowful. There is our little squaw will help us to set up a capital wigwam, while the new house is building."

"But the nice table that you made, Louis, and the benches and shelves!"

"Never mind, Cathy, we will have better tables, and benches, and shelves too. Never fear, *ma chère*, the same industrious Louis will make things comfortable. I am not sorry the old shanty is down; we shall have a famous one put up, twice as large, for the winter. After the corn is

---

[1] The girdled pines are killed by barking them round, to facilitate the clearing.

planted we shall have nothing else to do but to think about it."

The next two or three days was spent in erecting a wigwam, with poles and birch bark; and as the weather was warm and pleasant, they did not feel the inconvenience so much as they would have done had it been earlier in the season. The root-house formed an excellent store-house and pantry; and Indiana contrived, in putting up the wigwam, to leave certain loose folds between the birch-bark lining and outer covering, which formed a series of pouches or bags, in which many articles could be stowed away out of sight.[1]

While the girls were busy contriving the arrangements of the wigwam, the two boys were not idle. The time was come for planting the corn; a succession of heavy thunder-showers had soaked and softened the scorched earth, and rendered the labour of moving it much easier than they had anticipated. They had cut for themselves wooden trowels, with which they raised the hills for the seed. The corn planted, they next turned their attention to cutting house-logs; those which they had prepared had been burned up; so they had their labour to begin again.

The two girls proved good helps at the raising; and in the course of a few weeks they had the comfort of seeing a more commodious dwelling than the former one put up. The finishing of this, with weeding the Indian corn, renewing the fence, and fishing, and trapping, and shooting partridges and ducks and pigeons, fully occupied their time this summer. The fruit season was less abundant this year than the previous one. The fire had done this mischief, and they had to go far a-field to collect fruits during the summer months.

It so happened that Indiana had gone out early one

[1] In this way the winter wigwams of the Indians are constructed so as to give plenty of stowing room for all their little household matters, materials for work, &c.

morning with the boys, and Catharine was alone. She had gone down to the spring for water, and on her return was surprised at the sight of a squaw and her family of three half-grown lads, and an innocent little brown papoose.[1] In their turn the strangers seemed equally astonished at Catharine's appearance.

The smiling aspect and good-natured laugh of the female, however, soon reassured the frightened girl, and she gladly gave her the water which she had in her birch dish, on her signifying her desire for drink. To this Catharine added some berries, and dried venison, and a bit of maple sugar, which was received with grateful looks by the boys; she patted the brown baby, and was glad when the mother released it from its wooden cradle, and fed and nursed it. The squaw seemed to notice the difference between the colour of her young hostess's fair skin and her own swarthy hue; for she often took her hand, stripped up the sleeve of her dress, and compared her arm with her own, uttering exclamations of astonishment and curiosity; possibly Catharine was the first of a fair-skinned race this poor savage had ever seen. After her meal was finished, she set the birchen dish on the floor, and restrapping the papoose in its cradle prison, she slipped the basswood-bark rope over her forehead, and silently signing to her sons to follow her, she departed. That evening a pair of ducks were found fastened to the wooden latch of the door, a silent offering of gratitude for the refreshment that had been afforded to this Indian woman and her children.

Indiana thought, from Catharine's description, that these were Indians with whom she was acquainted; she spent some days in watching the lake and the ravine, lest a larger and more formidable party should be near. The squaw, she said, was a widow, and went by the name of Mother Snow-storm, from having been lost in the woods,

[1] An Indian baby; but "papoose" is not an Indian word. It is probably derived from the Indian imitation of the word "*babies*."

when a little child, during a heavy storm of snow, and nearly starved to death. She was a gentle, kind woman, and, she believed, would not do any of them hurt. Her sons were good hunters; and though so young, helped to support their mother, and were very good to her and the little one.

I must now pass over a considerable interval of time, with merely a brief notice that the crop of corn was carefully harvested, and proved abundant, and a source of great comfort. The rice was gathered and stored, and plenty of game and fish laid by, with an additional store of honey.

The Indians, for some reason, did not pay their accustomed visit to the lake this season. Indiana said they might be engaged with war among some hostile tribes, or had gone to other hunting grounds. The winter was unusually mild, and it was long before it set in. Yet the spring following was tardy, and later than usual. It was the latter end of May before vegetation had made any very decided progress.

The little loghouse presented a neat and comfortable appearance, both within and without. Indiana had woven a handsome mat of bass bark for the floor; Louis and Hector had furnished it with very decent seats and a table, rough, but still very respectably constructed, considering their only tools were a tomahawk, a knife, and wooden wedges for splitting the wood into slabs. These Louis afterwards smoothed with great care and patience. Their bedsteads were furnished with thick, soft mats, woven by Indiana and Catharine, from rushes which they cut and dried; but the little squaw herself preferred lying on a mat or deer-skin on the floor before the fire, as she had been accustomed.

A new field had been enclosed, and a fresh crop of corn planted, and was now green and flourishing. Peace and happiness dwelt within the loghouse;—but for the regrets that ever attended the remembrance of all they had left and lost, no cloud would have dimmed the serenity of those who dwelt beneath its humble roof.

The season of flowers had again arrived,—the earth, renovated by the fire of the former year, bloomed with fresh beauty,—June, with its fragrant store of roses and lilies, was now far advanced,—the anniversary of that time when they had left their beloved parents' roofs, to become sojourners in the lonely wilderness, had returned. Much they felt they had to be grateful for. Many privations, it is true, and much anxiety they had felt; but they had enjoyed blessings above all that they could have expected, and they might, like the Psalmist when recounting the escapes of the people of God, have said,— "Oh that men would therefore praise the Lord for his goodness, and the wonders that he doeth for the children of men." And now they declared no greater evil could befal them than to lose one of their little party, for even Indiana had become as a dear and beloved sister; her gentleness, her gratitude and faithful trusting love, seemed each day to increase. Now, indeed, she was bound to them by a yet more sacred tie, for she knelt to the same God, and acknowledged, with fervent love, the mercies of her Redeemer. She had made great progress in learning their language, and had also taught her friends to speak and understand much of her own tongue; so that they were now no longer at a loss to converse with her on any subject. Thus was this Indian girl united to them in bonds of social and Christian love.

Hector, Louis, and Indiana had gone over the hills to follow the track of a deer which had paid a visit to the young corn, now sprouting and showing symptoms of shooting up to blossom. Catharine usually preferred staying at home, and preparing the meals against their return. She had gathered some fine ripe strawberries, which, with plenty of stewed rice, Indian meal cake, and maple sugar, was to make their dinner. She was weary and warm, for the day had been hot and sultry. Seating herself on the threshold of the door, she leaned her back against the door-post, and closed her eyes. Perhaps the poor child's thoughts were wandering back to her far-off, never-to-be-forgotten home, or she might be thinking of the hunters and their game. Suddenly a vague, undefinable feeling of dread stole over her mind: she heard no steps, she felt no breath, she saw no form; but there was a strange consciousness that she was not alone— that some unseen being was near, some eye was upon her. I have heard of sleepers starting from sleep the most profound when the noiseless hand of the assassin has been raised to destroy them, as if the power of the human eye could be felt through the closed lid.

Thus fared it with Catharine: she felt as if some unseen enemy was near her; and, springing to her feet, she cast a wild, troubled glance around. No living being met her eye; and, ashamed of her cowardice, she resumed her seat. The tremulous cry of her little grey squirrel, a pet which she had tamed and taught to run to her and nestle in her bosom, attracted her attention.

"What aileth thee, wee dearie?" she said, tenderly, as the timid little creature crept, trembling, to her breast. "Thy mistress has scared thee by her own foolish fears. See now, there is neither cat-a-mount nor weasel here to seize thee, silly one;" and as she spoke she raised her head, and flung back the thick clusters of soft fair hair that shaded her eyes. The deadly glare of a pair of dark eyes fixed upon her met her terrified gaze, gleaming with sullen ferocity from the angle of the door-post, whence the upper part of the face alone was visible, partly concealed by a mat of tangled, shaggy, black hair. Paralysed with fear, the poor girl neither spoke nor moved; she uttered no cry; but pressing her hands tightly across her breast, as if to still the loud beating of her heart, she sat gazing upon that fearful appearance, while, with stealthy step, the savage advanced from his lurking-place, keeping, as he did so, his eyes riveted upon hers, with such a gaze as the wily serpent is said to fascinate his prey. His hapless victim moved not; whither could she flee to escape one whose fleet foot could so easily have overtaken her in the race? where conceal herself from him whose wary eye fixed upon her seemed to deprive her of all vital energy?

Uttering that singular, expressive guttural which seems with the Indian to answer the purpose of every other exclamation, he advanced, and taking the girl's ice-cold hands in his, tightly bound them with a thong of deer's hide, and led her unresistingly away. By a circuitous path through the ravine they reached the foot of the mount, where lay a birch canoe, rocking gently on the waters, in which a middle-aged female and a young girl were seated. The females asked no questions, and expressed no word indicative of curiosity or surprise, as the strong arm of the Indian lifted his captive into the canoe, and made signs to the elder squaw to push from the shore. When all had taken their places, the woman, catching up a paddle from the bottom of the little vessel, stood up, and with a few rapid strokes sent it skimming over the lake.

The miserable captive, overpowered with the sense of her calamitous situation, bowed down her head upon her knees, and concealing her agitated face in her garments, wept in silent agony. Visions of horror presented themselves to her bewildered brain—all that Indiana had described of the cruelty of this vindictive race, came vividly before her mind. Poor child, what miserable thoughts were thine during that brief voyage!

Had the Indians also captured her friends? or was she alone to be the victim of their vengeance? What would be the feelings of those beloved ones on returning to their home and finding it desolate! Was there no hope of release? As these ideas chased each other through her agitated mind, she raised her eyes all streaming with tears to the faces of the Indian and his companions with so piteous a look, that any heart but the stoical one of an Indian would have softened at its sad appeal; but no answering glance of sympathy met hers, no eye gave back its silent look of pity—not a nerve or a muscle moved the cold apathetic features of the Indians, and the woe-stricken girl again resumed her melancholy attitude, burying her face in her heaving bosom to hide its bitter emotions from the heartless strangers.

She was not fully aware that it is part of the Indian's education to hide the inward feelings of the heart, to check all those soft and tender emotions which distinguish the civilized man from the savage.

It does indeed need the softening influence of that powerful Spirit, which was shed abroad into the world to turn the hearts of the disobedient to the wisdom of the just, to break down the strongholds of unrighteousness, and to teach man that he is by nature the child of wrath and victim of sin, and that in his unregenerated nature his whole mind is at enmity with God and his fellow-men, and that in his flesh dwelleth no good thing. And the Indian has acknowledged that power,—he has cast his idols of cruelty and revenge, those virtues on which he prided himself in the blindness of his heart, to the moles and the bats; he has bowed and adored at the foot of the Cross;— but it was not so in the days whereof I have spoken. [1]

[1] Appendix K.

CHAPTER 12

"Must this sweet new-blown rose find such a winter
Before her spring be past?"

BEAUMONT AND FLETCHER.

THE little bark touched the stony point of Long Island. The Indian lifted his weeping prisoner from the canoe, and motioned to her to move forward along the narrow path that led to the camp, about twenty yards higher up the bank, where there was a little grassy spot enclosed with shrubby trees—the squaws tarried at the lake-shore to bring up the paddles and secure the canoe.

It is a fearful thing to fall into the hands of an enemy, but doubly so, when that enemy is a stranger to the language in which we would plead for mercy—whose God is not our God, nor his laws those by which we ourselves are governed. Thus felt the poor captive as she stood alone, mute with terror, among the half-naked dusky forms with which she now found herself surrounded. She cast a hurried glance round that strange assembly, if by chance her eye might rest upon some dear familiar face, but she saw not the kind but grave face of Hector, nor met the bright sparkling eye of her cousin Louis, nor the soft, subdued, pensive features of the Indian girl, her adopted sister—she stood alone among those wild gloomy-looking men; some turned away their eyes as if they would not meet her woe-stricken countenance, lest they should be moved to pity her sad condition; no wonder that, overcome by the sense of her utter forlornness, she hid her face with her fettered hands and wept in despair. But the Indian's sympathy is not moved by tears and sighs; calmness, courage, defiance of danger and contempt of death, are what he venerates and admires even in an enemy.

The Indians beheld her grief unmoved. At length the old man, who seemed to be a chief among the rest, motioned to one of the women who leant against the side of the wigwam, to come forward and lead away the stranger. Catharine, whose senses were beginning to be more collected, heard the old man give orders that she was to be fed and cared for. Gladly did she escape from the presence of those pitiless men, from whose gaze she shrunk with maidenly modesty. And now when alone with the women, she hesitated not to make use of that natural language which requires not the aid of speech to make itself understood; clasping her hands imploringly, she knelt at the feet of the Indian woman, her conductress— kissed her dark hands and bathed them with her fast flowing tears, while she pointed passionately to the shore where lay the happy home from which she had been so suddenly torn.

The squaw, though she evidently comprehended the meaning of her imploring gestures, shook her head, and in plaintive earnest tone replied in her own language, that she must go with the canoes to the other shore,—and she pointed to the north as she spoke. She then motioned to the young girl—the same that had been Catharine's companion in the canoe—to bring a hunting knife, which was thrust into one of the folds of the birch-bark of the wigwam. Catharine beheld the deadly weapon in the hands of the Indian woman with a pang of agony as great as if its sharp edge was already at her throat. So young—so young, to die by a cruel bloody death! what had been her crime?—how should she find words to soften the heart of her murderess? The power of utterance seemed denied— she cast herself on her knees and held up her hands in silent prayer; not to the dreaded Indian woman, but to Him who heareth the prayer of the poor destitute—who alone can order the unruly wills and affections of men.

The squaw stretched forth one dark hand and grasped the arm of the terror-struck girl, while the other held the weapon of destruction; with a quick movement she severed the thongs that bound the fettered wrists of the pleading captive, and with a smile that seemed to light up her whole face she raised her from her prostrate position, laid her hand upon her young head, and with an expression of good-humoured surprise lifted the flowing tresses of her sunny hair and spread them over the back of her own swarthy hand; then, as if amused by the striking contrast, she shook down her own jetty-black hair and twined a tress of it with one of the fair haired girl's—then laughed till her teeth shone like pearls within her red lips. Many were the exclamations of childish wonder that broke from the other females, as they compared the snowy arm of the stranger with their own dusky skins; it was plain that they had no intention of harming her, and by degrees distrust and dread of her singular companions began in some measure to subside.

The squaw motioned her to take a seat on a mat beside her, and gave her a handful of parched rice and some deer's flesh to eat; but Catharine's heart was too heavy; she was suffering from thirst, and on pronouncing the Indian word for water, the young girl snatched up a piece of birch-bark from the floor of the tent, and gathering the corners together, ran to the lake, and soon returned with water in this most primitive drinking vessel, which she held to the lips of her guest, and she seemed amused by the long deep draught with which Catharine slaked her thirst; and something like a gleam of hope came over Catharine's mind as she marked the look of kindly feeling with which she caught the young Indian girl regarding her, and she strove to overcome the choking sensation that would from time to time rise to her throat, as she fluctuated between hope and fear. The position of the Indian camp was so placed that it was quite hidden from the shore, and neither could Catharine see the mouth of the ravine, nor the steep side of the mount that her brother and cousin were accustomed to ascend and descend in their visits to the lake shore, nor had she any means of making a signal to them even if she had seen them on the beach.

The long, anxious, watchful night passed, and soon after sunrise, while the morning mists still hung over the lake, the canoes of the Indians were launched, and long before noon they were in the mouth of the river. Catharine's heart sunk within her as the fast receding shores of the lake showed each minute fainter in the distance. At midday they halted at a fine bend in the river, where a small open place and a creek flowing down through the woods afforded them cool water; and here they found several tents put up and a larger party awaiting their return. The river was here a fine, broad, deep and tranquil stream; trees of many kinds fringed the edge; beyond was the unbroken forest, whose depths had never been pierced by the step of man—so thick and luxuriant was the vegetation that even the Indian could hardly have penetrated through its dark swampy glades: far as the eye could reach, that impenetrable interminable wall of verdure stretched away into the far off distance.

On that spot where our Indian camp then stood, are now pleasant open meadows, with an avenue of fine pines and balsams; showing on the eminence above, a large substantial dwelling-house surrounded by a luxuriant orchard and garden, the property of a naval officer,[1] who with the courage and perseverance that mark brave men of his class, first ventured to break the bush and locate himself and his infant family in the lonely wilderness, then

[1] Lieut. Rubidge, whose interesting account of his early settlement may be read in a letter inserted in Captain Basil Hall's Letters from Canada.

far from any beaten road or the haunts of his fellow-men.

But at the period of which I write, the axe of the adventurous settler had not levelled one trunk of that vast forest, neither had the fire scathed it; no voices of happy joyous children had rung through those shades, nor sound of rural labour nor bleating flock awakened its echoes.

All the remainder of that sad day, Catharine sat on the grass under a shady tree, her eyes mournfully fixed on the slow flowing waters, and wondering at her own hard fate in being thus torn from her home and its dear inmates. Bad as she had thought her separation from her father and mother and her brothers, when she first left her home to become a wanderer on the Rice Lake Plains, how much more dismal now was her situation, snatched from the dear companions who had upheld and cheered her on in all her sorrows! But now she was alone with none to love or cherish or console her, she felt a desolation of spirit that almost made her forgetful of that trust that had hitherto always sustained her in time of trouble or sickness. She looked round, and her eye fell on the strange unseemly forms of men and women, who cared not for her, and to whom she was an object of indifference or aversion: she wept when she thought of the grief that her absence would occasion to Hector and Louis; the thought of their distress increased her own.

The soothing quiet of the scene, with the low lulling sound of the little brook as its tiny wavelets fell tinkling over the mossy roots and stones that impeded its course to the river, joined with fatigue and long exposure to the sun and air, caused her at length to fall asleep. The last rosy light of the setting sun was dyeing the waters with a glowing tint when she awoke; a soft blue haze hung upon the trees; the kingfisher and dragon-fly, and a solitary loon, were the only busy things abroad on the river; the first darting up and down from an upturned root near the water's edge, feeding its younglings; the dragon-fly hawking with rapid whirring sound for insects, and the loon, just visible from above the surface of the still stream, sailing quietly on companionless, like her who watched its movements.

The bustle of the hunters returning with game and fish to the encampment roused many a sleepy brown papoose, the fires were renewed, and the evening meal was now preparing,—and Catharine, chilled by the falling dew, crept to the enlivening warmth. And here she was pleased at being recognised by one friendly face—it was the mild and benevolent countenance of the widow Snowstorm, who, with her three sons, came to bid her to share their camp fire and food. The kindly grasp of the hand, the beaming smile that was given by this good creature, albeit she was ugly and ill-featured, cheered the sad captive's heart. She had given her a cup of cold water and what food her log-cabin afforded, and in return the good Indian took her to her wigwam and fed, and warmed, and cherished her with the loving-kindness of a Christian; and during all her sojourn in the Indian camp she was as a tender mother over her, drying her tears and showing her those little acts of attention that even the untaught Indians know are grateful to the sorrowful and destitute. Catharine often forgot her own griefs to repay this worthy creature's kindness, by attending to her little babe and assisting her in some of her homely preparations of cookery or household work. She knew that a selfish indulgence in sorrow would do her no good, and after the lapse of some days she so well disciplined her own heart as to check her tears, at least in the presence of the Indian women, and to assume an air of comparative cheerfulness. Once she found Indian words enough to ask the Indian widow to convey her back to the lake, but she shook her head and bade her not think anything about it; and added, that in the fall, when the ducks came to the rice-beds, they should all return, and then if she could

obtain leave from the chief, she would restore her to her
lodge on the plains; but signified to her that patience was
her only present remedy, and that submission to the will of
the chief was her wisest plan. Comforted by this vague
promise, Catharine strove to be reconciled to her strange
lot, and still stranger companions. She could not help
being surprised at the want of curiosity respecting her
that was shown by the Indians in the wigwam, when she
was brought thither; they appeared to take little notice that
a stranger and one so dissimilar to themselves had been
introduced into the camp, for before her they asked no
questions about her, whatever they might do when she was
absent, though they surveyed her with silent attention.
Catharine learned, by long acquaintance with this people,
that an outward manifestation of surprise[1] is considered a
want of etiquette and good breeding, or rather a proof of
weakness and childishness. The women, like other
females, are certainly less disposed to repress this feeling
of inquisitiveness than the men, and one of their great
sources of amusement, when Catharine was among them,
was examining the difference of texture and colour of her
skin and hair, and holding long consultations over them.
The young girl and her mother, those who had paddled
the canoe the day she was carried away to the island,
showed her much kindness in a quiet way. The young
squaw was grand-daughter to the old chief, and seemed
to be regarded with considerable respect by the rest of the
women; she was a gay lively creature, often laughing, and
seemed to enjoy an inexhaustible fund of good humour.
She was inclined to extend her patronage to the young
stranger, making her eat out of her own bark dish, and
sit beside her on her own mat. She wove a chain of the
sweet-scented grass with which the Indians delight in
adorning themselves, likewise in perfuming their lodges
with bunches or strewings upon the floor. She took great

[1] See Appendix L.

pains in teaching her how to acquire the proper attitude of sitting, after the fashion of the Eastern nations, which position the Indian women assume when at rest in their wigwams.

The Indian name of this little damsel signified the Snow-bird. She was, like that lively restless bird, always flitting to and fro from tent to tent, as garrulous and as cheerful too as that merry little herald of the spring.

Once she seemed particularly attracted by Catharine's dress, which she examined with critical minuteness, evincing great surprise at the cut fringes of dressed doeskin with which Indiana had ornamented the border of the short jacket which she had manufactured for Catharine. These fringes she pointed out to the notice of the women, and even the old chief was called in to examine the dress; nor did the leggings and mocassins escape their observation. There was something mysterious about her garments. Catharine was at a loss to imagine what caused those deep guttural exclamations, somewhat between a grunt and a groan, that burst from the lips of the Indians, as they one by one examined them with deep attention. These people had recognised in these things the peculiar fashion and handiwork of the young Mohawk girl whom they had exposed to perish by hunger and thirst on Bare Hill, and much their interest was excited to know by what means Catharine had become possessed of a dress wrought by the hand of one whom they had numbered with the dead. Strange and mysterious did it seem to them, and warily did they watch the unconscious object of their wonder.

The knowledge that she possessed of the language of her friend Indiana, enabled Catharine to comprehend a great deal of what was said; yet she prudently refrained from speaking in the tongue of one, to whose whole nation she knew these people to be hostile, but she sedulously endeavoured to learn their own peculiar dialect, and in this she succeeded in an incredibly short time, so that she was soon able to express her own wants, and converse a little with the females who were about her.

She had noticed that among the tents there was one which stood apart from the rest, and was only visited by the old chief and his grand-daughter, or by the elder women. At first she imagined it was some sick person, or a secret tent set apart for the worship of the Great Spirit; but one day when the chief of the people had gone up the river hunting, and the children were asleep, she perceived the curtain of skins drawn back, and a female of singular and striking beauty appeared standing in the open space in front. She was habited in a fine tunic of white dressed doeskin richly embroidered with coloured beads and stained quills, a full petticoat of dark cloth bound with scarlet descended to her ancles, leggings fringed with deer-skin knotted with bands of coloured quills, with richly wrought mocassins on her feet. On her head she wore a coronet of scarlet and black feathers; her long shining tresses of raven hair descended to her waist, each thick tress confined with a braided band of quills dyed scarlet and blue; her stature was tall and well-formed; her large, liquid, dark eye wore an expression so proud and mournful that Catharine felt her own involuntarily fill with tears as she gazed upon this singular being. She would have approached nearer to her, but a spell seemed on her; she shrunk back timid and abashed beneath that wild melancholy glance. It was she, the Beam of the Morning, the self-made widow of the young Mohawk, whose hand had wrought so fearful a vengeance on the treacherous destroyer of her brother. She stood there, at the tent door, arrayed in her bridal robes, as on the day when she received her death-doomed victim. And when she recalled her fearful deed, shuddering with horror, Catharine drew back and shrouded herself within the tent, fearing again to fall under the eye of that terrible woman. She remembered how Indiana had told her that since that fatal marriage-feast she had been kept apart from the rest of the tribe,—she was regarded by her people as a sacred character, a great *Medicine*, a female *brave*, a being whom they regarded with mysterious reverence. She had made this great sacrifice for the good of her nation. Indiana said it was believed among her own folk that she had loved the young Mohawk passionately, as a tender woman loves the husband of her youth; yet she had not hesitated to sacrifice him with her own hand. Such was the deed of the Indian heroine—and such were the virtues of the unregenerated Greeks and Romans!

CHAPTER 13

"Now where the wave, with loud unquiet song,
Dash'd o'er the rocky channel, froths along,
Or where the silver waters soothed to rest,
The tree's tall shadow sleeps upon its breast."

COLERIDGE.

THE Indian camp remained for nearly three weeks on this spot,[1] and then early one morning the wigwams were all taken down, and the canoes, six in number, proceeded up the river. There was very little variety in the scenery to interest Catharine; the river still kept its slow flowing course between low shores, thickly clothed with trees, without an opening through which the eye might pierce to form an idea of the country beyond; not a clearing, not a sight or sound of civilized man was there to be seen or heard; the darting flight of the wild birds as they flitted across from one side to the other, the tapping of the woodpeckers or shrill cry of the blue jay, was all that was heard, from sunrise to sunset, on that monotonous voyage. After many hours a decided change was perceived in the current, which ran at a considerable increase of swiftness, so that it required the united energy of both men and women to keep the light vessels from drifting down the river again. They were in the Rapids,[2] and it was hard work

---

[1] Now known by the name of Campbelltown, though there is but one log-house and some pasture fields; it is a spot long used as a calling place for the steamer that plies on the Otonabee, between Gore's Landing on the Rice Lake and Peterborough, to take in fire-wood.

[2] Formerly known as Whitla's Rapids, now the site of the Locks.

to stem the tide, and keep the upward course of the waters. At length the Rapids were passed, and the weary Indian voyagers rested for a space on the bosom of a small but tranquil lake.[1] The rising moon shed her silvery light upon the calm waters, and heaven's stars shone down into its quiet depths, as the canoes with their dusky freight parted the glittering rays with their light paddles. As they proceeded onward the banks rose on either side, still fringed with pine, cedar and oaks. At an angle of the lake the banks on either side ran out into two opposite peninsulas, forming a narrow passage or gorge, contracting the lake once more into the appearance of a broad river, much wider from shore to shore than any other part they had passed through since they had left the entrance at the Rice Lake.

Catharine became interested in the change of scenery, her eye dwelt with delight on the forms of glorious spreading oaks and lofty pines, green cliff-like shores and low wooded islands; while as they proceeded the sound of rapid flowing waters met her ear, and soon the white and broken eddies rushing along with impetuous course were seen by the light of the moon; and while she was wondering if the canoes were to stem those rapids, at a signal from the old chief, the little fleet was pushed to shore on a low flat of emerald verdure nearly opposite to the last island.[2]

Here, under the shelter of some beautiful spreading black oaks, the women prepared to set up their wigwams. They had brought the poles and birch-bark covering from the encampment below, and soon all was bustle and business; unloading the canoes, and raising the tents. Even

[1] The little lake about a mile below Peterborough and above the Locks, formerly girt in by woods of pine and beech and maple, now entirely divested of trees and forming part of the suburbs of the town.

[2] Over the Otonabee, just between the rapids and the island, a noble and substantial bridge has been built.

Catharine lent a willing hand to assist the females in bringing up the stores, and sundry baskets containing fruits and other small wares. She then kindly attended to the Indian children, certain dark-skinned babes, who, bound upon their wooden cradles, were either set up against the trunks of the trees, or swung to some lowly depending branch, there to remain helpless and uncomplaining spectators of the scene.

Catharine thought these Indian babes were almost as much to be pitied as herself, only that they were unconscious of their imprisoned state, having from birth been used to no better treatment, and moreover they were sure to be rewarded by the tender caresses of loving mothers when the season of refreshment and repose arrived; but she alas! was friendless and alone, an orphan girl, reft of father, mother, kindred and friends. One Father, one Friend, poor Catharine, thou hadst, even He— the Father of the fatherless.

That night when the women and children were sleeping, Catharine stole out of the wigwam, and climbed the precipitous bank beneath the shelter of which the lodges had been erected. She found herself upon a grassy plain, studded with majestic oaks and pines, so beautifully grouped that they might have been planted by the hand of taste upon that velvet turf. It was a delightful contrast to those dense dark forests through which for so many many miles the waters of the Otonabee had flowed on monotonously; here it was all wild and free, dashing along like a restive steed rejoicing in its liberty, uncurbed and tameless.

Yes, here it was beautiful! Catharine gazed with joy upon the rushing river, and felt her own heart expand as she marked its rapid course, as it bounded murmuring and fretting over its rocky bed. "Happy, glorious waters! you are not subject to the power of any living creature, no canoe can ascend those surging waves; I would that I too, like thee, were free to pursue my onward way—how soon would I flee away and be at rest!" Such thoughts perhaps might have passed through the mind of the lonely captive girl, as she sat at the foot of a giant oak, and looked abroad over those moonlit waters, till, oppressed by the overwhelming sense of the utter loneliness of the scene, the timid girl with faltering step hurried down once more to the wigwams, silently crept to the mat where her bed was spread, and soon forgot all her woes and wanderings in deep tranquil sleep.

Catharine wondered that the Indians in erecting their lodges always seemed to prefer the low, level, and often swampy grounds by the lakes and rivers in preference to the higher and more healthy elevations. So disregardful are they of this circumstance, that they do not hesitate to sleep where the ground is saturated with moisture. They will then lay a temporary flooring of cedar or any other bark beneath their feet, rather than remove the tent a few feet higher up, where a drier soil may always be found. This either arises from stupidity or indolence, perhaps from both, but it is no doubt the cause of much of the sickness that prevails among them. With his feet stretched to the fire the Indian cares for nothing else when reposing in his wigwam, and it is useless to urge the improvement that might be made in his comfort; he listens with a face of apathy, and utters his everlasting guttural, which saves him the trouble of a more rational reply.

"Snow-bird" informed Catharine that the lodges would not again be removed for some time, but that the men would hunt and fish, while the squaws pursued their domestic labours. Catharine perceived that the chief of the laborious part of the work fell to the share of the females, who were very much more industrious and active than their husbands; these, when not out hunting or fishing, were to be seen reposing in easy indolence under the shade of the trees, or before the tent fires, giving themselves little concern about anything that was going on. The squaws were gentle, humble, and submissive; they bore without a murmur pain, labour, hunger, and fatigue, and seemed to perform every task with patience and good humour. They made the canoes, in which the men sometimes assisted them, pitched the tents, converted the skins of the animals which the men shot into clothes, cooked the victuals, manufactured baskets of every kind, wove mats, dyed the quills of the porcupine, sewed the mocassins, and in short performed a thousand tasks which it would be difficult to enumerate.

Of the ordinary household work, such as is familiar to European females, they of course knew nothing; they had no linen to wash or iron, no floors to clean, no milking of cows, nor churning of butter.

Their carpets were fresh cedar boughs spread upon the ground, and only renewed when they became offensively dirty from the accumulation of fish bones and other offal, which are carelessly flung down during meals. Of furniture they had none, their seat the ground, their table the same, their beds mats or skins of animals,—such were the domestic arrangements of the Indian camp.[1]

In the tent to which Catharine belonged, which was that of the widow and her sons, a greater degree of order and cleanliness prevailed than in any other, for Catharine's natural love of neatness and comfort induced her to strew the floor with fresh cedar or hemlock every day or two, and to sweep round the front of the lodge, removing all unseemly objects from its vicinity. She never failed to wash herself in the river, and arrange her hair with the comb that Louis had made for her; and took great care of the little child, which she kept clean and well fed. She loved this little creature, for it was soft and gentle, meek and

[1] Much improvement has taken place of late years in the domestic economy of the Indians, and some of their dwellings are clean and neat even for Europeans.

playful as a little squirrel, and the Indian mothers all looked with kinder eyes upon the white maiden, for the loving manner in which she tended their children. The heart of woman is seldom cold to those who cherish their offspring, and Catharine began to experience the truth, that the exercise of those human charities is equally beneficial to those who give and those that receive; these things fall upon the heart as dew upon a thirsty soil, giving and creating a blessing. But we will leave Catharine for a short season, among the lodges of the Indians, and return to Hector and Louis.

CHAPTER 14

"Cold and forsaken, destitute of friends,
And all good comforts else, unless some tree
Whose speechless charity doth better ours,
With which the bitter east-winds made their sport
And sang through hourly, hath invited thee
To shelter half a day. Shall she be thus,
And I draw in soft slumbers?"

BEAUMONT AND FLETCHER.

IT was near sunset before Hector and his companions returned on the evening of the eventful day that had found Catharine a prisoner on Long Island. They had met with good success in hunting, and brought home a fine half-grown fawn, fat and in good order. They were surprised at finding the fire nearly extinguished, and no Catharine awaiting their return. There, it is true, was the food that she had prepared for them, but she was not to be seen; supposing that she had been tired of waiting for them, and had gone out to gather strawberries, they did not at first feel very anxious, but ate some of the rice and honey, for they were hungry with long fasting; and taking some Indian meal cake in their hands, they went out to call her in, but no trace of her was visible. They now became alarmed, fearing that she had set off by herself to seek them, and had missed her way home again.

They hurried back to the happy valley—she was not there; to Pine-tree Point—no trace of her there; to the edge of the mount that overlooked the lake— no, she was not to be seen; night found them still unsuccessful in their search. Sometimes they fancied that she had seated herself beneath some tree and fallen asleep; but no one imagined the true cause, having seen nothing of the Indians.

Again they retraced their steps back to the house; but they found her not there. They continued their unavailing search till the moon setting left them in darkness, and they laid down to rest, but not to sleep. The first streak of dawn saw them again hurrying to and fro, calling in vain upon the name of the loved and lost companion of their wanderings. Desolation had fallen upon their house, and the evil which of all others they had most feared, had happened to them.

Indiana, whose vigilance was more untiring, for she yielded not so easily to grief and despair, now returned with the intelligence that she had discovered the Indian trail, through the big ravine to the lake shore; she had found the remains of a wreath of oak leaves which had been woven by Catharine, and probably been about her hair; and she had seen the mark of feet, Indian feet, on the soft clay, at the edge of the lake, and the furrowing of the shingles by the pushing off of a canoe. It was evident that she had been taken away from her home by these people. Poor Louis gave way to transports of grief and despair; he knew the wreath, it was such as Catharine often made for herself, and Mathilde, and petite Louise, and Marie; his mother had taught her to make them; they were linked together by the stalks, and formed a sort of leaf chain. The remembrance of many of their joyous days of childhood made Louis weep sorrowful tears for happy days, never to return again; he placed the torn relic in his breast, and sadly turned away to hide his grief from Hector and the Indian girl.

Indiana now proposed searching the island for further traces, but advised wariness in so doing. They saw, however, neither smoke nor canoes. The Indians had departed while they were searching the ravines and flats round Mount Ararat, and the lake told no tales. The following day they ventured to land on Long Island, and on going to the north side saw evident traces of a temporary encampment having been made. This was all they could do, further search was unavailing; as they found no trace of any violence having been committed, they still cherished hopes that no personal harm had been done to the poor captive. It was Indiana's opinion that, though a prisoner, she was unhurt, as the Indians rarely killed women and children, unless roused to do so by some signal act on the part of their enemies, when an exterminating spirit of revenge induced them to kill and spare not; but where no offence had been offered, they were not likely to take the life of an helpless, unoffending female.

The Indian is not cruel for the wanton love of blood, but to gratify revenge for some injury done to himself, or to his tribe; but it was difficult to still the terrible apprehensions that haunted the minds of Louis and Hector. They spent much time in searching the northern shores and the distant islands, in the vain hope of finding her, as they still thought the camp might have been moved to the opposite side of the lake.

Inconsolable for the loss of their beloved companion, Hector and Louis no longer took interest in what was going on; they hardly troubled themselves to weed the Indian corn, in which they had taken such great delight; all now seemed to them flat, stale, and unprofitable; they wandered listlessly to and fro, silent and sad; the sunshine had departed from their little dwelling; they ate little, and talked less, each seeming absorbed in his own painful reveries.

In vain the gentle Indian girl strove to revive their drooping spirits; they seemed insensible to her attentions, and often left her for hours alone. They returned one evening about the usual hour of sunset, and missed their meek, uncomplaining guest from the place she was wont to occupy. They called, but there was none to reply—she too was gone. They hurried to the shore just time enough to see the canoe diminishing to a mere speck upon the waters, in the direction of the mouth of the river; they called to her in accents of despair, to return, but the wind wafted back no sound to their ears, and soon the bark was lost to sight, and they sat them down disconsolately on the shore.

"What is she doing?" said Hector; "this is cruel to abandon us thus."

"She has gone up the river, with the hope of bringing us some tidings of Catharine," said Louis.

"How came you to think that such is her intention?"

"I heard her say the other day that she would go and bring her back, or die."

"What! do you think she would risk the vengeance of the old chief whose life she attempted to take?"

"She is a brave girl; she does not fear pain or death to serve those she loves."

"Alas!" said Hector, "she will perish miserably and to no avail; they would not restore our dear sister, even at the sacrifice of Indiana's life."

"How can she, unprotected and alone, dare such perils? Why did she not tell us? we would have shared her danger."

"She feared for our lives more than for her own; that poor Indian girl has a noble heart. I care not now what befals us, we have lost all that made life dear to us," said Louis gloomily, sinking his head between his knees.

"Hush, Louis, you are older than I, and ought to bear these trials with more courage. It was our own fault, Indiana's leaving us, we left her so much alone to pine after her lost companion; she seemed to think that we did not care for her. Poor Indiana, she must have felt lonely and sad."

"I tell you what we will do, Hec.—make a log canoe. I found an old battered one lying on the shore, not far from Pine-tree Point; we have an axe and a tomahawk,—what should hinder us from making one like it?"

"True! we will set about it to-morrow."

"I wish it were morning, that we might set to work to cut down a good pine for the purpose."

"As soon as it is done, we will go up the river; anything is better than this dreadful suspense and inaction."

The early dawn saw the two cousins busily engaged chopping at a tree of suitable dimensions, and they worked hard all that day, and the next, and the next, before the canoe was hollowed out, and then, owing to their inexperience and the bluntness of their tools, their first attempt proved abortive; it was too heavy at one end, and did not balance well in the water.

Louis, who had been quite sure of success, was disheartened; not so Hector.

"Do not let us give it up; my maxim is perseverance; let us try again, and again—aye! and a third and a fourth time. I say, never give it up, that is the way to succeed at last."

"You have ten times my patience, Hec."

"Yes! but you are more ingenious than I, and are excellent at starting an idea."

"We are a good pair then for partnership."

"We will begin anew; and this time I hope we shall profit by our past blunders."

"Who would imagine that it is now more than a month since we lost Catharine!"

"I know it, a long, long, weary month," replied Louis, and he struck his axe sharply into the bark of the pine as he spoke, and remained silent for some minutes. The boys, wearied by chopping down the tree, rested from their work, and sat down on the side of the condemned canoe to resume their conversation. Suddenly Louis grasped Hector's arm, and pointed to a bark canoe that appeared making for the westernmost point of the island. Hector started to his feet, exclaiming, "It is Indiana returned!"

"Nonsense! Indiana!—it is no such thing. Look you, it is a stout man in a blanket coat."

"The Indians?" asked Hector inquiringly.

"I do not think he looks like an Indian; but let us watch. What is he doing?"

"Fishing. See now, he has just caught a fine bass—another—he has great luck—now he is pushing the canoe ashore."

"That man does not move like an Indian—hark! he is whistling. I ought to know that tune. It sounds like the old *chanson* my father used to sing;" and Louis, raising his voice, began to sing the words of an old French Canadian song, which we will give in the English as we heard it sung by an old lumberer.

"Down by those banks where the pleasant waters flow,
Through the wild woods we'll wander, and we'll chase the buffalo.
And we'll chase the buffalo."

"Hush, Louis! you will bring the man over to us," said Hector.

"The very thing I am trying to do, mon ami. This is our country, and that may be his; but we are lords here, and two to one—so I think he will not be likely to treat us ill. I am a man now, and so are you, and he is but one, so he must mind how he affronts us," replied Louis laughing.

"I wish the old fellow was inclined to be sociable. Hark, if he is not singing now! aye, and the very chorus of the old song,"—and Louis raised his voice to its highest pitch as he repeated,

"Through the wild woods we'll wander,
And we'll chase the buffalo—
And we'll chase the buffalo."

"What a pity I have forgotten the rest of that dear old song. I used to listen with open ears to it when I was a boy. I never thought to hear it again, and to hear it here of all places in the world!"

"Come, let us go on with our work," said Hector, with something like impatience in his voice; and the strokes of his axe fell once more in regular succession on the log; but Louis's eye was still on the mysterious fisher, whom he could discern lounging on the grass and smoking his pipe. "I do not think he sees or hears us," said Louis to himself, "but I think I'll manage to bring him over soon"—and he set himself busily to work to scrape up the loose chips and shavings, and soon began to strike fire with his knife and flint.

"What are you about, Louis?" asked Hector.

"Lighting a fire."

"It is warm enough without a fire, I am sure."

"I know that, but I want to attract the notice of yonder tiresome fisherman."

"And perhaps bring a swarm of savages down upon us, who may be lurking in the bushes of the island."

"Pooh, pooh! Hec.:—there are no savages. I am weary of this place—anything is better than this horrible solitude." And Louis fanned the flame into a rapid blaze, and heaped up the light dry branches till it soared up among the bushes. Louis watched the effect of his fire, and rubbed his hands gleefully as the bark canoe was pushed off from the island, and a few vigorous strokes of the paddle sent it dancing over the surface of the calm lake.

Louis waved his cap above his head with a cheer of welcome as the vessel lightly glided into the little cove, near the spot where the boys were chopping, and a stout-framed, weather-beaten man, in a blanket coat, also faded and weather-beaten, with a red worsted sash and worn mocassins, sprung upon one of the timbers of Louis's old raft, and gazed with a keen eye upon the lads. Each party silently regarded the other. A few rapid interrogations from the stranger, uttered in the broad patois of the Lower Province, were answered in a mixture of broken French and English by Louis.

A change like lightning passed over the face of the old man as he cried out—"Louis Perron, son of my ancient compagnon."

"Oui! oui!"—with eyes sparkling through tears of joy, Louis threw himself into the broad breast of Jacob Morelle, his father's friend and old lumbering comrade.

"Hector, son of la belle Catharine Perron,"—and Hector, in his turn, received the affectionate embrace of the warm-hearted old man.

"Who would have thought of meeting with the children of my old comrade here at the shore of the Rice Lake?— oh! what a joyful meeting!"

Jacob had a hundred questions to ask: Where were their parents? did they live on the Plains now? how long was it since they had left the Cold Springs? were there any more little ones? and so forth.

The boys looked sorrowfully at each other. At last the old man stopped for want of breath, and remarked their sad looks.

"What, mes fils, are your parents dead? Ah well! I did not think to have outlived them; but they have not led such healthy lives as old Jacob Morelle—hunting, fishing, lumbering, trapping,—those are the things to harden a man and make him as tough as a stock-fish—eh! mes enfans, is it not so?"

Hector then told the old lumberer how long they had been separated from their families, and by what sad accident they had been deprived of the society of their beloved sister. When they brought their narrative down to the disappearance of Catharine, the whole soul of the old trapper seemed moved—he started from the log on which they were sitting, and with one of his national asseverations, declared "That la bonne fille should not remain an hour longer than he could help among those savage wretches. Yes, he, her father's old friend, would go up the river and bring her back in safety, or leave his grey scalp behind him among the wigwams."

"It is too late, Jacob, to think of starting to-day," said Hector. "Come home with us, and eat some food, and rest a bit."

"No need of that, my son. I have a lot of fish here in the canoe, and there is an old shanty on the island yonder, if it be still standing,—the Trapper's Fort I used to call it some years ago. We will go off to the island and look for it."

"No need for that," replied Louis, "for though I can tell you the old place is still in good repair, for we used it this very spring as a boiling house for our maple sap, yet we have a better place of our own nearer at hand—just two or three hundred yards over the brow of yonder hill. So come with us, and you shall have a good supper, and bed to lie upon."

"And you have all these, boys!" said Jacob opening his merry black eyes, as they came in sight of the little log-house and the field of green corn.

The old man praised the boys for their industry and energy. "Ha! here is old Wolfe too," as the dog roused himself from the hearth and gave one of his low grumbling growls. He had grown dull and dreamy, and instead of going out as usual with the young hunters, he would lie for hours dozing before the dying embers of the fire. He pined for the loving hand that used to pat his sides, and caress his shaggy neck, and pillow his great head upon her lap, or suffer him to put his huge paws upon her shoulders, while he licked her hands and face; but she was gone, and the Indian girl was gone, and the light of the shanty had gone with them. Old Wolfe seemed dying of sorrow.

That evening as Jacob sat on the three-legged stool,

smoking his short Indian pipe, he again would have the whole story of their wanderings over, and the history of all their doings and contrivances.

"And how far, mes enfans, do you think you are from the Cold Springs?"

"At least twenty miles, perhaps fifty, for it is a long long time now since we left home, three summers ago."

"Well, boys, you must not reckon distance by the time you have been absent," said the old man. "Now I know the distance through the woods, for I have passed through them on the Indian trail, and by my reckoning as the bee flies, it cannot be more than seven or eight miles—no, nor that either."

The boys opened their eyes. "Jacob, is this possible? So near, and yet to us the distance has been as great as though it were a hundred miles or more."

"I tell you what, boys, that is the provoking part of it. I remember when I was out on the St. John, lumbering, missing my comrades, and I was well-nigh starving, when I chanced to come back to the spot where we parted; and I verily believe I had not been two miles distant the whole eight days that I was moving round and round, and backward and forward, just in a circle, because, d'ye see, I followed the sun, and that led me astray the whole time."

"Was that when you well-nigh roasted the bear?" asked Louis, with a sly glance at Hector.

"Well, no; that was another time; your father was out with me then." And old Jacob, knocking the ashes out of his pipe, settled himself to recount the adventure of the bear. Hector, who had heard Louis's edition of the roast bear, was almost impatient at being forced to listen to old Jacob's long-winded history, which included about a dozen other stories, all tagged on to this, like links of a lengthened chain; and was not sorry when the old lumberer, taking his red nightcap out of his pocket, at last stretched himself out on a buffalo skin that he had brought up from the canoe, and soon was soundly sleeping.

The morning was yet grey when the old man shook himself from his slumber, which, if not deep, had been loud; and after having roused up a good fire, which, though the latter end of July, at that dewy hour was not unwelcome, he lighted his pipe, and began broiling a fish on the coals for his breakfast; and was thus engaged when Hector and Louis wakened.

"Mes enfans," said Jacob, "I have been turning over in my mind about your sister, and have come to the resolution of going up the river alone without any one to accompany me. I know the Indians; they are a suspicious people, they deal much in stratagems, and they are apt to expect treachery in others. Perhaps they have had some reason; for the white men have not always kept good faith with them, which I take to be the greater shame, as they have God's laws to guide and teach them to be true and just in their dealing, which the poor benighted heathen have not, the more's the pity. Now, d'ye see, if the Indians see two stout lads with me, they will say to themselves, there may be more left behind, skulking in ambush. So, boys, I go to the camp alone; and, God willing, I will bring back your sister, or die in the attempt. I shall not go empty-handed; see, I have here scarlet-cloth, beads, and powder and shot. I carry no fire-water; it is a sin and a shame to tempt these poor wretches to their own destruction; it makes fiends of them at once."

It was to no purpose that Hector and Louis passionately besought old Jacob to let them share the dangers of the expedition; the old man was firm, and would not be moved from his purpose.

"Look you, boys," he said, "if I do not return by the beginning of the rice harvest, you may suppose that evil has befallen me and the girl; then I would advise you to take care for your own safety, for if they do not respect my grey head, neither will they spare your young ones. In such case, make yourselves a good canoe—a dug-out[1] will do—and go down the lake till you are stopped by the rapids;[2] make a portage there; but as your craft is too weighty to carry far, e'en leave her and chop out another, and go down to the Falls;[3] then, if you do not like to be at any further trouble, you may make out your journey to the Bay[4] on foot, coasting along the river; there you will fall in with settlers who know old Jacob Morelle—aye, and your two fathers—and they will put you in the way of returning home. If I were to try ever so to put you on the old Indian trail in the woods, though I know it myself right well, you might be lost, and maybe never return home again. I leave my traps and my rifle with you; I shall not need them: if I come back I may claim the things; if not, they are yours. So now I have said my say, had my *talk*, as the Indians say. Farewell. But first let us pray to Him who alone can bring this matter to a safe issue." And the old man devoutly kneeled down, and prayed for a blessing on his voyage and on those he was leaving; and then hastened down to the beach, and the boys, with full hearts, watched the canoe till it was lost to their sight on the wide waters of the lake.

[1] Log canoe.
[2] Crook's Rapids.
[3] Heeley's Falls, on the Trent.
[4] Bay Quinté.

CHAPTER 15

"Where wild in woods the lordly savage ran."

DRYDEN.

WHAT changes a few years make in places! That spot over which the Indians roved, free of all control, is now a large and wide-spreading town. Those glorious old trees are fast fading away, the memory only of them remains to some of the first settlers, who saw them twenty-five years ago, shadowing the now open market-place; the fine old oaks have disappeared, but the green emerald turf that they once shaded still remains. The wild rushing river still pours down its resistless spring floods, but its banks have been levelled, and a noble bridge now spans its rapid waters. It has seen the destruction of two log-bridges, but this new, substantial, imposing structure bids fair to stand from generation to generation. The Indian regards it with stupid wonder: he is no mechanic; his simple canoe of birch bark is his only notion of communication from one shore to another. The towns-people and country settlers view it with pride and satisfaction, as a means of commerce and agricultural advantage. That lonely hill, from which Catharine viewed the rapid-flowing river by moonlight, and marvelled at its beauty and its power, is now the Court-house Hill, the seat of justice for the district,—a fine, substantial edifice; its shining roof and pillared portico may be seen from every approach to the town. That grey village spire, with its groves of oak and pine, how invitingly it stands! those trees that embower it, once formed a covert for the deer. Yonder scattered groups of neat white cottages, each with its garden of flowers and fruit, are spread over what was once an open plain, thinly planted with poplar, oaks, and pine. See, there is another church; and nearer, towards the west end of the town, on that fine slope, stands another, and another. That sound that falls upon the ear is not the rapids of the river, but the dash of mill wheels and mill dams, worked by the waters of that lovely winding brook which has travelled far through woods and deep forest dingles to yield its tribute to the Otonabee. There is the busy post-office, on the velvet carpet of turf; a few years, yes, even a few years ago, that spot was a grove of trees. The neat log building that stood then alone there, was inhabited by the Government Agent, now Colonel Macdonald, and groups of Indians might be seen congregated on the green, or reposing under the trees, forming meet subjects for the painter's pencil, for he knew them well, and was kind to them.

The Indian only visits the town, once the favourite site for his hunting lodge, to receive his annual government presents, to trade his simple wares of basket and birch-bark work, to bring in his furs, or maybe to sell his fish or venison, and take back such store goods as his intercourse with his white brethren has made him consider necessary to his comforts, to supply wants which have now become indispensable, before undreamed of. He traverses those populous, busy streets, he looks round upon dwellings, and gay clothes, and equipages, and luxuries which he can neither obtain nor imitate; and feels his spirit lowered—he is no more a people—the tide of intellect has borne him down, and swept his humble wigwam from the earth. He, too, is changing: he now dwells, for the most part, in villages, in houses that cannot be moved away at his will or necessity; he has become a tiller of the ground, his hunting expeditions are prescribed within narrow bounds, the forest is disappearing, the white man is everywhere. The Indian must also yield to circumstances; he submits patiently. Perhaps he murmurs in secret; but his voice is low, it is not heard; he has no representative in the senate to take interest in his welfare, to plead in his behalf. He is anxious, too, for the improvement of his race: he gladly listens to the words of life, and sees with joy his children being brought up in the fear and nurture of the Lord; he sees with pride some of his own blood going forth on the mission of love to other distant tribes; he is proud of being a Christian; and if there be some that still look back to the freedom of former years, and talk of "the good old times," when they wandered free as the winds and waters through those giant woods, they are fast fading away. A new race is rising up, and the old hunter will soon become a being unknown in Canada.

There is an old gnarled oak that stands, or lately stood, on the turfy bank, just behind the old Government-house (as the settlers called it), looking down the precipitous cliff on the river and the islands. The Indians called it "the white girl's rest," for it was there that Catharine delighted to sit, above the noise and bustle of the camp, to sing her snatches of old Scottish songs, or pray the captive exile's prayer, unheard and unseen.

The setting sun was casting long shadows of oak and weeping elm athwart the waters of the river; the light dip of the paddle had ceased on the water, the baying of hounds and life-like stirring sounds from the lodges came softened to the listening ear. The hunters had come in with the spoils of a successful chase; the wigwam fires are flickering and crackling, sending up their light columns of thin blue smoke among the trees; and now a goodly portion of venison is roasting on the forked sticks before the fires. Each lodge has its own cooking utensils. That jar embedded in the hot embers contains sassafras tea, an aromatic beverage, in which the squaws delight when they are so fortunate as to procure a supply. This has been brought from the Credit, far up in the west, by a family who have come down on a special mission from some great chief to his brethren on the Otonabee, and the squaws have cooked some in honour of the guests. That pot that sends up such a savoury steam is venison pottage, or soup, or stew, or any name you choose to give the Indian mess that is concocted of venison, wild rice, and herbs. Those tired hounds that lay stretched before the fire have been out, and now they enjoy the privilege of the fire, some praise from the hunters, and receive withal an occasional reproof from the squaws, if they approach their wishful noses too close to the tempting viands.

The elder boys are shooting at a mark on yonder birch-tree; the girls are playing or rolling on the grass; "The Snow-bird" is seated on the floor of the wigwam braiding a necklace of sweet grass, which she confines in links by means of little bands of coloured quills; Catharine is working mocassins beside her;—a dark shadow falls across her work from the open tent door—an exclamation of surprise and displeasure from one of the women makes Catharine raise her eyes to the doorway; there, silent, pale, and motionless, the mere shadow of her former self, stands Indiana—a gleam of joy lights for an instant her large lustrous eyes. Amazement and delight at the sight of her beloved friend for a moment deprive Catharine of the power of speech; then terror for the safety of her friend takes the place of her joy at seeing her. She rises regardless of the angry tones of the Indian woman's voice, and throws her arms about Indiana as if to shield her from threatened danger, and sobs her welcome in her arms.

"Indiana, dear sister! how came you hither, and for what purpose?"

"To free you, and then die," was the soft low tremulous answer. "Follow me."

Catharine, wondering at the calm and fearless manner with which the young Mohawk waved back the dusky matron who approached as if with the design of laying hands upon her unwelcome guest, followed with beating heart till they stood in the entrance of the lodge of the Bald Eagle; it was filled with the hunters, who were stretched on skins on the floor reposing in quiet after the excitement of the chase.

The young Mohawk bent her head down and crossed her arms, an attitude of submission, over her breast as she stood in the opening of the lodge; but she spoke no word till the old chief waving back the men, who starting to their feet were gathering round him as if to shield him from danger, and sternly regarding her, demanded from whence she came and for what purpose.

"To submit myself to the will of my Ojebwa father," was the meek reply. "May the daughter of the Bald Eagle's enemy speak to her great father?"

"Say on," was the brief reply, "the Bald Eagle's ears are open."

"The Bald Eagle is a mighty chief, the conqueror of his enemies and the father of his people," replied the Mohawk girl, and again was silent.

"The Mohawk squaw speaks well; let her say on."

"The heart of the Mohawk is an open flower, it can be looked upon by the eye of the Great Spirit. She speaks the words of truth. The Ojebwa chief slew his enemies, they had done his good heart wrong; he punished them for the wrong they wrought; he left none living in the lodges of his enemies save one young squaw, the daughter of a brave, the grand-daughter of the Black Snake. The Bald Eagle loves even an enemy that is not afraid to raise the war-whoop or fling the tomahawk in battle. The young girl's mother was a *brave*." She paused, while her proud eye was fixed on the face of her aged auditor. He nodded assent, and she resumed, while a flush of emotion kindled her pale cheek and reddened her lips,—

"The Bald Eagle brought the lonely one to his lodge, he buried the hatchet and the scalping knife, he bade his squaws comfort her; but her heart was lonely, she pined for the homes of her fathers. She said, I will revenge my father, my mother, and my brothers and sisters; and her heart burned within her: but her hand was not strong to shed blood, the Great Spirit was about my Ojebwa father; she failed, and would have fled, for an arrow was in her flesh. The people of the Bald Eagle took her, they brought her down the great river to the council hill, they bound her with thongs and left her to die. She prayed, and the Great Spirit heard her prayer and sent her help. The white man came; his heart was soft; he unbound her, he gave water to cool her hot lips, he led her to his lodge. The white squaw (and she pointed to Catharine) was there, she bound up her wounds, she laid her on her own bed, she gave her meat and drink, and tended her with love. She taught her to pray to the Good Spirit, and told her to return good for evil, to be true and just, kind and merciful. The hard heart of the young girl became soft as clay when moulded for the pots, and she loved her white sister and brothers, and was happy. The Bald Eagle's people came, when my white brothers were at peace, they found a trembling fawn within the lodge, they led her away, they left tears and loneliness where joy and peace had been. The Mohawk squaw could not see the hearth of her white brothers desolate; she took the canoe, she came to the lodge of the great father of his tribe, and she says to him, 'Give back the white squaw to her home on the Rice Lake, and take in her stead the rebellious daughter of the Ojebwa's enemy, to die or be his servant; she fears not now the knife or the tomahawk, the arrow or the spear: her life is in the hand of the great chief.'" She sank on her knees as she spoke these last words and bowing down her head on her breast remained motionless as a statue.

There was silence for some minutes, and then the old man rose and said:—

"Daughter of a brave woman, thou hast spoken long,

and thou hast spoken well; the ears of the Bald Eagle have been open. The white squaw shall be restored to her brother's lodge—but thou remainest. I have spoken."

Catharine in tears cast her arms around her disinterested friend and remained weeping—how could she accept this great sacrifice? She in her turn pleaded for the life and liberty of the Mohawk, but the chief turned a cold ear to her passionate and incoherent pleading. He was weary—he was impatient of further excitement—he coldly motioned to them to withdraw; and the friends in sadness retired to talk over all that had taken place since that sad day when Catharine was taken from her home. While her heart was joyful at the prospect of her own release, it was clouded with fears for the uncertain fate of her beloved friend.

"They will condemn me to a cruel death," said Indiana, "but I can suffer and die for my white sister."

That night the Indian girl slept sweetly and tranquilly beside Catharine; but Catharine could not sleep; she communed with her own heart in the still watches of the night—it seemed as if a new life had been infused within her. She no longer thought and felt as a child; the energies of her mind had been awakened, ripened into maturity as it were, and suddenly expanded. When all the inmates of the lodges were profoundly sleeping, Catharine arose,—a sudden thought had entered into her mind, and she hesitated not to put her design into execution. There was no moon, but a bright arch of light spanned the forest to the north; it was mild and soft as moonlight, but less bright, and cast no shadow across her path; it showed her the sacred tent of the widow of the murdered Mohawk. With noiseless step she lifted aside the curtain of skins that guarded it, and stood at the entrance. Light as was her step, it awakened the sleeper; she raised herself on her arm and looked up with a dreamy and abstracted air as Catharine, stretching forth her hand in tones low and tremulous, thus addressed her in the Ojebwa tongue:—

"The Great Spirit sends me to thee, O woman of much sorrow; he asks of thee a great deed of mercy and goodness. Thou hast shed blood, and he is angry. He bids thee to save the life of an enemy—the blood of thy murdered husband flows in her veins. See that thou disobey not the words that he commands."

She dropped the curtain and retired as she had come, with noiseless step, and lay down again in the tent beside Indiana. Her heart beat as though it would burst its way through her bosom. What had she done?—what dared? She had entered the presence of that terrible woman alone, at the dead hour of night! she had spoken bold and presumptuous words to that strange being whom even her own people hardly dared to approach uncalled-for! Sick with terror at the consequences of her temerity, Catharine cast her trembling arms about the sleeping Indian girl, and hiding her head in her bosom, wept and prayed till sleep came over her wearied spirit. It was late when she awoke. She was alone: the lodge was empty. A vague fear seized her: she hastily arose to seek her friend. It was evident that some great event was in preparation. The Indian men had put on the war-paint, and strange and ferocious eyes were glancing from beneath their shaggy locks. A stake was driven in the centre of the cleared space in front of the chief's lodge: there, bound, she beheld her devoted friend; pale as ashes, but with a calm unshaken countenance, she stood. There was no sign of woman's fear in her fixed dark eye, which quailed not before the sight of the death-dooming men who stood round her, armed with their terrible weapons of destruction. Her thoughts seemed far away: perhaps they were with her dead kindred, wandering in that happy land to which the Indian hopes to go after life; or, inspired with the new hope which had been opened to her, she was looking to Him who has promised a crown of life to such as believe in His name.

She saw not the look of agony with which Catharine
regarded her; and the poor girl, full of grief, sunk down at
the foot of a neighbouring tree, and burying her face
between her knees, wept and prayed—oh! how fervently!
A hope crept to her heart—even while the doom of
Indiana seemed darkest—that some good might yet accrue
from her visit to the wigwam of the Great Medicine squaw.
She knew that the Indians have great belief in omens, and
warnings, and spirits, both good and evil; she knew that
her mysterious appearance in the tent of the Mohawk's
widow would be construed by her into spiritual agency;
and her heart was strengthened by this hope. Yet just now
there seems little reason to encourage hope: the war-
whoop is given, the war-dance is begun—first slow, and
grave, and measured; now louder, and quicker, and more
wild become both sound and movement. But why is it
hushed again? See, a strange canoe appears on the river;
anon an old weather-beaten man, with firm step, appears
on the greensward and approaches the area of the lodge.

The Bald Eagle greets him with friendly courtesy; the
dance and death-song are hushed; a treaty is begun. It is
for the deliverance of the captives. The chief points to
Catharine—she is free: his white brother may take her—
she is his. But the Indian law of justice must take its course;
the condemned, who raised her hand against an Ojebwa
chief, must die. In vain were the tempting stores of
scarlet cloth and beads for the women, with powder and
shot, laid before the chief: the arrows of six warriors
were fitted to the string, and again the dance and song
commenced, as if, like the roll of the drum and clangour of
the trumpet, they were necessary to the excitement of
strong and powerful feelings, and the suppression of all
tenderer emotions.

And now a wild and solemn voice was heard, unearthly
in its tones, rising above the yells of those savage men. At
that sound every cheek became pale: it struck upon the

ear as some funeral wail. Was it the death-song of the
captive girl bound to that fearful stake? No; for she stands
unmoved, with eyes raised heavenward, and lips apart—

"In still, but brave despair."

Shrouded in a mantle of dark cloth, her long
black hair unbound and streaming over her shoulders,
appears the Mohawk widow, the daughter of the Ojebwa
chief. The gathering throng fall back as she approaches,
awed by her sudden appearance among them. She
stretches out a hand on which dark stains are visible—it is
the blood of her husband, sacrificed by her on that day of
fearful deeds: it has never been effaced. In the name of
the Great Spirit she claims the captive girl—the last of that
devoted tribe—to be delivered over to her will. Her right
to this remnant of her murdered husband's family is
acknowledged. A knife is placed in her hand, while a
deafening yell of triumph bursts from the excited squaws,
as this their great high-priestess, as they deemed her,
advanced to the criminal. But it was not to shed the
heart's blood of the Mohawk girl, but to sever the thongs
that bound her to the deadly stake, for which that
glittering blade was drawn, and to bid her depart in
peace whithersoever she would go.

Then, turning to the Bald Eagle, she thus addressed
him: "At the dead of night, when the path of light spanned
the sky, a vision stood before mine eyes. It came from the
Great and Good Spirit, and bade me to set free the last of a
murdered race whose sun had gone down in blood shed by
my hand and by the hands of my people. The vision told
me that if I did this my path should henceforth be peace,
and that I should go to the better land and be at rest if I
did this good deed." She then laid her hands on the head
of the young Mohawk, blessed her, and enveloping herself
in the dark mantle, slowly retired back to her solitary tent
once more.

CHAPTER 16

"Hame, hame, hame,
Hame I soon shall be,
Hame, hame, hame,
In mine own countrie."—

Scotch Ballad.

OLD Jacob and Catharine, who had been mute spectators of the scene so full of interest to them, now presented themselves before the Ojebwa chief, and besought leave to depart. The presents were again laid before him, and this time were graciously accepted. Catharine in distributing the beads and cloth took care that the best portion should fall to the grand-daughter of the chief, the pretty good-humoured Snow-bird. The old man was not insensible to the noble sacrifice which had been made by the devoted Indiana, and he signified his forgiveness of her fault by graciously offering to adopt her as his child, and to give her in marriage to one of his grandsons, an elder brother of the Snow-bird; but the young girl modestly but firmly refused this mark of favour, for her heart yearned for those whose kindness had saved her from death, and who had taught her to look beyond the things of this world to a brighter and a better state of being. She said, "She would go with her white sister, and pray to God to bless her enemies, as the Great Spirit had taught her to do."

It seems a lingering principle of good in human nature, that the exercise of mercy and virtue opens the heart to the enjoyment of social happiness. The Indians, no longer worked up by excitement to deeds of violence, seemed disposed to bury the hatchet of hatred, and the lodge was now filled with mirth, and the voice of gladness, feasting, and dancing. A covenant of peace and good-will was entered upon by old Jacob and the chief, who bade Catharine tell her brothers that from henceforth they should be free to hunt the deer, fish, or shoot the wild fowl of the lake, whenever they desired to do so, "he the Bald Eagle had said so."

On the morrow, with the first dawn of day, the old trapper was astir; the canoe was ready, with fresh cedar boughs strewed at the bottom. A supply of parched rice and dried fish had been presented by the Indian chief for the voyage, that his white brother and the young girls might not suffer from want. At sun-rise the old man led his young charges to the lodge of the Bald Eagle, who took a kindly farewell of them. "The Snow-bird" was sorrowful, and her bright laughing eyes were dimmed with tears at parting with Catharine; she was a gentle loving thing, as soft and playful as the tame fawn that nestled its velvet head against her arm. She did not let Catharine depart without many tokens of her regard, the work of her own hands,—bracelets of porcupine quills cut in fine pieces and strung in fanciful patterns,[1] mocassins richly wrought, and tiny bark dishes and boxes, such as might have graced a lady's work-table, so rare was their workmanship.

Just as they were about to step into the canoe "the Snow-bird" reappeared, bearing a richly worked bark box, "From the Great Medicine," she said in a low voice, "To the daughter of the Mohawk *brave*." The box contained a fine tunic, soft as a lady's glove, embroidered and fringed, and a fillet of scarlet and blue feathers, with the wings and breast of the war-bird, as shoulder ornaments. It was a token of reconciliation and good-will worthy of a generous heart.

[1] Appendix M.

The young girl pressed the gifts to her bosom and to her lips reverentially, and the hand that brought them to her heart, as she said in her native tongue, "Tell the Great Medicine I kiss her in my heart, and pray that she may have peace and joy till she departs for the spirit-land."

With joyful heart they bade adieu to the Indian lodges, and rejoiced in being once more afloat on the bosom of the great river. To Catharine the events of the past hours seemed like a strange bewildering dream; she longed for the quiet repose of home; and how gladly did she listen to that kind old man's plans for restoring Hector, Louis and herself to the arms of their beloved parents. How often did she say to herself, Oh that I had wings like a dove, for then would I flee away and be at rest!—in the shelter of that dear mother's arms whom she now pined for with a painful yearning of the heart that might well be called home sickness. But in spite of anxious wishes, the little party were compelled to halt for the night some few miles above the lake. There is on the eastern bank of the Otonabee, a pretty rounded knoll, clothed with wild cherries, hawthorns and pine-trees, just where a creek half hidden by alder and cranberry bushes, works its way below the shoulder of the little eminence; this creek grows broader and becomes a little stream, through which the hunters sometimes paddle their canoes, as a short cut to the lower part of the lake near Crook's Rapids.

To this creek old Jacob steered his light craft, and bidding the girls collect a few dry sticks and branches for an evening fire on the sheltered side of the little bank, he soon lighted the pile into a cheerful blaze by the aid of birch bark, the hunter's tinder—a sort of fungus that is found in the rotten oak and maple-trees—and a knife and flint; he then lifted the canoe, and having raised it on its side, by means of two small stakes which he cut from a bush hard by, then spread down his buffalo robe on the dry grass. "There is a tent fit for a queen to sleep under, mes chères filles," he said, eyeing his arrangements for their night shelter with great satisfaction.

He then proceeded to bait his line, and in a few minutes had a dish of splendid bass ready for the coals. Catharine selected a large flat block of limestone on which the fish when broiled was laid; but old Jacob opened his wide mouth and laughed, when she proceeded to lay her bush table with large basswood leaves for platters. Such nicety he professed was unusual on a hunter's table. He was too old a forester to care how his food was dished, so that he had wherewithal to satisfy his hunger.

Many were the merry tales he told and the songs he sung, to wile away the time, till the daylight faded from the sky, and the deep blue heavens were studded with bright stars, which were mirrored in countless hosts deep deep down in that calm waveless river, while thousands of fireflies lighted up the dark recesses of the forest's gloom. High in the upper air the hollow booming of the nighthawk was heard at intervals, and the wild cry of the nightowl from a dead branch, shouting to its fellow, woke the silence of that lonely river scene.

The old trapper stretched before the crackling fire, smoked his pipe or hummed some French voyageur's song. Beneath the shelter of the canoe soundly slept the two girls; the dark cheek of the Indian girl pillowed on the arm of her fairer companion, her thick tresses of raven hair mingling with the silken ringlets of the white maiden. They were a lovely pair—one fair as morning, the other dark as night.

How lightly did they spring from their low bed, wakened by the early song of the forest birds! The light curling mist hung in fleecy volumes upon the river, like a flock of sheep at rest—the tinkling sound of the heavy dewdrops fell in mimic showers upon the stream. See that red squirrel, how lightly he runs along that fallen trunk—how furtively he glances with his sharp bright eye at the intruders on his sylvan haunts! Hark! there is a rustling among the leaves—what strange creature works its way to the shore? A mud turtle—it turns, and now is trotting along the little sandy ridge to some sunny spot, where, half buried, it may lie unseen near the edge of the river. See that musk-rat, how boldly he plunges into the stream, and, with his oarlike tail, stems the current till he gains in safety the sedges on the other side.

What gurgling sound is that?—it attracts the practised ear of the old hunter. What is that object which floats so steadily down the middle of the stream, and leaves so bright a line in its wake?—it is a noble stag. Look at the broad chest, with which he breasts the water so gallantly; see how proudly he carries his antlered head; he has no fear in those lonely solitudes—he has never heard the crack of the hunter's rifle—he heeds not the sharp twang of that bow-string, till the arrow rankles in his neck, and the crimson flood dyes the water around him—he turns, but it is only to present a surer mark for the arrow of the old hunter's bow; and now the noble beast turns to bay, and the canoe is rapidly launched by the hand of the Indian girl—her eye flashes with the excitement—her whole soul is in the chase—she stands up in the canoe, and steers it full upon the wounded buck, while a shower of blows are dealt upon his head and neck with the paddle. Catharine buries her face in her hands—she cannot bear to look upon the sufferings of the noble animal. She will never make a huntress—her heart is cast in too soft a mould. See they have towed the deer ashore, and Jacob is in all his glory,—the little squaw is an Indian at heart—see with what expertness she helps the old man; and now the great business is completed, and the venison is stowed away at the bottom of the canoe—they wash their hands in the river and come at Catharine's summons to eat her breakfast.

The sun is now rising high above the pine-trees, the

morning mist is also rising and rolling off like a golden veil
as it catches those glorious rays—the whole earth seems
wakening into new life—the dew has brightened every leaf
and washed each tiny flower-cup—the pines and balsams
give out their resinous fragrance—the aspens flutter and
dance in the morning breeze and return a mimic shower of
dew-drops to the stream—the shores become lower and
flatter—the trees less lofty and more mossy—the stream
expands and wide beds of rushes spread out on either side
—what beds of snowy water-lilies—how splendid the rose
tint of those persicaria that glow so brightly in the morn-
ing sun—the rushes look like a green meadow, but the
treacherous water lies deep below their grassy leaves—the
deer delights in these verdant aquatic fields, and see what
flocks of red-wings rise from among them as the canoe
passes near—their bright shoulder-knots glance like
flashes of lightning in the sun-beams.

This low swampy island, filled with drift-wood, these
grey hoary trees, half choked and killed with grey moss
and lichens—those straggling alders and black ash look
melancholy—they are like premature old age, grey-headed
youths. That island divides the channel of the river—
the old man takes the nearest, the left hand, and now they
are upon the broad Rice Lake, and Catharine wearies her
eye to catch the smoke of the shanty rising among the trees
—one after another the islands steal out into view—the
capes, and bays, and shores of the northern side are
growing less distinct. Yon hollow bay, where the beaver
has hidden till now, backed by that bold sweep of hills that
look in the distance as if only covered with green ferns,
with here and there a tall tree, stately as a pine or oak—
that is the spot where Louis saw the landing of the Indians
—now a rising village—Gore's Landing. On yon lofty hill
now stands the village church, its white tower rising
amongst the trees forms a charming object from the lake,
and there a little higher up, not far from the plank road,

now stand pretty rural cottages—one of these belongs to the spirited proprietor of the village that bears his name. That tasteful garden before the white cottage, to the right, is Colonel Brown's, and there are pretty farms and cultivated spots; but silence and loneliness reigned there at the time of which I write.

Where those few dark pines rise above the oak groves like the spires of churches in a crowded city, is Mount Ararat.[1] The Indian girl steers straight between the islands for that ark of refuge, and Catharine's eyes are dimmed with grateful tears as she pictures to herself the joyful greeting in store for her. In the overflowings of her gladness she seizes the old man's rugged hand and kisses it, and flings her arms about the Indian girl and presses her to her heart, when the canoe has touched the old well-remembered landing place, and she finds herself so near, so very near her lost home. How precious are such moments—how few we have in life—they are created from our very sorrows—without our cares our joys would be less lively; but we have no time to moralize—Catharine flies with the speed of a young fawn, to climb the steep cliff-like shoulder of that steep bank, and now, out of breath, stands at the threshold of her log-house—how neat and nice it looks compared with the Indians' tents—the little field of corn is green and flourishing—there is Hector's axe in a newly-cut log—it is high noon—the boys ought to have been there taking their mid-day meal, but the door is shut. Catharine lifts the wooden latch, and steps in—the embers are nearly burned out to a handful of grey ashes—old Wolfe is not there—all is silent—and Catharine sits down to still the beating of her heart and await the coming up of her slower companions, and gladdens her mind with the hope that her brother and Louis will soon be home—her eye wanders over every old familiar object—all things seem much as she had left them, only the maize is in

[1] Appendix N.

the ear and the top feather waves gracefully with the summer breeze—it promises an abundant crop; but that harvest is not to be gathered by the hands of the young planters—it was left to the birds of the air and the beasts of the field—to those humble reapers who sow not, neither do they gather into barns, for their Heavenly Father feedeth them. While the two girls busied themselves in preparing a fine roast of venison old Jacob stalked away over the hills to search for the boys, and it was not long before he returned with Hector and Louis.

I must not tell tales, or I might say what tears of joy were mingled with the rapturous greetings with which Louis embraced his beloved cousin; or I might tell that the bright flush that warmed the dusky cheek of the young Indian, and the light that danced in her soft black eyes, owed their origin to the kiss that was pressed on her red lips by her white brother. Nor will we say whose hand held hers so long in his while Catharine related the noble sacrifice made for her sake, and the perils encountered by the devoted Indiana—whose eyes were moistened with tears as the horrors of that fearful trial were described—or who stole out alone over the hills, and sat him down in the hush and silence of the summer night to think of the acts of heroism displayed by that untaught Indian girl, and to dream a dream of youthful love; but with these things, my young readers, we have nothing to do.

"And now, my children," said old Jacob, looking round the little dwelling, "have you made up your minds to live and die here on the shores of this lake, or do you desire again to behold your fathers' home? Do your young hearts yearn after the hearth of your childhood?"

"After our fathers' home!" was Louis's emphatic reply. "After the home of our childhood!" was Catharine's earnest answer. Hector's lips echoed his sister's words, while a furtive troubled glance fell upon the orphan stranger; but her timid eye was raised to his young face with a trusting look, as she would have said, "Thy home shall be my home, thy God my God."

"Well, mon ami, I believe, if my old memory fails me not, I can strike the Indian trail that used to lead to the Cold Springs over the pine hills. It will not be difficult for an old trapper to find his way."

"For my part, I shall not leave this lovely spot without regret," said Hector. "It would be a glorious place for a settlement—all that one could desire—hill, and valley, and plain, wood and water. Well, I will try and persuade my father to leave the Cold Springs, and come and settle hereabouts. It would be delightful, would it not, Catharine, especially now we are friends with the Indians."

With their heads full of pleasant schemes for the future, our young folks laid them down that night to rest. In the morning they rose, packed up such portable articles as they could manage to carry, and with full hearts sat down to take their last meal in their home—in that home which had sheltered them so long—and then, with one accord, they knelt down upon its hearth, so soon to be left in loneliness, and breathed a prayer to Him who had preserved them thus far in their eventful lives, and then they journeyed forth once more into the wilderness. There was one, however, of their little band they left behind: this was the faithful old dog Wolfe. He had pined during the absence of his mistress, and only a few days before Catharine's return he had crept to the seat she was wont to occupy, and there died. Louis and Hector buried him, not without great regret, beneath the group of birch-trees on the brow of the slope near the corn-field.

CHAPTER 17

"I will arise, and go to my father."—

New Testament.

IT is the hour of sunset; the sonorous sound of the cattle bells is heard, as they slowly emerge from the steep hill path that leads to Maxwell and Louis Perron's little clearing; the dark shadows are lengthening that those wood-crowned hills cast over that sunny spot, an oasis in the vast forest desert that man, adventurous, courageous man, has hewed for himself in the wilderness. The little flock are feeding among the blackened stumps of the uncleared chopping; those timbers have lain thus untouched for two long years; the hand was wanting that should have given help in logging and burning them up. The wheat is ripe for the sickle, and the silken beard of the corn is waving like a fair girl's tresses in the evening breeze. The tinkling fall of the cold spring in yonder bank falls soothingly on the ear. Who comes from that low-roofed log cabin to bring in the pitcher of water, that pale, careworn, shadowy figure that slowly moves along the green pasture, as one without hope or joy; her black hair is shared with silver, her cheek is pale as wax, and her hand is so thin, it looks as though the light might be seen through if she held it towards the sun? It is the heart-broken mother of Catharine and Hector Maxwell. Her heart has been pierced with many sorrows; she cannot yet forget the children of her love, her first-born girl and boy. Who comes to meet her, and with cheerful voice chides her for the tear that seems ever to be lingering on that pale cheek,—yet the premature furrows on that broad, sunburnt, manly brow speak, too, of inward care? It is the father of Hector and Catharine. Those two fine, healthy boys, in homespun blouses, that are talking so earnestly, as they lean across the rail fence of the little wheat field, are Kenneth and Duncan; their sickles are on their arms; they have been reaping. They hear the sudden barking of Bruce and Wallace, the hounds, and turn to see what causes the agitation they display.

An old man draws near; he has a knapsack on his shoulders, which he casts down on the corner of the stoup; he is singing a line of an old French ditty; he raps at the open door. The Highlander bids him welcome, but starts with glad surprise as his hand is grasped by the old trapper.

"Ha, Jacob Morelle, it is many a weary year since your step turned this way." The tear stood in the eye of the soldier as he spoke.

"How is ma chère mère, and the young ones?" asked the old man, in a husky voice—his kind heart was full. "Can you receive me, and those I have with me, for the night? A spare corner, a shake-down, will do; we travellers in the bush are no wise nice."

"The best we have, and kindly welcome; it is gude for saer een to see you, Jacob. How many are ye in all?"

"There are just four, beside myself,—young people; I found them where they had been long living, on a lonely lake, and I persuaded them to come with me."

The strong features of the Highlander worked convulsively, as he drew his faded blue bonnet over his eyes. "Jacob, did ye ken that we lost our eldest bairns, some three summers since?" he faltered, in a broken voice.

"The Lord, in his mercy, has restored them to you, Duncan, by my hand," said the trapper.

"Let me see, let me see my children. To him be the praise and the glory," ejaculated the pious father, raising his bonnet reverently from his head; "and holy and blessed be his name for ever. I thought not to have seen this day. Oh! Catharine, my dear wife, this joy will kill you."

In a moment his children were enfolded in his arms. It is a mistaken idea that joy kills, it is a life restorer. Could you, my young readers, have seen how quickly the bloom of health began to reappear on the faded cheek of that pale mother, and how soon that dim eye regained its bright sparkle, you would have said that joy does not kill.

"But where is Louis, dear Louis, our nephew, where is he?"

Louis whose impetuosity was not to be restrained by the caution of old Jacob, had cleared the log fence at a bound, had hastily embraced his cousins Kenneth and Duncan, and in five minutes more had rushed into his father's cottage, and wept his joy in the arms of father, mother, and sisters by turns, before old Jacob had introduced the impatient Hector and Catharine to their father.

"But while joy is in our little dwelling, who is this that sits apart upon that stone by the log fence, her face bent sadly down upon her knees, her long raven hair shading her features as with a veil," asked the Highlander Maxwell, pointing as he spoke to the spot where, unnoticed and unsharing in the joyful recognition, sat the poor Indian girl. There was no paternal embrace for her, no tender mother's kiss imprinted on that dusky cheek and pensive brow—she was alone and desolate, in the midst of that scene of gladness.

"It is my Indian sister," said Catharine, "she also must be your child;" and Hector hurried to Indiana and half leading, half carrying the reluctant girl, brought her to his parents and bade them be kind to and cherish the young stranger, to whom they all owed so much.

I will not dwell upon the universal joy that filled that humble dwelling, or tell the delight of Kenneth and Duncan at the return of their lost brother and sister, for my story hurries to a close.

Time passes on—years, long years have gone by since the return of the lost children to their homes, and many changes have those years effected. The log-houses have fallen to decay—a growth of young pines, a waste of emerald turf with the charred logs that once formed part of the enclosure, now, hardly serve to mark out the old settlement—no trace or record remains of the first breakers of the bush, another race occupy the ground. The traveller as he passes along on that smooth turnpike road that leads from Cobourg to Cold Springs, and from thence to Gore's Landing, may notice a green waste by the road-side on either hand, and fancy that thereabouts our Canadian Crusoes' home once stood—he sees the lofty wood-crowned hill, and sees in spring-time, for in summer it is hidden by the luxuriant foliage, the little forest creek, and he may if thirsty, taste of the pure fresh icy water, as it still wells out from a spring in the steep bank, rippling through the little cedar-trough that Louis Perron placed there for the better speed of his mother when filling her water jug. All else is gone. And what wrought the change?—a few words will suffice to tell. Some travelling fur merchants brought the news to Duncan Maxwell, that a party of Highlanders had made a settlement above Montreal, and among them were some of his kindred. The old soldier resolved to join them, and it was not hard to prevail upon his brother-in-law to accompany him, for they were all now weary of living so far from their fellow-men; and bidding farewell to the little log-houses at Cold Springs, they now journeyed downwards to the new settlement, where they were gladly received, their long experience of the country making their company a most valuable acquisition to the new colonists.

Not long after the Maxwells took possession of a grant of land, and cleared and built for themselves and their family. That year Hector, now a fine industrious young man, presented at the baptismal font as a candidate for baptism, the Indian girl, and then received at the altar his newly baptized bride. As to Catharine and Louis, I am not sufficiently skilled in the laws of their church to tell how the difficulty of nearness of kin was obviated, but they were married on the same day as Hector and Indiana, and lived a happy and prosperous life; and often by their fireside would delight their children by recounting the history of their wanderings on the Rice Lake Plains.

APPENDIX A

SARAH CAMPBELL, of Windsor, who was lost in the woods on the 11th of August, 1848, returned to her home on the 31st, having been absent twenty-one days. A friend has sent us a circumstantial account of her wanderings, of the efforts made in her behalf, and her return home, from which we condense the following statements:—

It appears that on the 11th of August, in company with two friends, she went fishing on the north branch of Windsor-brook; and that on attempting to return she became separated from her companions, who returned to her mother's, the Widow Campbell, expecting to find her at home. Several of her neighbours searched for her during the night, without success. The search was continued during Sunday, Monday, and Tuesday, by some fifty or sixty individuals, and although her tracks, and those of a dog which accompanied her, were discovered, no tidings of the girl were obtained. A general sympathy for the afflicted widow and her lost daughter was excited, and notwithstanding the busy season of the year, great numbers from Windsor and the neighbouring townships of Brompton, Shipton, Melbourne, Durham, Oxford, Sherbrooke, Lennoxville, Stoke, and Dudswell, turned out with provisions and implements for camping in the woods, in search of the girl, which was kept up without intermission for about fourteen days, when it was generally given up, under the impression that she must have died, either from starvation, or the inclemency of the weather, it having rained almost incessantly for nearly a week of the time. On the 31st her brother returned home from Massachusetts, and with two or three others renewed the search, but returned the second day, and learned to their great joy that the lost one had found her way home the evening previous.

On hearing of her return, our correspondent made a visit to Widow Campbell, to hear from her daughter the story of her wanderings. She was found, as might be supposed, in a very weak and exhausted condition, but quite rational, as it seems she had been during the whole period of her absence. From her story the following particulars were gathered:—

When first lost she went directly from home down "Open Brooke," to a meadow, about a mile distant from where she had left her companions, which she mistook for what is called the "*Oxias* opening," a mile distant in the opposite direction. On Sabbath morning, knowing that she was lost, and having heard that lost persons might be guided by the sun, she undertook to follow the sun during the day. In the morning she directed her steps towards the East, crossed the north Branch, mistaking it for "Open Brooke," and travelled, frequently running, in a south-east direction (her way home was due north) seven or eight miles till she came to the great Hay-meadow in Windsor. There she spent Sabbath night, and on Monday morning directed her course to, and thence down, the South Branch in the great Meadow.

After this, she appears to have spent her time, except while she was searching for food for herself and dog, in walking and running over the meadow, and up and down the south branch, in search of her home, occasionally wandering upon the highlands, and far down towards the junction of the two main streams, never being more than seven or eight miles from home.

For several days, by attempting to follow the sun, she travelled in a circle, finding herself at night near the place where she left in the morning. Although she often came across the tracks of large parties of men, and their recently-erected camps, and knew that multitudes of people were in search of her, she saw no living person, and heard no sound of trumpet, or other noise, except the report of a gun, as she lay by a brook, early on Thursday morning, the sixth day of her being lost. Thinking the gun to have been fired not more than half a mile distant, she said she "screamed and run" to the place from whence she supposed the noise came, but found nothing. Early in the day, however, she came to the camp where this gun was fired, but not until after its occupants had left to renew their search for her. This camp was about four miles from the great meadow, where she spent the Sabbath previous. There she found a fire, dried her clothes, and found a partridge's gizzard, which she cooked and ate, and laid down and slept, remaining about twenty-four hours.

In her travels she came across several other camps, some of which she visited several times, particularly one where she found names cut upon trees, and another in which was a piece of white paper. Except three or four nights spent in these camps, she slept upon the ground, sometimes making a bed of moss, and endeavouring to shelter herself from the drenching rains with spruce boughs. For the two first weeks she suffered much from the cold, shivering all night, and sleeping but little. The last week she said she had got "toughened," and did not shiver. When first lost she had a large trout, which was the only food she ate, except choke-berries, the first week, and part of this she gave to her dog, which remained with her for a week, day and night. The cherries, which she ate greedily, swallowing the stones, she found injured her health; and for the last two weeks she lived upon cranberries and wood sorrel. While the dog remained with her, she constantly shared her food with him, but said she was glad when he left her, as it was much trouble to find him food.

On Thursday of last week she followed the south towards the junction with the north branch, where it appeared she had been before, but could not ford the stream; and in the afternoon of Friday crossed the north, a little above its junction with the south branch, and following down the stream, she found herself in the clearing, near Moor's Mill. Thence directing her steps towards home, she reached Mr. McDale's, about a mile from her mother's, at six o'clock, having walked five miles in two hours, and probably ten miles during the day. Here she remained till the next day, when she was carried home, and was received by friends almost as one raised from the dead. Her feet and ankles were very much swollen and lacerated; but strange to say, her calico gown was kept whole, with the exception of two small rents.

Respecting her feelings during her fast in the wilderness, she says she was never frightened, though sometimes, when the sun disappeared, she felt disheartened, expecting to perish; but when she found, by not discovering any new tracks, that the people had given over searching for her, she was greatly discouraged. On the morning of Friday, she was strongly inclined to give up, and lie down and die; but the hope of seeing her mother stimulated her to make one more effort to reach home, which proved successful. When visited, she was in a state of feverish excitement and general derangement of the system, and greatly emaciated, with a feeble voice, but perfectly sane and collected.

It is somewhat remarkable that a young girl (aged seventeen), thinly clad, could have survived twenty-one days, exposed as she was to such severe storms, with no other food but wild berries. It is also very strange that she should have been so frequently on the tracks of those in search of her, sleeping in the camps, and endeavouring to follow their tracks home, and not have heard any of their numerous trumpets, or been seen by any of the hundreds of persons who were in search for her.

A more dismal result than the deprivations endured by Sarah Campbell, is the frightful existence of a human creature, called in the American papers, the "Wild Man of the far West." From time to time, these details approach the terrific, of wild men who have grown up from childhood in a state of destitution in the interminable forests, especially of this one, who, for nearly a quarter of a century, has occasionally been seen, and then either forgotten, or supposed to be the mere creation of the beholder's brain. But it appears that he was, in March, 1850, encountered by Mr. Hamilton, of Greene County, Arkansas, when hunting. The wild man was, likewise, chasing his prey. A herd of cattle fled past Mr. Hamilton and his party, in an agony of terror, pursued by a giant, bearing a dreadful semblance to humanity. His face and shoulders were enveloped with long streaming hair, his body was entirely hirsute, his progression was by great jumps of twelve or thirteen feet at a leap. The creature turned and gazed earnestly on the hunters, and fled into the depths of the forest, where he was lost to view. His footprints were thirteen inches long. Mr. Hamilton published the description of the savage man in the *Memphis Inquirer*. Afterwards several planters deposed to having, at times, for many years, seen this appearance. All persons generally agreed that it was a child that had been lost in the woods, at the earthquake in 1811, now grown to meridian strength, in a solitary state. Thus the possibility of an European child living, even unassisted, in the wilderness, is familiar to the inhabitants of the vast American continent. Although we doubt that any human creature would progress by leaps, instead of the paces familiar to the human instinct. It is probable that the wild man of the Arkansas is, in reality, some species of the oran-outang, or chimpanzee.

APPENDIX B

Page 47.—*"where Wolf Tower now stands."*

The Wolf Tower is among the very few structures in Canada not devoted to purposes of strict utility. It was built by a gentleman of property as a *belle vue*, or fanciful prospect residence, in order to divert his mind from the heavy pressure of family affliction. It was once lent by him to the author, who dwelt here some time during the preparation of another house in the district.

APPENDIX C

Page 74.—". . . *as civilization advances.*"

Formerly the Rice Lake Plains abounded in deer, wolvès, bears, raccoons, wolverines, foxes, and wild animals of many kinds. Even a few years ago, and bears and wolves were not unfrequent in their depredations; and the ravines sheltered herds of deer; but now the sight of the former is a thing of rare occurrence, and the deer are scarcely to be seen, so changed is this lovely wilderness, that green pastures and yellow cornfields now meet the eye on every side, and the wild beasts retire to the less frequented depths of the forest.

From the undulating surface, the alternations of high hills, deep valleys, and level table-lands, with the wide prospect they command, the Rice Lake Plains still retain their picturesque beauty, which cannot be marred by the hand of the settler even be he ever so devoid of taste; and many of those who have chosen it as their home are persons of taste and refinement, who delight in adding to the beauty of that which Nature had left so fair.

APPENDIX D

Page 103, *note*.

"I will now," says our Indian historian, "narrate a single circumstance which will convey a correct idea of the sufferings to which Indians were often exposed. To obtain furs of different kinds for the traders, we had to travel far into the woods, and remain there the whole winter. Once we left Rice Lake in the fall, and ascended the river in canoes as far as Belmont Lake. There were five families about to hunt with my father on his ground. The winter began to set in, and the river having frozen over, we left the canoes, the dried venison, the beaver, and some flour and pork; and when we had gone further north, say about sixty miles from the white settlements, for the purpose of hunting, the snow fell for five days in succession, to such a depth, that it was impossible to shoot or trap anything; our provisions were exhausted, and we had no means of procuring any more. Here we were, the snow about five feet deep, our wigwam buried, the branches of the trees falling all about us, and cracking with the weight of the snow.

"Our mother (who seems, by-the-bye, from the record of her son, to have been a most excellent woman) boiled birch-bark for my sister and myself, that we might not starve. On the seventh day some of us were so weak they could not guard themselves, and others could not stand alone. They could only crawl in and out of the wigwam. We parched beaver skins and old mocassins for food. On the ninth day none of the men could go abroad except my father and uncle. On the tenth day, still being without food, the only ones able to walk about the wigwam were my father, my grandmother, my sister, and myself. Oh, how distressing to see the starving Indians lying about the wigwam with hungry and eager looks!—the children would cry for something to eat! My poor mother would heave bitter sighs of despair, the tears falling profusely from her cheeks as she kissed us! Wood, though in plenty, could not be obtained on account of the feebleness of our limbs. My father would at times draw near the fire and rehearse some prayer to the gods. It appeared to him that there was no way of escape; the men, women, and children, dying; some of them were speechless, the wigwam was cold and dark, and covered with snow!

"On the eleventh day, just before daylight, my father fell into a sleep; he soon awoke, and said to me: 'My son, the good Spirit is about to bless us this night; in my dream I saw a person coming from the east walking on the tops of the trees; he told me we should obtain two beavers about nine o'clock. Put on your mocassins, and go along with me to the river, and we will hunt beaver, perhaps, for the last time.' I saw that his countenance beamed with delight and hope; he was full of confidence. I put on my mocassins and carried my snow-shoes, staggering along behind him about half a mile. Having made a fire near the river, where there was an air-hole through which the beaver had come up during the night, my father tied a gun to a stump with the muzzle towards the air-hole; he also tied a string to the trigger, and said, 'Should you see the beaver rise pull the string, and you will kill it.' I stood by the fire, with the string in my hand; I soon heard the noise occasioned by the blow of his tomahawk; he had killed a beaver and brought it to me. As he laid it down, he said, 'Then the great Spirit will not let us die here;' adding, as before, 'if you see the beaver rise, pull the string;' and he left me. I soon saw the nose of one, but I did not shoot. Presently, another came up; I pulled the trigger, and off the gun went. I could not see for some moments for the smoke. My father ran towards me with the two beavers, and laid them side by side; then, pointing to the sun,—'Do you see the sun?' he said; 'the great Spirit informed me that we should kill these two about this time in the morning. We will yet see our relatives at Rice Lake. Now let us go home, and see if our people are yet alive.' We arrived just in time to save them from death. Since which we have visited the same spot the year the missionaries came among us.

"My father knelt down, with feelings of gratitude, on the very spot where we had nearly perished. Glory to God! I have heard of many who have perished in this way far up in the woods."—*Life of George Copway, written by himself,* p. 44.

APPENDIX E

Page 121.—". . . *on first deciding that it was a canoe.*"

The Indians say, that before their fathers had tools of iron and steel in common use, a war canoe was the labour of three generations. It was hollowed out by means of fire, cautiously applied, or by stone hatchets; but so slowly did the work proceed, that years were passed in its excavation. When completed, it was regarded as a great achievement, and its launching on the waters of the lake or river was celebrated by feasting and dancing. The artizans were venerated as great patriots. Possibly the birch-bark canoe was of older date, as being more easily constructed, and needing not the assistance of the axe in forming it; but it was too frail to be used in war, or in long voyages, being liable to injuries.

The black stone wedges, so often found on the borders of our inland waters, were used by the Indians in skinning the deer and bear. Their arrow-heads were of white or black flint, rudely chipped into shape, and inserted in a cleft stick. A larger sort were used for killing deer; and blunt wooden ones were used by the children, for shooting birds and small game.

APPENDIX F

Page 128.—". . . *the Christian mind revolts with horror.*"

There is, according to the native author, George Copway, a strong feeling in the Indians for conversion and civilization, and a concentration of all the Christianised tribes, now scattered far and wide along the northern banks of the lakes and rivers, into one nation, to be called by one name, and united in one purpose—their general improvement. To this end, one of the most influential of their chiefs, John Jones, of Dover Sound, offered to give up to his Indian brethren, free of all cost, a large tract of unceded land, that they might be gathered together as one nation.

In the council held at Saugeen, where were convened Indian chiefs from lakes St. Clare, Simcoe, Huron, Ontario, and Rice, and other lakes, it was proposed to devise a plan by which the tract owned by the Saugeens could be held for the benefit of the Ojebwas, to petition Government for aid in establishing a manual-labour school, and to ascertain the general feeling of the chiefs in relation to forming one large settlement at Owen's Sound. At this meeting forty-eight chiefs were assembled.

There is much to admire in the simple, earnest, and courteous style of the oration delivered by Chief John Jones, and will give to my readers some idea of the intelligence of an educated Indian:—

"Brothers, you have been called from all your parts of Canada, even from the north of Georgian Bay. You are from your homes, your wives, and your children. We might regret this, were it not for the circumstances that require you here.

"Fellow-chiefs and brothers, I have pondered with deep solicitude our present condition and the future welfare of our children, as well as of ourselves. I have studied deeply and anxiously, in order to arrive at a true knowledge of the proper course to be pursued to secure to us and our descendants, and even to those around us, the greatest amount of peace, health, happiness, and usefulness. The interests of the Ojebwas and Ottawas are near and dear to my heart; for them I have often passed sleepless nights, and have suffered from an agitated mind. These nations, I am proud to say, are my brothers, many of them bone of my bone; and for them, if needs be, I would willingly sacrifice anything. Brothers, you see my heart." [Here he held out a piece of white paper, emblematical of a pure heart.]

"Fellow-chiefs and warriors, I have looked over your wigwams throughout Canada, and have come to the conclusion that you are in a warm place [*query*, too hot to hold you]. The whites are kindling fires all round you [*i.e.* clearing land].

"One purpose for which you have been called together, is to devise some plan by which we can live together, and become a happy people; so that our dying fires may not go out, *i.e.* our people become extinct, but may be kindled, and burn brightly, in one place. We now offer you any portion of the land we own in this region, that we may smoke the pipe of peace, and live and die together, and see our children play and be reared on the same spot. We ask no money of you. We love you; and because we love you, and feel for you, we propose this.

"My chiefs, brothers, warriors. This morning" [the speaker now pointed with his finger towards the heavens], "look up and see the blue sky: there are no clouds; the sun is bright and clear. Our fathers taught us, that when the sky was without clouds, the Great Spirit was smiling upon them. May he now preside over us, that we may make a long, smooth, and straight path for our children. It is true I seldom see you all, but this morning I shake hands with you all, in my heart.

"Brothers, this is all I have to say."

APPENDIX G

Page 140.—". . . *and aimed a knife at his throat*."

The period at which these events are said to have occurred was some sixty or eighty years ago, according to the imperfect chronology of my informant. At first, I hesitated to believe that such horrible deeds as those recorded could have taken place almost within the memory of men. My Indian narrator replied—"Indians, no Christians in those days, do worse than that very few years ago,—do as bad now in far-west."

The conversion of the Rice Lake Indians, and the gathering them together in villages, took place, I think, in the year 1825, or thereabouts. The conversion was effected by the preaching of missionaries from the Wesleyan Methodist Church; the village was under the patronage of Captain Anderson, whose descendants inherit much land on the north shore on and about Anderson's Point, the renowned site of the great battle. The war-weapon and bones of the enemies the Ojebwas are still to be found in this vicinity.

APPENDIX H

Page 152.—*"This place she called Spooke Island."*

Spooke Island. A singular and barren island in the Rice Lake, seventh from the head of the lake, on which the Indians used formerly to bury their dead, for many years held as a sacred spot, and only approached with reverence. Now famous for two things, *picnics* and *poison ivy, rhus toxicodendron,*—many persons having suffered for their temerity in landing upon it and making it the scene of their rural festivities.

APPENDIX I

Page 166.—*"and nothing but fire."*

The Indians call the Rice Lake, in allusion to the rapidity
with which fires run over the dry herbage, the Lake of the
Burning Plains. Certainly, there is much poetical fitness
and beauty in many of the Indian names, approximating
very closely to the figurative imagery of the language of
the East; such is "Mad-wa-osh," the music of the winds.

APPENDIX K

Page 180.—*"but it was not so in the days whereof I have spoken."*

From George Copway's Life.

Converted Indians are thus described in the "Life" of their literary countryman, George Copway:—

Chippewas of the River Credit.—These Indians are the remnant of a tribe which formerly possessed a considerable portion of the Home and Gore Districts, of which, in 1818, they surrendered the greater part for an annuity of 532*l.* 10*s.* reserving only certain small tracts at the River Credit; and at Sixteen and Twelve Miles Creeks they were the first tribe converted to Christianity. Previous to the year 1823 they were wandering pagans. In that year Peter Jones, and John his brother, the sons of a white by a Mississaga woman, having been converted to Christianity, and admitted as members of the Wesleyan Methodist Church, became anxious to redeem their countrymen from their degraded state of heathenism and spiritual destitution. They collected a considerable number together, and by rote and frequent repetitions, taught the first principles of Christianity to such as were too old to learn to read, and with the Lord's Prayer, the Creed, and Commandments, were thus committed to memory. As soon as the tribes were converted they perceived the evils attendant on their former state of ignorance and vagrancy. They began to work, which they had never done before; they recognised the advantage of cultivating the soil; they gave up drinking, to which they had been greatly addicted, and became sober, consistent, industrious Christians.

J. Sawyer, P. Jones, Chiefs; J. Jones, War-chief.

The *Chippewas of Alnwick* were converted in 1826-7. They were wandering pagans, in the neighbourhood of Belleville, Kingston, and Gananoque, commonly known as Mississagas of the Bay of Quinté; they resided on Grape Island, in the Bay of Quinté, six miles from Belleville. They resided eleven years on the island, subsisting by hunting and agriculture. Their houses were erected partly by their own labour and by the Wesleyan Missionary funds; these consist of twenty-three houses, a commodious chapel and school, an infant school, hospital, smithy, shoemaker's shop and joiner's. There are upwards of 300 of these Indians.

The chiefs are—Sunday; Simpson; G. Corrego, chief and missionary interpreter.

Rice Lake Chippewas.—In 1818 the greater part of the Newcastle and Colborne districts were surrendered, for an annuity of 940*l*. These Indians have all been reclaimed from their wandering life, and settled in their present locations, within the last ten or twelve years.[1] The settlement is on the north side of the lake, twelve miles from Peterborough. Number of Indians, 114; possessing 1,550 acres, subdivided in 50-acre lots.

Chiefs—Poudash, Copway, Crow.

Deer were plenty a few years ago, but now only few can be found. The Ojebwas are at present employed in farming instead of hunting; many of them have good and well-cultivated farms; they not only raise grain enough for their own use, but often sell much to the whites.

[1] I think G. Copway is incorrect as to the date of the settling of the village, as it was pointed out to me in 1832. Note,—In the year 1822 the larger part of the Indian village on Anderson's Point was built and cultivated.

APPENDIX L

Page 187.—". . . *that an outward manifestation of surprise.*"

A young friend, who was familiar with Indian character from frequent intercourse with them in his hunting expeditions, speaking of their apparent absence of curiosity, told me that, with a view to test it, he wound up a musical snuff-box, and placed it on a table in a room where several Indian hunters and their squaws were standing together, and narrowly watched their countenances, but they evinced no sort of surprise by look or gesture, remaining apathetically unmoved. He retired to an adjoining room, where, unseen, he could notice what passed, and was amused at perceiving, that the instant they imagined themselves free from his surveillance, the whole party mustered round the mysterious toy like a parcel of bees, and appeared to be full of conjecture and amazement, but they did not choose to be entrapped into showing surprise. This perfect command over the muscles of the face, and the glance of the eye, is one of the remarkable traits in the Indian character. The expression of the Indian face, if I may use so paradoxical a term, consists in a want of expression—like the stillness of dark deep water, beneath which no object is visible.

APPENDIX M

Page 220.—*"bracelets of porcupine quills cut in fine pieces and strung in fanciful patterns."*

The Indian method of drawing out patterns on the birch bark, is simply scratching the outline with some small-pointed instrument, Canadian thorn, a bodkin of bone, or a sharp nail. These outlines are then pierced with parallel rows of holes, into which the ends of the porcupine quills are inserted, forming a rich sort of embroidery on the surface of the bark.

The Indian artistes have about as much notion of perspective, or the effects of light and shade, as the Chinese or our own early painters; their attempts at delineating animals, or birds, are flat, sharp, and angular; and their groups of flowers and trees not more graceful or natural than those on a china plate or jar; nevertheless, the effect produced is rich and striking, from the vivid colours and the variety of dyes they contrive to give to this simple material, the porcupine quills. The sinew of the deer, and some other animals, furnish the Indian women with thread, of any degree of fineness or strength. The wants of these simple folk are few, and those easily supplied by the adaptation of such materials as they can command with ease, in their savage state.

APPENDIX N

Page 225.—*"is Mount Ararat."*

Mount Ararat, the highest elevation on the Rice Lake Plains, for nearly two years the residence of the Authoress and her family.

Explanatory Notes

These explanatory notes deal with two kinds of material in *Canadian Crusoes*: direct quotations and allusions, and references to specific events, people, and places. Of the direct quotations and allusions, the most numerous reflect the training and education that Thomas Strickland and his wife gave their children and the wide reading that the family library and other libraries nearby made possible. In both the text and the epigraphs that head each chapter, quotations from their daily reading abound. The Bible is the most quoted source, but the plays of Shakespeare and of Beaumont and Fletcher, and the works of earlier and contemporary English, Scottish, and Irish writers are also represented. Many of the references Mrs. Traill makes to events, people, and places are themselves explained within the text of *Canadian Crusoes* and therefore require no additional notes. Notes have been provided, however, for historical events like the Battle of Culloden and exploits of the Stuarts, to whom the Strickland sisters were so devoted; for the people in the Peterborough area whom Mrs. Traill mentions by name; and for a few places such as the St. John River or Kilvert's Ravine of which either the identity or location is unclear. The notes are keyed to the text by page and line numbers.

1.2-5   *"The morning ... lash'd on the shore"*]
          James Hogg, "The Emigrant," 1819, ll. 1-4; the
          poem was published in collections of both Hogg's
          works and Jacobite songs throughout the
          nineteenth century; in *The Jacobite Minstrelsy*, for
          example, the opening lines read:

255

MAY morning had shed her streamers on
   high,
O'er Canada, opening all pale on the sky!
Still dazzling and white was the robe that she
   wore,
Except where the mountain wave lash'd on
   the shore.

See *The Jacobite Minstrelsy*. Glasgow: R. Griffin,
1829, p. 335.

2 .14-16   *"without the Lord . . . vain"*] Compare Psalm 127:1,
"Except the LORD build the house, they labor in
vain that build it: except the LORD keep the city,
the watchman waketh *but* in vain." See *The
Interpreter's Bible*. Vol. 4. New York and
Nashville: Abingdon Press, 1955, p. 667.

2 .21   *the famous battle of Quebec*] The Battle of the
Plains of Abraham, where on 13 Sept. 1759, the
British under Major-General James Wolfe
defeated the French under Lieutenant-General
Louis-Joseph de Montcalm, Marquis de
Montcalm.

4 .7   *of the same religion*] Many of the Scottish soldiers
who served in British North America were
Roman Catholic.

6 .30-7.1   *a Testament . . . the truths of the Gospel*] Referring to
the New Testament, Mrs. Traill expresses a
traditional, albeit erroneous, Protestant notion
that Roman Catholic laymen were not allowed to
read the Bible. See *Twentieth Century Encyclopedia
of Catholicism*. Vol. 60: *What is the Bible?* By Henri
Daniel-Rops. J. R. Foster trans. New York:
Hawthorn Books, 1958, pp. 10-13.

18 .2   *"Fear not, ye are of more value than many sparrows"*]
Compare Matthew 10:31 and Luke 12:7. See *The
Interpreter's Bible*. Vol. 7. 1951, p. 372, and Vol. 8.
1952, p. 223.

20 .23-25   *"There was a voice of woe . . . because they were not"*]
Compare Jeremiah 31:15, "Thus saith the
LORD; A voice was heard in Ramah,
lamentation, *and* bitter weeping; Rachel weeping
for her children refused to be comforted for her
children, because they *were* not." See *The
Interpreter's Bible.* Vol. 5. 1956, pp. 1031-32.

20 .31-34   *"Oh, were their tale . . . fancy's endless dreams de-
part"*] John Malcolm, "Lines on the Loss of a
Ship," ll. 25-28; this popular poem about a ship
that sailed away and "was never heard of more"
was reprinted in the *Cobourg Star* in 1835 under
the title of "The Cast-Away Ship"; in this version
the first four lines of the last stanza read,

Oh! were her tale of sorrow known,
   'Twere something to the broken heart;
The pangs of doubt would then be gone,
   And Fancy's endless dreams depart!

In "Memorials The Stricklands," Mrs. Traill also
uses these lines when she tells the story of the
disappearance of "Captain W____," the fiancé
of her sister Elizabeth; he had "command of a
fine new East Indiaman" which "was launched
under bright auspices but from that hour of
parting from the English shores, . . . was heard
of no more." See *Cobourg Star*, 13 May 1835, p. 1,
and PAC, TFC, Vol. 7, pp. 10879-80.

22 .3   *Sackville's Mill-dike*] An 1848 map of the
Newcastle and Colborne District shows a sawmill
south of Rice Lake towards its west end; in 1850
James Sackville owned this mill and occupied lot
31 on the 8th Concession; in "Rice Lake Plains—
The Wolf Tower," Mrs. Traill locates "Sackville
Mill" west of Wolf Tower. See OTAR, Hamilton
Township Census 1850, RG 21, Sheet 29, and
"Forest Gleanings. No. III." *Anglo-American
Magazine*, 1 (1852), 418.

23¹.1   *Black's Landing*] Named after William Black, who kept a tavern there, Black's Landing was located at the west end of Rice Lake where the town of Bewdley is today.

30 .32-35   *"Consider the fowls . . . they"*] Compare Matthew 6:26, "Behold the fowls of the air: for they sow not, neither do they reap, nor gather into barns; yet your heavenly Father feedeth them. Are ye not much better than they?" See *The Interpreter's Bible*. Vol. 7, pp. 321-22.

34 .15-17   *Charles Stuart . . . the young Chevalier Charles Edward*] Charles Edward Louis Philip Casimir (1720-88), the Young Pretender, was the grandson of James II, who succeeded his brother, Charles II, as King of England in 1685.

34 .25-31   *some great battle . . . Oliver Cromwell*] At Worcester on 3 Sept. 1651, Oliver Cromwell's Roundheads defeated Charles II and his Royalists, who were mostly Scottish, in the last pitched battle of the Civil War.

35 .2-4   *he hid . . . with . . . one of his own brave officers . . . great oak*] After his defeat at Worcester, Charles II became a fugitive; on 6 Sept. 1651, he joined William Carlos (or Careless), a Royalist officer who was himself escaping from the Commonwealth forces, in his hiding place in an oak tree in the woods near Boscobel House. See *DNB*. Vol. 3, pp. 1014-15.

35 .5   *he was in the house of one Pendril, a woodman*] William Penderel and his five sons all helped Charles II to escape after his defeat at Worcester; William hid the king in Boscobel House; his son Richard hid him in Hobbal Grange; although the Penderels have sometimes been called poor woodmen, they were, in fact, substantial yeomen. In an article on the Strickland family written towards the end of her life, Mrs. Traill claimed

that through her grandmother Strickland she was descended from a "Pendril . . . one of the brave honest Shropshire lads whose inflexible loyalty was proof against *all* temptation and threats to betray their fugitive King when hard pressed by the soldiers of the Parliament after the defeat of his army at Worcester, he was a hunted homeless wanderer seeking refuge in the woods of Boscobel"; in the same article she says that William Pendril, "the Woodman . . . cut the young King's lovelocks with his billhook, the better to hide his cavalier bearing, and dressed him in his own coarse green jerkin and leathers and hobnailed shoes, guiding him through the bosky dells of that far famed wood, the recesses and haunts of which he knew so well." See *DNB*. Vol. 15, pp. 734-35, and PAC, TFC, Vol. 7, p. 10845, "Our Grandmother's Stories."

35 .25   *his poor father*] Charles I; he was beheaded on the orders of Oliver Cromwell and his followers on 30 Jan. 1649.

36 .2-4   *Prince Charles . . . the battle of Culloden*] On 16 Apr. 1746, the Duke of Cumberland, the son of George II, and his troops fought Prince Charles Edward, the Young Pretender, and his Scottish followers at Culloden; the defeat of the Jacobites ended both their rebellion and their hope of restoring the Stuarts to the British throne.

36 .9   *General Wolfe*] Major-General James Wolfe, who died at the Battle of the Plains of Abraham, was the commander-in-chief of the land forces that took part in the expedition against Quebec in 1759. See *DCB*. Vol. 3, pp. 666-74.

37 .9-11   *bears . . . like the lambs in the old nursery tale*]Visions of a land of plenty where food and drink proliferate without man's labour or effort have appeared in literature since mediaeval times; the

meat usually offered is that of fowl, geese, or pigs, although in *Songs of the Bards of the Tyne* (1849), one poem includes "Legs of mutton" growing on trees. The similarity between Mrs. Traill's wording and that of Susanna Moodie's reference in *Roughing It in the Bush* (1852) to "the story told in the nursery, of the sheep and oxen that ran about the streets, ready roasted, and with knives and forks upon their backs," suggests that the Stricklands had their own version of the tale. See, for example, "The Land of Cokaygne," ll. 102-10. In *Early Middle English Verse and Prose*. Ed. J.A.W. Bennett and G. V. Smithers. Oxford: Clarendon Press, 1966, pp. 141-42; A. L. Morton. *The English Utopia*. London: Lawrence and Wishart, 1969, p. 36; and Susanna Moodie. *Roughing It in the Bush; or, Life in Canada*. London: Richard Bentley, 1852, Vol. 1, p. xi.

38 .31   *the St. John*] This is probably the St. John River in New Brunswick; there are also, however, at least four rivers of that name in Quebec.

39 .2-3   *"Sufficient unto the day . . . evil thereof"*]Compare Matthew 6:34; the complete verse reads, "Take therefore no thought for the morrow: for the morrow shall take thought for the things of itself. Sufficient unto the day *is* the evil thereof." See *The Interpreter's Bible*. Vol. 7, p. 324.

43 .24-25   *"Wolf's Crag," for so the children had named the . . . spot*] The Traill family also called the spot "Wolf's Crag"; they may have taken the name from Sir Walter Scott's *The Bride of Lammermoor* (1819), where the only inheritance of the Master of Ravenswood is a tower named Wolf's Crag. See "Forest Gleanings. No. III." *Anglo-American Magazine*, 1 (1852), 418.

45^2 .3   *G. Ley*] G. Ley, a neighbour of the Traills who

died on 13 Aug. 1893, owned lots 27-31 on the
8th Concession of Hamilton Township.

46 .10   *"bright, boundless, and free"*] Unidentified.

49 .13-14   *"God hath . . . the wilderness"*] Compare Psalm
78:19; Catharine is recalling the psalmist's
description of the Jews, who, after their
miraculous escape from Egypt, found themselves
in the desert without food and "spake against
God; they said, Can God furnish a table in the
wilderness?" See *The Interpreter's Bible*. Vol. 4, p.
418.

49 .26   *"children in the wood"*] There are several versions
in both poetry and prose of the story of two
orphaned children who, victims of a designing
uncle, were left to die in the woods. Mrs. Traill
learned her version, which was one of her
favourite stories, from Betty Holt, her mother's
old nurse. See *The Osborne Collection of Early
Children's Books, 1566-1910*. Comp. Judith St.
John. Toronto: Toronto Public Library, 1966,
pp. 22-23, and Catharine Parr Traill. *Cot
and Cradle Stories*. Toronto: Briggs, 1895, p. 48.

53 .2-4   *They . . . exclaimed with the patriarch Jacob, "How
dreadful is this place"*] Compare Genesis 28:17; on
the way from Beer-sheba to Haran, Jacob,
awaking from a dream in which he saw God and
heard Him speak, "was afraid, and said, How
dreadful *is* this place! this *is* none other but the
house of God, and this *is* the gate of heaven." See
The Interpreter's Bible. Vol. 1. 1952, p. 691.

54 .2-3   *"Oh for a lodge . . . shade"*] William Cowper, *The
Task*, 1784, Book 2: "The Time-Piece," ll. 1-2; in
Southey's edition of Cowper's works, the lines
read: "OH for a lodge in some vast wilderness, /
Some boundless contiguity of shade." See *The
Works of William Cowper, Esq. Comprising His*

Poems, Correspondence, and Translations. Ed. Robert Southey. Vol. 9. London: Baldwin and Cradock, 1836, p. 97.

58 .31-32   *"The world was all . . . Providence their guide"*]John Milton, *Paradise Lost*, 1667, Book XII, ll. 646-47; when Adam and Eve left *"Eden,"* "The World was all before them, where to choose / Thir place of rest, and Providence thir guide." See *The Works of John Milton*. Vol. 2, Pt. 2. Ed. Frank Allen Patterson. New York: Columbia University Press, 1931, p. 401.

61³.1   *Kilvert's Ravine*] Richard Kilvert was living on the property in the 1830s, but his name does not appear in the 1850 census of Hamilton Township. In "Rice Lake Plains—The Wolf Tower," Mrs. Traill refers to "Thilvert's Ravine" east of Wolf Tower, the death of Mrs. Thilvert, and the departure of her husband and children; the difference in spelling is probably a compositorial error due to a misreading of Mrs. Traill's handwriting. She repeats the same story of "Kilvert's ravine" in "Floral Studies." See "Forest Gleanings. No. III." *Anglo-American Magazine*, 1 (1852), 418, and PAC, TFC, Vol. 3, p. 3510.

63 .20-23   *the old song:—"Oh! the golden days of good Queen Bess . . . latch"*] The exact source of this song has not been located; there are various songs about "good Queen Bess," however, including one by W. Collins (1721-56), that has as a line in its chorus "O! the golden days of good Queen Bess"; one stanza of one version of this song also has the phrase "doors only latched." See *The Minstrelsy of England. A collection of English Songs*. Ed. Edmondstoune Duncan. Vol. 2. London: Augener, [1909], pp. 240-41.

68 .24-28   *the mighty thunder-peal . . . "a mighty voice"*]
Compare Psalm 68:33, where the psalmist urges
that praises be sung to God, "To him that rideth
upon the heavens of heavens, *which were* of old;
lo, he doth send out his voice, *and that* a mighty
voice." See *The Interpreter's Bible*. Vol. 4, p. 360.

83 .2-11   *"Aye from the sultry heat . . . their drowsy song"*]
Samuel Taylor Coleridge, "Songs of the Pixies,"
1796, ll. 25-34; the version that appeared in
Poems on Various Subjects (1796) reads:

> Aye from the sultry heat
> We to the cave retreat
> O'ercanopied by huge roots intertwin'd
> With wildest texture, blacken'd o'er with age:
> Round them their mantle green the ivies bind,
>   Beneath whose foliage pale
>   Fann'd by the unfrequent gale
> We shield us from the Tyrant's mid-day rage.

> Thither, while the murmuring throng
> Of wild-bees hum their drowsy song.

See *The Complete Poetical Works of Samuel Taylor
Coleridge Including Poems and Versions of Poems
Now Published for the First Time. In Two Volumes.*
Ed. Ernest Hartley Coleridge. Vol. 1: *Poems.*
1912; rpt. Oxford: Clarendon Press, 1968, pp.
41-42.

86¹.1   *Joe Harris*] In 1850 Joe Harris owned lot 21 on
the 8th Concession of Hamilton Township; a
United Empire Loyalist, Harris is the "old Joe" of
Susanna Moodie's *Roughing It in the Bush*. See
OTAR, Hamilton Township Census 1850, RG 21,
Sheet 27.

87 .19   *Mount Ararat*] Genesis 8:4; after the flood, the

ark which contained Noah and all that were with him came to rest "upon the mountains of Ararat." See *The Interpreter's Bible*. Vol. 1, p. 544. Mrs. Traill describes the Canadian Mount Ararat in detail in "Rice Lake Plains—The Wolf Tower." See "Forest Gleanings, No. III." *Anglo-American Magazine*, 1 (1852), 418.

91¹.2   *Alfred Hayward*] In 1850 Captain Alfred Hayward (1810-66) owned lots 16 and 17 on the 9th Concession of Hamilton Township; these lots in Gore's Landing fronted on Rice Lake. See OTAR, Hamilton Township Census 1850, RG 21, Sheet 27.

101 .2-3   *"The soul of the wicked desireth evil; his neighbour findeth no favour in his eyes"*] Compare Proverbs 21:10. See *The Interpreter's Bible*. Vol. 4, p. 904.

103¹.1   *George Copway*] Born near the mouth of the Trent River, George Copway (1818-69) was a Mississauga or Ojibwa who became a Methodist missionary. In *Canadian Crusoes* Mrs. Traill is quoting with some alterations, and paraphrasing from, *Recollections of a Forest Life; or, The Life and Travels of Kah-ge-ga-gah-bowh or George Copway, Chief of the Ojibway Nation* (London: Gilpin, [1850]), an edition of *The Life, History, and Travels of Kah-ge-gah-bowh (George Copway), a Young Indian Chief of the Ojebwa Nation* published originally in 1847. See *DCB*. Vol. 9, pp. 419-21.

112 .2-5   *"Here the wren . . . to our cell"*] Samuel Taylor Coleridge, "Songs of the Pixies," 1796, ll. 5-8; the version that appeared in *Poems on Various Subjects* (1796) reads:

Here the wren of softest note
    Builds its nest and warbles well;
Here the blackbird strains his throat;
    Welcome, Ladies! to our cell.

See *The Complete Poetical Works of Samuel Taylor Coleridge*. Vol. 1, p. 40.

120 .2   *"Go to the ant"*] Compare Proverbs 6:6, "Go to the ant, thou sluggard; consider her ways, and be wise." See *The Interpreter's Bible*. Vol. 4, p. 818.

129 .23   *"God's gift to the weak"*] Caroline Anne Bowles Southey (Mrs. Southey), "The Reed-Sparrow's Nest," 1829, l. 18; describing the location of the nest, the narrator says, "'Twas an instinct unerring (God's gift to the weak) / Taught the poor little builder this covert to seek." See *The New Year's Gift; and Juvenile Souvenir*. Ed. Mrs. Alaric Watts. London: Longman, Rees, Orme, Brown, and Green, 1829, pp. 209-11.

130 .2-3   *"Oh, come and hear . . . the Dark Ladye"*] Samuel Taylor Coleridge, "The Dark Ladie," 1799, ll. 15-16; the version that appeared in the *Morning Post*, 21 Dec. 1799, reads: "O come and hear the cruel wrongs / Befel the dark Ladie!" See *The Complete Poetical Works of Samuel Taylor Coleridge*. Vol. 2: *Dramatic Works and Appendices*, p. 1053.

132¹.1   Anderson's Point] The point was named after Captain Charles Anderson (1786-1844), a veteran of the War of 1812-14, who came to Rice Lake c. 1819 and married an Indian woman.

138 .26-27   *A second Judith*] Judith, widow of Manasses of Bethulia, beheaded Holophernes, the leader of the Assyrians who were invading Judaea, and thus saved the Israelites from defeat at the hands of Nebuchadnezzar, king of Assyria; her story is told in Judith, one of the books of the Apocrypha. See, for example, "The Apocrypha." In *The New English Bible with the Apocrypha*. Oxford and Cambridge University Presses, 1970, pp. 68-85.

141 .9   *a lamb of his "extended fold"*] Compare John 10:16;

Mrs. Traill is probably recalling Jesus' parable about himself as the good shepherd: "And other sheep I have, which are not of this fold: them also I must bring, and they shall hear my voice; and there shall be one fold, *and* one shepherd." See *The Interpreter's Bible*. Vol. 8, p. 627.

141¹.2   *Mosang Poudash*] Mosang Poudash or Paudash (c. 1818-c. 1893) was a Mississauga or Ojibwa Indian of Rice Lake. See J. Hampden Burnham. "The Coming of the Missassagas." In *The Valley of the Trent*. Ed. Edwin C. Guillet. Toronto: Champlain Society, 1957, pp. 9-10.

142 .2   *"The horn of the hunter is heard on the hill"*]Louisa Matilda Jane Montagu ("Julia") Crawford, "Kathleen Mavourneen," 1835, l. 2. See *Metropolitan Magazine*, 14 (September 1835), p. 66.

146 .31-32   *joy . . . over one sinner that repenteth*]Compare Luke 15:10; Jesus concludes the parable of the lost coin with the statement: "Likewise, I say unto you, there is joy in the presence of the angels of God over one sinner that repenteth." See *The Interpreter's Bible*. Vol. 8, p. 269.

146¹.1-2   *a . . . family of the name of Brown*] Captain Alexander Brown (d. 1848) came to Canada from Cavan, Ireland, in 1821; in 1850 his family occupied lot 17 on the 8th Concession of Hamilton Township, the farm next to Mt. Ararat. See OTAR, Hamilton Township Census 1850, RG 21, Sheet 3.

152¹.7   *William Falkner*] In 1850 William Falkner (1782-1854) owned lot 14 on the 9th Concession of Hamilton Township; one of the first settlers in the area, he arrived in 1833. See OTAR, Hamilton Township Census 1850, RG 21, Sheet 26.

155 .12-13   *they were in the hands of Him who can say to the tempest-tossed waves, "Peace, be still"*] Compare

Mark 4:39; Jesus and his disciples are crossing the sea of Galilee when a storm arises, and the disciples, afraid, waken the sleeping Christ. "And he arose, and rebuked the wind, and said unto the sea, Peace, be still. And the wind ceased, and there was a great calm." See *The Interpreter's Bible*. Vol. 7, p. 710.

157 .2   *"Scared by the red and noisy light"*] Samuel Taylor Coleridge, "Fire, Famine, and Slaughter," 1798, l. 55. See *The Complete Poetical Works of Samuel Taylor Coleridge*. Vol. 1, p. 239.

165 .14-15   *"That winter, cold winter, was past, / And that spring, lovely spring, was approaching at last"*] Mrs. Traill quotes these unidentified lines in at least two other works; in her journal, she describes the hepatica as a "harbinger of Spring" that "tells us that Winter, / Cold winter is past / And that Spring lovely spring / Is returning at last," and in *Pearls and Pebbles*, she calls the "Chipping Sparrow" one of "the earliest harbingers of spring; 'They tell us that winter, cold winter, is past, / And spring, lovely spring, is arriving at last.'" See PAC, TFC, Vol. 3, p. 3506, Mrs. Traill's Journal 1831-1895, and *Pearls and Pebbles; or, Notes of an Old Naturalist*. Toronto: Briggs, Montreal: Coates, and Halifax: Huestis, 1894, pp. 69-70.

171 .2-5   *"I know a lake . . . disturb the strand"*]Fitz-James O'Brien, "Loch Ina, A Beautiful Salt-Water Lake, in the County of Cork, near Baltimore," 1845, ll. 1-6; the first published version of these lines reads:

I know a lake
Where the cool waves break,
And softly fall on the silver sand—
And no steps intrude

On that solitude,
And no voice, save mine, disturbs the strand—

See *Nation* (Dublin), 26 July 1845, p. 683.

177 .14-16 *"Oh that men . . . children of men"*] Compare Psalm 107:8, "Oh that *men* would praise the LORD *for* his goodness, and *for* his wonderful works to the children of men!" See *The Interpreter's Bible*. Vol. 4, p. 573.

181 .2-3 *"Must this sweet new-blown rose find such a winter / Before her spring be past"*] John Fletcher, *The Night-Walker; or, The Little Thief*, 1640, I.iii.34-35; the version that appeared in the collected *Works of Beaumont & Fletcher* edited by Alexander Dyce reads, "Must my sweet new-blown rose find such a winter / Before her spring be near?" See *The Works of Beaumont & Fletcher; The Text Formed from a New Collation of the Early Editions. With Notes and a Biographical Memoir by the Rev. Alexander Dyce*. In Eleven Volumes. Vol. 11. London: Edward Moxon, 1846, p. 136.

184^1.1 *Lieut. Rubidge*]Charles Rubidge (1787-1873), a naval officer on half pay, immigrated to Upper Canada in 1819 and took up lands in Otonabee Township in 1820; he thus became one of the first settlers in the area. One of his letters describing his settlement was included by Basil Hall in *Travels in North America, In the Years 1827 and 1828*. See *DCB*. Vol. 10, pp. 635-36, and Basil Hall. *Travels in North America, In the Years 1827 and 1828. In Three Volumes*. Edinburgh: Cadell, and London: Simpkin and Marshall, 1829, Vol. 1, pp. 324-39.

191 .2-5 *"Now where the wave . . . sleeps upon its breast"*] Samuel Taylor Coleridge, "Songs of the Pixies," 1796, ll. 69-72; the version that appeared in *Poems on Various Subjects* (1796) reads:

Or where his wave with loud unquiet song
Dash'd o'er the rocky channel froths along;
Or where, his silver waters smooth'd to rest,
The tall tree's shadow sleeps upon his breast.

See *The Complete Poetical Works of Samuel Taylor Coleridge*. Vol. 1, p. 43.

197 .2-8   *"Cold and forsaken . . . in soft slumbers"*]Francis Beaumont and John Fletcher, *The Coxcomb*, 1647, IV.ii.37-43; the version that appeared in Dyce's edition reads:

Cold and forsaken, destitute of friends,
And all good comforts else, unless some tree,
Whose speechless charity must better ours,
With which the bitter east winds made their sport
And sung through hourly, hath invited her
To keep off half a day? Shall she be thus,
And I draw in soft slumbers?

See *The Works of Beaumont & Fletcher*. Vol. 3, p. 180.

202 .14-21   *an old French Canadian song . . . "And we'll chase the buffalo"*] No "old French Canadian song" that resembles Mrs. Traill's has been identified; her song, however, does bear some resemblance to "Shoot the Buffalo," an Anglo-American song. See one version of this in *Folk Song: USA*. Ed. Alan Lomax. New York: Duell, Sloan, and Pearce, 1947, p. 103.

209 .2   *"Where wild in woods the lordly savage ran"*] John Dryden, *The Conquest of Granada, Part I*, 1672, I.i.209; Almanzor states that he is "as free as Nature first made man / 'Ere the base Laws of Servitude began / When wild in woods the noble Savage ran." See *The Works of John Dryden*. Vol. 11. Ed. John Loftis and David Stuart Rodes.

Berkeley: University of California Press, 1978, p. 30.

210 .13-14　　*the Government Agent, now Colonel Macdonald*] Alexander McDonell (1786-1861) was an immigration and Crown Land agent in Peterborough from 1827 until 1843; in 1837 he was colonel of the 2nd battalion of Northumberland militia. See *DCB*. Vol. 9, p. 483.

218 .4　　*"In still, but brave despair"*] Felicia Hemans, "Casabianca," 1829, l. 24; at the Battle of the Nile, the boy Casabianca, "In still, yet brave despair," stands alone "on the burning deck" of his ship and waits in vain to hear its captain, his father, who has already been killed, order his son to abandon his "post of death." See Felicia Hemans. *The Forest Sanctuary: With Other Poems. The Second Edition, with Additions.* Edinburgh: William Blackwood, and London: T. Cadell, 1829, pp. 243-45.

219 .2-5　　*"Hame, hame . . . mine own countrie"*] Allan Cunningham, "Hame, Hame, Hame," 1810, ll. 1-2; the first published version of these lines reads: "Hame, hame, hame, Hame fain wad I be, / O hame, hame, hame, to my ain countrie!" See *Remains of Nithsdale and Galloway Song.* Ed. R. H. Cromek. London: T. Cadell and W. Davies, 1810, p. 169.

221 .13-14　　*Oh that I had wings like a dove . . . rest*] Compare Psalm 55:6, where the psalmist sings: "And I said, Oh that I had wings like a dove! *for then* would I fly away, and be at rest." See *The Interpreter's Bible.* Vol. 4, p. 289.

225 .2　　*the . . . proprietor of the village that bears his name*] Gore's Landing was named after Thomas Gore (c. 1818-58), an Irishman, who in 1850 lived on lot 15 in the 8th Concession of Hamilton

Township. See OTAR, Hamilton Township Census 1850, RG 21, Sheet 27.

225 .4   *Colonel Brown's*] Lieutenant-Colonel Robert Brown immigrated to the Peterborough area in 1830 and moved with his family to Gore's Landing in 1847; the family was related to Thomas A. and Frances Stewart, Mrs. Traill's close friends. See Norma Martin, Catherine Milne, and Donna McGillis. *Historic Gore's Landing: A Walking Tour.* Second Edition. 1983, p. 5.

226 .4-7   *it was left to the birds of the air . . . feedeth them*] Compare Matthew 6:26; in a discussion about trust and anxiety, Jesus says: "Behold the fowls of the air: for they sow not, neither do they reap, nor gather into barns; yet your heavenly Father feedeth them." See *The Interpreter's Bible.* Vol. 7, p. 321.

227 .1-2   *"Thy home . . . my home, thy God my God"*] Compare Ruth 1:16; Ruth, the Moabite, refuses to leave Naomi, her mother-in-law, when she decides to return to the land of Judah: "And Ruth said, Entreat me not to leave thee, *or to return from following after thee:* for whither thou goest, I will go; and where thou lodgest, I will lodge: thy people *shall be* my people, and thy God my God." See *The Interpreter's Bible.* Vol. 2. 1953, p. 837.

228 .2   *"I will arise, and go to my father"*] Compare Luke 15:18. See *The Interpreter's Bible.* Vol. 8, p. 275.

229 .8   *Bruce and Wallace*] The Highlanders, supporters of the Jacobite cause, have appropriately named their hounds after King Robert "the Bruce" (1274-1329) and William Wallace (1272?-1305), both of whom were heroic defenders of Scottish independence.

Bibliographical Description of
Authoritative Editions

A bibliographical description follows of the 1852 London: Hall, Virtue edition of *Canadian Crusoes*, the copy-text of the CEECT edition; of the 1859 London: Hall, Virtue edition of *Canadian Crusoes*; and of the 1882 Nelson edition of *Lost in the Backwoods*. In these transcriptions, the differences between sizes of capitals within a single line are not noted, and the form (thin/thick, swelled, etc.) and the length (short, full measure, etc.) of rules are not specified.

1852 London: Hall, Virtue

Title-page: CANADIAN CRUSOES. | 𝔄 𝔗𝔞𝔩𝔢 | OF | THE RICE LAKE PLAINS. | BY | CATHARINE PARR TRAILL, | AUTHORESS OF "THE BACKWOODS OF CANADA," ETC. | EDITED BY AGNES STRICKLAND. | [rule] | ILLUSTRATED BY HARVEY. | [rule] | LONDON: | ARTHUR HALL, VIRTUE, & CO. | 25, PATERNOSTER ROW. | 1852.

This title-page is reproduced as an illustration in the CEECT edition.

Size of leaf: 163 × 103 mm.

Collation: foolscap 8°, π^2 b^4 $^2\pi$1 B-2A^8, 191 leaves, pp. *i-v* vi-xi *xii-xiv 1* 2-350 *351-353* 354-368

273

Contents: p. [i] title-page, p. [ii] printer's imprint, p. [iii] dedication, p. [iv] blank, pp. [v]-xi preface, p. [xii] blank, p. [xiii] list of engravings, p. [xiv] blank, pp. [1]-350 text, p. [351] appendix, p. [352] blank, pp. [353]-368 appendices, on p. 368 colophon

In some copies the list of engravings precedes the preface.

Head-titles: PREFACE. p. [v]
THE | CANADIAN CRUSOES. p. [1]
APPENDIX. p. [353]

Running-   From pp. 2-350 "THE CANADIAN CRUSOES."
titles: appears on each page. From pp. 354-368 "APPENDIX." appears on each page.

Notes: Twelve steel-plate engravings have been tipped in, one as frontispiece and the others facing pp. 22, 40, 98, 120, 164, 198, 263, 270, 320, 326, 347. In the "List of Engravings," the engraving that is the frontispiece is said to be facing p. 336. These illustrations are printed on paper different from the text. They are "ATTACK ON THE DEER," frontispiece; "LOUIS CONFESSING HIS DECEPTION OF CATHARINE," p. 22; "THE FIRST BREAKFAST," p. 40; "CATHARINE FOUND BY THE OLD DOG," p. 98; "WOLF FINDING THE WOUNDED DOE," p. 120; "HECTOR BRINGING THE INDIAN GIRL," p. 164; "KILLING WILD FOWL," p. 198; "INDIAN WOMAN AT THE DOOR OF THE HUT," p. 263; "CATHARINE CARRIED OFF," p. 270; "INDIANA BEFORE THE BALD EAGLE," p. 320; "INDIANA AT THE STAKE," p. 326; and "RETURN HOME," p. 347.

The casing is in diagonal fine wave grain cloth; its colour varies: dull green, brown, purple, saturation moderate. Front and back covers are blind stamped with a double line around the edges; an inner frame, top and bottom, of branch, leaf, and scallop; and a central triangular pattern of three branches with leaves. The spine is gilt stamped. At the top stands "THE | CANADIAN | CRUSOES." and at the bottom "HALL, VIRTUE, | & C?". Between them is a fir tree surrounded by a flight of birds in S-formation. The tree's roots that enclose the initials "J. L." extend to the bottom lettering. Against the trunk of the tree stands a trophy comprising a spear, a deer head with antlers, a hatchet, two fish, a hanging duck, a bow or fishing pole, and a paddle or spade all tied together with a ribbon. There are plain yellow end-papers. One copy in the OTP Osborne Collection has on the back end-paper a small rectangular ticket: "Bound by | Westleys & Co. | Friar Street, | London."

The OKQ copy, the OONL copy, and one OTP Osborne Collection copy have bound in a 32-page gathering of advertisements, entitled "A List of New Works and New Editions published by Arthur Hall, Virtue & Co." This list is not dated, but on p. 28 *Canadian Crusoes* is advertised as being "In preparation," while on p. 31 a "New Christmas Book," "The Illustrated Year Book," with an article on the "Industrial Exhibition, 1851," is advertised. The OTU copy has a 16-page gathering of advertisements, entitled "A Catalogue of Instructive and Amusing Works for the Young." This catalogue is dated 1 Nov. 1853 and includes an advertisement for *Canadian Crusoes* with quotations from reviews that appeared in *Tait's Edinburgh Magazine* and the *Guardian*.

Copies: OKQ Lorne Pierce Collection PS8489 R35 C3;
OONL PS8439 T7 C3; OTP Osborne Collection —
two copies (no call numbers); OTU B11.6880

Each of the copies listed above was microfilmed for
CEECT by the Central Microfilming Unit of the
Public Archives of Canada.

1859 London: Hall, Virtue

Title-page: CANADIAN CRUSOES. | 𝔄 𝔗𝔞𝔩𝔢 | OF | THE
RICE LAKE PLAINS. | BY | CATHARINE
PARR TRAILL, | AUTHORESS OF "THE
BACKWOODS OF CANADA," ETC. |
EDITED BY AGNES STRICKLAND. | [rule]
| ILLUSTRATED BY HARVEY. | [rule] |
SECOND EDITION. | LONDON: | ARTHUR
HALL, VIRTUE, & CO. | 25, PATERNOSTER
ROW. | 1859.

Size of leaf: 172 × 106 mm.

Collation: foolscap 8°, π^2b^4 B-Z^8 2A^6, 188 leaves, pp. *i-v* vi-xi
xii 1 2-344 *345-347* 348-362 *363-364*

Contents: p. [i] title-page, p. [ii] printer's imprint, p. [iii]
dedication, p. [iv] list of engravings, pp. [v]-xi
preface, p. [xii] blank, pp. [1]-344 text, p. [345]
appendix, p. [346] blank, pp. [347]-362 appen-
dices, on p. 362 colophon, p. [363] advertisement,
p. [364] blank

Head-titles: PREFACE. p. [v]
THE | CANADIAN CRUSOES. p. [1]
APPENDIX. p. [347]

Running-   From pp. 2-344 "THE CANADIAN CRUSOES."
titles: appears on each page. From pp. 348-362
"APPENDIX." appears on each page.

Notes: The same twelve steel-plate engravings as in the
1852 edition have been tipped in, one as frontis-
piece and the others facing pp. 21, 40, 98, 119,
162, 195, 260, 266, 315, 321, 342. In the "List of
Engravings," "Attack On The Deer," the engraving
that is sometimes used as the frontispiece, is said to
be facing p. 331. The frontispiece varies, however,
and when an illustration is used as the frontispiece,
it does not appear on the page indicated in the
"List of Engravings." These illustrations are
printed on paper different from the text.

There are at least two casings for this edition. One
casing is bead grain cloth medium orange, satura-
tion moderate. Front and back covers are blind
stamped with two lines around the outside and leaf
and branch designs on each side and at the bottom.
The spine reproduces that of the 1852 in every
detail. There are plain yellow end-papers. One
copy in OTU has on the back end-paper a small
diamond-shaped ticket bearing "BOUND BY |
WESTLEYS | & Co. | LONDON.". The other
casing is pebble grain cloth, medium red in colour,
saturation moderate. Front and back covers are
blind stamped with four lines and a floral pattern
around the edges. The front cover also has, within

the border, a gilt stamped wreath and "CANADIAN CRUSOES.". The spine is gilt stamped: a floral design at top, followed by a square cross design with side extensions, "CANADIAN CRUSOES.", the square cross and floral designs repeated, a shield enclosing a wheel and surrounded by branches and leaves, an epergne with floral attachments, and "ILLUSTRATED.".

All copies examined contain an advertisement for *A Peep Into the Canadian Forest; With a History of the Squirrel Family*, by Mrs. Traill, on p. [363]. The leaf on which it is printed is conjugate with the first leaf of gathering 2A. One OTU copy has "A Catalogue of Instructive and Amusing Works for the Young," which advertises as "In preparation" a "New and Cheaper Edition" of *Canadian Crusoes* (p. 3).

There was a second issue of this edition in 1862, and sheets from the 1859 were issued as a new undated American edition some time between 1864 and 1872.

Copies: OONL PS8439 T7 C3 1859; OTU B11.6535 (two copies)

A third OTU copy (PS8489 R35 C3) was microfilmed for CEECT by the Central Microfilming Unit of the Public Archives of Canada.

1882 Nelson

Title-page: LOST | IN THE BACKWOODS. | 𝔄 𝔗𝔞𝔩𝔢 𝔬𝔣 𝔱𝔥𝔢 𝔠𝔞𝔫𝔞𝔡𝔦𝔞𝔫 𝔉𝔬𝔯𝔢𝔰𝔱. | By | MRS. TRAILL, | Author of "In the Forest," &c. | [rule] | WITH

THIRTY-TWO ENGRAVINGS. | [rule] |
𝕷onꝺon: | T. NELSON AND SONS,
PATERNOSTER ROW. | EDINBURGH; AND
NEW YORK. | [rule] | 1882.

Size of leaf: 179 × 117 mm.

Collation: 8°, 1⁸ 2-20⁸, 160 leaves, pp. *i-vii* viii *9* 10-31 *32*
33-77 *78* 79-115 *116* 117-124 *125-126* 127-140 *141*
142-155 *156* 157-166 *167* 168-179 *180* 181-195
196 197-200 *201-202* 203-212 *213-214* 215-217
218 219-230 *231-232* 233-234 *235-236* 237-239
240 241-253 *254* 255-265 *266* 267-270 *271-272*
273-274 *275* 276-288 *289* 290-300 *301* 302-312
313 314-319 *320*

Contents: p. [i] blank, p. [ii] illustration, p. [iii] title-page, p.
[iv] blank, p. [v] preface, p. [vi] blank, p. [vii] list of
illustrations, p. viii illustrations cont'd., pp. [9]-319
text, p. [320] blank

Head-title: LOST IN THE BACKWOODS. p. [9]

Headlines: Each numbered page carries a different headline
applying to the content of that page. A selection of
these follows: p. 10, "PAST AND PRESENT.";
p. 17, "IN THE FLOWERY MONTH OF JUNE.";
p. 33, "IN SEARCH OF THE WANDERERS.";
p. 49, "FAITH AND WORKS."; p. 65,
"VOLATILE LOUIS."; p. 81, "LOOKING
FORWARD."; p. 97, "MELANCHOLY
FOREBODINGS."; p. 113, "PRACTICAL
KNOWLEDGE."; p. 129, "NECESSITY AND
INVENTION."; p. 145,"CATHARINE'S FEARS.";

p. 161, "A RUDE PIECE OF POTTERY.";
p. 177, "A PRIMITIVE KILN."; p. 193, "THE
BRAVE SQUAW."; p. 209, "WORDS OF
KINDNESS AND LOVE."; p. 225, "WINTER
WORK."; p. 241, "IN A PLACE OF SAFETY.";
p. 257, "A GLEAM OF HOPE."; p. 273,
"DOMESTIC ECONOMY OF THE INDIANS.";
p. 291, "BEFORE THE GREAT CHIEF.";
p. 305, "THE NIGHT SHELTER.".

Notes: There are thirty-two illustrations. Most are incor-
porated within the type-pages. Twelve come from
the 1852 edition. There are seven full-page
illustrations, each printed on an unnumbered recto
with blank verso; these are integral to the gather-
ings and fit in the foliation and pagination. The
illustrations are "A CANADIAN TRAPPER,"
frontispiece, p. [ii]; "THE WOODPECKER," p. 21;
"LOUIS CONFESSING HIS DECEPTION,"
p. 27; "THE FIRST BREAKFAST,"
p. 43; "THE SENTINEL WOLF," p. 76;
"CATHARINE FOUND BY THE OLD DOG,"
p. 92; "WILD BEES," p. 100; "THE GRAY
SQUIRREL," p. 105; "THE WOLVERINE,"
p. 106; "THE ATTACK ON THE DEER," p. 111;
"PECCARIES," p. 118; "RAFTS ON THE ST.
LAWRENCE," p. 125; "THE WOUNDED DOE,"
p. 142; "HECTOR BRINGING THE INDIAN
GIRL," p. 151; "COB OF INDIAN CORN,"
p. 160; "A MOCCASIN," p. 164; "SHOOTING
WILD FOWL," p. 181; "DEATH OF THE
CHIEF'S SON," p. 190; "CANADIAN LAKE
SCENERY," p. 201; "CHIPPEWA INDIANS OF
THE PRESENT DAY," p. 213; "A SNOW-
SHOE," p. 222; "CHITMINKS," p. 229; "AT
WORK IN THE FOREST," p. 231; "A FOREST

ON FIRE," p. 235; "VISIT OF THE INDIAN FAMILY," p. 245; "CATHARINE CARRIED OFF," p. 252; "KINGFISHER AND DRAGON FLY," p. 260; "AN INDIAN CRADLE," p. 268; "AN INDIAN CAMP," p. 271; "INDIANA BEFORE THE BALD EAGLE," p. 294; "INDIANA AT THE STAKE," p. 299; and "THE RETURN HOME," p. 316.

In the lower corner of each signed leaf, the figure 721 appears in parentheses. This is probably the stereotype identification number for this book.

The casing is in diagonal ribbed fine grain cloth. Some copies are medium brown in colour, others reddish orange, saturation moderate. The front cover is stamped, top and bottom, with two black lines, the outside line being thicker than the inside. There is a blind stamped illustration of five Indians around a campfire with trees in the background and left foreground and a small bird in the upper right foreground. The Indians are in gilt. The title appears below this, "LOST IN THE BACKWOODS.", with "L" and "B" in gilt. Below this some copies have "BY THE | AUTHOR OF | 'AFAR IN THE FOREST'". The back cover carries a black design of branch, flowers, and Nelson's device; in some copies a child holds the device. The spine has black trees at the top followed by "LOST | IN THE | BACKWOODS", with "L" and "B" in gilt, a gilt stamped illustration of a man lighting a pipe (the same figure as appears in the frontispiece), and, at the bottom, "BY THE | AUTHOR OF | 'AFAR IN THE FOREST'" in black.

There were numerous impressions of this edition.

Copies: OONL PS8439 T7 C35; OTNY — two copies (no call numbers)

One OTNY copy was microfilmed for CEECT by the Central Microfilming Unit of the Public Archives of Canada.

Published Versions of the Text

The following is a list of editions, impressions, and issues of *Canadian Crusoes*. At least one location is given for each entry. The locations marked with a # indicate that these copies were microfilmed for CEECT. Under each edition are listed its impressions and issues; the information on the title-page of each first impression is transcribed. Subsequent impressions and issues are given in chronological order, with undated versions appearing at the end of every list. New features on the title-pages of these versions are given. Notes explain further distinguishing characteristics of each version.

1852

First English Edition

First Impression

Canadian Crusoes. A Tale of the Rice Lake Plains. By Catharine Parr Traill, Authoress of "The Backwoods of Canada," Etc. Edited by Agnes Strickland. Illustrated by Harvey. London: Arthur Hall, Virtue, & Co., 25, Paternoster Row, 1852.
   Note: See above, pp. 273-76, for a full bibliographical description of this edition.

1853

First American Edition (reset)

First Impression

The Canadian Crusoes. A Tale of the Rice Lake Plains. By Catharine
Parr Traill, Authoress of "The Backwoods of Canada," Etc.
Edited by her sister, Agnes Strickland. Illustrated by Harvey.
New York: C. S. Francis & Co., 252 Broadway; Boston:
Crosby, Nichols & Co., 1853.
Copy: OTMC #
Note: The illustrations from the London, 1852 are tipped in.
The colophon reads "Stereotyped by Billin & Bros., 20
N. William St."

Subsequent Impressions

The Canadian Crusoes. New York: C. S. Francis and Co.; Boston:
Crosby, Nichols and Co., 1854.
Copy: OONL
Note: The colophon in the New York, 1853 has been
removed and does not reappear in subsequent impres-
sions.

The Canadian Crusoes. New York: C. S. Francis and Co.; Boston:
Crosby, Nichols and Co., 1856.
Copy: OOC

The Canadian Crusoes. New York: C. S. Francis and Co., 554
Broadway; Boston: Crosby, Nichols and Co., 1859.
Copy: Private

The Canadian Crusoes. Boston: Crosby, Nichols, Lee and Co.,
1861.
Copy: OTMC

The Canadian Crusoes. Boston: Crosby and Nichols, 1862.
Copy: OPETP

The Canadian Crusoes. Boston: Crosby and Ainsworth; New
York: Oliver S. Felt, 1866.
Copy: OKQ

The Canadian Crusoes: A Tale of the Rice Lake Plains. By Catharine Parr Traill, Author of "Stories of the Canadian Forest," etc. Edited by her sister, Agnes Strickland. Boston: Hall and Whiting, 1881.
Copy: OOCC
Note: The preliminaries as well as the title-page have been reset. The Harvey illustrations have not been included.

The Canadian Crusoes. Boston: Crosby and Nichols, n.d.
Copy: OPET (two copies)
Note: This impression was published some time before the dissolution of the Crosby and Nichols partnership in 1864.

The Canadian Crusoes. Boston: Woolworth, Ainsworth and Co.; New York: A. S. Barnes and Co., n.d.
Copy: NcD
Note: This impression was published some time between Woolworth's replacement of Crosby in 1868 and the move of the Woolworth, Ainsworth firm to New York in 1870.

1859

Second English Edition (reset)

First Impression

Canadian Crusoes. A Tale of the Rice Lake Plains. By Catharine Parr Traill, Authoress of "The Backwoods of Canada," Etc. Edited by Agnes Strickland. Illustrated by Harvey. Second Edition. London: Arthur Hall, Virtue, & Co., 25, Paternoster Row, 1859.
Note: See above, pp. 276-78, for a full bibliographical description of this edition.

Second Issue

Canadian Crusoes. London: J. S. Virtue, 294, City Road, and 26,
  Ivy Lane, 1862.
  Copy: OONL
  Note: The printer's imprint is no longer present on the verso
    of the title-leaf, but it has been retained at the foot of
    p. 362. The advertisement for *A Peep Into the Forest* is
    included.

1864-1872

Second American Edition

First Impression

Canadian Crusoes. New York: Virtue and Yorston, 12 Dey Street,
  n.d.
  Copy: OPET
  Note: This is an issue of the second English edition. It was
    published some time between 1864 and 1872 when J. S.
    Virtue and John C. Yorston were business partners in
    New York.

1882

Third English Edition (reset)

First Impression

Lost in the Backwoods. A Tale of the Canadian Forest. By Mrs. Traill,
  Author of "In the Forest," &c. With Thirty-Two Engravings.

London: T. Nelson and Sons, Paternoster Row, Edinburgh; and New York, 1882.

Note: See above, pp. 278-82, for a full bibliographical description of this edition.

Subsequent Impressions

Lost in the Backwoods. London: T. Nelson and Sons, 1884.
Copy: OPAL
Note: This impression appeared in Nelson's "Daring Adventure Library."

Lost in the Backwoods. London: T. Nelson and Sons, 1886.
Copy: NSWA

Lost in the Backwoods. London: T. Nelson and Sons, 1890.
Copy: OTU
Note: This impression appeared in Nelson's "Our Boys' Select Library."

Lost in the Backwoods. London: T. Nelson and Sons, 1892.
Copy: OTNY
Note: This impression appeared in Nelson's "Our Boys' Select Library."

Lost in the Backwoods. London: T. Nelson and Sons, 1896.
Copy: OPET
Note: This impression appeared in Nelson's "Our Boys' Select Library."

Lost in the Backwoods. London: T. Nelson and Sons, 1901.
Copy: OPET
Note: This impression appeared in Nelson's "Our Boys' Select Library."

Altered Plates — First Impression

Lost in the Backwoods. By Mrs. Traill. London, Edinburgh, Dublin,

& New York: Thomas Nelson and Sons, n.d.
Copy: OOCC (two copies)
Note: This impression was published in 1909 in Nelson's "Travel Series."

Altered Plates — Second Impression

Lost in the Backwoods. London, Edinburgh, and New York: Thomas Nelson and Sons, n.d.
Copy: OTU
Note: This impression was published in 1923 in Nelson's "Blue Star Series."

1923

First Canadian Edition (reset)

First Impression

Canadian Crusoes. A Tale of the Rice Lake Plains. By Catharine Parr Traill. Edited by Agnes Strickland and Illustrated by G. A. Neilson. Toronto: McClelland and Stewart, [1923].
Copy: OONL
Note: The verso of the title-leaf carries the date.

NOTE
A Swedish adaptation of *Canadian Crusoes* was published in 1865: *Indiana eller ett år i Amerikas urskogar*. Berättelse för barn, bearbetad efter ‚Canadian Crusoes‘. Öbro. 1865. The title translates as "*Indiana, or, one year in America's primeval forests*. An account for children adapted from *Canadian Crusoes*." See Dr. Hermann Ullrich, *Robinson und Robinsonaden. Bibliographie, Geschichte, Kritik*, Teil I, *Bibliographie*, 1898; rpt. Nendeln/Liechtenstein: Kraus Reprint, 1977, p. 211.

Emendations in Copy-text

This list records all the emendations made in this edition to its 1852 Hall, Virtue copy-text (A), except those noted in the introduction as having been made silently. In this list, B stands for the 1859 Hall, Virtue edition; C, the 1882 Nelson; and Ed, for the emendations made by the editor that corrected errors in the copy-text not previously rectified in either B or C. Each entry in this list is keyed to the page and line number of the CEECT edition. In each entry the reading of the CEECT edition is given before the]; the source of this reading immediately after the]; to the right of the semi-colon that immediately follows either B, C, or Ed, the original reading as found in the copy-text is recorded. A solidus, /, indicates a line-end hyphen.

5 .31	wanting] C; wanted
6 .5	young] B; you
7 .27	castilleja coccinea] castilegia coccinea (C) and castilleja (Ed); enchroma
7 .29	trillium grandiflorum] C; trillium
7 .32	cypripedium] C; cyprepedium
8 .30	and plucked] B; aud plucked
13 .36	sounds] B; sound
13 .37	were] B; was
18 .8	paillasses] B; paliasses
27 .6	the wild grape vine] C; the vine
27[1].1	*Celastrus scandens*] C; *Solanum dulcamara*
29 .26	unheeded] C; unheeding
29 .30	but was now] C; but now
32 .10-11	May-apples (*Podophyllum peltatum*)—I] C; May-apples—I
36 .7	times; but] Ed; times; (but
37 .19	but they] B; but that they
38 .24	bear.] B; bear."

39 .27	moon] B; moonlight
41 .12	grizzly] C; grisly
43[1].1-3	footnote: The . . . canoes.] Ed; [The . . . canoes.] *embedded in text*
45[1].1	*Euchroma*] Ed; *Erichroma*
51 .33-34	big stone] B; bigstone
56[1].1-2	footnote: A . . . creeks.] Ed; [A . . . creeks.] *embedded in text*
58 .8	Beaver Meadow] C; Beaver-/meadow
59 .19	oaks (*Quercus alba* and *Quercus nigra*), diversified] C; oaks, diversified
60 .14	bases] C; basis
61 .5	*castilleja coccinea*] *Castilegia coccinea* (C) and *castilleja* (Ed); *enchroma*
61 .6	lupine (*Lupinus perennis*) and] C; lupine and
61 .7	*trillium*; dwarf roses (*Rosa blanda*) scent] C; *trillium* roses scent
61 .9-10	(*Saxifraga nivalis*)] C; footnote: Saxifraga nivalis.
61.13-14	spiceberry (*Gaultheria procumbens*); the] C; spiceberry; the
61.16-17	orange lilies (*Lilium Philadelphicum*)] C; martagon lilies
61[1].1	Indian bean . . . (*Apios tuberosa*)] C; Pyrola rotundifolia, P. asarifolia
62[1].1	*Podophyllum peltatum*] C; *Pedophyllum palmata*
64 .29	Duncan] Ed; Donald
69 .31	these] Ed; this
70 .6	day] C; night
70 .17-18	bee-hives] C; bees
71 .5	latter] C; last
71 .7	palatable] B; palateable
75 .7	one] C; some
81 .11	Catharine] B; Catherine
82 .15	"but] B; " but
84 .23	St. John] C; St. John's
86 .17	and] B; an

87 .31	marks] C; remarks
88 .12	would] B; should
92 .29	and the fur stretched] C; and stretched
93¹.1	footnote: *Comptonia asplenifolia*, a . . . family.] C; *omitted*
100 .6	drank of] B; drank some of
101 .20	day. A] B; day A
109 .30	fancied] C; fancy
116².1	*Gaultheria*] Ed; *Gualtheria*
126 .3	masquinonjé] Ed; masquinonjè
126 .19	bow and arrow] C; bows and arrows
127 .6	"for] C; for
128 .13	frame; on the mat she] B; frame on the mat; she
130 .29	Louis] B; Lewis
132 .15	herself] B; myself
136 .3	were] C; was
139 .6	one who, her spirit] B; one, whose spirit
139 .25	the tents] C; their tents
140 .4	bound, and ready to] C; bound, to
140 .17	was as] B; was that as
143 .24	die!] B; die?
144 .3	religious] B; religions
146 .21	Catharine] B; Catherine
147 .23-24	butter-nut-trees (*Juglans cinerea*) on] C; butter-nut-trees on
147 .24	bagful of nuts] C; bag full
148 .18	alder (*Alnus incuna*)] C; elder
148 .18-19	cranberries (*Viburnum opulus*), dogwood] C; cranberries, dogwood
149 .28	cedar] B; redar
152 .14	and] B; aud
157 .19	knots] B; knotts
158 .26	*couteau-de-chasse*] B; *couteau-du-chasse*
163 .17	great] C; entire
165 .17	wood-thrush] C; thrush
168 .7	them."] B; them.
173 .23	chief part of] C; chief of
181 .28	forlornness] C; friendliness

183 .33	Catharine's] C; her
184 .5	brother and cousin] C; brothers
185 .28	mossy] C; massy
185 .36	younglings] B; youngings
186 .3	sailing] C; sailed
190 .8	folk] C; folks
190 .10	had not hesitated] B; had hesitated not
191¹.1	Campbelltown] Ed; Cambelltown
191¹.3	Otonabee] B; Otoanbee
193 .13	loving] C; living
194 .4	a] B; one
197 .10	companions] C; cousin
198 .36	neither] B; no
204 .29	so?"] Ed; so?
206 .18	St. John] C; St. John's
207 .25	empty-handed] B; single-handed
212 .24	deprive] C; deprives
212 .26	takes the place] C; takes place
217 .31	they] C; it
218 .20	heart's] B; heart's
221 .11	Hector, Louis] C; her brothers
224 .11	persicaria] Ed; perseicarias
224 .33	Gore's] C; Gores'
225 .1	belongs] B; belong
226 .16	their] C; its
226 .30	fathers'] B; father's
229 .6	Duncan] Ed; Donald
229 .34	Duncan] Ed; Donald
230 .14	embraced] B; embraeed
230 .14	Duncan] Ed; Donald
230 .36	Duncan] Ed; Donald
231 .10	Cobourg] Ed; Coburg
231 .23	Duncan] Ed; Donald
235 .12	clothes] B; elothes
239 .3-4	deer, wolves] B; deer wolves
244 .14	Saugeen] Ed; Sangeeny
244 .15	Simcoe] Ed; Samcoe

244 .17	Saugeens] Ed; Sangeenys
249 .8	Home] Ed; Elome
249 .11	Sixteen and Twelve Miles Creeks] B; sixteen and twelve miles creeks
249 .15	Mississaga] B; mississaga
250 .1-2	1826-7. They] B; 1826-7 They
250 .3	Gananoque] Ed; Gannoyne
250 .4	Quinté] Ed; Quintè
250 .5	Quinté] Ed; Quintè
250 .16	Colborne] Ed; Colburn
250 .23	Poudash] Ed; Pondash

Line-end Hyphenated Compounds in Copy-text

The compound or possible compound words that appear in this list were hyphenated at the end of a line in the copy-text used for this edition of *Canadian Crusoes*. They have been resolved in the CEECT edition in the manner indicated below. In order to decide how to resolve these words, examples of their use within the lines of the copy-text itself were sought. When, however, these compounds or possible compounds were not used other than at the end of a line in the copy-text, the *Compact Edition of the Oxford English Dictionary* was consulted for examples of how they were spelled in the eighteenth and nineteenth centuries, and their resolution based on this information. The words in this list are keyed to the CEECT edition by page and line number; a word appears each time it has been resolved in the copy-text.

2 .1	log-house	32 .13	squaw-berries
4 .26	backwoodsmen	32 .14	bird-cherries
5 .33	sister-in-law	35 .21-22	chopping-block
6 .21	Frenchwoman	40 .23	dogwood
6 .22	well-regulated	46 .22	torch-light
8 .10	red-bird	51 .4	terror-blanched
12 .18-19	white-thorn	51 .26	deep-drawn
12 .22	twin-flowered	52 .26	far-off
21 .6	footsteps	57 .9	woodchucks
22 .29	hunting-grounds	58 .18	forest-trees
22¹.5	garden-fence	60 .27	table-land
24 .13	kind-hearted	62 .21	woodchucks'
28 .14	dead-falls	63 .16-17	Indian-fashion
29 .26	white-headed	67 .13	home-sick
32 .2	woodchuck	73 .21	bow-string
32 .3	chitmunks	73 .28	long-bow
32 .10-11	May-apples	74 .16	catamount

75 .11	woodchucks	169 .34	store-house
80 .9	fresh-cut	172 .9	spring-flowers
87 .36	deer-skin	172 .23	pine-woods
91 .13	bread-roots	173 .20	root-house
92 .3	deer-sinew	174 .21	house-logs
92 .14	woodchuck	178 .3	door-post
98 .4	Race-course	181 .17	half-naked
99 .6	wood-covered	184 .30	dwelling-house
99 .32	grape-vines	185 .33	kingfisher
105 .34	Whip-poor-will;	186 .17	log-cabin
107 .5	late-flowering	187 .26	grand-daughter
110 .33	fever-thirst	189 .6	grand-daughter
116 .28	winter-green	197 .28	overlooked
117[1] .3	Thesha-mon-e-doo	203 .33	weather-beaten
119 .20	golden-winged	205 .6	to-day
120 .14	golden-yellow	207 .26	fire-water
131 .22	water-fowl	209 .14	log-bridges
136 .29	Spartan-like	213 .30	war-whoop
137 .35	war-dance	217 .13-14	war-whoop
140 .11	Bare-hill	219 .14	Snow-bird
147 .23	butter-nut-trees	219 .19	Snow-bird
153 .5	drift-wood	220 .33	war-bird
154 .10	copper-tinted	221 .5	spirit-land
159 .3-4	deer-hide	221 .21	pine-trees
159 .7	cane-bottomed	223 .17	bow-string
159 .20	shuttle-cock	223 .36	pine-trees
161 .10	table-land	224 .18	drift-wood
161 .17-18	hand-sleighs	225 .21-22	cliff-like
162 .35-36	butter-nut	225 .23	log-house
163 .30	log-house	225 .26	newly-cut
164 .2-3	sugar-making	228 .8	wood-crowned
164 .8	boiling-place	228 .18-19	low-roofed
165 .1	red-headed	234 .36	recently-erected
165 .3	quakerly-looking	240 .24	birch-bark
165 .7	shore-side	244 .22	forty-eight
165 .18	passenger-pigeon	250 .11	shoemaker's
165 .21	winter-green	252 .6	small-pointed

Line-end Hyphenated Compounds in CEECT Edition

This list records compounds hyphenated at the end of a line in this edition of *Canadian Crusoes* that should be hyphenated in quotations from it. All other line-end hyphenations should be recorded as single words. The words in this list are keyed to the CEECT edition by page and line number; a word appears each time it is hyphenated at the end of a line.

2 .1	block-house	61 .12	winter-green
3 .29	re-union	62 .1	moss-covered
7 .27	painted-cup	63 .16	Indian-fashion
10 .30	red-headed	64 .13	thunder-clouds
12 .18	white-thorn	64 .19	spinning-wheel
13 .16	silver-barked	70 .17	bee-hives
15 .5	high-principled	70 .19	bee-hunter
21 .11	birch-trees	71 .2	mud-pouts
27 .19	hen-house	71 .3	water-mussels
30 .6	sleeping-chamber	75¹.1	May-apple
32 .10	May-apples	77 .36	long-trained
32 .16	butter-nuts	86 .6	Pine-tree
35 .21	chopping-block	98¹.1	winter-green
35 .27	hard-hearted	99 .16	wood-crowned
40 .31	sweet-scented	99 .26	hiding-places
43 .8	tin-pot	100 .1	hiding-place
43 .34	leather-wood	100 .11	terror-struck
45 .11	white-belled	105 .35	night-hawk
51 .28	land-mark	108 .13	landing-place
55 .21	log-house	116 .15	dead-falls
57 .27	wild-flowers	118 .26	Nee-chee
57 .35	to-day	119 .19	wood-duck
59 .17	table-land	129 .19	north-west

131 .2	duck-shooting	174 .9	birch-bark
133 .12	war-knife	174 .15	thunder-showers
138 .7	horror-stricken	180 .6	woe-stricken
148 .33	high-bush	183 .27	birch-bark
149 .17	egg-shells	188 .5	Snow-bird
151 .16	fishing-line	189 .22	well-formed
151 .28	Sugar-Maple	203 .32	stout-framed
159 .3	deer-hide	205 .21	log-house
159 .32	Snow-shoe	209 .23	Court-house
161 .17	hand-sleighs	210 .20	birch-bark
162 .35	butter-nut	212 .12	birch-tree
163 .11	birch-bark	216 .29	death-dooming
163 .21	fur-merchant	217 .13	war-whoop
163 .35	hunting-grounds	220 .27	Snow-bird
164 .2	sugar-making	222 .18	night-hawk
164 .11	bass-woods	222 .19	night-owl
164 .14	hand-sleigh	222 .33	dew-drops
166 .27	Oak-hills	225 .15	well-remembered
169 .35	hiding-place	225 .21	cliff-like
171 .29	gas-lighted	228 .18	low-roofed
172 .4	root-house	228 .24	heart-broken
172 .25	pine-woods	237 .18	foot-prints

Historical Collation

This list records variant readings that affect meaning between the CEECT edition of *Canadian Crusoes* and each of the 1852 Hall, Virtue, the 1859 Hall, Virtue, and the 1882 Nelson editions. In this list, A stands for the 1852, B for the 1859, and C for the 1882. Each entry in this list is keyed to the page and line number of the CEECT edition. In each entry the reading of the CEECT edition is given before the]; after the] the variant reading or readings and the source or sources of each are recorded. Thus the entry "11.5-6 bright sparkling] sparkling > C" indicates that at p. 11, ll.5-6 "bright sparkling" appears in the CEECT edition, but that the 1882 Nelson edition contains the variant reading "sparkling." And the entry "7.27 castilleja coccinea] enchroma > A-B; castilegia coccinea > C" indicates that on p. 7, l.27 where the CEECT edition reads "castilleja coccinea," each of the 1852 and the 1859 Hall, Virtue editions has the variant reading "enchroma," and the 1882 Nelson "castilegia coccinea." When appropriate in passages of more than six words, ellipsis dots have been used to shorten the entry.

1 .9	hills . . . clothed] hills, clothed > B-C
1 .10	though] *omitted* > B-C
1 .11	gave] display > B-C
1 .12	the maple] the useful and beautiful maple > C
1 .12-13	beech, hemlock, and others] beech, and hemlock > B-C
1 .14	of pure refreshing water] *omitted* > B-C
1 .15	from whence the spot has derived] whence it derives > B-C
1 .17	time] period > B-C
1 .19	small farms] clearings > C
1 .20	which owned] which previously owned > B-C
1 .24-27	To . . . one.] *omitted* > B-C

1 .29	the Ontario] Lake Ontario > C
2 .8	wheels] paddles > C
2 .14	without] unless > B-C
2 .14	city] house > C
2 .25	with sick and disabled men] *omitted* > B-C
2 .25	lodged] billeted > C
2 .29	which consisted] consisting > B-C
2 .36	little] *omitted* > C
3 .6	corps] regiment > C
3 .9	them] it > C
3 .18-22	while . . . ami] *omitted* > B-C
3 .35	the daughter] a daughter > C
4 .4	with . . . nature] *omitted* > B-C
4 .9	the Ontario] Lake Ontario > C
4 .22-23	settle themselves down at once as] settle as > B-C
4 .27	but] *omitted* > B-C
5 .5	older] earlier > C
5 .9	the Ontario] Lake Ontario > C
5 .17	slowly] *omitted* > C
5 .31	wanting] wanted > A-B
5 .31	homesteads] homestead > C
5 .33	even] *omitted* > B-C
6 .5	young] you > A
7 .9	the pearl] a pearl > C
7 .13-14	which . . . fairyland] *omitted* > B-C
7 .16-18	Louis . . . tell] *omitted* > B-C
7 .27	castilleja coccinea] enchroma > A-B; castilegia coccinea > C
7 .28	of the lily-like] on the lily-like > B
7 .29	grandiflorum] *omitted* > A-B
8 .5	were] was > C
8 .14	melodies] sounds > C
8 .23	eye] eyes > C
8 .24	was] were > C
8 .33	Louis] *omitted* > C
9 .11	the top of] *omitted* > B-C
9 .17	on her] in her > C

9 .17-18   the poor sick thing] her > B-C
9 .19   petite] *omitted* > B-C
9 .21   them] *omitted* > C
10 .8   now] *omitted* > B-C
11 .1   all] *omitted* > B-C
11 .5-6   bright sparkling] sparkling > C
11 .6   rill.] rill, or the hurrying to and fro of the turkeys among the luxuriant grass. > C
11 .15   handle] handles > C
11 .32   dinners] dinner > C
12 .2   But here] But there > C
12 .16   from] at > C
12 .19   and of the] and the > B-C
13 .5   and thorns] thorns > B-C
13 .28   had now forcibly struck] forcibly struck > B-C
13 .36   sounds] sound > A
13 .37   were] was > A
15 .12   the kinder] *omitted* > B-C
15 .22   spoke] told > B-C
15 .35   morrow] future > C
17 .20   for] *omitted* > B-C
17 .20   that night] *omitted* > B-C
18 .2   sparrows."] sparrows." — *St. Luke.* > C
19 .12   giddy] *omitted* > C
20 .10   our] the > C
20 .11   dispositions] disposition > C
20 .35-36   the Cold Springs] Cold Springs > C
21 .15-21   as . . . rhyme] *omitted* > B-C
22 .3   is now] was > C
22 .4   has] had > C
22 .17   a] the > B-C
22¹.1-7   This . . . hop.] *omitted* > C
23 .25   these] those > C
23².1-4   Now . . . beauties . . . prospect.] Now . . . beauty . . . prospect. > B; *omitted* > C
24 .15   bedewed] dropped on > C
25 .1   partridge] partridge's > C

25 .3   partridge] ruffed grouse > C
27 .6   flexile] flexible > C
27 .6   wild grape] *omitted* > A-B
27 .11   shingles] shingle > C
27[1].1   *Celastrus scandens*] *Solanum dulcamara* >A-B
27[2].1-3   The . . . Gardens.] *omitted* > C
29 .26   unheeded] unheeding > A-B
29 .30   was] *omitted* > A-B
29 .33   the second] their second > C
32 .11   (*Podophyllum peltatum*)] *omitted* > A-B
37 .6   Well, they] They > B-C
37 .12   Well now,] *omitted* > B-C
37 .19   but they] but that they > A
37 .22   kindle up] kindle > B-C
37 .27-30   You . . . without.] *omitted* > B-C
37 .32   burnt] burned > C
38 .5   but] *omitted* > C
38 .6-7   began . . . and] *omitted* > C
38 .7   he] *omitted* > B-C
38 .8   and the] the > B-C
38 .21   quarter] quarters > C
39 .14   and miles] *omitted* > B-C
39 .21   so hopeful] hopeful > B-C
39 .27   moon] moonlight > A
39 .32   which] *omitted* > B-C
40 .2   track] tract > C
40 .25   a grisly beast] the head of a black elk > C
40 .28   oak, dashed] oak, and dashed > C
41 .26   wandering] wanderings > C
41 .32   a full] full a > B-C
42 .28   the fall] autumn > C
42 .33   often] sometimes > B-C
43 .5   the Cold Springs] Cold Springs > C
43 .8   in] *omitted* > B-C
43 .14   manufacturing] constructing > B-C
43 .19   the] their > C
43 .19   that] *omitted* > B-C
43 .20   his cousin's] her > B-C

43 .24	trunk] birch tree > C
43 .28	are ragged] ragged > B-C
44 .6	The] A > B-C
45 .18-19	These . . . nature, and] *omitted* > B-C
45 .20	the picturesque] picturesque > B-C
45 .24	yet] *omitted* > B-C
45¹.1	*Euchroma*] *Erichroma* > A-C
45².1-4	The . . . Esq.] *omitted* > C
46 .5	and neither] neither > B-C
46 .13	all the mysteries of it] its mysteries > B-C
46 .18	was used] used > B-C
46 .33	that] *omitted* > B-C
47 .16	sprung] she sprang > C
47 .17	sunk] sank > C
47¹.1	See . . . Appendix.] *omitted* > C
48 .5	fish-hook] a fish-hook > B-C
48 .17-20	A . . . feet] A waterfall dashing from the upper part of the bank fell headlong in spray and foam > C
48 .21	pebbles] fragments > C
49 .5	fish, and this] fish. This > B-C
49 .6	that] *omitted* > B-C
49 .6	kindling up] kindling > B-C
50 .14	and so] so > B-C
50 .25	heavily] *omitted* > B-C
50 .27-28	a greater degree of] greater > B-C
51 .3-4	can . . . if] *omitted* > B-C
52 .21	gone] gone to join his companions > C
52 .21	crushing] crashing > C
52 .23	some] a > C
53 .2	terrors] terror > C
53 .14	wakened] awakened > B-C
53 .23	were] was > C
53 .24	rich berries] fruit > C
56 .24	berries] fruit > C
56 .25	be soon] soon be > B-C
58 .13-15	It . . . have] Persons who lose their way in the pathless woods have > B-C

58 .16	is] it is > C
58 .24	his] its > C
59 .4-5	their . . . of] *omitted* > B-C
59 .7	his cousin to assist] to assist his cousin > B-C
59 .19	(*Quercus . . . nigra*)] *omitted* > A-B
59 .32	course] sweep > C
60 .2	steep] deep > B-C
60 .14	bases] basis > A-B
60 .24-25	oak . . . pines] oak or a few stately pines growing upon it > B-C
60 .26	merely] *omitted* > B-C
61 .5	*castilleja coccinea*] *enchroma* > A-B; *Castilegia coccinea* > C
61 .6	(*Lupinus perennis*)] *omitted* > A-B
61 .7	*trillium . . . scent*] *trillium* roses scent > A-B
61 .11	the fall] autumn > C
61 .13-14	(*Gaultheria procumbens*)] *omitted* > A-B
61 .16-17	orange lilies (*Lilium Philadelphicum*)] martagon lilies > A-B
61¹.1	Indian . . . *tuberosa*)] Pyrola rotundifolia, P. asarifolia > A-B
62 .22	while] wild > B-C
62¹.1	*Podophyllum peltatum*] *Pedophyllum palmata* > A-B
63 .16	bed] beds > C
63 .17-28	This . . . rich.] *omitted* > B-C
63 .32	bed] beds > C
63 .34	was] were > C
63 .36	silk or damask] damask or silk > B-C
64 .3	dry] the dry > B-C
64 .3-4	plenty . . . there] *omitted* > B-C
64 .5	and this] this > B-C
64 .12	even . . . still] *omitted* > B-C
64 .25	eye] eyes > C
64 .33	sunk] sank > C
65 .6	sprang] springs > C
65 .14	the fulness] fulness > C
66 .7	and joyfully] joyfully > B-C

67 .24	that] who > B-C
67 .24	whose heart] but > B-C
67 .34-35	by its intense brightness] *omitted* > B-C
68 .9	thunder-peal] thunder-peals > C
68 .25	thunder-peal] thunder-peals > C
69 .5-6	"If . . . hither."] *omitted* > B-C
69 .7	father] fathers > C
69 .9	and Catharine] She > B-C
69 .31	and these] and this > A; these > B-C
69 .32	with] at > B-C
69 .34	and for] for > B-C
70 .6	day] night > A-B
70 .17-18	bee-hives] bees > A-B
70 .24	sunbeam] sunbeams > C
70 .27	the fall] autumn > C
71 .5	latter] last > A-B
73 .19	woodchucks] woodchuck > C
74[1].1	three] few > C
75 .7	one] some > A-B
75[1].1	*Podophyllum peltatum*—May-apple, or Mandrake.] *omitted* > C
76 .14-15	the fall] autumn > C
76[1].4	furthest] farthest > C
79 .1	it glanced] the arrow glanced > C
81 .8	would] could > C
81 .18- 82.6	"Yes . . . help."] *omitted* > B-C
83 .6-11	Round . . . song.] *omitted* > B-C
83 .19	Don't teaze, ma belle.] *omitted* > B-C
84 .9	holes] hole > C
84 .23	St. John] St. John's > A-B
84 .25	ma belle] *omitted* > B-C
85 .1-2	gather . . . rice] hunt the peccary, which is, as you know, a kind of wild boar, and whose flesh is very good eating > C
86 .17	and] an > A
86[1].1-4	Now . . . family.] *omitted* > C

87 .26-27   regular blaze on the trees] blaze, as it is called, on
             the trees, by cutting away pieces of the outer bark
             > B-C
87 .31   marks] remarks > A-B
87 .34   viz.] namely > C
88 .12   and they] they > B-C
88 .12   would] should > A
88 .12   warm] warmly > B-C
89 .10   were] was > C
90 .5   and floated] and in spring floated > C
91[1].1-3   This . . . traveller.] *omitted* > C
92 .29   the fur] *omitted* > A-B
93 .13   an . . . scale] tea > B-C
93 .15   plant] shrub > C
93 .20   could] might > B-C
93 .34   live coals] hot embers > C
93[1].1   *Comptonia . . . family.*] *omitted* > A-B
94 .3   and . . . them] *omitted* > B-C
94 .12   all their] their > B-C
94 .14-16   About . . . out.] *omitted* > B-C
95 .26   bear] a bear > C
96 .17   They] One > C
96 .18   bushes.] bushes, while the others kept further
             along the shore. > C
96 .22   Well] After closely examining what I suppose
             was one of our footmarks > C
97 .9   safe] save > B
98 .17   and] *omitted* > B-C
98 .23   were] was > C
98 .24   fresh] were fresh > C
98 .32   liberal] a liberal > C
100 .6   drank of] drank some of > A
100 .7   laid] lay > C
100 .11-12   terror-struck] terror-stricken > B-C
100 .19   asleep] fast asleep > B-C
100 .32   their] the > C
101 .8   dews] dew > C

101 .9	summer's] summer > C
102 .7	lighted] ventured to light > C
102 .8	much venison] much of the venison > C
103 .11	chance] evil chance > C
103¹.1-10	George . . . grounds . . . another . . . transgresses . . . *himself.*] George . . . ground . . . another's . . . trangress . . . *himself.* > B; *omitted* > C
104 .23	befel] were to befall > C
105 .26	eye] eyes > C
105 .27	ear] ears > C
105 .31	she] it > B-C
106 .22	dosed] then dozed > C
107 .7	the fall] autumn > C
107 .26	masses] mass > C
108 .29-33	her hands . . . painful:] Her hands and feet were fastened by thongs of deer-skin to branches of the tree, which had been bent downward for that purpose. Her position was a most painful one. > C
109 .7	the wolf, and] *omitted* > C
109 .21	sunk] sank > C
109 .30	fancied] fancy > A-B
114 .36	produces] produce > C
115 .1	beside] besides > C
115 .12-13	was . . . *vive,* and] *omitted* > B-C
115 .18	and Louis was] and was > B-C
116 .4	soup] soups > C
116 .7	furthest] farthest > C
117 .5	*dulçamara,* or] *omitted* > C
117 .28	congeners] companions > B-C
117¹.1-8	By . . . has . . . *Missionary.*] By . . . had . . . *Missionary.* > B; *omitted* > C
118 .1	and when] when > B-C
118 .20-23	the sheath . . . wrought] the sheath of deer-skin he carried his knife in, was made and ornamented by her hands; also the case for his arrows, of birch-bark, she wrought > B-C

119 .12	but] *omitted* > C
119 .23	but] *omitted* > B-C
119 .23	showed] indicated > B-C
119 .29	occupation] occupations > B-C
119 .30	I . . . narrative.] *omitted* > B-C
120 .17	was] were > C
120 .22	just] *omitted* > B-C
120 .26-27	not disposed] indisposed > B-C
120 .28	they] *omitted* > B-C
121 .16	vessel] canoe > C
122 .28	his] the > B-C
122 .28	that] *omitted* > B-C
122 .29	in the air] *omitted* > B-C
122 .32	sung] sang > B-C
122 .35	sound] sounds > C
123 .24	great] as great > B-C
123 .24	Edinburgh] an Edinburgh > C
123 .27	with apparent ease] *omitted* > B-C
123 .29	enjoyment] delight > B-C
124 .8	after all] *omitted* > C
124 .20	was] would be > C
124 .22	very] *omitted* > C
124 .27	knee] knees > C
124 .30	the doe-skin] doe-skin > C
124 .31-32	but not very unbecoming] *omitted* > B-C
124 .36	parts] part > C
125 .2	cutting] *omitted* > B-C
125 .34	sung] sang > B-C
125 .35	that] which > B-C
126 .19	bow and arrow] bows and arrows > A-B
126 .26	and milking of] milking > B-C
126 .34	down] *omitted* > B-C
127 .17	that offered] *omitted* > B-C
127 .28	And] *omitted* > B-C
127 .36	was] were > C
127 .36	a sacrifice] sacrifices > C
128 .3-4	deeds of blood] bloodshed > B-C

128 .10	and sharpened] sharpened > B-C
128 .11	over which] over it > B-C
128 .12	then] *omitted* > B-C
128 .24	and] *omitted* > B-C
128 .24-25	by small] in small > C
130 .12	that] *omitted* > B-C
131 .8	was] *omitted* > B-C
131 .8	finished by] concluded with > B-C
131 .20	sins] sin > C
131 .26	any of] *omitted* > B-C
131 .27	that] *omitted* > B-C
131 .28	these they dried] dried them > B-C
131 .29	that] *omitted* > B-C
131 .29	Orkney] the Orkney > C
131 .37	and for] and > B-C
132 .14	father's] father > C
132 .15	herself] myself > A
132 .19	with] in > B-C
132 .20-21	and her eyes . . . stretched] She raised her eyes, and stretched her arms > B-C
132¹.1-2	the Indian] an Indian > C
132¹.3	site] scene > C
133 .4	their movements] the movements of the Indians > C
133 .5	the Indians] they > C
133 .17	seemed] *omitted* > B-C
133 .18	seeming] seemed > B-C
133 .18-19	as far as . . . quite] apparently > B-C
133 .20	and] *omitted* > B-C
133 .30	and] *omitted* > B-C
133 .30	may as well] will now > B-C
133 .32-134.1	though . . . friends] *omitted* > B-C
134 .12	beside] besides > C
135 .34	he . . . flesh] his flesh must be > C
136 .3	were made] was made > A-B
136 .28-29	plunged . . . firmness] saw his son bound to the

fatal post and pierced by the arrows of his own tribe > C

136 .30	that] the > C
136 .33	fearful rite] horrible rite > C
137 .4	pressed] he pressed > C
137 .17	pitched] had pitched > C
138 .15	plunged the knife into] saw the arrows pierce > C
138 .21	those] These > C
138 .27	Indian girl] chief's daughter > C
139 .6	who, her] whose > A
139 .11	eye] eyes > C
139 .20-22	till . . . work] *omitted* > B-C
139 .24	back] *omitted* > C
139 .25	collect] to collect > C
139 .25	the tents] their tents > A-B
139 .27	they were tired of blood-shedding;] *omitted* > B-C
139 .30	one] a > C
139 .34	and clothed] clothed > B-C
140 .4	and ready] *omitted* > A-B
140 .7	unperceived] *omitted* > C
140 .10	council] counsel > B
140 .17	as] that as > A
140 .23	And she told] telling > B-C
140 .27	that] and > B; and that > C
140 .28-29	and . . . it] and replaced by the spirit of love > B-C
140 .29	the child] a child > C
141 .6	and leading] drawing > B-C
141[1].1	me] the author > C
141[1].2	who] He > C
141[1].2	an] a > C
141[1].4-7	Mosang . . . copying.] *omitted* > C
142 .15	shore, and] shore, where the Indians assembled under the boughs of some venerable trees, and round the evening fires related the deeds of the preceding day, and > C

142 .16	their] their own > C
142 .17	sufficiency] a sufficiency > C
142 .18	following day] morrow > C
142 .21	that] *omitted* > B-C
142 .26-28	and . . . heroism?] *omitted* > B-C
143 .2	they had been] were > B-C
143 .3-4	or . . . seen] *omitted* > B-C
143 .10	when . . . and] where > B-C
144 .2	for] of > C
144 .2	ill] evil > C
144 .21	sung] sang > B-C
146¹.1-3	A . . . farm.] *omitted* > C
147 .3	beside] besides > C
147 .22	Beside] Besides > C
147 .23	(*Juglans cinerea*)] *omitted* > A-B
147 .24	bagful of nuts] bag full > A-B
147 .33	council] counsel > B-C
148 .1	heard] had heard > C
148 .10	them] them that > C
148 .18	alder (*Alnus incuna*)] elder > A-B
148 .19	(*Viburnum opulus*)] *omitted* > A-B
148 .19	and, as] as > B-C
148 .20	further, and] farther > B; further > C
148 .21	cedar] with cedar > B-C
148 .21	with] *omitted* > B-C
148 .27	and the] The > B-C
148 .27	very] *omitted* > B-C
148 .30	banks] bank > C
148 .33	and the brilliant] the brilliant > B-C
149 .24	pounced upon, and] *omitted* > B-C
149 .33	chucked] threw > C
150 .27	to them] them > C
151 .18	coals] embers > C
151 .22	stones] a stone > C
151 .22	nut-crackers] a nut-cracker > C
151 .23	stretched] then stretched > C
151 .25	the two girls] Catharine and Indiana > C

151¹.1-2   Sugar . . . Esq.] *omitted* > C
152 .9-10   used the Indian people] the Indian people used
                > C
152 .15   shores] shore > C
152¹.1   The Beaver] *omitted* > C
152¹.5-12   This . . . developed.] *omitted* > C
152³.1   Appendix H.] *omitted* > C
153 .25   ivory] ivory-white > C
153 .28   lingered on] clung to > C
154 .27   harbinger] harbingers > C
155 .36   them] themselves > C
157 .5   excepting] except > C
157 .20   but] *omitted* > B-C
158 .6   plunging it] plunging the spear > C
160 .7   that] *omitted* > B-C
160 .31   This circumstance gives] giving > B-C
160 .32   this] the > B-C
160¹.1-3   One . . . Authoress.] *omitted* > C
161 .14   that] *omitted* > B-C
161 .29   maybe a] *omitted* > B-C
163 .17   great] entire > A-B
164 .1   little] *omitted* > B-C
164 .13   and] *omitted* > C
164 .16   could] would > C
164 .22   long] *omitted* > C
164 .22   remain on] remain longer on > C
164 .29-30   that came] which came > C
164 .30   that never] which never > B-C
164 .31   and Indiana] Indiana > B-C
164 .32   birds] birds' > C
165 .12-13   and for . . . ears,] *omitted* > B-C
165 .15   that] *omitted* > B-C
165 .17   wood-thrush] thrush > A-B
165 .18   passenger-pigeon] passenger pigeons > C
165 .29   has] have > B-C
165 .30   and Hector] Hector > B-C
166 .1   the house] their house > C

166 .1	which] *omitted* > B-C
166 .8	which] *omitted* > B-C
166 .9	which] this > B-C
166 .20	and the] The > B-C
166 .20	were sitting] sat > B-C
166[1].1	Appendix I.] *omitted* > C
168 .21	which] *omitted* > B-C
169 .5	that] *omitted* > B-C
169 .30	applause] approval > C
169 .35	would] could > B-C
170 .2	also from] that > B-C
171 .23	fires] fire > C
172 .26	the] with the > B-C
172 .28	fires] fire > C
172[1].6	near] nearly > C
173 .3	fires] fire > C
173 .8	fires] fire > C
173 .13	and] *omitted* > B-C
173 .23	part] *omitted* > A-B
174 .3	was] were > B-C
176 .24	very decent] *omitted* > B-C
176 .35	and was] which was > B-C
177 .9-10	Much they felt they had] They felt they had much > B-C
177 .12	above all that] beyond what > B-C
177 .13	they might] might > B-C
177 .35	which, with plenty of] to add to the > B-C
177 .36	was to make] for > B-C
178 .2	her back] *omitted* > C
178 .5	never-to-be-forgotten] unforgotten > B-C
178 .14	lid] lids > C
178 .20	run to her and] *omitted* > B-C
179 .3	his] its > C
179 .11-12	deer's hide] deer-hide > C
180[1].1	Appendix K.] See Appendix K. > B; *omitted* > C
181 .22	eye] eyes > C
181 .28	forlornness] friendliness > A-B

183 .5	terror-struck] terror-stricken > C
183 .32	and] *omitted* > C
183 .33	Catharine's] her > A-B
184 .4	neither could Catharine] Catharine could neither > C
184 .5	brother and cousin] brothers > A-B
184 .16	where . . . and] and landed on a small open place where > C
184 .17	and here] here > C
184 .27-185.6	On . . . echoes.] *omitted* > C
184¹.1-2	Lieut. . . . Canada.] *omitted* > C
185 .16	But now] Now that > C
185 .18	that trust] the trust > C
185 .23	that] *omitted* > B-C
185 .28	mossy] massy > A-B
186 .3	sailing] sailed > A-B
186 .7	and the] the > B-C
186 .11	and] *omitted* > B-C
186 .13-14	the beaming] and the beaming > C
186 .14	was given] were given > C
186 .16-17	what food] such food as > B-C
186 .17	and in] in > B-C
186 .18	and warmed] warmed > B-C
186 .20	and during] During > B-C
186 .20	she] the widow Snowstorm > B-C
186 .21	over] to > B-C
186 .26	some of] *omitted* > B-C
186 .27	preparations of] *omitted* > B-C
186 .35	the fall] autumn > C
187 .6-7	could not help being] was > B-C
187 .8	that was shown] evinced > B-C
187 .11-13	for . . . attention] *omitted* > B-C
187 .23	those] *omitted* > B-C
187 .30	was inclined to extend] extended > B-C
187 .31	making] by making > B-C
187 .32	chain of] chain for her of > B-C
187¹.1	See Appendix L.] *omitted* > C

188 .7	to and fro] *omitted* > B-C
188 .13	which she] she > B-C
188 .21	them] her dress > C
188 .25	know] learn > B-C
188 .31	that] *omitted* > B-C
189 .10-11	she . . . skins] the curtain of skins was > B-C
189 .12	standing] *omitted* > B-C
189 .22	her stature] She > C
189 .23	eye] eyes > C
190 .4	character, a] character, entitled the > B-C
190 .8	folk] folks > A-B
190 .10	not hesitated] hesitated not > A
191 .18	woodpeckers] woodpecker > C
191^1.1-4	Now . . . Campbelltown . . . fire-wood.] Now . . . Cambelltown . . . fire-wood. > A-B; *omitted* > C
191^2.1	Formerly . . . Locks.] *omitted* > C
192 .5	waters] water > C
192 .9	pine, cedar] pines, cedars > C
192^1.1-3	The . . . town.] *omitted* > C
192^2.1-2	Over . . . built.] *omitted* > C
193 .13	loving] living > A-B
193 .15-16	an orphan girl] *omitted* > B-C
193 .16	reft] bereft > C
194 .2-3	perhaps might have] *omitted* > B-C
194 .4	a] one > A
194 .5-6	the overwhelming] an overwhelming > C
194 .20	either arises] arises either > C
194 .34	these] those > C
195 .16	upon] on > B-C
195 .31	that] *omitted* > B-C
195 .31	took] she took > B-C
196 .6	those human] human > B-C
196 .7	that] who > C
197 .10	companions] cousin > A-B
197 .20	very] *omitted* > B-C
197 .20	some] *omitted* > B-C
197 .21-22	and taking] Then taking > B-C

197 .23-24	They . . . that] Fearing > B-C
197 .28	no] *omitted* > B-C
197 .29	still] *omitted* > B-C
198 .3	having seen nothing] nothing having been seen > C
198 .4	Indians.] Indians since they had proceeded up the river. > C
198 .8	laid] lay > C
198 .11-13	Desolation . . . them.] *omitted* > B-C
198 .14	more] *omitted* > B-C
198 .15	so] *omitted* > B-C
198 .19	woven . . . about] worn by Catharine in > B-C
198 .22-23	It . . . people.] *omitted* > B-C
198 .29-31	The . . . he] Louis > B-C
198 .36	neither] no > A
199 .5-7	This . . . found] but > B-C
199 .8-9	they still . . . captive] *omitted* > B-C
199 .10	she] Catharine > B-C
199 .15	an] a > B-C
200 .11	this] it > B-C
200 .13	with] in > B-C
200 .22-24	"Alas . . . life."] *omitted* > B-C
201 .11	and they] they > B-C
201 .13	and then] but > B-C
201 .20	a third and a fourth] a fourth and a fifth > C
202 .29	I . . . sociable.] *omitted* > B-C
203 .35	sprung] sprang > C
204 .24-29	"What . . . so?"] *omitted* > B-C
204 .30	then] *omitted* > B-C
205 .1-3	la . . . Yes,] *omitted* > B-C
205 .13	for though] though > B-C
205 .15	yet] *omitted* > C
205 .30	and caress] caress > B-C
205 .31	upon her] on her > B-C
206 .4	mes enfans] *omitted* > B-C
206 .17	what] *omitted* > B-C
206 .18	St. John] St. John's > A-B

206 .34   was] he was > C
206 .36   that] *omitted* > B-C
207 .4-5   which . . . loud] *omitted* > B-C
207 .8   on the coals] *omitted* > C
207 .10   "Mes enfans," said Jacob,] *omitted* > B-C
207 .11   sister, and] sister," said he, "and > B-C
207 .25   empty-handed] single-handed > A
209 .4-211 .22 WHAT . . . turf that they once shaded still remains. . . . oaks . . . That sound . . . Macdonald, and groups of Indians might be seen . . . for he . . . indispensable, before undreamed of. . . . unseen.] WHAT . . . turf they once shaded remains. . . . oak . . . The sound . . . Macdonald. Groups of Indians might be then seen . . . he . . . indispensable. . . . unseen. > B; *omitted* > C
212 .7   lay] lie > C
212 .24   deprive] deprives > A-B
212 .26   the place] place > A-B
213 .7   arms . . . breast] arms over her breast, an attitude of submission > C
213 .32   eye was] eyes were > C
215 .2   open] opened > B-C
215 .4   around] round > B-C
217 .10   in] at > C
217 .21   dance and death-song are] dance ceases and the death-song is > C
217 .26   were] are > C
217 .29   were] are > C
217 .30   commenced] commence > C
217 .31   they] it > A-B
217 .34   was] is > C
217 .36   that] the > C
217 .36   became] becomes > C
217 .36   struck] strikes > C
218 .1   Was] Is > C

218 .18	deemed] deem > C
218 .19	advanced] advances > C
218 .19	was] is > C
218 .21	bound] bind > C
218 .22	was] is > C
218 .24	addressed] addresses > C
220[1].1	Appendix M.] *omitted* > C
221 .11	Hector, Louis] her brothers > A-B
221 .27	light] little > C
221 .35	then] he > C
222 .3	then proceeded to bait] baited > B-C
222 .4	coals] fire > C
222 .30	lightly] gaily > B-C
222 .32	upon] on > B-C
223 .19	of] from > C
223 .25	are] is > C
223 .34	eat her] their > B-C
224 .27	and bays] bays > B-C
225 .1	belongs] belong > A
225 .21-22	steep cliff-like] cliff-like > C
225 .23	stands] she stands > C
225 .32	up] *omitted* > C
225[1] .1	Appendix N.] *omitted* > C
226 .1	with] in > C
226 .6	their] the > C
226 .16	their] its > A-B
226 .25	but] *omitted* > C
226 .30	fathers'] father's > A
227 .1	as] as if > C
227 .3	mon ami] *omitted* > B-C
227 .10	Well] *omitted* > B-C
228 .3	*New Testament*] *St. Luke* > C
228 .22	is shared] shared > C
228 .22	is pale] pale > C
228 .23	is so] so > C

229 .19-22   "How . . . A] "Can you receive me, and those I
             have with me, for the night?" asked the old man,
             in a husky voice — his kind heart was full. "A >
             B-C

229 .24-25   it . . . you] *omitted* > B-C

229 .26   beside] besides > B-C

230 .9   that] *omitted* > B-C

230 .30   child;" and] child." > C

230 .30-31   and half . . . brought] led > B; and taking her
             by the hand led > C

230 .34-37   I . . . close.] *omitted* > B-C

231 .6   hardly] scarcely > B-C

231 .14   and sees in] and in > B-C

231 .32   new] new-come > C

231 .36   That year] *omitted* > B-C

232 .2   As to] *omitted* > B-C

232 .2-4   I . . . they] *omitted* > B-C

232 .6   and lived . . . life] They lived happy and
             prosperous lives > C

232 .7   fireside] firesides > C

233 .1- 253 .5   Appendix A - Appendix N] *omitted* > C

Appendices

1
AGNES STRICKLAND'S PREFACE TO THE 1852 EDITION

IT will be acknowledged that human sympathy irresistibly responds to any narrative, founded on truth, which graphically describes the struggles of isolated human beings to obtain the aliments of life. The distinctions of pride and rank sink into nought, when the mind is engaged in the contemplation of the inevitable consequences of the assaults of the gaunt enemies, cold and hunger. Accidental circumstances have usually given sufficient experience of their pangs, even to the most fortunate, to make them own a fellow-feeling with those whom the chances of shipwreck, war, wandering, or revolutions have cut off from home and hearth, and the requisite supplies; not only from the thousand artificial comforts which civilized society classes among the necessaries of life, but actually from a sufficiency of "daily bread."

Where is the man, woman, or child who has not sympathised with the poor seaman before the mast, Alexander Selkirk, typified by the genius of Defoe as his inimitable Crusoe, whose name (although one by no means uncommon in middle life in the east of England,) has become synonymous for all who build and plant in a wilderness, "cut off from humanity's reach?" Our insular situation has chiefly drawn the attention of the inhabitants of Great Britain to casualties by sea, and the deprivations of individuals wrecked on some desert coast; but it is by no means generally known that scarcely a summer passes over the colonists in Canada, without losses of children from the families of settlers occurring in the vast forests of the backwoods, similar to that on which the narrative of the Canadian Crusoes is

321

founded. Many persons thus lost have perished in the wilderness; and it is to impress on the memory the natural resources of this country, by the aid of interesting the imagination, that the author of the well-known and popular work, "The Backwoods of Canada," has written the following pages.

She has drawn attention, in the course of this volume, to the practical solution* of that provoking enigma, which seems to perplex all anxious wanderers in an unknown land, namely, that finding themselves, at the end of a day's toilsome march, close to the spot from which they set out in the morning, and that this cruel accident will occur for days in succession. The escape of Captain O'Brien from his French prison at Verdun, detailed with such spirit in his lively autobiography, offers remarkable instances of this propensity of the forlorn wanderer in a strange land. A corresponding incident is recorded in the narrative of the "Escape of a young French Officer from the depôt near Peterborough during the Napoleon European war." He found himself thrice at night within sight of the walls of the prison from which he had fled in the morning, after taking fruitless circular walks of twenty miles. I do not recollect the cause of such lost labour being explained in either narrative; perhaps the more frequent occurrence of the disaster in the boundless backwoods of the Canadian colonies, forced knowledge, dearly bought, on the perceptions of the settlers. Persons who wander without knowing the features and landmarks of a country, instinctively turn their faces to the sun, and for that reason always travel in a circle, infallibly finding themselves at night in the very spot from which they started in the morning.

The resources and natural productions of the noble colony of Canada are but superficially known. An intimate acquaintance with its rich vegetable and animal productions is most effectually made under the high pressure of difficulty and necessity. Our writer has striven to interest children, or rather young people approaching the age of adolescence, in the natural history of this country, simply by showing them how it is possible for children to make the best of it when thrown into a state of destitution as

*See Appendix A; likewise p. 310 [CEECT, p. 206].

forlorn as the wanderers on the Rice Lake Plains. Perhaps those who would not care for the berry, the root, and the grain, as delineated and classified technically in books of science, might remember their uses and properties when thus brought practically before their notice as the aliments of the famishing fellow-creature, with whom their instinctive feelings must perforce sympathise. When parents who have left home comforts and all the ties of gentle kindred for the dear sakes of their rising families, in order to place them in a more independent position, it is well if those young minds are prepared with some knowledge of what they are to find in the adopted country; the animals, the flowers, the fruits, and even the minuter blessings which a bountiful Creator has poured forth over that wide land.

The previous work of my sister, Mrs. Traill, "The Backwoods of Canada, by the Wife of an Emigrant Officer," published some years since by Mr. C. Knight, in his Library of Useful Knowledge, has passed through many editions, and enjoyed, (anonymous though it was,) too wide a popularity as a standard work for me to need to dwell on it, further than to say that the present is written in the same *naïve*, charming style, with the same modesty and uncomplaining spirit, although much has the sweet and gentle author endured, as every English lady must expect to do who ventures to encounter the lot of a colonist. She has now devoted her further years of experience as a settler to the information of the younger class of colonists, to open their minds and interest them in the productions of that rising country, which will one day prove the mightiest adjunct of the island empire; our nearest, our soundest colony, unstained with the corruption of convict population; where families of gentle blood need fear no real disgrace in their alliance; where no one need beg, and where any one may dig without being ashamed.

2
NELSON'S PREFACE TO THE 1882 EDITION

THE interesting tale contained in this volume of romantic adventure in the forests of Canada, was much appreciated and enjoyed by a large circle of young readers when first published, under the title of "The Canadian Crusoes." After being many years out of print, it will now, we hope and believe, with a new and more descriptive title, prove equally attractive to our young friends of the present time.

EDINBURGH, 1882.